What people are saying ab

"Like Bruce Springsteen in his song *Wrecking Ball*, Bill Zaferos reminds the reader to "hold tight to your anger." To be motivated by it. To not blink when it stares back in the mirror. Zaferos' brilliant tour de force about a narrator unwilling to compromise moral dignity and intellectual honesty in the face of a sagging and torpid world is a must-read for those of us who realize that to not be pissed off is to not be paying attention.
—Thomas Peele, 2017 Pulitzer Prize winning author

"Bill Zaferos' **Poison Pen** will appeal to fans of the odd and absurd. Each sentence is loaded with humor, heart, and meaning."
— Lisa Kaiser, author, *I Never Wanted to be a Rock Star*

"Bill Zaferos' novel **Poison Pen** is funny—outrageously so, as its misanthropic protagonist from small-town Wisconsin stumbles from disaster into catastrophe."
—David Luhrssen, *Shepherd Express*

"**Poison Pen** by Bill Zaferos is a page-turner. Mr. Zaferos is a wonderful storyteller and masterful writer. This is a ride you don't want to miss. From the beginning of the book and throughout, he builds the characters such that you, the reader, feel empathy for them. You will cheer and laugh, and at times choke up with tears. I did not want the story to end, but—and I don't think I am giving anything away when I say—the ending will leave you with a satisfied smile. Bravo, Mr. Zaferos."
– Nick Chiarkas, author of the award-winning novel, *Weepers*

"There are times we all wish we could respond to life's absurdities with the cynicism, wit and audacity of Zaferos' protagonist. **Poison Pen** is a gift for those of us who pay for our TicTacs and ignore hitchhikers."
—Jerry Stockfisch, reporter/editor, *Tampa Tribune, Tampa Bay Times*

POISON PEN

(A novel)

Published by Three Towers Press
An imprint of HenschelHAUS Publishing, Inc.
www.henschelHAUSbooks.com

ISBN: 978159598-659-7
E-ISBN: 978159598-663-4
AUDIO ISBN: 98159598-674-0
LCCN: 2018948560

Author photo: Todd Daquisto, Milwaukee
Typography: WaterStreet Creative

To Audrey, who pushed me.
To Melanie, who encouraged me.
To Lish, who said I had to finish it.
To Tracey, who always supported me.
And to Jerry, who made it better.

POISON PEN

(A novel)

Bill Zaferos

Three Towers Press

Milwaukee, Wisconsin

Chapter 1:
What My Sorry Life Was Made Of

There's no easy way to explain why a guy like me would decide to pick up a young hitchhiker on a spring afternoon in the new century. But then there's no easy way to explain why a guy like me would bother to get out of bed at all. Both acts require more work than I'm normally prepared to devote to such tasks.

As I woke on that particular day, my eyes had barely focused on the Roger Maris poster on the far wall of my bedroom when I knew I was in for another bad day. I didn't mind the bad days. I was used to them and I didn't like surprises. A good day was likely to throw me off balance.

But this one was off to a particularly spectacular start. I had a funny feeling even before I heard the sound of breaking glass in another room. I have this rule: If I wake up facing the Roger Maris poster instead of the Farrah Fawcett poster (Yes, that one! I saved mine all these years!), I'm superstitious enough to believe that my day is already swirling about in seas of excrement.

I've never actually tested that theory, since most of my days seem awful by any 20th century, and certainly 21st century, American standard, and I never wake up to Farrah's image unless I've been having one of those dreams again. Anyway, the idea that waking up to Farrah means an improvement in my life's condition gives me something to hang on to.

For some people, the bad days seem to be based on trivial inconveniences that come in streaks of two or three. These difficult stretches aren't really much to endure as tests of faith and patience go. Maybe the ATM machine eats their card and they're forced to put a client lunch on a dangerously stressed credit card. Or perhaps traffic holds them up and makes them pick up a late charge at their child's corporately owned daycare center.

Follow those modern tragedies with pre-emption of a favorite TV show for something as ridiculous as a presidential declaration of war, and you've got a full-scale personal disaster. Can't a guy even watch TV in peace

1

without being confronted with the problems of the outside world, the victim wonders, stewing until alcohol-induced drowsiness forces him to an early bed followed by a cruel 6 a.m. alarm clock.

Oh yeah. That's sheer hell.

The thing is, my bad days tended to come in a series of years, so this one wasn't unexpected. In fact, I greeted it with the same sense of security with which other people might get from any old routine. The sameness, the absolute predictability of some catastrophe seemed to me to be as normal as any nine-to-five suburban-white-picket-fence wife-and-two-kids rut.

My life was always about crisis management, and I accepted it as routine. It was easier that way, and I had long since lost the will to fight.

I'm not sure I would ever have known what to do with a pleasant day of reading a book in a park or holding the hand of a small niece or nephew as we walk through the zoo or playing fetch with the family Golden Retriever. I was always convinced, in fact, that I would have squandered any opportunity for a nice day because I just couldn't appreciate one.

Some might say I suffered from depression, but that's too dramatic. I suffered from chronic indifference.

The crisis of indifference I suffered was part of what little identity I had. I had always wanted to be somebody. I mean a guy who could get rich with his own TV show and tell all the old bullies they could go to hell. In this TV age, one must come to grips with the fact that they will never even be important enough to be a has-been guest on Hollywood Squares. It is important to realize early that whatever you thought you would become when you were 16, you won't.

By then you'd have realized that the bullies had won. An early recognition system helps reduce frustration, heartbreak and effort. My motto is that if you set a goal and work hard every day, nothing happens. Once you understand that, the stress of participating in the human drama diminishes precipitously. You are free to watch television and sleep on the couch.

Still, I always believed that never having been important is better than being someone important and then having your star fall into that vast hoi polloi sea of faceless souls. I'd hate to have to know I used to be "somebody." I can't imagine how painful it must be to have any recognition and then lose it, to have waiters look at you like you were nuts when you talked about your days hanging around with Bogie.

For me, it was always better never to have been a part of things to begin with than to bore people with embellished war stories of incidents that are no longer relevant. I never would have believed that the events that unfold here would have led me to the type of notoriety that is normally denied the nobodies.

But even the nobodies need stimulus of some kind. So the fact that my grandfather was smashing dishes downstairs in the kitchen gave me a sense of calm. For at least one more day, I would not be confronted with the notion of quiet, normal waking hours. Thank goodness.

My grandfather, now in his eighties, lived with me through some odd skip in the family genetic structure that took both of my parents to their graves with different kinds of horrible, disfiguring diseases which made death a welcome, if early, exit from their own string of bad days.

I took Grampa in when Gramma died of hopelessness and boredom, although the coroner listed the death as natural causes.

I lived in a small burg in central Wisconsin called Hammertown, named, of course, for the city's main industry until the 1970s recession, which was the manufacture of hammer heads.

Hammertown made hammer heads for 127 years before the economy forced it to close its doors for good. Our town didn't make the whole hammer, just the metal head. The hammer handles were made at a factory in our sister city 10 miles away—no, not Handletown, but Little Rose. The name of our tiny town was a bit unusual in this part of the state, since there seemed to be some little-known state law that required most rural municipalities to be named like bad country and western bands.

As for Hammertown, the name of the high school football and basketball teams is, of course, the Hammerheads, which was more in keeping with a nautical than a manufacturing theme, but no one minded since sharks are a sufficiently predatory creature to create the image of a winning team. I'm not sure what the town would have done if the main industry was the manufacture of feather dusters.

But for years, Hammertown meant hammers, and so the hammer motif permeated the personality of the town. Bars had names like the "Hammer It Inn," and "Mike Hammer's," and drunks still thought it was funny when told their wives they were hammered. Oddly enough, Hammertown didn't have a hardware store, which meant that anyone who actually needed a hammer would have to travel to nearby Little Rose.

The hammer factory building reopened when a computer manufacturer bought the building in the early 21st century for the manufacture of microchips for expensive and sophisticated laptops that big city executives had to carry with them or be shunned as losers. No one in Hammertown could afford to buy one of these devices, let alone find a use for them since internet connections in Hammertown were laughably deficient.

But the factory kept the locals in beer money and prevented the town from complete economic collapse. The locals called the factory "The Chips," and every time I hear that nickname I get hungry for potato chips. Ruffles, specifically, because they have ridges.

You don't meet a lot of new people when you live in Hammertown. If you're over 25, your best chance to find a meaningful relationship, which meant getting drunk and getting laid on a regular basis with the same person, is to go to your ten-year high school reunion and pick off the retread divorced people.

That may be why I was never married. I hated the reunions. But it isn't that simple. I got burned, of course, like everybody else. My story is a bizarre one I must share in order to make some sense of my dismal outlook.

It was high school, the seventies, it was first love, and Carol Ann Doefler and I figured—no, we knew—we'd be getting married. Doesn't every young high school couple in love think that? So I insisted we wait until we were married until we decided to, as the Raspberries sang, "go all the way." But I spent a lot of time on third base, as it was known among us Hammerheads, and apparently we got sloppy, because she got pregnant. I offered to marry her and get a job at the hammer factory even though I figured I was destined for greater things. She said no, got the abortion, dumped me and screwed the first guy she dated after me, then called me the next day to let me know what she did.

That kind of killed any developing sense of romance or trust I might have had.

As for marriage, I never got close, although I had a long-term arrangement with a waitress at the IHOP. It was a kind of symbiotic relationship, if two social parasites can be said to have symbiosis. It was almost purely a physical release when we spent time together and little more.

We didn't believe in quality time, long walks in the woods and staring moon-eyed at one another over Beaujolais in front of a fireplace. All we had in common was that we were unattractive people on physical, psychological and emotional levels that have yet to be explored by even the best therapists and medical professionals.

The relationship was as colorless as the rest of my life. It wasn't even good sex. But it was the only thing people like us could expect, and we took what we could get.

When the IHOP finally closed, she got a job at a truck stop in another town and became the long-haul companion of a red-bearded New Jersey galoot named Rolf. I sometimes walk by the boarded-up windows of the IHOP and reminisce about the smell of maple syrup that permeated her matted blond hair.

So it goes, as Kurt Vonnegut would say.

I love Vonnegut. His economy with words, his simple declarative sentences and his bemused way of observing his world made him a real-life truth teller. I always thought that if I could just write like Vonnegut, just one book, I might break the family pattern of desolation and sheer boredom, my family's heirloom, that had passed down to me from two generations of ennui and listlessness. The book idea wasn't bad.

Well, maybe it was kind of cheesy, now that I think about it. It was about how some geologists dig deep for oil in the Southern California desert when they discover a strange creature that looks like a demon. Then another. And the deeper they dig, the more demons they uncover until they realize they've discovered the Gates of Hell.

The book idea died because after a few pages of typing I became too distracted by the overwhelming notion that even my own imagination was bereft of any idea that would be of interest to the general public. I tried and tried to write, but no dice. *Hell's Gates*, the name of the book, would go undiscovered. And largely unwritten.

That was my life: No book, no fame, nobody, no dice.

That's my own catch-phrase. Vonnegut uses "so it goes," or "hi ho." I always liked to put "no dice" at the end of my sentences when I was trying to make a point. I thought it was a nice literary technique, even an homage to Vonnegut. No dice. As usual, I don't measure up.

But I digress. It's a habit of mine. Anyway, I even used the phrase "no dice" in *Hell's Gate*.

It went like this: "The demon beast-thing grabbed Dr. Block by the head and stuck out a long, slimy green barbed tongue, which it proceeded to stick in the good doctor's ear. Dr. Block raised his eye heavenward, but was suddenly confronted with the fact that his superior intellect, which told him there was no God or Devil, had betrayed him. He prayed for protection, but no dice."

OK, so it wasn't Hemingway. That was my best shot at literary recognition.

I myself was always a bit religious, despite occasional misgivings which were generated by the circumstances of my miserable existence. Religion provided me with comfort because, in essence, it says that our only mission on Earth is to save our souls and be nice to people. When you break it down to that basic tenet, life doesn't seem so bad when you don't have a swimming pool in the back yard or you have to drink cheap beer instead of good wine.

In any event, on the morning in question, long after the *Hell's Gate* project had been abandoned, Grampa was looking frantically for his Metamucil again. Grampa had become increasingly paranoid in his golden years, and his outbursts were as reliable as his Social Security checks. He once believed that Gerald Ford was speaking to the annual Hammertown Chamber of Commerce dinner as part of a secret plan to complete a mob hit on him. It never occurred to Grampa why Ford or even the most ruthless hitman would want to kill him.

He was, after all, worthless and hardly worth the effort of killing, even for sport.

I, on the other hand, had been considering taking out a contract on him myself if for no other reason than to reduce my interaction with the crabby hippie neighbors who constantly complained about Grampa's nude sunbathing. Grampa thought exposure to the full sunlight would help him live longer.

I could never understand why he would want to do that. Live longer, that is. But the neighbors did not care for his therapy and they sometimes bitched to me about it.

On the other hand I could understand why the neighbors could not enjoy Grampa's nudist tendencies. But I couldn't stand their yappy little Yorkshire Terriers that barked at any movement within 300 yards at 6 a.m. So when they asked me to make Grampa put on clothes, I just said: "No dice."

The neighbors on either side of my house had quirks of their own. To the south there was a man who was referred to by locals as "Foilhead Eddie" because, of course, he constantly wore foil under his wool cap. I once went into Eddie's house because he asked me to help him move some furniture.

The place was littered with stacks of newspapers and guns and random paraphernalia and clocks. All the clocks were set to different times, and at least three police radios squawked in a constant chatter that made it sound like they were deranged parrots talking to each other. Despite his oddities, for the most part Eddie kept to himself, although he and Grampa would sometimes have long chats over at his house.

As for the neighbors with the yappy dogs, I never knew their names and didn't care to find out. They were a couple who drove expensive SUVs and kept weird hours, and it was said that the wife, or whatever she was, read palms and used healing crystals to treat minor ailments. I sometimes wondered if she could cure my life. The only odd thing about their house was that the lights always seemed to be on in the basement, even when they were gone.

Sometimes at night I tried to peer into their windows, but they were covered by two layers of gauze curtains which distorted all images and more or less prevented nosy neighbors from finding out too much.

My Grampa was, as they say, all I had left, and I loved him for whatever reason that blood ties make any person love another whom they would ordinarily avoid on a city bus. But on this day Grampa was convinced that I had hidden his Metamucil in an attempt to make him die a slow, excruciating, colorectal cancerous death. As opposed to the slow, regular death that had already stumbled upon us with all the subtlety of a drunken burglar.

Whatever his reasoning, he needed his fix. Now. And his screaming almost sounded like the mantra of an insane Hare Krishna being dragged out by airport security.

"Where's the goddamned Metamucil? The Metamucil, goddammit. Where's the Metamucil? The Metamucil, goddammit. You're trying to give me the ass cancer by hiding my Metamucil. If I get the ass cancer I want to be shot. I'm not going to spend the rest of my life with a bag coming out of my gut. But that's what you want, isn't it? You bastard!"

"Grampa, if you get the ass cancer at your age the only bag they'll give you is a body bag," I said, handing him the jar of brand-name psyllium fibers he had somehow missed while rooting through the kitchen cabinets. "I think you have already evacuated what's left of your intestines, anyway. There no place for cancer to go."

He ignored me, quickly mixed his elixir and drank it with the gusto of a Skid Row drunk guzzling Sterno.

"It's not just the cancer. I also like to shit. You gotta problem with that? You gonna deny me a good shit?"

"Not at all," I said. "Everybody has to be good at something. Frankly, I think you're the best shitter in the world. I might see if the sewerage district has some kind of award for a guy like you. I know The Reader's Digest wouldn't exist without people like you. They should at least recognize you in some way."

"Fine," he said, a grainy, orange mustache above his lip. "Mock the one thing that gives me joy."

He stripped right there in the kitchen, and left his clothes in a heap on the floor. Then he spoke again. "I'm thinking about starting to wear a monocle," he said. "Don't try to stop me. If you're not going to let me have a giraffe, I get to wear the monocle."

With that, he walked outside to get his sun soaking for the day. Such remarks did not bear response. Besides, what would I say? That I never told him he couldn't have a giraffe? That I had no opposition to his wearing a monocle?

His departure to the back yard allowed me to open the newspaper to the only section that interested me anymore. No, not the sports section. Sports were ruined for me after they broke Roger Maris's single-season record for home runs. That and the designated hitter soured me on baseball, and I never cottoned to football. Too many 300 pound linebackers standing around waiting for the results of a replay.

But the obituaries. Now that's where there's real life-and-death action. I'm not especially afraid of death myself. It doesn't make me sad. In fact, if it is possible to have neutral feelings about the end of life, I'm neutral. Death is just boredom in a smaller box.

If what they taught me in Sunday school was true, and I still believed it, I just might go to heaven. Jesus said there were mansions waiting for us in heaven. It might be interesting to live in a heavenly mansion.

It would be a nice change of scenery, anyway. There would be more to clean, that's for sure. But the concept of eternal life itself also made me a bit uncomfortable. What do you do with all that time? Do they have good books there? Do I have to go through eternity without ever getting laid again?

In spite of my misgivings about heaven and life itself, there are times, although they are few and far between, when I swear I can see and feel the glory of God Himself. Like when Maris hit number 61 when I was a kid.

But there are plenty of other days when I feel like I'm staring into the maw of Hades with an invitation in my hand. Mostly, though, my life has been reduced to a sort of militant indifference.

Even baseball, once a passion bordering on compulsion from childhood to adulthood, lost its charm for me in the last player strike in 1994. I already mentioned the designated hitter, a tool of the devil if there ever was one. But I really didn't care about millionaire owners and millionaire players arguing over billions of dollars.

The betrayal for me was that the season stopped during the players strike. In my mind, if you didn't have baseball, you might as well not have summer. There were no games to listen to late at night on the porch from faraway places like Philadelphia and New York and Chicago and Milwaukee. There was no reason to sit out on the porch without a ballgame. The strike destroyed my lifestyle, such as it was, and I knew I could no longer trust even baseball.

When the strike occurred, my last connection to society was pretty much broken. And when that creep Mark McGwire broke Maris' record, I just saw him as unworthy. Turns out he apparently used drugs. Figures.

In any event, I liked to read the obituaries in the local paper, the *Hammertown Telegraph-Herald*, to separate the deceased into categories of those who led useful lives and those whose lives were utterly meaningless to anyone outside their small circles of family, friends and coworkers.

People who led meaningful lives got headlines like: "Smith, Who Headed Asthma Foundation, Dies at 68" or "Butterfly Expert Jones, 53, Killed in Crash." It's safe to say that despite having served in a war, Grampa's life will go in the useless bin. I expected to see my own obit in a few years if you get newspapers delivered to those heavenly mansions.

Sometimes I bought *The New York Times* at the gas station just to check out the recently deceased bigwigs. But whether in the *Telegraph-Herald* or *The Times*, you can recognize obituarial tributes to the very important immediately. What usually goes unnoticed, however, is the obit of the unimportant. If you're not important, only your name and a brief biography, embellished by grieving family members, appears with the time and location of your funeral service.

I loved reading the crime reports, too, because it showed me what happened when people like me try to make something of themselves and fail. It made me feel superior to them because they had screwed up, and that was a feeling with which I was not well accustomed. But at least those people got in the paper with a kind of infamous notoriety.

The crime page documented the mishaps in people's lives, and the obituary page is the last reminder they were even here. The obituary page, for most people, is like the telephone book. It's the only record of their ever having existed.

I've still tried to write a book about my own miserable life thinking that maybe, just maybe, the act of creativity will convince me (if not some agent or publisher) that I'm still alive, or at least that I'm not dead yet. They say you should write about something you know. So, having abandoned *Hell's Gate*, I'm writing about losers like me.

If you're reading this, then I must have been successful. It meant a lot of sacrifice, because there are a lot of reruns to watch on TV, and you don't watch them writing books you know no one will ever read. Assuming they're published in the first place.

Chapter 2
Why There Are So Few Hitchhikers

I made my living, if you could call it a living, writing what used to be called "poison pen" letters. For $50, I would write a letter to your enemy guaranteed to leave psychic scars that would last a lifetime. I always wanted to have some super power when I was a kid. It would be cool to have ESP, super strength or even the talent of the guy in the Fantastic Four who could turn himself into a fireball.

I didn't get any of those powers. But I did have the power of the poison pen, and I could make the guarantee of leaving those lifetime psychic scars because, well, who knows how long a psychic scar really lasts?

It's just good marketing.

I had no requests for letters that day though, so I was free to relax. Grampa, naked in his hammock and sleeping, had managed through his snores to agitate the hippie neighbors' terriers, which were yapping wildly. I didn't much care about what was going on outside, because "The Beverly Hillbillies" were coming on soon. I had to prepare with some cheese sticks and beer.

I always thought that the best sitcoms ever made were created in the 1960s. That's why I watch them again and again. But I sometimes wonder what it must have been like to be a television executive in the '60s approaching the network president with ideas for a new fall line-up.

How do you tell a man with that much power that you've got a show about a guy who looks like Frankenstein and thinks everyone else is weird? Or a show about a talking horse who drives a laundry truck and ends up trying out for the Los Angeles Dodgers? And of course, there were Jed, Granny, Jethro, Ellie Mae and the see-ment pond.

Watching those shows may not have led to a fulfilling life to some people, but that's what my life was made of then. Reruns, cheese sticks and beer.

That was before I met the hitchhiker.

So I guess it's time we looked into this little matter. Once again, in some attempt to explain the events that brought my life into such disarray, we must begin to look into my state of mind.

In short, if life was a business, I believed I was pure overhead. I contributed nothing to the bottom line of humanity. No joy. No great invention that cured acne. I just was. The biggest event in my life was getting my picture in my high school yearbook. Of course, posterity will show, should I become an assassin, that the last known photo of me included greasy white pimples, a ridiculous cowlick and a wispy mustache.

I will concede, then, that I had some serious self-esteem issues.

But I did one thing well, and I knew it. I wrote devastating poison pen letters.

Perhaps you'd like to see a little evidence of my venomous writing prowess. I'll show you some examples later in this screed. I'm sure the quality of the missives will surprise those of you who have read this far into my memoirs. When I get focused, I could actually twist a phrase or two right into the hearts of my targets.

But it's really not meanness that motivated me, although I admit that bitterness, nastiness and a general dislike for the human race did make me more creative and bring the bile closer to my fingertips. It's just it was the one thing I seemed to be good at. In my darker moments I think my poison pen letters were the only way that a guy like me could make any impression on the world at all. If I behaved nicely or if I had written greeting cards, who would have noticed a gnome like me?

What's kind of sad is that writing those letters really used to bring me to life. It's kind of pathetic, I guess. But I enjoyed settling scores for people who had real enemies and real lives. The problem was, there weren't enough of them. It wasn't an issue of income. At $50 apiece, there wasn't much to be earned from these letters. Since I received a reasonable, if small, settlement from my mother's doctor's liability insurance company—the doctor had misdiagnosed her disease and caused her to die miserably and prematurely—I could get by, just barely.

But my talents as a writer were not always in great demand, especially in a small town, and I had experience in very little that allowed me to get a big piece of the American pie. I suppose I could have charged a lot more for the letters. I should have. Most people couldn't write their own ransom notes, so diatribes as devastating as mine were worth a fortune in a semi-literate society. But the truth is, I enjoyed writing the poison pen letters, so I kept my fee low. I guess I you could say I gave a volume discount for spite. The more letters I had to write, the happier I was.

So you're wondering what all this has to do with picking up hitchhikers. Trust me, it has everything to do with picking up hitchhikers. First, I was attracted to the idea of hitchhikers, people who just hopped on the road and set a course for adventure, as they used to say on TV.

But the rarity of the breed was very intriguing to me.

You don't really see hitchhikers anymore. Most of them have been skinned alive and chopped to little bits by serial killers. I guess the hitchhiker herd has been pretty much thinned out by the natural selection of other people's psychoses. The hitchhikers who did survive were probably serial killers themselves. They wound up with collections of human fingers, the digits of their weaker or less-cunning colleagues, in the trunk of their stolen cars until they made some mistake that alerted even the most incompetent small-town law enforcement officers.

That's my theory about why you don't see hitchhikers much anymore.

And that's precisely what made me stop and pick her up. It seemed like it might lead to some weird fun. I don't mean that I intended to dismember her. That would have created a mess and would have been too much work. But I thought it might break up my sad routine.

Besides, if I had had any kind of killer instinct I would have put it to better use, like shooting the writers of awful TV jingles. But my life was one long rut. Why not do something wild to break out? Either way, whether she was a serial killer or potential victim of one, a hitchhiker, especially a young woman, reeked of danger. I thought she might even have had a hidden machete for use in a hostage situation. I'd never been a hostage before, so I guess it was the danger of it all that made me slow down, and it was the exhilaration of some strange new experience to come that made me pull over and open the door to let her in.

I had been on my way to the grocery store for the cheese sticks and Milwaukee's Best beer, and I had to hurry to pick it up before *The Beverly Hillbillies* started. But the sight of a hitchhiker made me look twice. I made a split-second decision to give her a ride when I saw her standing on the side of the road. Where she wanted to go, I didn't know or care, since all of my appointments had been cancelled for the day other than watching the Hillbillies. As it turned out, my adventure, my walk on the wild side, my key to a new and interesting life, just needed a ride to Kmart.

"You know where it is?" she asked. "It's the one by the frontage road near Old Mill Avenue. Right near the Hee Haw Lounge."

"You look at the way I'm dressed and ask if I know where the Kmart is?" I replied. "Yeah, I'm familiar with the establishment, and I have even found myself at the Hee Haw on occassion. They make great Mai Tais. I suppose you're some sort of Kmart senior associate. I can tell by your smock you're a top executive."

That sort of sarcasm usually ended most of the conversations I ever had with strangers, especially women. I learned early that the same wit that made me a good poison pen writer made me a bad candidate to sit peacefully in bars and cafes. My mouth was a trouble magnet, and depending on my target, it has also been a fist magnet.

She ignored my barb. In fact, she seemed to like it, even savor it. She smiled at me, licked her teeth, and crossed her legs, and I knew I was in some kind of trouble. I was highly intrigued.

"Actually, I'm president of the company," she said. "You can call me K. I just wanted to see how my employees live. It's very depressing. They punch clocks and drive gas-guzzling cars to tiny, ratty houses where they store what's left of their broken dreams. I can barely wait to get back to my Jaguar and my mansion."

Return fire. Not a great shot, really, but I wasn't used to even that much repartee. And I certainly wasn't used the way she seemed to warm up to me. Who knew what she was thinking? She certainly wasn't intimidated by me, a fat, sarcastic loser in a beat-up Toyota Tercel who was, with the exception of being an employee of Kmart, pretty much the person she was describing.

She was somewhere between 17 and 23, an age spread that was not worth the risk of trying any funny business. Beneath her Kmart smock was a tight blue knit blouse that refused to cover her navel.

It did not appear that she was dressed according to Kmart code.

She stared into the abyss of my eyes and she wasn't frightened at all. If the eyes are the window to the soul, all she could see in my windows was a deep, dark, chasm. But a person like this, man or woman, looks at all frightening things with the same kind of enthusiasm they would a roller coaster ride.

If you haven't already guessed, there was a lot in my life for an outsider to be afraid of.

She wasn't afraid of anything. That's why she got in the car in the first place. Despite her bravery, I must have embarrassed her about the smock because she decided to explain herself.

"Look Fat Boy, I don't work at Kmart and I'm a little insulted that you could look at me and think that," she said. "For your information I borrowed the smock when I saw it lying on a counter at Kmart. I had uses for it."

"Of course you're not a Kmart employee. I figured you were some kind of FBI operative investigating bootleg Beanie Babies or Pez dispensers."

"Well, I thought you might be an undercover cop, but even undercovers have to have some physical conditioning," she said. "It's real attractive how your belly button sticks out between your belt and the bottom of your T-shirt. Since you're not a cop, I can tell you. I use the smock to shoplift from Kmart."

"That's ingenious," I said. "I bet you can steal a bunch of Mike and Ikes if you get a Walgreen's smock. You're a criminal mastermind."

"And you're an overweight, sarcastic loser."

"Ah, then we've met before. You seem to know everything about me."

"Just shut up and drive, Fat Boy. We've got work to do."

"Yeah, we've got work to do. Hey, if we knock off a Dairy Queen, can I get a Peanut Buster Parfait?"

This was becoming entertaining. But she got quiet when she lit a joint and we just drove for a while, down the frontage road and toward the Kmart.

So that's why I picked up this specimen of that endangered species known as the hitchhiker. I was setting my own course for adventure. I still don't know whether it was a good idea or not, and I still don't know if it was fun or not. But I do know this: In the end, the whole incident brought me as close to having an identity, even getting acceptance by the rest of humanity, as I would ever get.

Chapter 3
Stealing Tic Tacs

So we chugged into the Kmart parking lot. Me, with no idea what I was doing, and in full knowledge that I would miss the Hillbillies, and her, with an apparent scheme but no obvious plans to let me know what it was.

"Are we here to steal?" I asked.

"You go into a bar to drink. You go into a whorehouse to screw. And you go into Kmarts to steal," she explained. "Only I'm not going to steal anything. You are."

"I've done a lot of stupid things, and I've done a lot that I regret, although the regrets mostly surround the things I haven't done, but anyway, I don't steal," I explained to someone I knew for about five minutes but who already had some weird pull over me. I was now babbling.

"That's why your life is boring," she said. "You don't take any chances."

"How did you know my life was boring, and yes, I suppose I could make it more interesting by taking a hostage or sniping from a bell tower, but I don't much like to raise my excitement level much past the occasional train robbery," I said. "I don't even know your real name. Not that I have the slightest confidence that you'd give me anything less than a fictional nom de guerre."

"Look, this isn't dangerous. It's fun," she said. "And maybe the excitement will give that fat-encrusted heart of yours a jump-start. Go on. Get in there and steal something for mama. Mama wants a Tic Tac. You can steal me a Tic Tac, can't you?"

For some reason, music began rising in my head. It was The Clash singing the Bobby Fuller Four's "I Fought the Law." Of course, The Law always won. I could just see myself getting nailed for pilfering Tic Tacs from a Kmart. Strangely enough, just visualizing the scene made it somehow appealing. What was I going to lose with such a daring exploit?

My career? My reputation? The respect of my peers? The love of my family? It all started to make sense. I was going to commit an act of treason against the ordinary, law-abiding self-government I had caged myself in. I was gonna bust out—and with Tic Tacs!

Who could have thought a discreet breath mint in a convenient small pack could change a life?

And, gee whiz, stealing those Tic Tacs could even get me laid once I had safely determined she was of age. I felt like Cagney. Top o' the world, Ma!

"Peppermint or spearmint?" I asked.

"Wintergreen," she chirped. "I'll wait here by your Tercel."

And so I walked across that parking lot, my Rubicon. When I came back with those Tic Tacs, my life would mean more than just the next TV rerun. It would mean something altogether different. Just what, I wasn't quite sure.

I entered the store and smiled broadly at the old coot who greeted me. I remembered that Grampa used to work in this very Kmart as a greeter until he showed up one day holding a rubber snake and dressed only in his smock and an adult diaper wrapped around his head like a turban. Kmart management invited Grampa never to return, even as a customer.

But this wasn't about Grampa. This was my moment under the dark sun.

I was cool. I took a few laps around the store, pretending to look at sporting goods and sports wristwatches and hardware. Finally, I made it to the electronics section, where I grabbed a three-pack of old noir movie DVDs and some batteries. I headed for the checkout line, where the impulse items are stored. There I spied the quarry. They didn't have wintergreen. She'd have to settle for peppermint.

The woman in front of me was buying a toilet seat and some bananas, so the obligatory price check gave me my chance to move. With a little legerdemain I had learned from a magician at Boy Scout camp, the Tic Tacs were mine. I slipped them into the pocket of my windbreaker and when it was my turn to pay, I calmly gave the clerk a twenty dollar bill for the DVDs and batteries.

She gave me the change, and I headed toward the door. I fought the law and I won.

But just as I walked out the front door and into the glass foyer area with the bubblegum machines and the cheesy 25-cent kiddy rides, I heard a voice behind me.

"Sir ... Ah, sir, could I have a word with you?" said the voice, which belonged to a large man in a blue fake-cop uniform that made security guards feel important.

I turned around innocently, surprised and confused.

"What can I do for you, officer?" I inquired. "Stock tips? Career counseling?"

"I'm not an officer," he said sharply. "But I am store security. One of our employees spotted you stealing something at the checkout. I'd like to take you in the back room and look in your pockets."

"Which employee saw me?" I demanded. I couldn't have been seen. Half the employees were asleep or hungover or indifferent or even working out their own theft schemes. "I want to face my accuser."

He pointed to a young woman standing near the cash register. There she was. My new friend. In her Kmart smock. She was pointing at me accusingly and angrily, as though her entire sense of civility had been destroyed by what she had seen.

"I think it was a Tic Tac," she said. "Wintergreen if I'm not mistaken. Check that ratty windbreaker of his. It's probably buried in lint and used Kleenex."

"There must be some kind of mistake," I said, making me only the three billionth shoplifter to use that line. "I had every intention of purchasing these refreshing mints, but I was distracted by the wide array of consumer items available at the checkout line alone. Why, anyone would be dazzled and at least momentarily confused by the very sight of these impulse items."

The pretensions of classiness didn't work. I should have pretended I was just nuts.

My mistake. The security guard just took me firmly by the elbow and ushered me to the rear of the store, just past the automotive department where a tire "blow-out sale" was taking place.

I was hauled to a dusty back room that looked like it was used alternately for eating and sex during employee breaks. A dirty table with fast food cartons left on it sat in the middle, with a cluttered desk in one corner, empty boxes in another, and pillows against the wall.

Best of all, for those interested in entertaining sudden romantic impulses, it had no windows and a lock on the door. The guard asked me to sit down at the desk while he called the police. Thus began my career as a criminal, a classification which dropped me just a peg or two beneath my life-long station as societal barnacle.

Chapter 4
Crime and Punishment

In the time it takes to eat an entire container of Tic Tacs, the real cops, or a cop anyway, arrived. Obviously, the quick response indicated that the great jaywalking crackdown had come to an end in this sorry burg. I had been noisily escorted to a windowless office—"See what happens when you steal Tic Tacs, folks?" the imbecile had shouted as he took me into custody—and told me to sit down and keep quiet. The Kmart cop had called the police and told them they "had a customer." He seemed very delighted with his security guard humor.

"Get it, boy? You were supposed to be our customer, and now you're theirs," he said, suddenly affecting a redneck southern accent and exaggerating a deep, throaty laugh that sounded like he was saying "ah-hyuah, ah-hyuah, ah-hyuah." "Yessiree, now yer gon' be their customer. Hope they got a rubber hose to get some answers out of you."

"I'll give them any answers they want. I'll tell them anything. I just pray they don't ask me for the frequency," I said, feigning hysteria and insanity. I found that you could confuse, and even frighten, idiots into a ponderous silence if you spoke cryptically to them and alluded to conspiracies they had heard about on late night AM radio.

I had no idea where my new friend was. I guessed that while Barney Fife had me locked up in the office for Grand Theft Tic Tac, K was busy stuffing small electronic devices and clothing into a bag before she hit the road again. That was probably the whole plan, to get me nailed while she enjoyed the bounty of the American consumer society free of charge.

Meanwhile, here I was trapped in a room with someone with an even lower station in life than my own, and I was still suffering humiliation. Apparently convinced that I was not some kind of dangerous foreign agent or space alien with a "frequency," he broke the silence for more charming banter.

"You're fat," he said, winding up for what was likely to be a carnival of statements of the obvious dressed up as insults. "Your T-shirt is ripped and you're a loser. You stole Tic Tacs. Stole Tic Tacs. Man, that is so low. Yer mama would be real proud of you."

I don't know what it is about rural cops and would-be cops that makes them adopt the faux Southern accent. I was curious, but I thought asking this guy about it would be as rewarding as asking a parakeet for directions to the Grand Canyon. Besides, by now my powers as a professional humiliator kicked in, partly in defense and partly as a means of entertainment.

I normally never faced my victims, so this would be a treat. I figured I'd go for the throat.

Although the written word was my true medium, I could still dish out verbal abuse when the need arose, although I was never as eloquent as on paper.

"I know why you're angry, and I can understand fully," I said. "You're not angry at me. You're angry because you couldn't catch a fly ball or hit a curve, which meant that athletics, the only way to make money for morons like you, was out right at the start. And it meant you never got to date anyone in high school because you certainly couldn't rely on your looks, brains or potential earning power. You're angry because your own mother was ashamed of you after you dropped out of high school, and even your cousin stopped having sex with you—and she wasn't getting it anywhere else. You're angry because the only difference between that cop costume you've got on and the orange smocks worn by your colleagues is that you have to be able to read to work your way up to the smock. I know you're bitter because you'll never be trusted to wear a badge that didn't come in a plastic bubble at and say 'Visit Wall Drug,' and that as a result you will be a member of the permanent underclass, driving used cars that leak oil and break down on the way to the drag strip so you've got to drink your six-pack on the side of the road while you wait for a friend named Ox to pick you up and take you to some roadhouse where you will get drunk because there is no possible way you're going to get laid and, well, alcohol really is your only release, isn't it?

"And that will lead to more complications. Fights. Fists through windows. A stern lecture from mom. Maybe a trip to the hoosegow and some counseling whose purpose you couldn't begin to understand. Am I right?

Come on. You can talk to me. I can even recommend a shrink to help you face the fact that your life is so worthless you might just as well never have been born. That's the first step—facing your failure as a human."

"You got a real smart mouth, asshole," was his elegant riposte. I was hoping for a little more. But I should have known better.

"Call me a real smart mouth just as long as you don't say I have a real pretty mouth, Tex," I cheerily responded. "I know all about repressed guys like you. But it's good that we can talk like this. It helps to work things out."

Just then, the real John Law walked in, which was probably lucky for me since the discussion was likely to take a more violent turn in a moment or two. But now I was going to feel the full force of the law. I had thought I could steal the Tic Tacs and still get home in time for the Hillbillies.

No dice. What a day.

"Hey, Rip," said the cop. "Whattya got here?"

I couldn't believe it. The guard's name was Rip. He was worse off than I thought. He had a dog's name, for pity's sake. Maybe I was too rough on him, I thought. That was until he opened his mouth again.

"This smelly fat queer tub of shit here was stealing Tic Tacs, just like all smelly fat queer tubs of shit do when they're not screwing monkeys," he said, straightening up, contemptuous as Joe Friday.

"Tic Tacs, eh?" the officer said, looking at me as though he had just caught the famed Chicago murderer Richard Speck. He enunciated his words the way many in these parts do. Lots of contractions, and plenty of nasal tonalities. "Jeez, pal, you coulda made it all worth it by cadging a Chunky or somethin'. Guy like you, I'd figure he's at least a big enough crook for some Jujy Fruits or a couple of Ho-Hos, maybe. You got a name, Tic Tac?"

"Jean Valjean," I said. I assumed they wouldn't catch the humor. I was right.

"Well, John, I'm gonna have to see some kinda identification," the cop said.

"Well, officer, that's a problem, since I was only carrying cash when I left the house," I explained. "I would gladly pay five dollars to make this right. It would be quite a return for this establishment."

"I'm gonna assume that's not some kinda bribe, boy, aina?" the cop said indignantly. The word boy sounded like "boa." And he used my favorite colloquialism, "aina." That means "ya know?" in these parts. He continued.

"But widdout proper identification we're gonna have to take ya down t'the station house."

"I can assure you, officer, my identification is on top of my television at home, not at the station house," I said patiently. These guys didn't even know when they were being patronized. What kind of a town was I living in?

Just then, Rip piped in. "Yeah, his name's got to be Val-John, 'cuz that's just what a fat smelly monkey-screwin' French queer would be named," he posited. "He wouldn't make up a name like 'at. But that don't change the fact that he took Tic Tacs that didn't belong to him even if his name was Lyndon Burns Johnston. What would happen if any French scumbag could come in here and steal Tic Tacs?"

"People at the trailer park would have fresher breath?" I said. "And I think you meant Lyndon Baines Johnson. That must have been senior year history at your high school. You must have been an excellent student, Rip, as your erudition is quite remarkable. You are quite the historian and wordsmith. And there you go with the homosexual stuff again. Is there something you need to tell us? Maybe you've got some Streisand at home?"

"You callin' me a fag, Fat Boy?" he said, rising from his chair and approaching me in a threatening manner.

"Of course not, Rip. A fine specimen such as yourself could only be a discriminating lover of beautiful women, or at least cute female pigs," I explained. "I'm calling you a moron, or as I'm sure you would pronounce it, a moh-rohn. It means dummy, idiot, shit-for-brains. You know. I'm sure you've been called these things by your loved ones. Aina?"

"I know what moron means, Fat Boy. Just don't ever call me a fag."

So there you have it. I live in a place where even the security guards would rather be called stupid than gay. There was no doubt that an enlightened future was a long way off in these parts. But at least you could get *The New York Times* at the gas station. Civilization hadn't totally passed us by.

Meanwhile, up until now, no one had actually produced the breath mints in question. No one had searched me, and so far as I could tell my only crime was giving lip to a half-wit security guard named Rip. This must have occurred to the police officer, who, as a professional, slowly began to realize some evidence would be needed in order to prove the crime and haul me to the gaol.

Finally, he asked me to empty my pockets, and I did so gleefully. I pulled out the wads of hardened Kleenex which had been put to use on several occasions for purposes I'm sure they didn't care to think about. I pulled out two fives, eight singles, a few quarters and some three pennies, about what I needed to buy the beer and cheese sticks that were my original purpose.

"Well, it looks like yer goin' for a ride, fella," the cop said. "Tic Tacs. Tic Tacs."

"Can we go to the beach instead, officer? I'd love to get some sun," I said cheerfully, trying to lighten up the room a bit. No dice. The cop just glared at me. The worst part of all this was I actually needed a couple of Tic Tacs. My mouth tasted like what I imagined the store floor would taste like.

"No, why don't we go the human zoo, Fat Boy," he said. "You'll see a lot of interesting animals in cages, and you get t'be one of them."

"What time is the hose-down?" I asked, and he smacked me on the side of the head.

I thought he had gotten a little personal with that Fat Boy remark. That was the third time that day I'd been called Fat Boy, but I decided not to mention it, especially when the cop put the clamps on me and prepared to take me to his squad car. I was physically vulnerable, and I didn't care to find out whether he was one of the cops who had difficulty on the psychological tests. I had all kinds of crime cliches running through my mind, and I had an urge to read Raymond Chandler novels, smoke cigarettes and drink bourbon. Maybe they had Chandler books at the jail library. I'd even have settled for Hammett. I wondered if I got to keep a tin jail cup as a souvenir.

Rip opened the door of the office and the cop led me through the store with the handcuffs on, a lesson to other potential thieves. I decided to make the best of it, since people were already turning around to see what was happening. Meanwhile, a skinny guy with two skinny kids was shoving small hardware items into his Bermuda shorts, and I thought I'd give him some cover. Here I was, sticking it to The Man while a colleague in thievery was making a much larger haul than I had.

"Your goon squad can't silence me!" I shrieked. "I'm telling the truth and you know it. This store is part of a vast conspiracy to sell Taiwanese appliances that are infested with Asian cockroaches! There will be others like me brave enough to speak out. Put that microwave down, ma'am, they've got listening devices in there! They need your brain waves to communicate with each other and take your ideas! I know! I used to be able to make Tom Brokaw blink while he was doing the news, but they knew I was getting too powerful. This is what happens to those of us who fight! They want to control us with toaster ovens! Don't be fooled! The U.N. is in on this, and so are the trilateralists. They've even found a way to penetrate the foil barriers we wear under our hats to keep them from reading our bad thoughts.

"The Chia Pet is just a diversion to keep you from the truth about the lousy linens they sell here. Don't be fooled. They're watching you, and they know what you buy. It's all about cornering the market on chicken! How now brown shopping cart, the silver metal cow of the middle class! Don't touch me, I'm anti-matter. Touch me and you destroy the universe. I'm anti-matter. I'm anti-matter. It doesn't matter pitter patter mad hatter batter up!"

Then I reached down and exorcized the loudest, deepest belch I could conjure from the ninth circle of my digestive tract. As the air escaped I rolled my eyes back in my head and yelled:

"I'm the devil. I'm the devil. How 'bout some devil's food cake?"

With a performance like that, at least no one suspected I was accused of the ridiculous petty crime for which I was suffering this indignity. It's interesting. If you talk quietly in public, people will look at you and strain to hear you in the assumption that you're telling a secret. But if you start screaming, they'll look away. And they all looked away. I could have been Milton Berle for all they knew, but as I howled, the Bermuda shorts guy darted for the door with about a couple thousand dollars' worth of merchandise. Probably he needed these things for the family reunion on Cape Cod.

While I was being brought out, I saw the Bermuda shorts guy head out in a hurry and I scanned the store for my friend. She had apparently accomplished what she had set out to do while I acted as her unwitting screen. I'll never know what eerie power she used to cloud my mind into doing her will. Normally, I would have told her I just didn't feel like doing what she asked because it would be too much trouble. But then again, normally I would never have picked up a hitcher.

Still, I think I was hoping to get one more chance at human contact when I picked her up.

I had given up on people so long ago that I didn't remember that humans can be pretty entertaining company sometimes. She was entertaining all right. But now she was gone, and I was on my way to jail.

That's what I got for trying to return to the human race. But soon enough, I'd be faced with even more human contact, and I would become part of a huge plan to create a new religious game show with an existing pop culture icon.

But it will take some time to explain that twist of destiny that briefly turned me into somebody. Well, almost.

Chapter 5
A Funny Thing Happened on the Way to Jail

My humiliation was nearly complete as we left the store and headed for the nearby squad car. We bumped into four sweet-faced young boys of about seven or eight years old who I had thought were looking for quarters for the little elephant ride but instead were attempting to break open the little elephant's cash box.

"Busted," one of them shouted at me, followed by another, then another. "Busted, busted, busted, Fat Boy. Get a job and pay for stuff, you bum!"

One of them threw a rock at me and hit me in the back before the cop told them to beat it.

The cop opened the back door of the squad car, pushed my head down and told me to be careful not to bump it getting in. The kids were still taunting me as I slid into the back seat of the prowl car, but I said nothing to frighten them and even the score. They would be getting my view of the squad car soon enough. Instead, I simply puckered my lips and make kissing motions through the window. That would bug them all afternoon. It was the wrong thing to do, since they were only kids, but I correctly guessed I wasn't going to destroy their innocent world view. Homophobia, that horrible form of bigotry common to the ignorant, had already infected the young halfwits.

"Aggh, he's queer!" the largest one shouted in disgust. "He blew kisses at me."

"That makes you queer," said one of his young companions. "Now you'll get general herpes, like those TV commercials say. Your mom will have to put cream on your balls."

"Call me queer again and see what happens," said the larger one. "And it's genital, not general, you idiot."

"OK, fag, you should know," said his companion, running away, the large one and others in pursuit as we pulled away.

The cop shook his head in disgust.

"Them boys'll be sittin' where you're sittin' sooner than later," he said. "What kind of parents bring up kids that behave that way so young? Why, when I was young we didn't know what genital herpes was unless we got it at a whorehouse. Now they got TV commercials making it seem like it's almost a good idea. People just don't teach their kids values anymore, and TV has just wrecked 'em altogether with MTV and genital herpes commercials and condom commercials. Y'know, it all started with them athletes foot commercials in the '70s. If people had complained about them things in the first place, we wouldn't be seeing commercials for tampons and herpes and condoms while we're eating dinner."

I was far too concerned with my own predicament to worry about a local police officer's views on the collapse of western civilization. I wasn't worried about jail, since I had created my own little prison years ago, although my prison had cable TV, a DVR selection that allowed me to watch pornography any time I wanted and a comfortable couch that I didn't have to share with strangers.

But I wanted to know what happened to K, or whatever her name was. My view of the human condition was horrible enough so that I always expected the worst, most selfish impulses from people. That way I was never surprised when they behaved like the swine that they were.

Still, because of those cynical feelings I should have been smarter than to trust a stranger. A hitchhiker, even. What was I thinking?

Of course, her betrayal only served to deepen my bitterness about humanity and modern society. I sat seething in the back seat of the squad car, looking at billboards for car dealerships with George Washington, the Father of Our Country with white huckster's teeth grinning, saying: "I cannot tell a lie. These are the best prices in town!" I saw others advertising cheesy jewelry as a means of getting laid and one awful tribute to Rev. Dr. Martin Luther King, Jr. with a tagline that read, "I have a dream… of the lowest prices on lawn furniture in town!"

Just as I leaned my forehead against the window of the car in despair, the squawk box shook me out of my gloom.

"Ah, are you in the vicinity of the Hee Haw Lounge?" said the dispatcher, a woman with a metallic voice.

This cop picked up the mic and responded. "Yeah, I'm pretty close. But I got a passenger with me. What's up? Hookers invade the place again? Big rat trapped behind the bar?"

"We've got a disturbance there, white male, about 45, has been asked to leave but won't."

"It seems kind of early in the day for that sort of thing. What's the problem? It ain't closin' time."

"The owner, a gentleman named Blackie Browne, says this guy is depressing his patrons and he wants him out. He's also bothering some of the women at the bar."

"Jeez, we can't start kickin' people outta bars for being depressing and tryin' to pick up chicks," the cop said. "Isn't that why bars were created? What's the problem?"

"Ah, the owner thinks this gentleman may have a gun. He hasn't seen one, but the guy's talking like he might have one."

"Oh, goody, a depressed drunken lunatic with a gun. This don't sound like no trouble at all. All right, I'm heading over there, but I'd send back-up. And call the loon hatch so they can get the nets ready."

"On their way."

"I'm sorry, sir, but we've gotta pick up another fare before we head to the steel-barred hotel," the cop said to me over his shoulder. "Don't worry, though, you've got reservations and your room will be ready."

"Fine, but you're tipping the bellboy after this delay," I said. Screw it. I thought I might as well go with it and absorb the entire experience, try to have a little fun. "You know, I'm familiar with the Hee Haw, and you could just drop me off there and I'll find my way to your hotel later."

"No dice, Dillinger, but you'll stay put while I deal with Mr. Loonyhearts," he said, unwittingly stealing my line. Maybe I would have to change it if even cops used it. "Besides, this will be a nice chance to meet a new friend. I can even arrange to make him yer new roommate until you get bailed out."

As I looked out the window, I saw a billboard with Abe Lincoln on it.

The author of the *Gettysburg Address*, the savior of the union, martyr for freedom, was winking at passersby and hawking a local pizza parlor owned by a Russian immigrant named Leonid. Abe was saying: "I haven't had better pizza in four score and seven years!"

I wondered if the Romans had Julius Caesar's image on the walls of the Coliseum selling chariots with the timeless line: "You've tried the rest, now try the best." No American icon is sacred, and no historical figure can be prevented from pitching refrigerators. That's why I love America.

It wasn't long before we pulled into the parking lot of the Hee Haw, one of the few taverns without a hammer theme. There didn't appear to be any problem from the outside. A bar like the Hee Haw looks like a problem in and of itself. A sign on a pole at the street advertised Huber beer on tap, a clue that the establishment was quite elderly.

The building itself, a ghastly brick edifice painted sky blue, framed a large front window that had a neon image of an animated donkey kicking up its heels. It was the kind of place where the men's rooms had little signs over the urinals saying: "We aim to please. You please aim too."

I had been to the Hee Haw many times after my own forgetfulness or sleepiness caused me to neglect a purchase at Booby's Booze Ranch, the local beer depot, before it closed later that night. I didn't like going anywhere to drink with strangers, but if I needed a beer and it was late, I went to the Hee Haw. It was the kind of place where it always seemed like night, and everyone's face had an eerie blue tinge. Some of the regulars used the place as a living room, watching sitcoms and baseball games while their wives at home wondered how long it took them to go out and buy a pack of cigarettes.

Before noon, the Hee Haw was usually kind of quiet. It was the time of day when Blackie, the owner and one of the bartenders, caught up on his cleaning, cooked his books and laid bets with local bookies. The name Blackie fit his disposition perfectly, although his name was really Othmar. He wasn't particularly friendly to strangers, his outlook on life was almost as desolate as mine, and even when he knew you his demeanor wasn't exactly warm. His good nature had simply been worn down by too many silly, angry and violent drunks. The constant sight of the worst of human impulses had drained him of whatever sense of human charity he had been born with.

His idea of a kind gesture was to buy you a beer when you'd already had so many it didn't make a difference.

Because of Blackie's dark philosophy of human nature, he usually didn't involve himself with the police, whom he trusted just a little more than his patrons. He knew how to take care of the establishment's problem children if they misbehaved. He didn't believe in gun ownership, figuring that a gun in a room full of drunks is about the worst form of protection imaginable for a bar owner.

Instead, he had an oddly patient manner with drunks, whatever their mood, and he could usually quiet them or get rid of them with a few tender words or gestures. But there were a few times when more drastic measures were required.

The occasional violent action made people realize that Blackie was not to be trifled with. He once broke up an ugly bar fight by pulling a bullhorn out from behind the bar and announcing that drinks were free for all peaceful customers. Everyone lined up and Blackie obliged them. Then when the main cause of trouble came for his drink, Blackie pulled out a nail gun and sent an 8-penny through the fleshy part of the guy's hand and into the bar. They actually had to use a claw hammer to pull the nail out. Hilarious.

Blackie's decision to call to the police, then, meant something very unusual was taking place. What was taking place wasn't unusual from the standpoint of incidents in sleazy bars. What was unusual was that the source of the problem was a famous national TV game show host, Jerry Most, the Host You Like to Toast. Most was becoming something of a popular culture icon because of his friendly manner, bright smile and puckish sense of humor as host of a network game show called "Die Trying."

As the massive promotional campaign promised, "Die Trying" offered to "take contestants where no other game show had taken them—to the brink of death ... and beyond."

At stake was thousands of dollars in cash and valuable prizes, all of which could be gained by answering trivia questions and, ultimately, trying to cheat death in some ill-conceived stunt arranged by the show's producers.

Although no one had died on the show yet, several contestants had come close, particularly the pedestrian who failed to cross the Hollywood Freeway safely as part of the "Final Challenge Round." Live television had caught the unfortunate contestant/pedestrian as he was clipped at the knees by a Porsche Targa just short of the shoulder of the road. He was hospitalized for several weeks, and after months of extensive therapy he was walking almost normally. Since he got hit, he missed out on the jackpot of $1.2 million, but he still walked away, sort of, with a new range, a stereo system, a kayak and, ironically, a home workout center. Had he died, the prizes would have been awarded to a friend or relative or charity of the contestant's choice.

"Die Trying" had rejuvenated the game show genre after viewers grew tired of watching people sacrifice pride and dignity for a shot at big money. Questions and answer shows had long since died out, since too many viewers were confused by even simple history questions. By the end of the "Q&A format," as networks called them, the shows had grown so mundane that people were being awarded Jeep Grand Cherokees simply by correctly answering questions like: "Who was the first president of the United States?"

From the "Q&A format," the network masterminds cooked up a number of shows like "Cash for Your Pride" and "Dignity for Dollars," in which contestants won prizes by answering third-grade level trivia questions and then advancing to the "Hot Zone" where they dared each other to perform the most embarrassing acts on live TV. Though the TV execs thought the idea would be popular forever, the public grew weary of watching accountants and store clerks walk through shopping malls in diapers or dropping on all fours in a muddy pig sty at a children's zoo for a chance at cash and prizes.

And while men could never tire of watching women bear their breasts on television, those shows started losing the women's demo, and that was it. Something new was needed. A new level needed to be reached, and a young network executive dreamed up "Die Trying." After it cleared a dubious network legal department, the show was green-lighted and has been phenomenally popular ever since.

That meant, of course, that Jerry Most was phenomenally popular as well. So when he showed up drunk in a bar in a town in the middle of nowhere, it was likely to cause a stir. Any other gun-toting, drunken game show host might not have caused much concern. But when the guy hosts a show based on the notion of death as a penalty for losing, it can make everybody a little nervous.

The cop entered the Hee Haw. Blackie immediately put his index finger to his greasy lips, signaling for quiet. There, face down and motionless at the end of the bar, was a very drunk, semi-conscious Jerry Most. He was moaning softly and tapping his fingers rhythmically on the bar. And wouldn't you know it, sitting next to him was my friend K. She had apparently spotted Jerry as a new mark, and she was gently stroking his back and telling him everything would be all right while drinking a martini that had almost certainly been purchased with Most's money.

He didn't look like Jerry Most. At least not the guy on the TV show. He had no makeup on, his hair was greasy, and he was wearing khaki Dockers, a black Bruce Springsteen tour T-shirt and a tan corduroy sport jacket with dirty patches on the elbows. The cop approached him slowly, giving K a chance slip away and walk outside. K had a natural suspicion of cops, and could usually be counted on to disappear when they were with 100 feet of her. But the cop wasn't worried about her.

"Sir? Ah, mister, you OK?" the cop said, trying to shake Most awake.

"Physically, I'm fine, although quite drunk even at this early hour of the day," he said. "Spiritually and morally, I am quite ill. Is that a crime in this town? If so, then I plead guilty to having a bankrupt soul. And by the way, which town is this?"

"You tellin' me you don't know where ya' are?" the cop said.

"Of course. I am where I am most comfortable, the bar," he said. "Spiritually I am lost in a void I cannot escape. I search for meaning and ..." The cop cut him off.

"Look, we got a report says you were drunk. Frankly, that's Blackie's problem until you start breakin' things or hittin' people," the cop said. "But we also heard you might have a gun. You got a gun?"

Most raised his head.

"If you tell me which town I'm in, I'll tell you if I have a .357 Magnum in my left breast pocket," he said. "I'll tell you I brought it with me because I have been searching the country for an appropriate place to blow my brains out. So far, this little burg has a lot to recommend as a venue for such actions as suicide."

"Hoh-kay," the cop breathed deeply. "I'm gonna reach inta yer pocket and take the gun, if you don't mind. You don't have a problem with that, do you?"

"Die Trying," Most mumbled.

The cop suddenly got very excited. "Don'choo you fucking move," he said, drawing his own gun.

"What, are you going to shoot me? That's what I want, you stupid hick," Most said. "I didn't mean you would die trying to get the gun. I means that this would be a great challenge for my game show, "Die Trying." You know, relieve the suicidal drunk of his weapon. I've got to write this down."

"Just let me take the gun," the cop said, reaching in and pulling out what did indeed appear to be a brand-new .357 Magnum.

"Don't worry, I don't know how to use it anyway," Most said, cheering up a bit. "Say, officer, you saved my life. Now I can't kill myself. Well, thanks a lot. I must be off. There are many other small town bars to terrorize with my own personal demons and whatever weapons I can buy at their sporting goods stores."

"Well, since I'm sure you didn't bother to register this weapon, I'm gonna have ta take you in," the cop said. "You'll have to come along with me."

By now a back-up cop had arrived, but he wasn't needed. "Situation's under control," he said as he cuffed Most and lead him by the elbow toward the exit. He wanted to make the arrest himself because it isn't often police in Hammertown, Wisconsin, even get to see, let alone arrest, a national celebrity.

While all this was going on inside the bar with Most, K slipped out of the bar and saw me in the back of the squad car. She was carrying a backpack filled with merchandise she had pilfered from the Kmart. She was twirling in a little circle and holding the backpack at arm's length. She walked over and pressed her face against the glass, distorting her lips and nose and smearing her lipstick, a bright shade of tramp red, across the glass. She laughed and turned in a little taunting circle.

"Wanna kiss, baby?" she said. "I wanna kiss you cuz I know your breath is fresh as a peppermint Tic Tac. Or was that wintergreen?"

"From which vent of hell did you rise?" I asked. "Or are you simply possessed by an evil force?"

"Oh, come on, doll. Ain't this more fun than watchin' reruns and masturbating on your worn-out old couch?" she yelled through the glass in a sing-song voice.

"As opposed to having my eyelids ripped off, yeah, this is a blast," I said. "I'm so glad I offered you the ride. This has been a life-changing experience. Really. Thank you. Now would you please put your head beneath one of the wheels of this police car so that when we leave at least half of my problems will be solved."

"Yer just teasing me, I know it," she said, affecting a really annoying Lolita persona. "I betcher sweet on me. But we can't do anything about that right now. Howdja like ta see what I stoled before the cop comes out?

Nah, I don't wanna get ya too excited. You've got another treat in store, anyway. Yer goin' ta jail with a real celebrity. Jerry Most. Ya know, from 'Die Trying' ? He's in'nere drunk and they're gonna put him right in the same car with you."

"Terrific. Maybe he'll give me a personal challenge round and help me hang myself in jail," I said. "And no, I'm not particularly interested in your booty. I mean your loot, not your posterior."

"You talkin' dirty to me?" she said. "Posty rear sounds kinda sexial."

Just then, the door to the Hee Haw opened and Most and the cop emerged. K slipped away again, but I figured that I would see her again whether I wanted to or not. Most looked pretty wobbly, but he was chattering wildly, talking about feats by great men and how he could never measure up to Hugh Downs or Alex Trebek and complaining that he was being treated "like a common drunk."

I wasn't impressed by celebrity. I knew that even great movie and rock stars had wives who forced them to take out the garbage. They weren't any better off than I was, just wealthier.

So when Most entered the car I didn't piss myself in excitement or anything. I did worry that the motion of the car might make him puke on me. Of course, if he did I could always have sold the puke-spattered jeans to one of Most's many fans.

As they pushed him into the squad car Most's head bobbed as though he was on truth serum, but he was lucid enough to know he had company in the back seat. The squad pulled into traffic, and Most started speaking.

"Hello, and welcome to the squad car show. I'm Jerry Most, The Host You Like to Toast," he said. "We've got a great ride ahead of us today, so let's get ready to play. What's your name and where are you from? What do you like to eat? Can dogs read our minds? Hey officer, did I leave a tip for the barkeep?"

K was right. This was more interesting than lying on the couch all day. Even if I wasn't impressed by pop culture stars, riding to jail with a guy like Jerry Most was almost as entertaining as a rerun of "December Bride" with Spring Byington. I decided to go along with the drunk. Maybe I could even humiliate a so-called star. That might give me some psychic fuel to continue the struggle to go on living.

"Hi, Jerry," I said, mocking him excitedly. "Well, my name is Claude Rains, I'm from right here in Hammertown, and I sell electronic secrets to the Chinese. I'm a Pisces, I love beer, long walks on the beach and skinning cats alive. And no, dogs can't read your mind, but cats do have hypnotic abilities and can see through your clothes."

The cop chimed in. "Hey, Claude, I thought your name was John V. St. Jean. Have you got aliases? What th' hell's going on with you? You playin' straight?"

"Why would cats want to use X-ray vision to see through our clothes?" Most asked, looking delightfully confused. "Are you a nut case, Chubby? Jesus, am I going to the happy home with a guy who sweats under his tits? And I don't like cats."

"To answer your question, officer, I have no aliases, just one name: Pele. But you can call me Wanker. My friends call me Mojo. And as for you, Jerry, cats need to see through your clothes so they know where your flesh is softest so they can bite into it and finish you off the minute they decide they've had enough of you. They're the devil's pet, you know. It's in the Bible. Book of Jojo, I believe."

"Ain't no book of Jojo in the Bible, smart guy," the cop sneered.

"Maybe it was the Koran, or the Bhagavad Gita, or the Dead Sea Scrolls," I said. "I know some religious document said to steer clear of cats, and I've always considered it sound advice. Maybe it was my Grampa, I don't know. But I'll give you this much. Maybe they weren't referring to kitties. Maybe they were talking about lions or ocelots, beasts that eat people. Those could be the devil's pets, although we've anthropomorphized the lion into a terribly noble creature. Still, a lion would tear our throats out, given half the chance. But we still think of him as good old Leo."

"Ya know," said Most, perking up, then swallowing hard. "Ya know ...." He was fading, so he tried to get his sentence out as fast as possible, in one word.

"Fatguylikeyouwhoknowsaboutocelots," he slowed to enunciate. "Should ... be ... on ... my ... (hic) ... my show."

But before we could pursue this most interesting notion, Most delivered the puker's warning, the double-lipsmack. He nodded, eyes opening and closing slowly, desperately trying to focus. He made the mistake of looking out the window, which drunks should never do when the car is in motion. We stopped at a light, and he seemed to rally, closing his eyes hard.

Outside, a man in a pink bunny costume was passing out invitations to attend Easter services at a local church. He wore a sandwich sign that said "Jelly beans and Salvation Free!" I made a mental note to bring Grampa to Easter services at this church. No telling what kind of get-up he would concoct for a non-denominational church that used Easter bunnies as shills, but my guess is his miter would likely be taken out of mothballs for the occasion instead of his normal Santa Claus Easter costume.

Most could not have been less concerned about saving his soul at the moment, as he was trying to save his breakfast. As the light turned green and the squad moved again, he opened his eyes again, and then delivered the double-smack warning again. He smacked his lips once loudly and then twice. As a person who is familiar with the effects of alcohol poisoning, I knew what came next and moved as far to my end of the squad as I could. Bingo. Most puked against the back of the front seat, then again on the floor.

"Oh Jee-sus H. Goddammit. Son of a mother fucking bitch, the shit puked in my squad car," squealed the cop. "Hey, asshole, bigshot TV guy, yer gonna pay to get the smell out of this car. That smell's gonna bake in here permanently. Son of a bitch ..."

"Ah, I think it's customary for public safety officials, well, civilized human beings anyway, to ask if someone in Mr. Most's condition is all right and offer help," I offered. "I'm sure he'll be willing to pay for the damages, or die trying, once he feels better."

That time I had amused myself. Die trying. That's good. Sometimes I kill me.

"Yeah, well because I got you two clowns in my squad I can't go ta da car wash and clean up this mess," he said. "I gotta take you in and book ya first. Damn it all."

"You could always let us out here," I said. "We promise we'll be good. Right, Jerry?"

Jerry began snoring violently. Vomit dripped off of his chin and onto his T-shirt.

"If I let you two out of the car it would be at the edge of town where I'd give ya thirty seconds to run before I caught you and beatcher brains in," he said, sounding a bit like he was losing his temper. I actually started to think he might make good on the threat until I realized that beating our brains in would only further delay the clean-up of his precious squad car, one of only a few in Hammertown.

The stench was beginning to rise, though, and I breathed through my mouth to try to block the scent of half-digested booze and what appeared to be breakfast sausage. But my throat was beginning to tighten involuntarily. I gagged, but thankfully produced nothing.

"You fuckin' puke in here too an' there's gonna be a real unfortunate accident at the jail," said the cop, who now had turned on his warning lights and siren and was speeding. We were screeching through town as though he had picked up Charles Manson and Son of Sam. But all he had was a drunken game show host, a Tic Tac thief, and about a quart of vomit on the squad car interior.

I wondered if this is how the cop dreamed of his life when he was in cop school. He probably thought he'd be keeping the streets safe and putting away bad guys. Instead, he hauled away drunks and shoplifters, ticketed jaywalkers and got blown off when he tried to pick up women because they didn't want to date a cop, which was a nice way of saying he was an officious dork.

He couldn't be happy with how things ended up. And that made me wonder if my own shattered dreams, or lack of dreams at all, was actually the strongest thread of commonality I had with my fellow human beings. We all suffered humiliations as part of the price we paid to have a career or just make a living. The cop and the game show host were no different.

I didn't have much time to consider this state of affairs, because the cop took a sharp turn and Jerry plunked his head on my shoulder and began urinating in his khaki Dockers.

It took a minute for the cop to notice.

"Dear God, I better not be smellin' piss back dere," he said in a low growl.

"You are right, you better not, because if you, do you might puke, too," I said. "If you're asking if our friend has evacuated his bladder here in your squad car, or at least in his pants, I must report to you that he did, and that it is indeed urine that you are probably smelling at this moment. It smells as though he has been eating his vegetables, though.

"Actually, the piss makes a nice counter-point to the smell of the bile, doesn't it? To me it's reminiscent of a casserole my dear departed mother used to make. I didn't like it much, but it makes me happy to smell something that reminds me of her. It's like she's still in the kitchen."

The cop was now beginning to tum red, and I thought for a minute he might actually throw us both out of the car so he could go get it cleaned. No dice. He wanted to keep us as long as he could, just to punish us. But as we sped down the street and were just a few blocks from the station house, wouldn't you know it, the red lights at the railroad crossing went on and the safety arms came down. A train was coming. A freight train. A long freight train. I thought I was going to see an officer of the law break down and cry. But he maintained the angry posture.

"Why da hell is it every fuck-in' time ya gotta be somewheres, ya run into a train?" he breathed in a kind of low Clint Eastwood "make-my-day" tone.

"Well, what other time would you run into a train?" I volunteered. "When you're sitting on your couch at home? When you're sleeping in your office? Obviously you have to be going somewhere or you wouldn't be in your car and in a position to meet a train at a crossing."

He turned around, eyes narrow with hatred.

"I've always wondered what it would be like to split an asshole's tongue down da middle wit' a wire cutters," he said, suddenly turning spookily menacing. "Maybe I get to find out today."

"Well, you'd have to find an asshole first. I'm a pretty nice guy, actually," I said. Then I decided to shut up. He did, after all, carry a gun and a nightstick and have the force of law behind him. It seemed silly to wake up in a body cast and a split tongue for stealing Tic Tacs.

We both stared forward silently as Jerry snored like a snowmobile. Occasionally, he would wake slightly and gurgle up a little more puke, and the cop would just sigh heavily. Finally, the last rail car passed and in a few minutes we were at the station house. The cop opened the door to let me out. Then he went to Jerry's side and opened the door. Jerry, who had been leaning against the window since we stopped at the train, fell straight to the pavement.

What happened next is one of those things that still brings me joy in my darker moments. The cop, leaning in to survey the damage, accidently inhaled while looking at the mess. Anyone who's ever been in a bar knows you should never look at puke, even your own, unless you want to get sick.

The gendarme broke this most basic of rules. He looked at the mess, and he puked on the parking lot, and then he puked all over Jerry with what seemed to be an intentional second effort. Jerry, of course, never knew what hit him as he remained unconscious through the ordeal.

It is a saying amongst the lost creatures who frequent cheesy bars that there is nothing funnier than watching a guy puke. But there is something funnier: It is watching a guy puke on another guy, and it is especially humorous when one of the pukers wears a badge. And there is something ultimately funnier than watching a man puke on another: watching than same man slip and fall in the contents of his own digestive tract.

The poor cop could only manage one attempt at speech as he went down:

"Criiiymineeeeee."

Rather than be furious, he rose defeated. He got up quietly, picked up Jerry, and motioned for me to follow him into the station house.

After all I had been through, when all I wanted to do was watch "The Beverly Hillbillies" and drink beer, I believed I had truly been blessed. I got to watch two of the funniest and most disgusting incidents I have ever seen take place within a matter of seconds. It was truly a memory I would cherish for years, or, as some hockey player once said, it was a memory I'll never forget.

I would certainly think about this day every time I saw Jerry Most, the Host You Like to Toast, tormenting one of his contestants. Or every time I see that cop lecturing somebody about speeding or jaywalking or sniffing glue.

But now the fun part of my day was over. Even though my crime was minor, I was going to spend some time in jail until I got some bail money and identification. I was hoping that Grampa would be awake to answer the phone when I made the traditional jailhouse phone call. But as it turned out, I had such a nice conversation with Jerry, once he woke up, that I was willing to wait awhile.

Chapter 6
Confessions of a Game Show Host

Jerry Most was, by most accounts, a real asshole. I use the word not because I necessarily think that that kind of vulgarity is necessary. The English language is full of great words that are better than "asshole" and more acceptable. Take "rascal," or "rapscallion," for example. But we've become such an illiterate society that using words like that might cause you to be labeled a prissy or pretentious or faux intellectual, or worse yet in places like Hammertown, gay.

Anyway, the reason I use the word "asshole" to describe Jerry Most is because I read in *People* magazine that even his closest friends, what few there are, called him that. An asshole.

But part of Jerry's mass appeal was the fact that he was abusive to his contestants, and of course, in our society acts of public cruelty are humorous. His brand of ridicule entertained a nation that spent its day taking abuse from bosses, whom they resentfully referred to as "superiors" because their own insecurities lead them to believe that their bosses really were superior. After a day of taking flak, watching some poor slob get mocked on national TV made their emotional load a little lighter. Jerry Most's abusive nature reassured the public that they weren't alone in their desperate wish to be treated better by their bosses and the rest of the world.

Or that they weren't the only ones who wanted to humiliate someone they viewed as lesser than themselves.

But Jerry's game show persona was no act. It was all Jerry. No physical imperfection, no expression of nervousness and certainly no failure to correctly answer a question went unpunished. He even liked to refer to his barbs as "Most Toasties." But he treated those around him the same way as he treated his hapless contestants.

He was especially harsh on the weaker members of the herd. Once, he went on the air with a pronounced, Daffy Duck lisp, which he said was in honor of a quiet, shy young intern named Sally whom he named on camera.

The intern was known to be highly insecure about her condition, and as a result was terribly quiet around the studio. And when she introduced herself to Jerry as "Thally," Jerry went nuts.

"Can't understand a word the little goon says," Jerry told a national audience. "That lisp would even have some kind of cute, come-hither quality if she weren't so homely. One thing's for sure, you can't help but snicker when she's telling you ridiculous stories about boyfriends she's obviously made up. You've got to mop off the phone every time she uses it. I mean, where the hell do we get these people? Someone fire her right now for being a retard who can't talk. We don't need any retards spraying our phones with retard gob. Get her outta here! I mean it! Now let's play the game!"

Now that a national audience was aware of a sweet, passive young woman's speech impediment, Jerry invited the contestants, whom he called semi-humans, to play "Die Trying." "Frankly, I hope you all die, but only one can win," he said. "Maybe we should change the rules so we can kill all of you."

Backstage, Sally had broken past security, grabbed a fire axe and headed toward the stage yelling, "Ath-hole! Fucking ath-hole. I'll kill you, Mithter Motht" before she was tackled by a nearby producer.

Interestingly, Most was such a scary bastard that it is not surprising that even a woman with a fire axe in her hand and a bad agenda would maintain the respectful "Mister" before his miserable name. Sally was summarily fired on the spot for threatening to kill the host. She was dragged out of the building crying hysterically, screaming, "It'th not fair. It'th not fair."

"That man may be an asshole, a horrible prick, but you don't kill a man with such high ratings, you little shit. He's everyone's bread and butter," yelled the producer as they dragged Sally out.

"You just don't go after a man like Jerry Most with a fire axe," the producer -underling added under her breath: "A wooden stake would be more appropriate. Or maybe you just gouge out his eyes. Or feed him Drano."

Jerry's three marriages had ended with similar incidents. He was not above revealing the most intimate and embarrassing facts about any of his wives at any point in the show. Of his first wife, an aspiring actress named Candy Walker, he said that she had hammer toes that made her feet look like they belonged to a grizzly bear.

"And it was a real pain because she was always getting her toenails caught in the carpet," he said. "That wouldn't be so bad if she didn't drool during orgasms. I thought I was going to drown sometimes."

That marriage miraculously lasted a year. And when Candy left, Most referred to her as a "boozehound," although everyone who knew her said she seldom drank. Later, Most met a network news anchorwoman, Marilyn Hopper, who made the mistake of falling for him. It wasn't long before Most went on the show and started talking about "the whiteheads on her face that required three applications of base makeup to cover for the camera."

"I'm warning you, folks, don't get close to the TV when she's doing the news," he said. "Her very gaze could give you volcanic whiteheads, she's so contagious. Hey, honey, here's a news flash: Your zits are scaring the kids. Don't worry children, she can't get at you through the TV. Say, sweetie, before I get home tonight remember to use the belt sander on that puss or I won't be able to kiss you. And make sure you wash your greasy pillow case."

His third wife, a Southern deb named Antoinette "Toni" Jackson, who had previously gone unknown to the masses, thought she could change him with her strong personality, good breeding and steely will. This was, of course, a mistake, a mistake which made itself known where all the others had. On the show.

"You know, my wife Toni, excuse me, An-Twan-Ett, is the worst kind of redneck ever to be conceived by horny teenagers at a drive-in," he said. "This is a woman who actually farts loudly in bed, then spits in the air to make me put my head under the covers. She enjoys the smell of her own gas, for God's sake. I'm telling you, it smells like the kid she promised me died in her intestines. But that's not all. One night she was snoring so loud that the police came to the house thinking I was cutting her up with a chainsaw."

Toni was out of the house for good by the time that show was over.

It didn't have to be true for Most to say it. If it was plausible, that was good enough. That's why people who met him hated him almost instantly. I, on the other hand, found something to admire. For one thing, nobody screwed with a guy like Most. How many people in this world can claim such invulnerability and even have the money to back it up? In some ways, we were in the same business, and as far as using verbal torture, no one was better than Most. I couldn't wait for him to sober up so we could talk about some of the meanest, most horrible things we had done to another person. There were lots of laughs in store for the two of us, some real good times.

I thought for a moment that it would be just my luck for Grampa to show up right away and deny me the chance to talk shop with another master. But the thought of Grampa at the wheel reassured me that I would have a lot of time before I was sprung.

Jerry was only semi-conscious when he started rattling on about how much he hated his life. Of course, it was a little hard for me, a guy whose life revolved around cheese sticks, beer and TV reruns, to feel sorry for a guy who got paid a lot of dough to insult people, do very little work, and got laid every time his eyes landed on even the coldest women.

It turned out I underestimated Jerry's desire to make a change in his life. And I never could have guessed what he had in mind for me as part of his own personal redemption, his own self-guided journey to righteousness. As he lay on a bench at the back of the cell moaning softly, he seemed an unlikely candidate for such redemption.

On the other hand, maybe you've got to be lying on a bench softly moaning through an alcoholic haze before you become a candidate for atonement.

Jerry, Mr. Most, and I shared the cell with a worker from The Chips who had snapped and threatened his supervisor with, wouldn't you know it, a hammer. He was waiting for his wife to come and bail him out, and while he was waiting he decided he needed a little validation from me and the slowly awakening Jerry Most.

The guy was pacing back and forth in the front of the cell as I sat at Jerry's feet reading graffiti on the wall. From what I gathered from the graffiti, a gentleman called Big Jack had been there several times, unless I mistook the reason for the hash marks next to the message.

In addition, someone named Donnie had a giant penis, but I guessed that Donnie was the author of that statement. And, of course, there was the requisite name-calling. It turned out that several people, according to this Rosetta Stone of jail data, were fags, including a guy named "Stiv," who I instinctively did not want to meet no matter what his sexual orientation.

There was also art, the most interesting of which had a one-eyed Native American riding a Harley-Davidson motorcycle and following an eagle into the clouds. There was also a full-colored clown which was simply disturbing, especially when I noticed he had fangs and sharp hooks for hands.

I was starting to think about writing a message of my own when my train of thought was interrupted by the pacing hammer-wielder with a curious way of expressing himself. When he got angry, he used spoonerisms. That is, he sometimes scrambled the first letters of the last words he spoke in each sentence.

This was him: "Look, you know what it's like when a boss just rides you and rides you until you just wanna fash his smace in?" he said out of the blue. "Don't I have a right to wanna rip his face off and deed it to the fog?"

"Well, I've heard about marriages like that, but as I am self-employed I have never had the privilege of having a boss of any kind, especially one whom I wanted to maim," I said. "I'm not sure I would deed his face to the fog if I ripped it off in any event."

"Oh, man," he said. "You can't know what it's like. It's morse than warriage. At least with marriage you get sex once or twice a year. But work's different. See, this guy Steve, I went to high school with him, and he was OK, man, really OK. We used to go out into the woods and smoke dope and drink cheap vodka together and listen to the Moody Blues on a little portable tape recorder and talk about girls and look at the stars, man, pretend we were gonna be some kinda astronaut. That's a long time ago man, and we go way back. We even got the jobs together at the computer chip factory.

"We work together for five years, and everything's fine. Then he gets a promotion to floor supervisor, and he's all like, 'I'm better than you now.' I asked him to go out for beers with me once, and he said no, being hung over hurt productivity. Then he said he'd report me if I was hung over the next day. Threatened to make me pee in a cup just to make sure. I grabbed him by the smock and told him I was gonna piss right down his throat. Then he puts me on report.

"Can you believe it? On report? What kinda friend would do something like that?

"And fuck you, making fun of me with that deeding fog thing. You knew what I meant. "When I'm pissed I get my scretters lambled. So sucking fue me, asshole. Goddammit, I did it again. Calm down, Charlie, calm down."

"So that's your name? Charlie? Or are you speaking to some sort of invisible friend?" I asked.

"Yeah, it's Charlie. Charlie Schwandtske, from over in Little Rose," he said, sticking out a meaty hand. "What's yers?"

"I am Ironman," I said in a gravelly voice. "My apologies for making fun of your speech problem. I just thought you misspoke and I found it funny. You've got to look for laughs in a place like this, right?"

That was a mistake. I should never make reference to any heavy metal band or song with someone who finds the meaning of life under the hood of a car or in the lyrics of Deep Purple's "Smoke on The Water." The definition of boredom is listening to these specimens orate at length about how their favorite guitar-burning slasher was actually "classically trained." It always interested me that rock music fans often sought to legitimize the music by comparing it with classical music.

I'm not sure, if things were turned around, that Ludwig Von Beethoven would claim musical legitimacy by saying he had been trained by Eddie Van Halen. But my cellmate was not prepared for such a discussion. I had simply turned him on by mentioning a song he said was his "anthem."

"Hey, you mean yer name is like that song? 'Running as fast as they can. Iron-man lives again.' Man, me 'n' Steve used to listen to that in the woods, too. We both loved Peep Durple. Dammit. Deep Purple. But yer name ain't Ironman. I figure it's Heinz or something German."

"Actually, I think that it was Black Sabbath, not Deep Purple, who did 'Ironman,'" I said, regretting the words the minute they left my mouth. I had accidentally continued the conversation, a symptom of prison madness, no doubt.

"Could be Frank Sinatra, for all I care. It was a good song," he said. "Man, I wish I was Ironman right now. I'd Ironman that asshole Steve's face so his own mom didn't know who he was. I'd jam them iron rods into his eyes and then twist them around so his brains would leak out, if he has any, and then ..."

"Really, Charlie, I get the idea," I said. "And congratulations for expressing anger without using those spoonerisms. But listen, I don't know why I'm suggesting this. Maybe it's because I've been burned by assholes like Steve, too. Here's what I'm going to do for you, free of charge, even though I get usually get paid a nominal sum for this sort of thing. I'm going to write Steve a poison pen letter for you. Just pipe down."

"A poison pen letter? Shit, I thought you meant you were gonna kill him. What the living fuck can you do with a lasty netter?"

"Charlie, I'm not going to insult you, but with your limited intellectual resources, I'm guessing that writing was one tool you never learned to use," I said.

"Hell no. Once I learned the turret lathe, I figured I had a job for life. But when the hammer factory shut down I spent some time on unemployment and then welfare, but when the The Chips came I had to go back to school and learn computer stuff," he said. "Never had much use for writin'. They learned me what writin' I needed to know to graduate high school, but by now I've forgotten all that."

"Well, I can assure you, one of my letters will make Steve feel real bad," I said. Just to make it more attractive to him, I said: "You know, if I write it correctly, Steve may even want to kill himself. And that will save you the trouble."

"Nobody's going to commit suicide over a letter," said a third voice. It was Jerry, who apparently had been listening. "But I bet if I could get to this guy I could make him feel really ratty. In fact, if this guy doesn't cut his wrists after I'm done with him, I'll give you a hundred dollars."

"I don't know who you are, mister, but I can't lose either way with that deal. You serious?" Charlie said, apparently quieting down enough to speak normally.

"I'm not sure I'm quite sober enough to be serious, but yes, I will honor this arrangement," Jerry said.

Charlie turned to me, then to Jerry. "Look, maybe you can be real mean to Steve in front of everybody, then this fat guy can give him the letter he's gonna write," Charlie said, hopping up and down excitedly. "I like this. This is better than putting a steel bar in his head and using it like a handle and dragging him around the highway until he's wore down like a pencil eraser. Just a red smear on the highway, that's what Steve would be."

"I'm delighted I can brighten your miserable life, even if briefly," Jerry said. "But you will be honored to know you will be the last person for whom I will perform this service. After that, I'm going to find religion or something and start being more humane to those who are lesser than me. I've seen the light. Jail can be a very redemptive experience."

"Well, I'm not sure what you just said, but jail can be OK as long as you're not in a cell with a homo," Charlie said. "At least the wife ain't screechin' at ya in a cell."

"Does everything in this town revolve around fear of homosexuality?" I asked. "It's really getting tiresome."

"Look, pal," Jerry said. "A guy like me knows that fear of homosexuality creates some of the worst possible insults for males. You trying to take away one of my best bits?"

"I just thought that ... oh, never mind," I said. "It's not up to me to change the world. Not as long as I can watch 'The Rockford Files' every afternoon."

"You know, Charlie," Jerry said. "A guy like you would have been a great target for me in my soon-to-be former life. You're ignorant, you've got poor hygiene, you've never left this town, and your idea of high entertainment is watching the pregame show before Green Bay Packers games. But something inside me says take care of your enemy, and then start being nice."

"That'll kill your ratings," I warned. "You sure this little epiphany is a good idea?"

"It's time," Jerry said. "I know it."

"Well, as a man who hates all people, let me just tell you you're breaking my heart," I said. "I really thought you despised humanity as much as I did. I even thought we might form a partnership and travel the world taking out our frustrations of life on others. Maybe you're still intoxicated."

"I've made all the money I can make off the dickhead schtick, and I've lost three wives in the process," he said. "Maybe I can make a little more by turning myself into Dick Clark, the guy who used to do the New Year's Eve shows. I don't feel the need for people to love me, although becoming a beloved television figure wouldn't kill me. But I'm feeling the need to be a better person."

"Well, it's nice to know that you're motivated by such noble impulses as having made enough money," I said. "Most megastars such as yourself don't know when enough is enough. I'm proud of you, Jerome, even though I truly thought I had found my soul mate—and I don't mean that in a homosexual context. But before you give it all up, may I request that you have Charlie drive that steel rod through your head first? Honest, it wouldn't make a difference, but it would make me feel good."

Jerry shook off the lame sarcasm, but the conversation had helped Charlie get his bearings. It had taken him awhile, but Charlie started to understand that he was in the presence of celebrity. A celebrity, of course, had wisdom and intelligence and represented a chance to be king for a day.

It was dawning on Charlie that this might be the best day his life would offer him, and it included a chance to have a celebrity dress down an old friend and current nemesis, Steve.

"Wait a minute," Charlie said, getting excited now because of the recognition that he was in the presence of television greatness. "Aren't you that guy on 'The Price is Right?' No, wait. It's 'Jeopardy.' You're the guy on 'Jeopardy.' Hey, why are those questions so hard? You guys don't give away that much money, anyway. You should make the questions easier. Books of the Bible is a fine category, but you don't need all that science and literature stuff and what the hell is potpourri?"

"You are testing my newfound sense of kindness and patience confusing me with the pedestrian crap you have watched all your life," Jerry told him. "However, I will tell you that I am Jerry Most, that well-known host of the show, 'Die Trying,' a show you have no doubt viewed through a beery haze at some point in your miserable life. Sorry. As for making the questions easier, I suspect even the finest grade schools in this little shithole could not have prepared you for questions anymore difficult than, 'What time is it?' or 'What is your dog's name?'"

"Ooooh yeah," Charlie said. "Hey, now I know you. Say, did that one guy really get eaten by piranhas? It sure looked real, but I told my wife it was just some kind of magic fish-tank trick. Maybe you just switched and threw some homeless guy in the tank instead? Did it really happen?"

"I could produce the gentleman's bleached bones or introduce you to his widow, who drives a brand new Blazer as a reward for her husband's bravery, if you so desired," Jerry lied.

"The network kept the rights to the skeletal remains of that erstwhile Mark Spitz. The guy just didn't swim fast enough. Frankly, I told him he'd have a better chance in the Crips-Bloods gang fight crossfire. But it was his decision. Anyway, I was thinking about having his carcass mounted in my office until I decided to change my life this morning."

Jerry was making it all up, of course, but poor Charlie never thought to question him. It was too good a story, and Charlie was delighted.

"Fuckin'-A, it's really you," said Charlie. "Jerry Most. The Host Who Eats Toast! Do you think you could ever get me on your shame go? I've been cheating death my whole life, so I figure I could beat death on yer show easy, aina? Whattya say? My crew at work would be real proud. Hell, my wife might even start sleepin' with me again."

"Well, you'll have to be screened somehow to make sure you're worthy to risk death on television," Jerry said. "Are you prepared to acquaint yourself with the finer details of The French Revolution and its meaning to Western Civilization in exchange for a chance to be buried in a pit of wet cement and a shot at big cash and valuable prizes?"

"Are you kiddin' me?" Charlie said. "You could pour maple syrup all over my balls and let the yellow jackets come as long as I had a shot at a Dodge Dakota and maybe a trip to Cancun or the Bahamas for the wife. Man, Steve would know I wasn't just some asshole he could push around if I had a Dakota. Plus, I could use it to haul garbage to the dump every Saturday, and I wouldn't have to strap deers to the top of my Tercel when I went huntin'."

"Well, Charlie, other than jail we also have the Tercel in common. A fine car in the snow, um, aina?" I said, wearily entering the conversation and now hoping that Grampa would arrive soon. "Do you find it has the pick-up you need when robbing a gas station or dodging police while driving drunk?"

"Tercel's a piece of shit, my friend," he said. "All Hoyotas and Tondas are shit. American's the only way to go if you can afford it. Only a goofball would drive a Jap car of any kind if the bill collector wasn't chasin' him. B'lieve me, I wouldn't be drivin' no Tercel if could afford a nice American-made truck like one of them Chevys Bob Seger used to sing about on the Packer games. Like a rock, baby. That's American."

"Whatever the case may be," Jerry broke in, "I'm not sure you have the stuff it takes to be on my show, Charlie. You need more than the desire to drive a nice truck and the will to die trying to get it. You need to have some smarts, too. If I put a gun to your head, and I just might if you get on the show, could you name, say, the last three presidents or even all Three Stooges?"

"Presidents Huey, Dooey and Looey?" Charlie said, trying to make it sound like a joke just in case he was wrong. "I kind of stopped reading the papers when I got into a bar fight at the Hee Haw and someone broke a pool cue across my head. I lost a few teeth when I hit the ground, and even though the doctors said I was fine I never did read so good after that. Started thinking every day was Tuesday, too. And I kept gettin' dressed fer work on Saturdays."

"I'm guessin' you didn't read so good before that pool cue hit'cher cranium, but I betcha you didn't sound quite so stupid before somebody played Minnesota Fats with yer skull," Jerry said, exaggerating and mocking Charlie's accent. "But I kin offer you a consolation prize. How about a year's supply a Slim Jims? Don't tell me you don't like them Slim Jims. They're 100 percent beef, you know. Yummy, yummy. Taste real good sittin' there in your deer stand. I won't even make you cheat death. All you've got to do is shut the hell up. What do you say, pal?"

"Silence for Slim Jims? A year's supply. That's 365 Tuesdays ..."

Jerry caught himself and stopped suddenly. He was already failing his first test of being nicer, and worse yet he was picking on a man with the IQ of a single-cell organism. Hardly sporting. Or nice. Not that Charlie knew or cared he was being belittled. As far as he was concerned, being in the presence of a star like Jerry Most would be the high point of his adult life. In fact, he didn't even want the fabulous prizes that would have made him a real player at The Chips and humiliated Steve. He just wanted to be friends with a star, because if he was good enough to do that, well that kind of made him a star, too.

Already, Jerry was beginning to form the first of a series of ideas that he believed would make him more human and in doing so, change the lives of everyone in the cell, and Grampa's too. Jerry had begun to consider that insulting Charlie was like mocking the dog. Neither Charlie nor a dog had much comprehension of the English language. But just because Charlie didn't know he was being insulted, that didn't make it right to demean him. It dawned on Jerry that he would change his life by changing Charlie's.

"Charlie, has anyone ever called you Charles?" Jerry asked.

"Only the judge. Everybody else calls me Charlie or Buckethead, cuz my head rang like a bucket when that guy hit me with the stool pick," Charlie said. "My wife sometimes calls me Rock, cuz my head is as hard as my dick. And the kids, they call me Daddy. I mean my kids. The other kids ..."

"That's fine, my noble savage of a friend," Jerry said. "Things are going to be different for you from now on. You may quit your job at The Chips and curse your friend Steve with whatever barnyard epithet the contents of your buckethead can conjure. Because from now on, you will be my highly paid special assistant. You will be with me at all times, except when I am in bed or dating one of the many princesses who crave my attention.

"You will get me a beer when I want a beer, you will Simonize my Jaguar when it loses its sheen and you will do everything I ask of you. For that I am willing to pay you what I am sure will be more than you could imagine, and you and your family will move into the guest house on my estate in Santa Barbara. Of course, this means you will have to move to California. If you do this, Steve will die from jealousy. Do you have a problem with any of this? Would you like me to speak more slowly?"

Charlie was trying to comprehend all of this. His head tilted to the left, and his face twisted into a quizzical look similar to the one displayed by dogs when they hear high-frequency pitches. He had never lived anywhere other than Hammertown, and neither had any of his family.

In fact, he had never left the state of Wisconsin in his life. The most exotic trip of his life had been a jailbird's weekend in Milwaukee where he was arrested for jaywalking after a World Wrestling Federation match at the arena downtown on the first night. He never even got to the brewery tours.

"Mister," Charlie said, breathing heavily as he began to comprehend the implications of his chance meeting with a game show host in a rural jail in rural Wisconsin. "Mister, I'd dine yer shick if you let me do that stuff fer you. Don't be foolin' with me, cuz that would be mean."

"Charlie, meet Jerry Most, America's nicest game show host," he said. He rose from the bench and moved to hug Charlie, but Charlie moved back a little when he saw that Jerry's clothes were still moist with vomit.

By now, I was ready to vomit myself. The cop had brought us some jail baloney sandwiches when we came in, calling them part of the package. The cop had switched to his dress white uniform because the other one was drenched with Jerry's upchucked alcohol intake, and he didn't have another uniform available. But even with the baloney sandwich I was still hungry. I needed a cheese stick or two (or three).

I was way under quota for my daily cheese consumption, and it was time for me to start thinking about throwing a frozen pizza in the oven.

What was worse than listening to this tripe was the fact that my generous offer to write a letter had already been forgotten. I offered to write a devastating letter for a guy free of charge, something I had never done, and I get one-upped by a game show host who gives him an incredibly easy and high-paying job, along with a cushy place to live. It was just too easy to trump me.

Meanwhile, I was thinking, "'OK, Grampa, any time now.'" Jail had lost all of its charming novelty.

After a time, it became absolutely mind-numbing. I didn't even feel compelled to write some great piece of literature there like Dr. King's Letter from Birmingham Jail. The conversation between Jerry and Charlie no longer interested me, and I longed to be on my couch, dozing and watching "Dark Shadows".

But what was even more sickening than the real baloney was not in the sandwich but in Jerry's new personality, which I figured would last as long as it took to tell him that he would lose the show if he started behaving in a civilized manner.

Just as I was about to entertain a nice little depressive episode over my fate of picking up a hitcher and winding up in jail, the cop came back and said Grampa was here to bail me out.

"There somethin' wrong with your grampa?" the cop asked.

"Well, yes. But what makes you ask the question?"

"Well, it's just that he showed up here wearing an Abe Lincoln stove-pipe hat, string tie, white shirt and dark suit," the cop said. "It was kind of creepy, cuz' he's moving real slow like a robot. But that's not the weird part. He's got a Hawaiian grass skirt on. And one more thing."

"Yes?"

"He's not wearing anything under the skirt. Man, that's some tool he's got."

I sighed. It would be good to be back home. Normally, Grampa drove me kind of nuts, but today he was like the cavalry. As the cop opened the jail cell, he looked at Jerry and said if he was sober he could leave, too. He was going to forget the gun charge because Jerry was a national celebrity and as such presented no danger to society. Jerry and I were free. But our new friend wanted to leave, too.

"Not you, Buckethead," the cop said. "Yer wifey's gotta go to the bank and pick up yer bail money. You've still got some time to think about why you shouldn't go 'round trying to kill people with hammers, 'specially when they're yer superiors."

"Steve ain't superior to shog dit," Charlie said, grabbing the bars and shaking them. "He should be in here, not me. He's such an asshole."

Jerry turned back to Charlie and smiled. He walked back to the cell and put his hand on Charlie's hand.

"Don't worry, my friend, my Sancho Panza, my Watson, my Number One Son, my Tonto. I will make arrangements for your release as soon as I get settled at our friend's house," he said. "Be calm and know that Jerry Most is going to fix everything for everyone."

"Excuse me, which friend are you talking about?" I asked. "Are you suggesting that you'll be staying at my place? You know, I don't like strange people sitting on my couch. That sofa's kind of like my office."

"I will be staying with you," Jerry said. "And you will be well-compensated for the trouble because you will have access to the resources of Jerry Most. I'm actually hoping that your place is something of a dump. Because my stay with you will then become my time in the wilderness, a time when I can contemplate the deeper meaning of my existence."

"Fine. But you're buying the beer," I said.

All I needed now was for K to show up and ask to sleep in the basement.

Chapter 7
Pajama Party with a Celebrity

When we got to the front office area of the police station, we saw just what the cop had described. There was Grampa, bare-footed and grass-skirted. He was dressed in the black, 19th- century coat that you always see Abraham Lincoln wearing in the history books. He also wore a black stovepipe that looked as if it had been stolen from the wardrobe box of some '70s British glitter rock band.

"What the hell is this?" Jerry said. "Hey Abe, how was the play? Is the missus still such a Gloomy Gus? I'm sorry, that was in bad taste. Be nice, Jerry, be nice."

"That's my Grampa," I said. "Hello, grampa. Sorry to get you off the hammock. Did you get here OK? Any traffic or car trouble?"

Grampa said nothing. He simply took off the hat and bowed deeply. He straightened himself, and slowly and wordlessly motioned us toward the door with a broad and slow arc of his right arm. The he held the door for us and we emerged into the sunshine, free at last.

Grampa followed us slowly, walking erect, in more ways than one, and rhythmically tipping the hat to squirrels and crows and any other creature that happened to be in the area.

Grampa pointed to the area where his car was parked, and we drifted off in that direction, making sure to let Grampa keep up with us. Grampa had an immaculately kept car. It would have been worth thousands to a collector if it had been any other car. But it was a 1975 Chevrolet Vega. And it was yellow. And it had a red plaid interior. Whenever you got in Grampa's Vega, you always prayed that it didn't break down because it would take forever to explain the car's continued existence. Most people would have driven it over a cliff years ago, but Grampa loved his Vega.

"Hey, grampa, this is the second time today I've been thinking about Abe Lincoln," I said, trying to open him up just a little for Jerry's benefit since I was concerned that Grampa's behavior and getup might be a little off-putting. "They didn't hire you at the pizza place to pitch pizzas for them did they?"

Oh, God, they did. Wait until they find out that their Abe Lincoln pizza promoter was wandering the streets with his Italian sausage peeking out of a grass skirt.

Grampa remained silent. He simply nodded as he walked toward the car, and he continued to wave the hat.

"Hey, Gramps, Coolidge was the silent one. Lincoln spoke sometimes. Remember the Gettysburg Address?" Jerry said cheerfully. Grampa approached Jerry and handed him a coupon for half-off on a three-topping pizza at Leonid's Excellent Good Pizza. Jerry accepted the coupon, and that gave Grampa a chance to get close enough to begin sniffing Jerry like a dog. He started with the face and hands, then he turned Jerry around and started sniffing down his back until...

"Grampa. Jeez, you don't go around sniffing the asses of popular game-show hosts," I scolded.

Grampa stood straight again and tipped his hat to me. Then he let out a high-pitched whine, like that of a crying dog, and farted loud and long so that the rear end of the grass skirt billowed behind him. It was his way of telling me to fuck off in as subtle a way as he knew how.

"Could you just take us home?" I pleaded, my voice starting out high and going low for effect. "It's been a long day, I missed the Hillbillies and I'm starving, although for some reason any appetite for pizza I may have had has diminished considerably."

We got into the car, Jerry in front and me in the back, and just as Grampa was going to take off his hat to enter the car a tall, skinny man with a dirty chef's hat and a beard that covered his face to give him the look of a wild dog walked toward us. He approached the car slowly, apparently making sure it was Grampa—as though someone else in Hammertown was wearing a stovepipe hat—and upon positive identification he sprinted toward the car.

Now what? A car-jacking? A kidnapping? There was little left to make this day anymore difficult than it had already been. And it was only late afternoon time. There was still plenty of time for an alien abduction.

As it turned out, the man who appeared to be pursuing Grampa was indeed his employer, Leonid, the owner of Leonid's Excellent Good Pizza, a pizza parlor whose quirky name was the source of some amusement to the locals, or at least the literate ones. It was one of only two establishments that passed for a "sit-down" restaurant in Hammertown. The other was a Mexican place called "Pepe's" that was owned by a Greek named Giorgios Antonos.

The owner of "Excellent Good Pizza" was Leonid Golnikov, and he had escaped Communist Russia for a chance to "make big in America." He was still struggling with the language, but most people in Hammertown had grown accustomed to his heavy accent and occasional malaprop. Besides, he made great pizza, and he was almost always open.

In general, Leonid was a decent fellow, and as bad as Hammertown was, he still believed he was far better off than he was in Soviet Russia. He liked the local kids, and he often gave them odd jobs or even free pizza on a whim, which was not only a kind gesture, it was good politics in a town where there was little to do after sundown except vandalize, screw, smoke dope and drink cheap wine or vodka in the woods. Like some immigrants, Leonid had a fixation with American history far greater than "real" Americans, but he was especially fond of Abraham Lincoln.

"Lincoln freed slaves in America, and America freed me from the slavery that was Communist Russia," he said.

So when Grampa walked in a day or two prior to this nightmare in his Lincoln suit, Leonid offered to hire him on the spot, although it should have occurred to him that anyone who would walk around in a dark suit and stove-pipe hat was probably not good employment material.

"People trust Lincoln for good pizza, like I say on highway billboard," Leonid told the last of my blood relatives. "Give people coupons. Bring them into restaurant, and I will give you a good celery."

"I'm not much for celery, but I could help you out if you paid me in Metamucil," Grampa responded.

"OK, I find metal-music for you. Maybe I have one of the kids go get it at the Kmart. Here. Take coupons. Get rid of all of them, and I give you metal-music."

Thus was the deal sealed. It actually worked for the first day. For Grampa that initial shift of work was so uneventful that I didn't even know Grampa had gotten a job. But nothing lasts with Grampa before he gets what he calls "one of the bad ideas." So he took the remaining coupons from the day before, put on half of the Lincoln get-up, pulled off his pants, and pulled on the grass skirt. Once a member of the local Women's Club informed Leonid of Grampa's odd sales pitch, Leonid went looking for him. Now he had found him, and his normally genial nature was overtaken by a demeanor that might have frightened Ivan the Terrible.

Yelling and growling with a heavy dark beard, Leonid looked like Lon Chaney, Jr. during a full moon.

"You are insane man! Insane!" he screamed, beating on the top of the Vega. "I give you good celery and you wave penis at people. Abraham Lincoln never wave his penis. Now customers think people at my place work with penises. Why do you did this? Do you hate Leonid? Do you hate Russians? Are you a radical … I mean a racial!"

"You mean racist?" Jerry said, trying to calm the situation. "How could Abraham Lincoln be a racist? I mean he had some weird beliefs about black people but he freed the slaves, good sir. Did they tell you some kind of lies about Lincoln in those horrible commie schools? Dirty bastards. We should have nuked them during the coup attempt."

"When I get angry I speak too fast and wrong words come out, OK mister?" Leonid said, losing some steam. "No, Abraham Lincoln was greatest of American presidents. This man is not Lincoln. He is a hula girl in Lincoln's hat and suit, a disgrace to Civil War veterinarians. Shame, shame, shame, you, you hula Lincoln."

I did not care to enter this conversation. I simply pretended I was asleep in the back seat and tried hard to stifle snickers. Hula Lincoln? Grampa simply stared at Leonid with raised eyebrows, as though he was watching a chicken dance the Macarena. He had apparently chosen a strategy of bemused silence rather than his usual Dadaist babble. When Leonid had finished his tirade, Grampa slowly tipped the hat and entered the car. Leonid continued beating on the roof of the Vega.

"No more pizza for you, you hula Lincoln! You should be sent to the gulag for shaming Lincoln with waving penises," he screamed, but Grampa was already pulling out of the parking lot. He suddenly stopped the car, rolled down his window and looked straight at Leonid. Staring at him like a cigar store Indian, Grampa simply said: "You've tried the rest. Now try the best," and drove off.

Jerry sat silently, trying to figure out what the hell Grampa was talking about. I, of course, had long since grown accustomed to his non sequiturs and simply ignored them. Maybe Grampa, in his own little way, was trying to do Leonid a favor by giving him an even more hackneyed slogan for the pizza place. For the locals, at least, it would seem brand new.

In the end, it really didn't matter to me. I was finally going home. But first ...

"Hey, Grampa, stop off at the Booze Ranch, will you?" I asked firmly, to let Grampa know this was not the time to begin a fantasy that he was being chased by the Medellin drug cartel. I needed beer, and maybe even some cheap brandy to take the edge off this day.

"I will stop at said establishment under one condition, son of the fruit of my loins," he said. "You must not steal anything at all. Not even a seventy-five-cent bag of beer nuts, or one of those miniature liquor bottles, or a half-barrel of beer or a woman's red garter or the mustache of Burt Reynolds or nose of a dolphin. Nothing, do you understand? You must pay for everything. I will not make it a habit of visiting the jail with your bail money."

"Fuck you."

I'm sorry. I was just in no mood to crawl into Grampa's netherworld. My priorities were beer, cheese sticks and finally, bed. I might be up for one of the "Twilight Zone" reruns I they still showed late at night, but my attention span was decidedly short due to overstimulation. I needed to unplug.

We rolled into the Booze Ranch's parking lot, and I debarked from the car alone after borrowing $40 from Grampa, who made me take it from his teeth. Jerry, who had grown more quiet as the ride went on, did not wish to join me. "Get me a little nut roll or something, would you?" he asked vacantly in a soft voice.

Booby's Booze Ranch was one of the largest buildings on Hammertown next to The Chips and City Hall. It formerly been a family grocery store called "Hammertown Foods" run by an old institution named "Pops" who had gone out of business when a conglomerate came to Little Rose with its "miles and miles and aisles and aisles of low, low prices and big, big smiles."

The corporation was headquartered in Virginia, and the store was now called "Pops." A giant smiling, mustached grandfatherly caricature on top of the store greeted shoppers and made them feel like they were buying from an old friend, maybe even the real Pops. People flocked to the new Pops to shop for their radishes and breakfast cereal and eggs and ground chuck.

The Booze Ranch was a thriving business, and the owner, Booby O'Boyle, had contributed to the Hammertown visual arts scene by erecting a sixty-foot-tall neon cowboy lassoing liquor bottles. The neon sign lit up in a way to make it look like the lasso was actually moving, and the sight drew people from as far away as Dickeyville when it was first turned on.

Of course, once customers arrived, they bought intoxicants, mostly in the form of cheap sweet wines and pint-sized flasks of brandy and gin. And, of course, they drank their hooch under the neon lights of the cowboy and his lasso rather than wait and guzzle it at home.

There was pressure on the city to close the Booze Ranch, with the most active opposition coming from tavern owners at "Hammer It Inn" and "Mike Hammer's" who believed that people should get loaded in gin mills, not in liquor store parking lots. You could run into just about anyone at the Booze Ranch's parking lot, and I was hoping to run into no one.

Fortunately, it was a small crowd as the night was young. Only a few high school kids sat in their cars at the far end of the parking lot taking turns gulping lime vodka from a liter-sized bottle.

My mission was clear and would take little time. Beer, perhaps a case instead of a six-pack in the event Jerry had regained his taste for alcohol. Nut roll of some kind for Jerry, and maybe a small bottle of peppermint schnapps for Grampa.

In record time, I grabbed a small shopping cart and got everything I needed. I wheeled around the last aisle and headed past the champagne toward the cash register, and there she was. K. Or whatever her name was. I am not given to vulgarities, but goddammit, I just wanted to go back to my couch. Why her? Why now?

She was talking to Booby with her back to me, her hands on the counter with her elbows locked and her arms straight. She was rocking back and forth, shifting her weight rhythmically right foot to left foot, and so on. I did not want to see her. But I wanted beer and I had to pay for it.

Booby saw me, greeted me, and I gulped as she turned around.

"What can I do ya for?" Booby asked. K turned around, saw me and immediately tipped her head down and looked up at me with the sweet innocence of a succubus with a small child's arm in its mouth. I looked straight at her.

"Do you have any poison? I need to consume some immediately," I said. "Perhaps I could pretend to rob you and you could shoot me with the gun you stash behind the cash register." I picked up a schnapps bottle for Grampa's and waved it menacingly. "Look, I mean it, hand over everything in the cash register, then shoot me as I escape. I'm begging you."

"Hiya, Fat Boy," K said. "Miss me?"

"Yeah, the way I miss an abscessed tooth," I said. "Please return to the under-world. I command you in the name of God."

"Hey, you're talking to a very nice young lady," Booby said. "I'd rather have her around here than those vodka-puking high school kids in the parking lot. In fact, I'm thinkin' of hiring her. Somebody as cute as her would be good for business."

"Booby, I thought a hardened cynic like you knew not to mix business with his sick sexual predilections. And besides, you won't get anywhere with her," I said, although I wasn't so sure.

"Oh, I'm hardened, all right, buddy, and she's doin' the hard'ning," he said, guffawing wildly and slapping his thigh.

"Ya know, I think yer way too hard on me," K said to me, purring. "Why not give me a break and get to know me. Ya might like it."

"Hey, can I be hard on you, too?" Booby said. Although he was entertaining himself with the crude double entendres, he was no longer part of the conversation.

"What do you want from me? You've already gotten me to steal and spend most of the day in jail for the theft of a refreshing breath mint. Maybe you want to bust into a nuclear missile silo and play with the buttons," I said. "I have simply come to the conclusion that you are dangerous and to be avoided. Now, if you'll stand aside, I have a booze purchase to make. And please don't step on my feet with your cloven hooves."

I nudged her with the cart and moved toward the counter. I pulled out the twenties and handed them to Booby. She watched me quietly and suddenly started to cry. I could not tell if this was a fake or not, but either way it made me very uncomfortable. I have never appreciated being confronted with human emotion.

"I thought you were different from everybody else in this town," she said, a single tear running down her cheek.

"Yes, I am different from everybody else in this town. For one thing, I have never had sex with an animal of any kind although I did have relations with a waitress whose breath smelled like the inside of an owl cage," I said. "And I am also different in that I have apparently caught on to you and your tricks long before everybody else did."

"Take me home," she said. "We can have sex. I think I could love you."

Now I knew she was faking. For one thing, most women tend to find fat men with dirty T-shirts who have just spent the day in jail something of a turn-off. I had no reason to think she was different. In addition, I needed to be forewarned if I ever took a woman home as she and I might both be shocked by the graphic nature of the pornography spread all over my bedroom floor.

Plus, the Farrah poster was a bit embarrassing.

Still, the idea was intriguing. The notion of her growing to love me, of course, was ridiculous on its face. Either you love someone or you don't, and no one in this world has the time it would take to grow to love me. A redwood could grow to maturity in that time.

On the other hand, she represented the possibility of sex, a priority that ranked just below breathing with most men. I was no different, even if I hadn't had it in a while. She might have been evil. She may have gotten me time in jail. She may even have been planning to rob me blind in my own house. But she was offering the chance for sex, and I was, after all, a guy. The impulses from Brain Two convinced me that the risks were worth it, just as millions of other men have capitulated to those same impulses in discos and corner bars across the world at closing time.

"Y'know," I said, sighing. "You know, it's really cruel for you to talk that way. I am no more capable of attracting you sexually or in any way physically than I am of being named emperor. I can't help but think your statements are part of another scam the nature of which I will detect far too late to save myself. I do not believe you have my best interests at heart, and in fact, I believe you may simply be trying to taunt me into some new form of humiliation. Everything I know is telling me it is a bad idea to remain in your presence. And yet, and yet ..."

"Hey Hamlet," Booby said. "She wants the electric sausage. Don't stand here yammerin', take her home and do some hammerin'. Do the deed, ya lucky bum. I was hopin' I could have a go at her myself, but I gotta work 'til nine."

"Booby, you truly are a romantic," I said. "You should write poetry. You've got a good start with imagery like the electric sausage. Perhaps you could work in some references to the rubber headlights and the one-eyed sea snake."

"Ferget about Booby, baby," she said, pronouncing it "bay-bay." "I thought it was sweet you would steal for me. I didn't think you'd wind up in jail even after I turned you in. But I think you owe me one for giving you somethin' you'll remember for years to come."

"Getting my hand impaled by a drill press would be something I would remember for years to come, but I don't plan on doing that," I said. "So far, my experience today seems only somewhat less painful. Nevertheless, I am going to dig deep into the depths of my soul to find one last particle of trust that will allow me to take you home with me. I am still not convinced of the sex angle, but you should not assume I am uninterested, and even the fantasies this entire episode can generate will be far better than the pornography I purchase from the proprietor of this establishment."

"Talk about romantic, I think yer really knockin' her over comparin' her to whack-off books like that," Booby said, shaking his head, wiping off the counter and walking away.

"Look, bay-bay, I am gonna make you sooo happy," she said. "Just take me home and give me a place to crash. You'll see. I won't steal nuthin'. You can even search me. Don't you wanna search me?"

"I will take you home, but you must share the car with my grampa, who is a bit odd, and a hung-over, vomit-covered game show host whom I assume you might have already met when he was in a different state of mind at the tavern. Is this acceptable to you?"

She stuck her index finger in her mouth and pulled it out with a sucking sound. "Of course it is, silly," she said. "I just wanna be with you."

I added a half-pint of Jack Daniels for K, and we walked out to the car, Booby's hoots following us out. "Don't forget the man in the boat, pal," he yelled. "I know it's prob'ly been a while fer you. Ya gotta make her satisfied, too, ya know. Ya just can't come and go, if ya know what I mean. Hey, ya need condoms? I got them kind that are like a thousand tiny fingers urging her to let go, you know, with the ridges. Hey lady, maybe you need a bag to put over his puss. I got a bag. Use a plastic one, har, har."

That's what you get in Hammertown. Liquor store owners who are part bartender, part sex therapist, part comedian. It's why our lives in this burg are so fulfilling.

As we walked into the parking lot, K put both arms around my elbow as I carried the bag in my other arm. Since I only had two arms I would return to pick up the case of Milwaukee's Best beer. As we walked to the car she had her head up, neck stretched, looking at me with a big grin.

"This is gonna be fun fer you, I just know it," she said. "I'm a real tiger in bed."

"I almost fear to find out what your idea of fun is. But let me tell you straight out, I won't do anything that involves an animal," I said. "And I'm not referring to your tendency as a tigress."

"I don't mean that. It's the adventures we're gonna have," she said. "It's gonna be sooo cool. We're gonna make up fun things to do every day."

"Sure. I think we should plan to knock over some kid's lemonade stand tomorrow," I said. "Then we can shake down old people for their pill money. Or maybe we can push down a five-year-old and hit him up for protection money. "

When we got to the car, Grampa was explaining his rules of life while I went back to Booby's to get the case of beer. I had heard Grampa's rules before, and of course they made no sense, but I was somewhat interested in hearing Jerry's reaction to Grampa's aphorisms. His Abe Lincoln hat was between them, and Jerry was looking at him as though he was speaking Swahili.

"I always told that boy, if you ever fall behind the wall into another dimension, follow my voice. I have seen this successfully performed on the television," he said. "Also, if a dog tells you to kill the president, you are nuts and should seek a psychiatrist immediately as you should never even think such a thing. If a cat gives you such an order, however, he is speaking on orders from the High Priest of Cats, who is not to be trusted as has been proven so many times during the Animal Wars of the 1960s. Do you remember those? Bloody, bloody times. You've got to remember history, my friend. We would all be speaking chimpanzee if the good guys hadn't won."

"Yes, chimpanzee," Jerry said distantly. "That would be bad. All that teeth bearing and those dominance displays would mean dentists would rule the world."

I overheard the tail end of this conversation as I returned to the car with the beer. K was in the back seat taking swigs from the Jack Daniels bottle.

"Grampa, the man, Mr. Most, that is, is probably hung over, tired, and in need of sleep and a shower, so why do you persist in talking like a man who should be committed? It's obvious you're making this shit up to impress him," I said after I put the beer in the trunk and then squeezed in the car pushing K aside to get some room. "Isn't it bad enough for him without having to negotiate the minefields of your imagination?"

"It's no trouble, really," Jerry said, half dozing. "I like history. It's my favorite category on the show. You know, like, 'Who was the first Monkee to leave the band?' That was Mike Nesmith, of course."

Jerry was tuning in and out of our little frequency, but Grampa felt the need to explain himself. "The plan, boy, is to make him think he's dreaming this conversation," Grampa explained sternly. "It is a way to get to the real person and his mission. I learned this in the war while I worked intelligence."

"Grampa, shut up now or I shall kill you this instant with the ice scraper here in the back seat," I said. "It is only my firm belief in a vengeful God that prevents me from dashing your brains out. Your brains would make a real mess on your nice plaid interior and kill the already limited resale value of this automobile. So consider carefully before you speak again."

Grampa started to cry. That made two people in one day, and I believed them both to be faking. "I'm just an old man trying to tell others about my life," he whined. "I have a right to posterity, too. I have a right to tell my story."

"Fine, tell your story," I said. "But skip the space aliens and Russian spies and hookers with microfilm taped to their breasts and hyenas driving nitro-fueled dragsters and all that dreck. Just tell them you like to drink Metamucil, shit and bathe nude in the sun. Your life is not complicated. Shit and sun. Sun and shit."

"I thought he was kind of entertaining," said Jerry, blinking hard. He turned to face me and saw K. "Well, what do we have here? Is there a prostitution training school here in Hookertown? Will we be having group sex? Dammit. I'm sorry. New Jerry. New Jerry. Be nice. I meant to say how do you do, young lady? My name is Jerry Most. And you are?"

Up until now, I had not heard her name. Here I was, prepared to take her to the sack and I didn't know her name. I felt so cheap. So I waited in anticipation to hear just what her parents had dubbed this creature. She looked down, smiling, ever the coy little girl.

"I don't wanna say," she said.

"Fine," said Jerry. "I'm not all that interested. I barely know my own name right now."

"My name is Bond. James Bond," offered Grampa.

I smacked him in the back of the head with an auto club map of the Rocky Mountains and he squealed like a piglet.

After that, we drove in relative silence back to the house. Only the sound of an occasional snort from Jerry as he dozed and awoke, along with the screech of tires as Grampa took a left turn a little tight, competed with the other sounds of dusk in Hammertown. I was falling asleep myself, always a dangerous proposition with Grampa behind the wheel, when suddenly K said:

"It's Pinky Lee. My name. It's Pinky Lee. They named me that 'cuz I was so cute and pink when I was born and my mom wanted to name me Pinky. The Lee is for her mom, my Gramby. So that's it. Pinky Lee. Any questions? Go ahead and make fun now so I can scratch yer eyes out before we go any further."

The statement jolted me out of my trance, and then the contents of the statement forced me to stifle a snicker. "Pinky Lee? Isn't that just precious?" I said, momentarily losing interest in her until good old Brain Two sent a load of hormones up to Main Brain and reminded me of the primary imperative to have sex.

"Yes it is," said Jerry, back among the living. "It's precious and it's sweet. Pinky Lee has a certain Midwestern charm about it. It makes me smell freshly cut grass and searing boredom and teen pregnancy. There I go again. But in any event, nice to meet you, Pinky Lee. May I call you Miss Pinky? Perhaps not. That sounds a bit like one of those dreadful Muppets. How about Miss Lee?"

"Miss Lee would be just fine, Mr. Most," she said.

"They called you Pinky because you were cute and pink when you were born?" I said. "Well, I suppose it's better than being called Bloody Mess, which is also how you probably really looked when you were born."

"That's mean," she said.

"Yes, well, you're probably right. But now that we're all friends, we can retire to my home," I said. "Jerry, we can pick your car up at the bar in the morning. Blackie is unlikely to tow it, although the local youths may put their greasy fingerprints on it. You may sleep on the cot in my library. And, uh, Miss Lee, we can discuss your accommodations later. In the meantime, I suggest we drink beer, order Chinese and discuss the events which brought us all together. Jerry, you can get a change of clothes, although my size is quite a bit larger than yours. As for your current togs, we can either wash them or leave them out for the raccoons. I understand our raccoons can clean vomit off a shirt as well as any dry cleaner. Just throw them out in the back yard and we'll hose off the remains in the morning."

Grampa pulled into our driveway, sending the neighbors' terriers into spasms of yapping that made me wish I had my can of Mace. In the front yard of our other neighbor was an ominous site: Foilhead Eddie, a man we occasionally saw in his yard but who always seemed to be home, was lying flat on his back on his lawn. This could mean anything, but it probably meant trouble.

Grampa chose that moment to explain to Jerry and Pinky Lee that Foilhead Eddie was his friend and that he was harmless. Eddie never removed the foil/wool hat, even in the summer heat. He usually favored red plaid flannel shirts and denim overalls, but now he was wearing no shirt at all.

Grampa explained that Eddie did not wear the foil because for any nutty reason, such as being worried about satellites or spies or lasers reading his thoughts. He was nosy, but no threat to neighborhood serenity.

"Eddie just wants to keep his thoughts to himself, and the foil keeps them right in his head," Grampa explained. "The foil keeps the freshness in. Eddie said that whenever he takes the foil off for any period of time he winds up seeing his best ideas stolen and used for situation comedy plots. He wants royalties if they use his ideas but it's impossible to prove someone stole your thoughts. It is my belief that he is not crazy, because he does not believe other people are sending thoughts into his head. Rather, since he is sending thoughts into theirs, then those who hear them must be crazy."

From what Grampa had told me about Foilhead Eddie, he stayed up very late every night and appeared to have no visible means of support.

He sometimes worked in his one-car garage well into the wee hours, and he always had CNN on in his house at volumes loud enough to drown out the noise of a freight train. The nice part about that was I was always able to keep up with the news. He also seemed to have an unnatural interest in the hippies next door, although I always attributed that to a crush on Mrs. Hippie. I also often thought that if the Terriers wound up dead, Eddie would be a prime suspect.

Grampa liked Foilhead Eddie and often went to visit with him at what Eddie referred to as his "world headquarters." In fact, Foilhead Eddie was probably as close to a friend as Grampa had. Clearly, they were two kindred spirits in harmless eccentricity. The difference between Grampa and Foilhead Eddie, though, was that Grampa's craziness could have been described as a sort of forced whimsy. It seemed that Grampa's nutball act was some sort of affect to be used for purposes he kept to himself.

Foilhead Eddie, though, was the real thing. He was crazy, and, God bless America, he had more guns than just about any county in Texas, according to Grampa. This was the source of some concern, since I was never quite sure when Eddie would become Rambo and in his mind I would be some Vietcong colonel. In general, I avoided him, but I hoped that if he did put his arsenal to use he would spare me since I was the grandson of his only friend.

I will admit, however, that on at least one occasion I slipped an anonymous note under his door informing him that those Terriers were foreign spies and ordering him to destroy them at once. No dice.

This particular night was absolutely the wrong time for an encounter with Foilhead, so as we got out of the car we just cast our gazes in another direction, pretty much the same way you would when walking down the street and encountering a vagrant.

We stumbled through the door, walked in and started the process of trying to figure out what we were all doing together. Jerry just poked around, picking up the occasional knick-knack or staring at some of our paint-by-numbers pastoral scenes hanging on the wall.

Pinky Lee said she needed a shower, and without awaiting an invitation went to the upstairs bathroom.

I got Jerry some clothes, tossed them to him, and sent him into Grampa's room to change. I had some mail, mostly requests for poison pen letters, so business was picking up.

Meanwhile, having spent the day picking up strays, I had to find a way to feed and care for them, at least temporarily. I had a feeling that both Jerry and Pinky Lee—God it still makes me want to gag when I hear that name—were going to be around for a while.

This was fine, as long as they stayed off my couch and answered all of my questions.

And I had a lot of questions.

So, as Jerry changed, and Pinky Lee went to the bathroom and Grampa went to stare at the water running down the kitchen sink, I put on Miles Davis' "Birth of the Cool" to show my musical and intellectual superiority and sat down on my beloved couch.

But for once, I did not turn on the television. I had company, but I wasn't worried about being rude. I wanted to know what everyone was doing in my house, and there was a grilling to take place.

Chapter 8
Chinese Food and Beer and Conspiracies

"Have you ever wondered where your life was going? I mean, really going?" Jerry asked me as he settled into a director's chair that was one of the few pieces of furniture we had in the living room besides the couch and TV. "Have you ever awakened in the middle of the night and asked yourself, 'Where am I going? What am I doing? How will I be remembered?'"

Jerry, beer in hand, was apparently about to wax philosophical, with at least as deep a meaning as a drunk who's going for his second round with the bottle in one day. K—I mean Pinky Lee—was upstairs taking a shower, which made it hard for me to focus on Jerry's deep thoughts about meaning. There hadn't been a naked woman in the house since Gramma died.

"Well, yes, I used to wonder where my life was going until I found out I had already arrived at my destination," I said. "It turns out that my destiny was to lie on the couch all day and watch reruns until it was a civilized time of day to begin drinking. Now that I know where my life was headed, I try not to think about what could have been or what I might have done. I'm here. With Grampa, and cheese sticks and beer and TV. What else does this life have to offer?"

"See, with your attitude I think you're already lost," Jerry said. "There's got to be more. There is more. Do you really think I went to Rutgers to be a game show host? Rutgers! I could have been anything with a Rutgers degree."

"As long as you didn't decide to settle in the Midwest," I said. "I hate to tell you, but in these parts your education is impressive if you went to Wisconsin, Minnesota or Michigan and maybe Illinois. Northwestern is just a snooty small college with an attitude, of course. Nobody likes Northwestern. It doesn't even belong in the Big Ten or whatever they're calling that conference these days. And you can't attend a hyphen school, of course. No University of Michigan-Podunk if you want the big promotion. It's got to be the big state school in the state capitol and it should have a decent football team. No one here cares much about Rutgers. That was Ivy League, wasn't it, until they got accepted into the Big Ten? Whatever.

"Could their football team beat the Wisconsin Badgers? I think not. So don't try to impress me or anybody else around here with a 'Rutgers' education. You might as well say you went to the University of Jupiter."

"You miss my point," Jerry said, stating the obvious. I hadn't missed his point. I just chose to ignore it. "I think there's a greater meaning to all this and that I should be using whatever education I have to make this world a better place. I hadn't really thought about it until today.

"Now I understand why so many great books are written in prison. It all became clear to me in that cell. No matter how large or small, we will make a mark on this world, and I want mine to be a positive one. I want to make a difference."

"Studies show, one person can't make a difference," I said, matter-of-factly. "Don't let those good-government groups tell you differently. You may as well not bother. There's nothing but trouble in trying to help. Sit back. Drink your beer. Play the lottery. Watch TV. It's easy, and, well, you might just learn something about yourself. Your whole TV career is based on the notion of people with this lifestyle."

"Man, that's a great attitude. Why not just blow your brains out and get it over with?" Jerry said, getting a little frustrated. Here was one of the biggest jerks on Earth telling me to take a more positive attitude.

"What's with the game show host? Have a little epiphany on the road to Hammertown? I do not blow my brains out because there are so many reruns to watch," I explained. "'Hogan's Heroes,' 'Bewitched,' 'My Mother the Car,' 'Twilight Zone,' and certainly 'The Outer Limits' if it's on. There must be people like me in the world to maintain these shows' ratings and share and keep their legacy alive. I also could not bear to leave my poor grandpapa alone. He's so fragile, you know. But on a theological level, I do not blow my brains out because I firmly believe that God does not like people toying with their own life clocks. Kill yourself here, and your problems have just begun in the afterlife. No, sir, I do not intend to leave this world with my frontal lobe all over the shower door only to have demons raking my flesh for all eternity. I'll just stick around and take my chances.

"Actually, I don't kill myself because I'm already dead. I have nothing to do with this society, except eat its junk food and drink its beer. I might as well not be here. I am dead, you see. But the difference between me and the rest of the people who do what I do—work, sit entranced in front of the TV and drink beer every night—is that I know I'm dead. I know life is a sham. They think they're living, and I think that's sad.

"See, Jerry, the difference between you and me is we're both useless, except you have had to work hard to achieve your level of uselessness. Sure, you've got millions of dollars and you're adored by mouth-breathing proles all over America. But you're as dead and useless as I am. Except I didn't have to work at it. I just sit here watching TV, eating cheese sticks and drinking beer. My needs are simple. So which useless person is ahead in the deal?

"Me, the one who doesn't care and doesn't have to work at it? Or you, the one who is obsessed with his role in this meaningless existence? I know which one I'd take.

"I would like to add one more thing, Mr. Game Show Host. Blowing my brains out would be decidedly unimaginative. When I die, I want to be ripped apart by a troop of baboons. When I was a kid I seemed to remember from a TV show that they are very efficient killers, and I'm guessing there wouldn't be much suffering on my part unless they decided to keep me alive to keep the meat fresh. Have you ever seen a troop of baboons attack a leopard? It's a thing of sheer beauty and efficiency. Those four-inch fangs sink straight into the throat. No, sir, while I admit my life has been dull and uneventful, I want my death to be spectacular, and I think a baboon troop could make arrangements for just such a demise. Such a death would also provide me with an added benefit: I wouldn't have to work to make it happen. Just run a few steps and wait for the hoots to get closer."

Grampa jumped in when he heard me say something about baboons. "I used to know the King of Baboons, you know," he said. "Ornery fella. Always flashing his teeth and jumping up and down. Hooted, too. You know, 'Whooh, whooh, whooh.' I could get you pardoned if baboons jumped you."

Jerry sat for a moment, ignoring Grampa and pondering my profound statement. He switched his tongue back and forth inside his cheeks as though a clock pendulum had been installed in his mouth.

"This could be arranged," Jerry said suddenly. "I could put you out on an African plain and set the baboons loose on you, and the best part of it, you would be on the show. Maybe you could even win some prizes if you survived. Well, OK, maybe it would be too expensive to go to Africa. But we could probably get some baboons from somewhere. Not the zoo, though. We once threw a contestant into a lion cage and the stupid beasts were so zoned out from captivity that we couldn't wake them up long enough to get them to attack him. We wound up getting pictures of the guy sitting on their backs as they slept. He even gave one of them braids. We gave the guy a Chevy truck, a living room set, a bumper pool table and a fabulous trip to Hawaii. That and a lot of cash. But where could we get some real killer baboons to get you on the show?"

"What happened to the guy who wanted to be a sweetheart, a nice guy?" I asked. "Are you reverting to form? Will you soon be insulting our choice of carpeting and the pattern on the wall paper? Nice guys just don't send their new friends to bloody deaths by baboon on national TV. Look, let me explain it in different terms. I am not happy with my life, but I am reasonably content. My life has very little stress, save for those times when I have to coax my grandfather out of the neighbor's apple tree. An appearance on a TV show would only produce stress. I am stress-averse."

"I'm just saying that if that's what you want, I can arrange it," he said. "I'm trying to be a helper now, not a hurter. Don't turn your back on the nicest thing I've ever done for anybody. I'm offering to let you face baboon death on national TV as a favor to you."

"I'm going to forget the fact that 'hurter' isn't a word and ask what brought this turnabout. It couldn't just have been jail. It might have been the booze. And it certainly isn't the lovely scenery around Hammertown," I said. "And by the way. How in God's name did you wind up in Hammertown? At the Hee Haw, no less. Did you take a wrong turn on your way out of Hell and get stuck in our little Purgatory?"

While this conversation was taking place, Grampa was banging around in the kitchen.

The Chinese food we ordered for delivery from Little Rose was to arrive in a few minutes, and he had apparently been making something to go with it. He entered the room with a handful of spinach leaves.

"Makin' salad," he said proudly. "Special dressing, too."

Upstairs, Pinky Lee was still showering, and the notion that there was a naked woman in my bathroom continued to prove to be quite distracting while Jerry got deep with me. He and I were bonding, I guess, but I had another kind of bonding in mind, and not with a game show host.

"Look, let me tell you just how I wound up in Hammertown," Jerry said. "The show went on a three-month summer hiatus, which allowed me to take some vacation time."

"Of course, you came to Hammertown for its many tourist attractions. You didn't miss the Hall of Hammers, did you?" I said. "And they say that in addition to the liquor bottles scattered all around it the woods are filled with leprechauns. You've got to see those. The locals say they're easier to see if you drink a little beer with a turpentine chaser."

"Listen to me," Jerry said with deepening seriousness. "I have decided to blow my life up. Explode it. I'm not talking about killing myself or anything like that. But I haven't been any happier than you even though I drive a nice car and eat at restaurants even better than the Abe Lincoln place you've got here, if you can use your small town imagination to consider that. Sorry. Anyway, after the last show I just packed some clothes and some decent wine and took off. Went where the road took me. I was looking for whatever it is you're supposed to look for and never find. No staff. No company. Just Jerry Most.

"Look, pal, with everything I've got, it occurred to me that I'm just a game show host. I can't think of anything more useless to society, save for maybe TV weather people, lieutenant governors and school superintendents. Like them, I contribute nothing. I help no one. Sure, every once in a while a contestant on the show survives a dive off the cliffs of Acapulco or stays alert enough to escape carbon monoxide poisoning in a closed garage, and for their efforts their lives are changed by a sudden influx of cash and maybe a Dodge minivan with a DVD player in it to keep the kids quiet during those long drives across the Great Plains on the way to Colorado. But that doesn't have anything to do with me. Allan Ludden from 'Password' or Gene Rayburn from 'The Match Game' or even Tom Kennedy from 'You Don't Say' could do that. I'm simply a part in a large machine. If this part breaks, you replace it with another and no one notices. I suppose some of the new guys like Chuck Woolery couldn't do it. Death is something else altogether for them. Now, I will give you that the nature of 'Die Trying' would change without my savage bons mot, but people tune into see their fellow human beings cheat death, not me. Everyone worries about their own mortality, and it makes them feel good when they see someone face what appears to be certain death because it makes them feel like they might be immortal, too. And if a guy gets creamed, well, then they're grateful that it wasn't them. The whole world is based in schadenfreude.

"But none of this has anything to do with me. Which means outside of a game show I have very little identity of my own. I am who I am because I am the host of 'Die Trying.' Now, most people would think that's more than enough. Look at poor Charlie. Do you think going to jail is a real disruption in his lifestyle? Well, it is to the extent that he can't go to the bars while he's in there, but on the main, it's just another part of another day. Maybe Missus Charlie yells at him when he winds up in jail, but she yells at him all the time anyway. So in that way, jail is actually kind of a respite from Missus Charlie.

"But do you think Charlie ever sits awake at night and asks where his life is going, or who he is? Of course not. Because first and foremost, Charlie is a moron, and morons are not cursed with the tendency to be introspective. They just live their lives like insects. They exist, they go to work, they go to home, and sometimes they're happy and sometimes they're drunk and sometimes they're sad and then they are dead. But they are never worried about what it all meant. They weren't equipped for that. And in a lot of ways, I think they are happier than I ever could have been. Can you imagine how easy your life would be if you found auto racing interesting? Or if you thought country music was good?

"If you can do that, you can find entertainment in just about anything. Watching ants carry a moth to their colony or going to a tractor pull provide amusement and joy beyond their ability to comprehend. What a great way to live! They can go camping on the weekends and stare at the fire in a beer-soaked haze because fire is interesting to these people.

"That's because their brains are simple. And with simple minds come simple lives. And I submit that the simple life is the easy life, because you never have to worry about what you are contributing to society. They'll never be somebody, and they don't care. See, there are two kinds of people in the world—the performers and the audience. The audience just sits and watches and marvels. The performers, guys like you and me, have to worry about contributing something because our brains compel us to do something, to try to make our mark, or at least to reach some level of self-actualization that allows us to rationalize our shortcomings as society's performers while we sip Chardonnay and discuss foreign movies or the deeper meaning of Woody Allen's early movies as compared with his later works."

He paused and took in the music. Miles and the boys were playing "Boplicity." Grampa was in his room changing, and Pinky Lee was out of the shower and getting dressed. I wondered if she had a change of underwear. I wondered if she wore underwear.

"What are we listening to? Miles Davis?" Jerry continued. "Don't you understand that the fact that you are intelligent enough to listen to Miles Davis and actually enjoy the experience means you are a cut above the rest of the population? Again, let's go back to our friend, Charlie. Do you think he listens to Miles? Or Coltrane? Of course not. He thinks jazz is that musical wallpaper they play on those crappy 'smooth jazz' stations, and he doesn't like even that pablum. He thinks music reached its peak when Hank Williams Jr. did the Monday Night Football theme. His mind shuts out the complex, while our minds crave it because we want the intellectual challenge. But then we sit and listen and appreciate and we get depressed because we know we could never create something as beautiful as a work like 'Kind of Blue,' or strike an aching chord in your heart the way Springsteen can on a song like 'Thunder Road' or 'Darkness on the Edge of Town.' If people like Charlie love Springsteen, it's because they think he just sings about cars. There is no deeper meaning for them. And as for Miles or Coltrane or, God forbid, a symphony, these works are avoided because they are unnecessarily complicated and difficult to understand.

"My problem is I'm way too smart to be happy. When I graduated from Rutgers with my journalism degree, I figured I'd become a White House reporter and maybe even uncover the next Watergate. I took a job at a TV station in a small market in Texas and wound up covering barn fires until I got a job in a bigger market and wound up on the 'Action 12' anchor desk. I didn't know it, but the minute I had jumped on a career track and moved from market to market—I never called them cities, always markets—I was drifting farther and farther away from doing anything important with my life. I was just going to the bigger market for bigger money until I didn't even know why. Then came an opportunity to audition for what was then a new game show, 'Die Trying,' and I was so bored I thought, why not? Little did I know that I was in the perfect frame of mind to host such a show. I was indifferent and irreverent and I had a mean streak. Perfect for a guy urging others to defy their own deaths. So that's my legacy. That's all there is. I've done nothing except entertain millions of mouth-breathing illiterates who don't know any better than to turn off the TV and read a book."

Pinky Lee had come downstairs and she sat next to me on the couch during Jerry's soliloquy, then she rose again to get a beer. She brought me one and she brought Jerry another. "Whatcha talkin' about?" she said. "Football? Sex? Me?"

"We're talking about life's deeper meanings," I said. "Jerry seems to think there's more to life than TV and beer. It's a fascinating concept, but it's thoroughly un-tested and highly hypothetical. I myself am skeptical. But please go on, professor."

"Look, listen to me," Jerry said, becoming impatient. "I left California after the show was over because my complicated mind compelled me to find my connection to the rest of the world, to find my way to contribute something, to blow up my old world. See, the difference between you and me is I've realized my need to find my contribution, while you pretend to be happy watching TV as though you were one of those idiots. But you're not, and deep down I think you want to change all this. I hopped in my car and just drove from town to town on back highways looking to find my way. I suppose I was looking for Springsteen's legendary 'Thunder Road.'

"At first, I simply used my travels as a way to insult the locals and feel superior to them. But by the time I got to that bar—what was it, the Hee Haw—I realized I wasn't going to find it, whatever it was I was looking for, and that's why I got drunk. Because I thought I was beyond redemption, that I was going to be remembered as a rude game show host, that my mind would simply go to waste. And then I met Pinky Lee here, and then I met you, and then I met Charlie. And it all started to come together as I lay on that jail bench. I would change all of your lives through my unique powers as a game show host."

Unbeknownst to Jerry, as he was finishing his speech Grampa had been standing behind him listening. He was now wearing cutoff shorts that revealed skeletal but tan legs. He was wearing a black Mardi Gras feathered mask and a T-shirt that said: "Show Your Tits!"

"Salad's ready," he said. "Where's the Chinese? Do I have time to pinch a loaf before dinner? I've been saving up. Could be a real stinker, but I'll spray."

What came next was bizarre even by the standards of my grandfather. Because his words were still hanging in the air when he yanked down his shorts, squatted, and laid a little spiral pile of human dung on the carpet. He turned around, looked at his handiwork, and began clapping, applauding his effort.

"Boy, listening to this game show host fella really made me have to crap," he said. "Jeez, I thought I was the only one who was full of it."

Everyone sat stunned, apparently never having seen an elderly man in a "Show Your Tits" T-shirt and a Mardi Gras mask take a crap on the carpet. There was no protocol for a reaction. No one, except Grampa, who waddled into the kitchen to fetch a dustpan with which he could remove his artwork, was out of their chair. Nobody moved as he scraped the pile off the carpet.

He looked at it appreciatively, looked at the rest of us and said: "I wish I could save this one. It's a beaut." Then he walked outside with the pan and presumably laid the pile on our hippie neighbors' doorstep.

It was all over so fast that there was no time to scold him, no time to evacuate the room. We all just sat there as though we had all been exposed to radioactivity. Grampa returned, walked directly to the bathroom to clean himself, then rejoined the company as though nothing had happened. He was smiling broadly, clearly proud of himself. As promised, he sprayed Lysol all over the room. The place smelled like some fetid nursing home.

Still, it seemed Jerry's words had sunk in with Grampa, and it was good to know this conversation had its effect, that he had taken Jerry's words to heart. And yet, apparently something had happened to him when he came back into the room. Grampa took off the mask, and his face dropped into such a serious expression that I though he was going to move his bowels again right there in the living room. The thought of another clean-up was already turning my stomach.

But Grampa did something he hadn't done since Gramma was still alive. He spoke coherently about the real world, and he responded to a conversation that was actually taking place in the here and now.

His eyes got distant as everyone stared at him. Grampa sat on the floor, cross-legged, and closed his eyes. Now it appeared he was going to do some crazy Indian chief schtick. But instead, he just said one thing: "World War II."

Then he was silent for a minute.

"I was in World War II, you know," he said, as clearly as though he was a college professor. "When I got back, I didn't care to relive what I experienced there, and everybody said war stories were boring so I didn't tell any. I guess I had to put it behind me, anyway. Never saw any of my old buddies after I got back. Your grandmother didn't like going to those conventions and she wouldn't let me go alone because she said prostitutes would steal my money. So I never told my story. Your grandmother didn't want to hear about it. 'You're here with me now. There's no need to go back,' she'd say. But she never let me tell her. A few years before she died, I tried to tell her one last time, but she wouldn't have it. So I never spoke to her again. She died so quick I never even had a chance to end that foolishness and tell her I loved her, not that love is the same thing at my age as it was when I was younger.

"So I'm gonna say it to you, and I'll make this one quick, but I'll only say it once. France. Cold as hell. Snowing big white beautiful flakes, like on a Christmas card. We were fighting on and off all day, and finally marched through deep snow to establish our position. Dug trenches. Me and three other guys dug ours and fell right asleep the minute we put down our shovels. Couple hours later, we woke up and were covered in snow, at least six inches. It was getting dark, so we whistled to find out where everybody else was. No answer. Got out. Went to other trenches. Every man had been shot in every trench. Dead. Everyone, except my group. Turns out the Germans figured we were already dead because we were covered with snow. We lived. For what reason? To lie in hammocks with our penises pointing toward heaven?

"To kill enough enemy soldiers to win the war and then live the rest of our lives as useless veterans with stories no one wanted to hear?"

Why is it that it is always during these somewhat dramatic moments that something happens to break the spell? In this case, it was the doorbell announcing that the Chinese had arrived. I paid the driver and tipped him a dollar while the others moved to the kitchen table.

But it was probably the last time Grampa said anything that made any sense at all.

For now, however, he was serving his salad, a spinach and iceberg lettuce mixture with something he called an orange vinaigrette dressing. Pinky Lee had been silent through most of this, and in fact the silence was a little thick after Grampa's story and Jerry's sermon. She tried to break the silence with a little compliment for Grampa after he distributed the salads.

"This dressing's very good," she said. "What are these orange flecks in it?"

"What else?" he said, returning to character. "Metamucil. Gotta keep you all regular."

The sound of forks dropping was almost deafening, although Pinky Lee held onto hers. "It's real good, Grampa. Did you learn how to make this in the Army?" she said in a tone suggesting someone trying to coax a maniac to drop his gun.

"Just thought of it while I was staring into the sink before, young woman," he said. "Wanna see my tits?"

He raised his shirt before he got an answer and a collective groan rose from the table.

"'S'matter? Never been to New Orleans before? Everyone shows their tits in New Orleans," Grampa said. "Me 'n my friend Mike went down there once and we saw so many tits we thought we had died and gone to tit heaven. I always was a tit man, myself, and the notion of having a strange woman bear her breasts in front of a crowd always gave me tent pants. Know what I mean? Tent pants. Big pole in the middle holding the pants up? When I saw a woman's tits and I got tent pants, I used to tell Mike that I had tiny bears on unicycles riding around in the circus tent, which was in my pants. Of course, there were no tiny bears in there, nor were there tiny gorillas. There was just my balls and my penis. So sometimes when I see a woman's tits on TV, I think of the circus and little bears in pointy hats riding unicycles and monkeys riding on the backs of elephants.

"I've seen some tits lately, but I haven't seen the circus in a long time. I wonder if I saw a circus if that would remind me of tits the way tits remind me of the circus. Doesn't matter. Circus hasn't come to Hammertown for a long time and I'm not driving down to Milwaukee just to see if the circus gives me a boner. Saw one woman in New Orleans, though, a mature lady, to be sure, whose tits hung down to her belt. They peeked right out of the bottom of her midriff T-shirt. I wondered what would happen if she took her shirt off altogether and just twirled and twirled in a circle. Those things would have flown straight out and knocked over anyone they hit. I did not find those tits attractive, though."

The members of this little dinner party were looking at Grampa with a mixture of fascination and revulsion, as though he himself was the main act at a circus side-show filled with two-headed snakes, Lobster Boy and a variety of other ghastly sites. Ladies and gentleman, come one, come all and see the Grampa, The Amazing Giant Tit. Is he a man, or is he a tit? Decide for yourselves. You don't wanna miss this. No, sir, you cannot feel the Amazing Giant Tit. You can look but you cannot touch.

Clearly, Grampa was not going to get caught in the deep contemplative mood of the night as long as he was fixating on breasts. At least it didn't appear that he would. But then he put his shirt down and looked directly at me, then at Jerry, then at Pinky Lee. Everyone had resumed eating, but an edgy silence had settled over the room as everyone devoured Kung Pao chicken, egg rolls and egg foo yung. Grampa's eyes were as clear as I had ever seen them, and they had a focus that made it look like he was summoning every fiber of his being to concentrate on this very moment. That was not a good sign. This look could mean anything, so I thought I'd better say something immediately.

"Grampa, if you shit in your pants, I swear I am going to leave your battered body in a shallow grave in the woods," I warned. "These people have nowhere near the patience with you that ..."

"Shut up. Shut up. Shut up," he said. "Shut the hell up. You should all hear this. Now hear this. Now hear this. By now you might have asked yourself, why does this old fella show his tits and wave his penis under grass skirts and sunbathe naked? Because he is not among the sane? Does he do it because he is senile, or shell-shocked or maybe the military put implants in his head to make him do their bidding for the entertainment of some unseen force? Is he just an infirm, aging veteran? I am all of the above.

"But for my purpose it makes no difference. I was in a war, and I outlived my buddies. I was in a marriage and I outlived my wife. I had children, and I outlived them. All I have is the man I bailed out of jail today, my grandson. So I have determined that God has had some special purpose in mind for me, some way to make my life a lesson to others, or maybe give me the lead part in some incident where I inadvertently save the life of a child who grows up and cures cancer long after I am dead.

"But I am angry with God. I have been for some time. Y'see, God let me see my buddies die in the war, and he let me see my wife die, then my children, and that told me he had this divine plan. But he never told me what the plan was. He never gave me the chance to find out what I was supposed to do. So I got death all around me, and a mission that has remained a secret kept only by God. So in order to thwart the plans of the Almighty, I have engaged in a series of subversive acts against society that are actually designed to upset Him. My acts are like little pipe bombs in the public squares of Heaven. The angels cry, 'Oh, Lord, Grampa is at it again. He has spray-painted himself silver and declared himself Metal Man. How can he help our divine plans looking like a comic book character?' I have simply decided to so whatever pops into my head, no matter what God wants me to do. I've done enough.

"Maybe I should have known better than to try to read God's mind in the first place. Maybe there never was a plan that I fit into. But that's even more reason to do what I do. Because if there is no Divine Plan for me, if I have no reason to be here, I may as well have a good time and do whatever it is that crosses my mind, and to Hell with everyone else. And as you have seen, a great deal crosses my mind. Now, if someone would pass me the hot mustard, I will eat several egg rolls before I retire."

Grampa grabbed a dripping egg roll and looked at me. "By the way, if you are planning to have sex tonight with your prostitute friend here, don't worry about the noise. You are over 21, and I assume she is, too. I am also used to the low moans and squeaking bedsprings of your masturbatory practices. In fact, if you need costumes, you may borrow some of mine. I would suggest my Batman cape for the old 'damsel in distress' scenario."

I wasn't sure why Grampa was behaving this way. It could have been because there were so many new faces in his world, faces that were actually paying attention to him rather than looking away whenever he approached on the street. By now, everyone in Hammertown knew about his eccentricities. They had seen him dressed in military fatigues directing traffic because he had declared martial law. They had seen him show up at public City Council budget meetings in a werewolf mask.

"I am speaking for those who are stricken with lycanthropy," he had told the Hammertown City Council one year. "We need your help. We need a special werewolf recreation center where we can eat sheep and bay at an electric moon and play foosball and eat Milk Duds that get stuck in our werewolf teeth. We must not be denied that which we deserve. It is all up to youoooooooooooo."

After howling, he then ran off the stage and jumped out a window. Fortunately, the council chambers were on the first floor of the building.

On another occasion, he suggested that the city change its name to "Dildo Center of the Universe," because, he said, "everyone in this goddamned town is a dildo." The council stuck with Hammertown, although they thanked him for his input.

But I could not believe that I was the only one in Hammertown who had had about enough of his schtick. I once threatened to put him in a nursing home, only to find later that day that he had written his name in blood all over the upstairs hallway and said he was The Evil One.

A nursing home, I decided, could not hold such an imaginative and persistent man.

His behavior tonight was stranger than usual, inappropriate even for him. Perhaps he was just showing off. But I'm afraid I lost it.

"That's a very nice speech, Grampa. Say, why don't you tell them about the time when I was a kid when you shaved my old dog bald and wrote 'Hellhounds on my Trail' all over her with a magic marker?" I said. I looked at the others, who were growing more and more uncomfortable by the sentence. "We had to let the poor thing crap in the house during the day. If the neighbors had seen her they'd have called the cops. This whole concoction about thwarting God's plan is some rationalization for having his little fun. He thinks it helps him convince the military that he deserves extra money because he's nuts, and it allows him to behave with impunity. Grampa, I've been on to you for some time, and after tonight's performance you may want to consider a new act. The old one's getting stale. You're not nuts. You're not funny. But you are getting dull. You want to give everyone the chills? Behave normally for ten minutes."

Upon hearing this scolding, Grampa farted loudly. His report was so lengthy and full-octaved that it sounded as though it could have been heard all the way to The Chips if the acoustics were just right. Dinner was, of course, over at this point, and I was more than ready for bed.

"You sleepy?" I asked Pinky Lee.

"Not in the least," she said, grinning mischievously. Then she stifled a yawn.

"Great. Let's go upstairs," I said, a shot of adrenalin coursing though my veins and a huge rush of hormones joining the adrenalin for a high I would imagine to be similar to a dose, actually 37 doses, of heroin.

And with that, we all adjourned to our respective quarters. Jerry grabbed a book from my bookshelf that I couldn't see but which I think was a volume of "The Philokalia," a series of meditations by 5th-Century Orthodox aesthetics. I'm not sure why I bought it, and I had only glanced at it a few times, but I was glad Jerry found comfort in it.

"I gotta read to fall asleep," he said. "This looks like something I could learn from. Either that or it ought to put me out right away. G'night."

We bade Jerry goodnight and I closed the front door of the house without locking it. This was Hammertown, not New York City, after all. Before I did I looked outside and saw that Foilhead Eddie was still lying on his front lawn. I could tell he was not dead because he seemed to be flashing a light into the sky. No, I thought. I will have no part in this. I will close the door and forget what I have seen. Pinky Lee and I went upstairs and left Grampa at the table with the egg rolls and the white rice and the salads. He was playing with the food, pretending each greasy, hot mustard-covered egg roll was a tiny civilization that had incurred his wrath.

"And for your insolence, you must all be destroyed," he said, and jammed an entire hot mustard-covered egg roll in his mouth at once. "Tell all your puny friends and neighbors about what happens when you displease Gorgar! Gorgar must be worshiped and obeyed. Hah! Your pepperoni gun is useless against Gorgar's powers."

He made space ship and ray gun noises in his own private intergalactic battle for control of the universe. As it turned out, Gorgar, the Great Tormentor of the Universe, was shortly going to get his comeuppance from the hapless invisible denizens he had been picking on.

Chapter 9
The Gratuitous Sex Scene

All men lie about their sex lives. This is probably not a notion that alarms or surprises most people who are not still in high school. Men exaggerate to other men about women they have slept with and how many times. They lie to their wives about the number of women they've slept with before they were married, coming up with a credible number that is not zero but is as close as possible.

And, of course, men tell about their fantasies with each woman as though they were fact. When men describe themselves in the old sackeroo, every incident of premature ejaculation becomes a Herculean feat that leaves the poor woman tired and sore but begging for more.

So it should be said that the title of this very chapter is a lie. There was no sex on the night that Pinky Lee and I went upstairs to my bedroom. What began with some promise ended in confusion, ennui and maybe just a little testosterone-driven irritation.

It certainly seemed at the time that we were both going upstairs with the same idea in mind. At least I thought she had been hinting at it. But it turns out that my ability to respond to subtle cues and emotions of anyone other than Grampa had been so eroded by time that I did not realize she was in the infamous "cuddle" mood, a mood very much hated by very many men. The words, "Just hold me," spoken by a woman can turn the red-hottest of male lovers into an ice-cold pillar of resentment. Yes, they will hold their lady love, but only on the fading hope that the woman will cave and have sex.

When that doesn't work, they will finish holding their favorite gal, retreat to a bottle of their favorite alcohol and wonder why they didn't marry that horny love-slave girlfriend they screwed so many times in college.

Grampa had his own term for getting laid. He always called it "going to Bone Town."

"You gotta be like a dog, boy," he told me when I was 14. "You gotta keep sniffin'. You gotta bury that bone. You gotta go to Bone Town. Go there as many times as you like. It's a town that never sleeps. Now at your young age, Bone Town may have a population of one, that being you, and I think from all that Kleenex your mother says is under your bed that you know what I mean. But soon, you'll have company in Bone Town. And I'll tell you one thing, when you go to Bone Town with a girl, you'll want to become mayor or maybe even the king. I think I was mayor myself for a time before I met your grandmother. Your grandmother didn't like me calling it 'going to Bone Town.' She said it was crude. So in front of her I always tried to be discreet, referring Bone Town as Horny Land. This phrase may have had something to do with the fact that we did not sleep together for the last 20 years of her life. After a while I learned not to say Bone Town in front of ladies. You should call it 'making love.' Course, I only figured that out long after yer Gramma was dead."

Thus enlightened about my grandparents' sex life, I carried on through my adolescence.

I am of that unfortunate breed of human who has some smarts but certainly not looks. I had stature, but I was fat. I was not terribly active sexually during my formative years, or during my adult years, either, for that matter. If I did manage a date, most of my pursuits ended shortly after I made that first grope for the girl's breast in the movie theater parking lot.

When I finally had my first chance for a real live sexual encounter, my all-expenses-paid trip to Bone Town, I stopped way short of going downtown. That is, as I mentioned earlier, I did not consummate my relationship with my high school sweetheart, Carol Ann. At the age of 17, I sincerely believed we were in love, and I fervently believed we would spend an eternity together. So as a result, I turned into a good boy at the last minute and said, "Let's wait." Years later, I was still crazy about her but I hadn't seen her in years. So one night she phoned me out of the blue telling me she was screwing some college kid she met in a bar called "The Childe Harold." I no longer remember why the name of the bar was important, I just know I get a little touchy when someone brings up Byron.

Perhaps this was when my view of life and humanity began to deteriorate. It certainly didn't help my outlook. I lost my virginity with the IHOP waitress but I went bereft of any affections after she took off with the truck driver.

Obviously, I was creating a relationship in my mind with Pinky Lee already, a desperate measure, indeed, but a man in need of sex thinks strange thoughts.

We climbed the stairs to my bedroom and I opened the door ahead of her. I told her to wait outside the bedroom as I quickly gathered up dirty clothes and dirty books and threw them in the closet. I opened a window in an attempt to dilute the smells that I usually did not notice but which I am sure permeated the room, and I pulled the sheets up over the mattress and straightened the blanket.

"What're you doin' in there?" she said. "I'm sleepy. You makin' it pretty for me in there? So I can get some rest?"

"Well, I'm trying to clear out the detritus so that sleeping here is at least bearable, if not comfortable," I said.

"What's a 'titus' or 'detitus'?" she asked. "I don't like snakes. You got a snake in there?"

"It's 'detritus' and it means debris, garbage," I said. "It's a little messy in here and if I am going to be entertaining a crime goddess like you, I want to fix it up a bit. And yes, I've got a snake in here, but it's not the kind that tempted Eve, if you know what I mean."

"Just let me in. I don't care what it looks like in there. I wanna go to bed," she said.

I opened the door and with a sweep of my arm I invited her in. A copy of a magazine called *Big Ass Joggers* was sticking out from under the bed and I gave it a quick kick back into the darkness. Farrah looked down on us, smiling, while Maris went about the business of hitting his home run. And now, I thought, I was going to be hitting a homer of my own. Or so I thought.

"It looks like a high school kid lives in here," she said. "Who's that lady on the wall? And that baseball guy. Jeez, all ya need is pennants and some posters of metal bands."

"Yes, well, it does lack a certain adult touch," I said, embarrassed. "This is the room where I grew up, and somehow it makes me feel good to be surrounded by the same things that surrounded me when I was a kid. It just takes me back to a place when I thought I might have a shot at doing something in this world and becoming somebody."

"Well, if ya think feelin' sorry fer yerself is the way to seduce me, yer wrong," she said, sinking into the faux Southern accent she had used earlier.

"You can do anything you want to do, but all you do is watch TV and lay on that ratty couch. Have you even been laid in the last ten years?"

"I'm not feeling sorry for myself, I'm just saying ..." I started to explain, but she interrupted me by putting her index finger on my bottom lip.

"Look, I spotted you the minute I got into your car," she said, the Southern accent disappearing and replaced with a sharper, clipped Midwestern accent. "You're one of these guys who sits around all day making fun of other people when they're really just jealous because they feel like life is just one big party that they haven't been invited to. Well, I invited you to the party and all you do is whine."

"If we stay with your life as a party metaphor, then I must say your invitation, a shoplifting and jail escapade, left something to be desired," I said, getting defensive. "You might have started me off slow, maybe by vandalizing some gravestones or something."

I was losing steam. My responses were weak, and I was beginning to think she had a point. To continue the fight completely killed my chances of getting laid, but backing down would only prove that she was right and leave me vulnerable to more tortures and I still might not get laid. I considered my options, and went with the chance to have sex.

"You may have a point," I said, making a last-ditch effort to get my visa to Bone Town. "In many ways I simply have given up. I simply have seen no way to make life interesting or fun. So I decided to stop trying and live in my own little world. Up until now, it seemed to be working. But now I've got to rethink this. Thank you, Pinky Lee. Thank you. You may have changed my life."

I moved toward her and made an awkward attempt to kiss her. She didn't take evasive action, but her response was not warm. She held her lips tight against her teeth and gave the effect of kissing granite. This was not a good sign for an improved sex life. I took a step back.

"I'm sorry," I said. "It's just ..."

Dammit. Life was a lot easier before K or Pinky Lee or whatever the hell her name was. If I had simply passed her up and got my beer and cheese sticks I would not be tormented by my libido and the list of my shortcomings she had confronted me with. It looked like I would be sleeping with her, but doing little else. Then it occurred to me.

"I just want to be held," I said, making one last gambit. "I've lost contact with humanity, and I'm afraid you're my last hope to reconnect. I just need to be held."

I tried to well up some tears, but no dice. It was just as well, since I had already done such a good job of selling all this and she appeared to be buying. Although with this woman, you could never really tell what she was thinking.

"C'mere," she said, putting her hand on my shoulder, leading me to the foot of the bed and pushing my shoulder down gently so that we could both sit.

"Look, I think maybe we should just lie together and talk until we fall asleep," she said. "We can learn a lot from each other. Besides, if this works out we've got the rest of our lives for all the sex we want."

"Where have I heard that before?" I said, with just a trace of bitterness.

She made me turn around as she put one of my T-shirts on over her bra and panties. This really was killing me, but I was out of ideas. When she put on the T-shirt she reached into my dresser drawer and pulled out a pair of sweat pants. She instructed me to put them on.

"Those are for in case you get some bad ideas," she said. "Just keep telling yourself, 'I must not think bad thoughts, I must not think bad thoughts.'"

As usual, I would just think about baseball.

I was resigned, she was tired, and we both climbed into bed. She immediately noticed that there was a significant depression in the middle of the mattress from my weight and the hours I had spent sleeping there. She said it was OK because it would make us sleep closer together.

So, here I was, in bed with a pretty girl, much younger than me, and I had no control over what happened. Nothing was going to happen that she didn't want to happen.

She put her arms around me and held me. I had forgotten that I asked her to do that, and I wished I hadn't. I felt constrained. I felt stifled. I felt erect. Jeez, did I feel erect. But I was stuck in her tentacle-like embrace.

"I never did get to tell you why I was hitchhiking," she said. "It might interest you to know why a girl would so that in today's society."

I started to speak, but then I realized it. Oh shit. I hadn't brushed my teeth. I didn't think we'd do much talking if I didn't brush my teeth. By most standards, I was a slob. Since I didn't interact much with what I liked to call "mainstream" society, that is, people with jobs and families, I didn't pay much attention to regular hygiene. I showered when I got around to it, but I didn't mind going out not having done so.

But one thing my mother taught me was to always have clean teeth and fresh breath. It was the least I could do, she said, to try to get along. Grampa reinforced that in his own special way one day while I was flossing.

"Good boy," he said, when he saw me in the bathroom. "Floss those pearly whites. No one goes to Bone Town with green teeth. Make sure your breath is spring fresh, too. You don't want your words of love to smell like old trout."

Since this is one of the few rules that were ever driven into my head, I made sure to follow it. In fact, I was somewhat compulsive about it. Wouldn't you know it, Pinky Lee was just about to open up to me—and opening up is often just the long way to Bone Town—and my compulsion kicks in. I broke her embrace and got out of bed.

"What's the matter?" she said. "I thought we were gonna cuddle. I wanted to talk to you."

"I've got to brush my teeth," I said. "It's important. I ... I have bad breath. I don't want to make you sick." My humiliation was now complete.

"Oh, bay-bay," she said, falling into the faux Southern. "I ate Chinese, too, and I haven't brushed my teeth, either. C'mon back and talk to me."

"I have to," I said. "I'll be right back."

So I headed off toward the bathroom, walking as though I was walking those last few steps to the gallows. I wasn't getting this right. Just as I started falling into a really sweet depression, I tried to remind myself that I didn't care about this sort of thing anyway. I sang the song of the rejected male: I don't need her anyway. All I need is beer and TV. She could go to hell.

At this point it's important to explain that my teeth-cleaning ritual is detailed. Floss, waterpick, floss again and waterpick again. Then comes the brushing, every tooth getting at least ten strokes to all the way to the gum. Finally, there is the mouthwash and the final drink of water.

Rinse and spit. I conducted my ritual in a somewhat hurried fashion— still holding out hope that I could get lucky—and padded back to bed. Of course, she was sound asleep.

I looked at the poster of Maris. "Sorry, pal," I said. "No dingers tonight." I couldn't even bear to look at Farrah, not in my state, and I certainly could not relieve my desires, not with company in the room. This seemed as good a time as any to catch up on my poison pen letters. I'd had a few requests in that day's mail, and the mood seemed appropriate for anything that involved poison. I quietly slithered out of bed to my desk top.

I opened the letters while my computer booted up. The first one was very interesting. A political consultant had an unsuccessful client who wanted her money back because she believed it was his fault she had lost. Worse, they had been friends before the campaign, and this matter had strained their relationship considerably. He sent along a check for $100, far beyond my normal charge, because he said he heard I could rip someone's heart out. Well, I liked to think I could, anyway.

The client's letter detailed the target's weaknesses, including a bad temper and certain ethical lapses.

I thought for a moment, but this letter wrote itself.

"Dear Amanda:

"My business partner Marty showed me a copy of your letter in which you purport that he agreed to send you back the $10,000 retainer you paid us in connection with your ill-fated bid for judge.

"To say the least, I am shocked. I shouldn't be. I was shocked throughout the campaign by your unstable behavior and your total 'win at any cost' strategy. I was shocked by the feeble, sophomoric attempts at sarcasm you used in our last conversation on this matter. So being shocked by your actions is part of a pattern. But I was especially blown away by the fact that anyone who talked to me the way you did during your tirade last week would think for a minute that any shred of friendship was left.

"Let me be very clear: Our friendship has not, as you termed it, been threatened; it has been destroyed by your constant inability to maintain a civil tone or demeanor toward me. You failed to recognize the difference between a business relationship and a friendship, and we have been forced to re-evaluate both. It didn't come out well for you.

"The term apology is apparently foreign to you. Or perhaps you treat all of your friends to steady doses of brow-beating, screaming and threats. That being

the case, I'm sure your social calendar is well-packed with people who have terribly low self-esteem. In any event, it's too late for apologies. While I deeply believe in the concept of Christian charity and in turning the other cheek, I ran out of cheeks for you to slap long ago. Now I'm simply asking you to kiss my cheek, but not the one I turned, if you catch my meaning.

"Now, let's address the matter of our business relationship. You indicated that if we did not refund the money we earned, you would have no future business relationship with us. Let me assure you, we would rather declare bankruptcy and live in refrigerator boxes under a bridge than face the prospect of doing business with the likes of you again.

"On the matter of the refund, I would have made no such promise, and I am certain that Marty didn't. That's enough for me to know. If he had agreed to a refund, particularly after dealing with you for these long weeks and months, I would have shot him or hospitalized him for stress. Frankly, in an act of friendship, I might have considered giving you a refund. But since we have no friendship, that point is moot. However, I would happily endorse the idea of a refund if it was part of a guarantee that we would never see you again — unless we were running a race against you.

"Don't snicker. We'd beat you because we know too much about you.

"As you have never worked in the private sector, having derived your income from the public trough as a low-paid public defender, I understand why you would be confused about the notion of a refund for services performed. Let me explain. You may want to read this twice if it doesn't sink in the first time.

"While many of your colleagues in the legal community, those in the private sector, anyway, work on a contingency basis, we are neither attorneys nor do we ever work on contingency. We were on a retainer with you. If we were still on speaking terms I would ask you for the name of an attorney — OK, a successful and reputable attorney unlike yourself — who returned retainers.

"But on the matter of the money, let's review the facts. As your friends, we said we needed neither a contract nor a retainer in the first place. You were a friend, as we were prepared to work on a pay-as-you-go basis. You may further recall that you insisted on a paying us the retainer. It is entirely comical that you would now demand a return of the money you insisted we take in the first place.

"You made a snotty reference to our financial health, saying that giving back the $10,000 might hurt our cash flow. I would invite you to call our banker and check for yourself. Frankly, your $10,000 represents our annual greens fees at the country club. So this isn't really a matter of financing, is it?

"Finally, let me recommend that you seek some form of anger therapy immediately. Sure, being beaten badly at the polls and paying as much as you did for the privilege could really make someone angry. But if you treat all of your friends in the same hysterical manner you have treated us, I fear for those close to you.

"In one last act of friendship, we will offer you this bit of free political advice: If you ever run for judge again, don't run on the basis of your 'judicial temperament.'

"Sincerely,

"Your wealthy former political consultant."

Not my pithiest work, but good enough for the occasion.

Personally, I don't know that I like political consultants all that much. I've never met one, but I know enough about the image they seem to cultivate to think that one must have a certain vulpine personality to be truly successful in the business. It was not an important matter to me, since I couldn't remember the last time I voted. The only thing I know about elections is they pre-empt real television programming.

Having finished the letter, I looked over at Pinky Lee, and she was sleeping soundly despite the clicking of my keyboard. In fact, she was snoring lightly, a sign that she was sleeping soundly enough that maybe I could slide into bed quietly and just cop a little feel and ... No! What was I thinking? That's assault! My life wasn't exactly like that of famous TV game show host and now house guest Jerry Most, but I would never resort to groping a sleeping woman even if she was sleeping soundly in my bed and would never even notice what I was doing if I was quiet.

I stared at the Maris poster for strength and decided to go downstairs to get a beer. When I got to the fridge I happened to catch a glimpse of Foilhead Eddie through the kitchen window. He was standing in his backyard with a mirror and a flashlight and a walkie-talkie. He had a rifle in his hand. This meant he was "on patrol." I looked away and hoped to God the gun wasn't loaded. The day was already filled with far too much bad strangeness. I took the beer and headed back upstairs. I passed through the living room on the way.

It was dark, but Grampa was sitting in his chair, the place where he loved to sleep. Grampa hadn't slept in a bed since he broke his ribs testing his anti-gravity suit and falling off the roof of the garage.

Grampa was panting like a dog in the sun, and his face looked green and blue as the lights of the TV reflected on him in the dark living room. He was watching a pay-per-view movie called *"Tit Patrol."* It seemed to be some kind of war movie.

"You OK?" I asked.

"Just got bad heartburn and a huge boner," he said. "After dinner I ate an entire pepperoni and I seem to be paying for it. The pepperoni people are fighting back at their ruler, me, Gorgar himself, from beyond their graves in the very pit of my being. I shall prevail. Now be gone so that I may have a private moment with this fascinating motion picture."

He yelped like a little dog and continued panting.

I shrugged and left him alone. When I returned to my room, I realized that my typing had not roused Pinky Lee in any way, nor had my telepathic suggestions to her to throw off her clothes and beg me to make passionate love to her, so I thought I'd take my cuts at one more letter before I went to bed and tortured myself with the fact that I was sleeping in the same bed as a woman but I was powerless to do anything but sleep.

The next letter was from a local man who was in the midst of a nasty divorce from his wife of 16 years. Of course, it was ridiculously redundant to include the word "nasty" before the word divorce. I had never heard of any nice ones, and most took on the nature of knife fights on a Greek freighter. These were the letters I loved to write. It gave me such vicarious thrills to take sides and carve the heart out of the enemy.

While I wrote, I could not get the theme to "Mr. Ed" out of my head, only with different lyrics. "Divorce is divorce, of course, of course, and no one can talk though divorce, of course," and so on. While writing I mentally kept trying to rhyme divorce directly with horse. I kept coming back to the phrase, "face like a horse," but was otherwise unsuccessful in coming up with a suitable poetic finish.

It was getting late, but I thought I could get this one done before I resumed by position next to Pinky Lee. I started this way:

"Dear Horse Face:"

Hmmm. I wonder where that came from? I thought I might have to edit that out later. But I continued.

"Our long marriage together may have failed in the end, but I truly believe something good will come of it. That is because without you to nag me to mow the lawn or do the dishes, I have decided to use my extra time to dedicate my life to the creation of a machine which allows for time travel. Think of how this could benefit humankind. We could warn JFK not to go to Dallas. We could have Mr. and Mrs. Lincoln sit in another box. And we could go back to the day your father met your mother and taken him into an alley and beaten him senseless, giving him horrible scars that would have prevented your mother from ever looking at him.

"This, of course, would have resulted in your never having been born, and that alone would be worth the cost of this invention."

The nice part about these sorts of letters was that they could be generic. Everybody wishes they had never laid eyes on the other when they get divorced, and that allows artists such as myself freer use of the canvas. I didn't need to go much farther than the previous paragraph, but then again, I would never meet this woman, and I was a little down on women myself that night. I continued.

"But that's cruel. If you had never been born, there would have been so many things we shared together that would have been missed. Take robotic, uninspired sex. And those warm summer nights when we stayed up until the wee hours just talking, talking, talking. The neighbors got the wrong idea, of course, and called the cops because they misinterpreted our discussion as violent yelling. But over the years I really treasured the memory of having you stand over me with a bucket of water as I laid in bed in the event I fell asleep during one of your tirades. No, these are things I would not give up for the world."

It occurred to me as I wrote that sarcasm often does not come off in the written word because tone of voice and other physical cues are missing. But I continued because by the time people ask the courts to dissolve their union, even the word "hello" is viewed as some kind of insult. This stuff spoke for itself.

"And so, having been informed by your lawyer that you are asking for a divorce, I can only say that my faith in Almighty God has been restored. He has delivered me from the Gates of Hell, although Hell itself wouldn't be that bad if you were not there to share it with me.

"So let me just say that I will not contest this divorce in any way. You may have the house and the ugly art your mother bought us and the hideous furniture you snuck into the house while I was at work. You can have the lamps and the tables

and the chairs and even the TV, because these things are the ransom for my freedom, and when I turn them over to you I will be happy again. I simply want my clothes, my books, my guitar and my car.

"Farewell, my darling. We will probably never see each other again. But if I ever contract a terminal disease, I will ask for you to once again be at my side. Because you can make every day seem like it lasts forever.

"Yours in name only, Roger."

Such a productive end to such a strange day. I had to note that the Gates of Hell phrase had crept into the letter. I wondered if I wasn't a little preoccupied with that notion because of my book idea. I turned off my computer and slid into bed. All I could think of was Dorothy Parker's line about fresh hell. What sort of fresh hell awaited me tomorrow?

Obviously, my life outlook hadn't changed much in spite of all the excitement I had already experienced.

Chapter 10
The Pepperoni People Defeat Gorgar

I awoke the next morning in the middle of a dream in which I was making love to Pinky Lee, except she suddenly had the face of my mother. Before I had the time to analyze the Freudian horror of that situation, I realized that Jerry was pounding on the bedroom door as though he had set fire to the couch. Pinky Lee just rolled over and put a pillow on her head.

"Hey, you better get up," he shouted. "Something's definitely wrong with your grandfather."

"Is he on the roof again?" I asked. "Goddammit, if he's doing that Superman thing again, he's going to the most rat-infested nursing home I can find."

"No, he's not on the roof," Jerry said. "He's, um, well, he's not moving at all. I think ..."

Uh oh.

I threw on my bathrobe and ran downstairs. My anger had immediately turned to deep concern. I really did love Grampa even if he never did light a match in the bathroom after his famous bowel movements. I made it to the living room and I knew immediately when I saw him that he was dead. I knew it because most men would take their hand off their penis when someone walked into the room.

But there he was, pants down, wearing his "Show Your Tits" T-shirt with jaw agape. His hand was wrapped tightly around his penis. Very tightly. Rigor mortis had apparently set in.

After I got over the undignified sight, I immediately felt a little guilty. The heartburn. He had been having a heart attack the night before. At his age I should have known bad heartburn could be a sign of something more serious. It was just so hard to take anything about Grampa seriously. Maybe if I'd gotten him to a doctor he'd still be with us, masturbating in corners and wearing the monocle he so wanted.

Well, at least the ass cancer didn't get him.

I felt my bottom lip quiver a little bit and then I did something I hadn't done in years. I cried. It wasn't a loud, wailing cry. More of a subtle tear-down-the-cheek kind of cry, the kind you get when Old Yeller gets shot at the end of the movie. I blinked hard to prevent anyone from seeing this mawkish display.

"Aw, Grampa," I said, approaching his stiff carcass, kneeling and putting my hand on his cold paw, the one that wasn't holding his manhood. I began to giggle through the tears, the sight being rather unusual even if it did involve the death of a loved one.

"Aw, Grampa. You went out on your own terms, I guess. Chinese food, some pepperoni, a dirty movie and a chance to whack off. You died with your pants down, and somehow, I think that's how you would have wanted it. And you beat the ass cancer. Congratulations."

I almost expected him to answer me with some discussion of space aliens or something.

But he was silent as a statue, and just as cold. Jerry came over to me and put his hand on my shoulder consolingly. Pinky Lee, descending the stairs, immediately ran over to me and gave me a hug around the shoulders.

"You poor thing," she said. "You're the only one left of your kind now. Your people are all gone."

"Well, I don't know that the world's gene pool is any less well off because of it," I said. "But whatever he was, Grampa was interesting company, and he was my Grampa."

Jerry interrupted the sentimental scene.

"Hey, buddy, I, uh, I don't mean to be insensitive, but I think someone's going to have to get him out of here," Jerry said. "You know, a hearse or the coroner or something. You don't want him to—well, you know, you don't want him to start smelling up the place. Besides, having a dead guy in here is kind of creepy. I mean, look at his eyes. They follow you around the room. It's giving me the chills, a dead guy right in the living room. I should have gotten a room at the Hammertown Inn."

"Gee, I'm sorry my grandfather decided to pass away in an inconvenient spot," I said. "If you help me pull him out of this chair maybe we can drag him into a closet until the coroner gets here."

"Sorry," he said. "I'm not used to the presence of death."

"I thought that's what your stupid show was all about," I said. "'Die Trying.' Remember? Morons cheating death for cash and prizes?"

Jerry just sat on the couch. No one actually died on his show, so he probably really was creeped out by the corpse. He was obviously uncomfortable, and his eyes darted back and forth as though he expected the angel of death to return, this time for him. Pinky Lee was sobbing, but she had the sense to find a towel and drape it over Grampa's private parts. Now it really did look as though he had tent pants. His hand and that erection made the blanket bulge in a way that made it look as if there really was a tiny circus in there, just as he always said. The only thing that would have been more appropriate is if Grampa had died with one hand on his penis and the other flipping the bird at the world. Perhaps the undertaker could make that arrangement, I thought.

Grampa would have loved that parting shot.

It didn't take long for the coroner's van to arrive after I called, and when it did, it didn't take long for Foilhead Eddie to arrive. As the attendants pulled Grampa off the chair, almost dropping him at one point because they were trying so hard to stifle laughter, Eddie walked in the front door uninvited and he saluted.

"A fallen comrade in arms," Eddie said. "We will all miss him. He was a good soldier. He will be maintaining radio silence now, but he will always be with us."

Between the warm weather, the flannel shirt and the foil-lined wool cap, Eddie smelled like a fish that had been on the dock in the sun for several hours. Fortunately, he left quickly, saying he had work to do. The attendants pulled Grampa out of the chair and maneuvered him to the door. They maneuvered him into the coroner's van, placing him on his back even though he remained in his classic sitting masturbatory position. As they closed the door of the van, I could see Grampa's feet sticking up behind the glass. He seemed to be waving.

Funny, but in the old movies they used to refer to the coroner's van as a "meat wagon." I used to find that humorous. Not today, even if Grampa was leaving this world in a ridiculous pose.

As the van pulled away, Eddie ran out the door with a rifle, stopped dead on his front stoop, and pointed the gun skyward. He fired three times as Grampa was driven away.

"There's 18 more coming, good friend," he shouted after the slowly disappearing van. "You'll get those at your funeral."

As it turned out, he didn't.

"Good God, he'll probably fire them right into the box," I said under my breath.

It was just a day before that he was screaming at me for hiding his Metamucil. Just yesterday morning he was nakedly tanning himself in his hammock as the neighbors' terriers yapped. It wasn't even 24 hours since he bailed me out of jail and Leonid had screamed at him for being "Hula Lincoln." And now we had to plan his funeral. I assumed funeral directors did the bulk of it, but I was already thinking about what he should wear and who would come and who should write the obituary. That's probably when it would hit me that he was gone, when I did my daily reading of the obits. I didn't want Grampa to have one of those anonymous obits.

For the moment, we the living had to worry about breakfast. Pinky Lee was in the kitchen and had already rustled up some eggs and was scrambling them with a little cheese and a little black pepper. Jerry, still aching from the previous day's escapade, walked in to make some coffee. I turned on the television and sat down on my couch.

The Hillbillies were on, and it was a classic episode where Ellie Mae brought a gorilla home and Granny tried to teach it to do chores. This was just what I needed. Although normally the Hillbillies kept my attention throughout, the events of the past few hours caused my mind to wander. I started to think about what it would be like if I had a gorilla myself. I didn't think I could teach it to do chores, but maybe I could put a pointy little hat on him and tell people in town he was just a hairy clown visiting from the clown museum.

Then I realized: Grampa hadn't been dead more than a few hours, and already he seemed to be invading my thought process. Only Grampa would have considered a gorilla as a pet. Was some sort of genetic fluke manifesting itself upon me after the death of my last living relative?

Pinky Lee called in from the kitchen that breakfast was ready, but I wasn't hungry. I told them I wanted to be alone for a while in my room. I went back upstairs to write Grampa's obituary while the muse was with me. Because I didn't want him to be in a boring obit, I decided to embellish. No one on the *Hammertown Telegraph-Herald* staff would bother to check anyway.

I went back up to my room to type, and Pinky Lee's scent was still in the air, penetrating the normal stench of the room. I turned on the computer. No poison pen letters today, just a flattering obituary for my grandfather. And so it began:

"HAMMERTOWN—Donald Q. "Grampa" Peck, a self-proclaimed amateur pioneer in the study of colorectal cancer prevention and a World War II veteran, died in his sleep at home on Tuesday at an age believed to be about 85. Peck, who grew up in Milwaukee but moved to Hammertown after World War II, survived a harrowing onslaught during a battle in France after he and his unit dived into a trench and covered themselves in snow, pretending to be dead.

"After attacking the vulnerable troops, German soldiers departed the area, killing most of the men in Peck's battalion. Peck then led his small band on a counter-attack from behind that crippled German efforts in the area and resulted in the capture of more than 500 enemy soldiers. Peck refused any recognition for his part in the battle, saying any medals belonged to his fallen comrades who died in the battle."

Again, who was going to check this tale? I continued.

"Peck took a job at the former hammer factory after the war and worked there for more than 40 years before his retirement. His career at the factory was marked by his high productivity—he was named Hammer Man of the Year in 1960 for his high volume—and his penchant for keeping worker morale high by wearing strange costumes on the factory floor.

"Later in life, he funded his own research into the prevention of colorectal cancer, often wearing a white lab coat to Walgreens as he purchased stool softeners and other materials needed for his work. He was said to consume one-third of a jar of Metamucil each day, and he charted the timing and volume of each of his bowel movements for the last 37 years of his life. His research was turned over to the Mayo Clinic for study, although it is unknown whether the clinic made use of it. He is also said to have left his digestive tract to science for study.

"Although he is not shown in any credits for the television shows he claimed to have created, Peck often told associates that he influenced the creation of such popular 1960s and 1970s shows as 'Gomer Pyle, USMC,'

'Mannix,' 'My Mother the Car' and 'It Takes a Thief' through the fanciful tales he would tell his writer friends. He also claimed to have had bit roles on 'The Beverly Hillbillies' TV show, appearing once as a gorilla and once as a distant cousin from Hooterville named Clem.

"Peck could often be seen in downtown Hammertown wearing costumes that both amused and offended. He was arrested for disorderly conduct twice, once for wearing a chicken costume to Bob's Breakfast Bar and refusing to leave until they gave back 'his' eggs, and once for charging a $2 fee to read people's palms by licking their hands. Charges were dismissed both times.

"He had no known survivors."

I don't know why I added that last sentence. I just didn't think I needed to be recognized just because my grandfather had died. That's a heck of a reason to receive recognition. I didn't do anything; he was the one who had to die to get his name in the paper. I was nobody and I didn't deserve to have my name in the paper and hog the spotlight.

Having completed the record of Grampa's life with perhaps a few embellishments, it began to dawn on me again that he was gone. I was alone. The idea of being alone itself didn't bother me; it's how I preferred to live. But what seemed odd was that I was the last of a clan, a breed that would die out when my cholesterol-clogged arteries finally did me in.

But there was something else. Grampa lived as though he was immortal. He wasn't one of those sickeningly cuddly old geezers who they say is "full of life." He was totally indifferent to the rhythms of the world and the rules of society. He didn't seem immortal because he had such a strong life force, he seemed immortal because it seemed as though it would just never occur to him to die. He was as indifferent to death as he was to every other rule in life.

But death, any death close to you, makes you think about the bigger issues. It focuses you on what the hell it is you're doing here in the first place. I believed in God. I believed in heaven and hell, and I believed that people who asked for forgiveness went to heaven and those who didn't went to hell. I never asked Grampa how he felt about the afterlife. We usually didn't attend the local nondenominational church together, except on Easter and Christmas Eve. He liked to show up for services dressed as a raccoon for Christmas Eve and, of course, Santa Claus for Easter.

This both delighted and confused the children and drew dirty looks from parents who never seemed to be in on Grampa's jokes on the world. The minister ignored him altogether. It wasn't worth the scene Grampa would cause if he was in any way chastised for his dress.

But Grampa and I had never talked about death. In fact, we never really talked about life.

My parents died before the notion of death became enough of a curiosity for me to inquire about it. But I had to wonder what would happen if I was the only one in my family who went to heaven. Would I be responsible for pleading the case of the rest of my family to bring them in, too? Could I have an angel as my legal counsel? Could I trust Grampa not to try to get into heaven dressed as a Rockette once I had successfully argued for his admittance?

I had some personal concerns about heaven myself, as I mentioned earlier. It wasn't heaven that concerned me, actually, it was the length of time I would be there. What could you possibly do for an eternity? As much as I loved reruns, I couldn't watch them forever. Sex was probably a more difficult prospect there than it is on Earth. So what do you do with all that time? I also wondered if anyone could just opt out, just say, 'Lord, I don't want to go to heaven or hell. I just don't want to be anything anymore.' Just give me the blackness, I might ask, the non-existence. It's just a lot easier than trying to make plans for an eternity. But that attitude in and of itself was probably blasphemous and would draw me straight into the fiery furnace, I feared.

When I read the obituary I had written for submission to the *Hammertown Telegraph-Herald*, I started to wonder, too, about what Grampa's life had meant. As he suggested in his soliloquy the night before, was his life mission over when he helped capture those Germans in World War II, if, in fact, that's what really happened?

Was he free to do whatever he pleased after the war because there really was no other use for him? His offspring provided nothing for society, and it certainly didn't appear that I would accomplish anything beneficial in my lifetime. Perhaps he recognized all of this early on and decided just to have fun, or whatever it is you call it when you go work wearing a diaper and a feather headdress.

This thought process led me, of course, to some disturbing thoughts about why I was left on Earth. My sense of ambition, if I ever had one, had left me somewhere in college. I had attended the University of Wisconsin in Madison, but I found myself far more interested in beer and TV trivia than I was in my classes. I read a lot, probably more than any of my colleagues, and as a result I received an education but no diploma. After being placed on academic probation for the second time in my junior year, I called it quits. I figured I could go back to Hammertown and read books at my parents' house for free, so why should I spend all that money on room and board at a great university from which I had little chance of graduating?

I picked up the poison pen business when I sent a letter to the editor to the *Hammertown Telegraph-Herald* regarding a school superintendent whose salary I believed to be excessive. After the letter was published the superintendent sought me out with the intent to do bodily harm, but he thought better of it when I reminded him that he would lose both his job and a costly lawsuit if he laid one finger on me. He left town three months later, and I got credit.

With that, I had begun a small career.

As a result of the money from my mother's small estate and the poison pen letters, I never found myself on the career track. I never blew out of the university with plans to change the world, or at least make a lot of money and get my name on the social page in some big city newspaper. I never had to tum 40 and wonder why I hadn't achieved more or why younger and less deserving people were getting high paying jobs I couldn't touch. There was no mid-life crisis facing me. Mid-life looked to me just like young life did, and I assumed old age would look the same.

I just had never become "somebody."

I didn't understand what it meant to be happy, and I didn't necessarily think that a successful career and a lot of money could bring happiness. As a matter of fact, I wasn't even sure God meant for us to be happy here on Earth. Maybe life was simply something to be endured and, if you kept your faith throughout the ordeal, you would get into heaven where the real happiness awaited. I didn't know about that kind of happiness, or any kind of happiness, for that matter. I knew I was content. And that had always been good enough for me. But Grampa's death gave me a bit of a start. I certainly had never considered my place in the world before, and maybe it was time to start.

But I had to plan Grampa's funeral first. I had finally gotten hungry, so I went back downstairs. Jerry and Pinky Lee were sitting at the kitchen table.

"You OK, baby?" she said. "Want some eggs and toast?"

"Yeah, I'm fine. And yes, I'd love some eggs now," I said, pouring myself some coffee.

After a brief silence, Jerry looked up from his coffee and said: "So, he gonna leave you any money, big guy?" Pinky Lee shot him a nasty look.

"I'm glad you're focused on the important issues," I said, a little irritated. "Maybe you'd like to go through his dresser drawers and look for cash or jewelry. Maybe his shoes will fit you, or one of his suits."

"Hey, wait a minute, that's not what I meant," Jerry protested. "I meant how are you going to pay for a funeral? Or are you just going to haul him to a landfill?"

"You know, I'd really like to do two things, not necessarily in this order: First, I'd like to let this settle into my brain," I said. "Second, I want to eat breakfast. Eventually, I will worry about the funeral."

"Lay off, Mr. Game Show Host," Pinky Lee said. "His gramps just died and he's sad and he didn't get laid last night. He's the last of his family now. When he dies, his entire family will be extinct, and no one's ever gonna ..."

"Thanks, sweetie," I said. Why did I call her sweetie? "If you don't mind, I'd rather not think about the end of the line for my family. I'd dealing with enough issues today and I haven't even eaten my toast."

"I was just sayin'," she started again, but I interrupted.

"I know, I know, and I appreciate your concern, I really do, but it's all a little much right now," I said. "I'd kind of like to take a look at the paper and do the crossword puzzle and read the police reports. No obits for me today. A little too close to home, y'know."

"Look," Jerry said, moving his head closer to me across the table and staring me in the eye. "You've got to be practical, and that old man didn't have a big enough insurance policy to bury a squirrel. You don't have any money, either. So I'm asking what are you going to do for as funeral? I'll tell you what you're going to do. You 're going to give him the biggest funeral this dumpy little town had ever seen. And I'm paying for it. Me. Jerry Most. It's about time I did something nice for someone. And besides, I did kinda like the old guy."

Before I had time to ponder whether that was a gesture based on generosity or pure ego, there was a knock at the screen door, announcing the first of several visitors who would come to express their sympathy with cupcakes and soup and roasted chickens and home-made venison sausage. But this was no well-wisher. It was Charlie, our friend from the jail. He was wearing what appeared to be his best, and probably only, suit. It was light blue, and it may have been cotton or polyester or a blend of the two during its best days. Charlie's hair was combed with what appeared to be Vaseline and his paisley tie was tied so short it looked like a bib. The suit itself was shiny in parts, and it was so tight Charlie had to hold his arms away from his torso as though he had a body builder's physique.

Charlie looked through the screen door tentatively until he could spot Jerry. He smiled, showing a rack of rotting teeth that could have made a dentist rich.

"Reportin' for duty, sir," he said.

"What duty is that?" I asked.

"No, not you. I'm here for the game show host," he said. "I'm going to be his Pancho Sanza. Remember me, Jerry? We met in jail."

"You mean Sancho Panza, Reverend Spooner?" I asked wearily. "Or did you read the *Highlights Magazine* version?"

"I don't know from Sir Monte or a Reverend Spooner, but I did mean Pancho Sanza, Fat Boy," he said indignantly. "I read about Don Coyote in the *Classic Comics* when I was a kid. I always wanted to be Pancho Sanza."

"Fine, Pancho, or whatever your name is, would you care to join us in the eating of eggs and the planning of funerals?" I asked as he opened the screen door and walked in toward the kitchen.

"Funerals? I can't flan punerals," he said, flustered already. "Who died? The fat guy's blow up sex doll get punctured?"

"Whoa, hey, Charlie, is it? Or would you prefer Pancho?" Jerry broke in. "This man has suffered a terrible loss. His grandfather died in his sleep last night. In fact, they just took his body away to the funeral home. And that's why we're planning a funeral. A funeral which, by the way, I intend to pay for in full."

Jerry looked straight at me with his eyebrows raised, but I was in no position to argue. A funeral would cost an awful lot, but I hesitated to turn control of the event over to a TV game show host I had known for less than 24 hours.

"Don't worry, pal, Jerry's going to take care of everything," he said. "Charlie, you and I have work to do. I need you to drive me back to my car at the bar called ... uh, what was the name of that dreadful place?"

"The Hee Haw?" I said. "I hope you locked it and turned on your burglar alarm."

"Not to worry," Jerry said. "Charlie, take me to the Hee Haw. We'll get my car and then we'll make the preparations. You, pal, may stay here and allow your lovely young friend to help nurse you through your bereavement. Wink, wink, wink."

Suffering from as much stimulation as I was, sex had actually dropped fairly far down the priority list. I took a quick mental inventory: picked up a hitchhiker who convinced me to shoplift and I wind up in jail as she disappears. I meet a game show host who suggests I appear on his show to take a chance at being ripped apart by baboons in front of a national audience for a shot at great cash and prizes that could change my life. The hitcher returns, and winds up sleeping in my bed, but I don't have sex with her. Then Grampa dies masturbating in his favorite chair, apparently to a movie called "Tit Patrol." And all of this took place as the result of my craving for cheese sticks and beer and TV in a small town I didn't necessarily like on a planet that I wanted nothing to do with in the first place.

Now the game show host, who is trying to redeem his own miserable existence by doing nice things for people, is planning the funeral of an 80-something man who favored Lincoln stovepipe hats and hula skirts. As I considered all of this, my eyes must have glassed over a bit as I stared into space. Pinky Lee, who had done all of the dishes and was behaving as though she had lived in my house for years, came to me and put her hand on my shoulder.

"You look like a man who could use a back rub," she said. "Don't worry. Everything's gonna be OK. I got a feeling about this Jerry, and if he's anything like he is on TV, he's the kind of guy who can make things happen. Your Grampa's gonna have a great funeral."

"I don't know if that's good or bad," I said. "I'm sorry it took the death of my grandfather to motivate someone to give me a back rub, but I will most certainly take you up on the offer. I trust that in spite of yesterday's events you have no intention of lulling me to sleep and stealing my grandfather's meager belongings to sell for marijuana."

"Course not, silly," she said. "I wanna take care of you. I've never had anyone to take care of before."

"Well, then you may take care of me, provided we both agree on the definition of care," I said. "But since I am letting you inside what has previously been a life closed tighter than Hoxha's Albania, I just have one question you must answer."

"Sure, bay-bay," she said. There she went with the Southern accent again. "Whattya wanna know?"

"Who the hell are you?" I asked.

Chapter 11
Pinky Lee's Story

Everything I had done with this woman up until now had been an act of faith, faith being a commodity I did not tend to expend when it came to humanity. As a suspicious and cynical sort, I always assumed people were put on Earth to do three things: annoy me, harm me or cheat me. Few incidents in my life proved that theory incorrect.

So what magic had this young woman used to make her an aberration? I was still pondering the reason for picking up this hitchhiker. It had to be more than the idea of sleazy sex that caused me to pick her up in the first place. It had to be more than her verbal persuasion that got me to shoplift for her. By picking her up, had I tried to "explode" my life as Jerry had talked about? Did she represent an adventure I felt I'd been deprived of during my dull life?

These were issues to consider later over beer and Miles. The fact was, she was right there with me, and she was offering a back rub, and I was more than willing recipient. I had already slept with this woman, and she now represented the first true sensual human contact I had had since Gerald Ford's "Whip Inflation Now" program. But I had no idea who she was. My senses of suspicion and curiosity forced me to grill her. Of course, by doing so, I was only committing myself further to her. The act of questioning her simply drew me to her. Questioning her was a more intimate act that I myself had committed in years. If I had had any brains at all, I would have taken the back rub and remained as indifferent to her as I had to everyone else. No dice.

"So how did I come to find you hitchhiking in a miserable town like this that's at least five miles from the Interstate?" I asked. "Are you running drugs? Do you have a boyfriend who beats you up? Are you a Protestant? Catholic? Democrat or Republican? Are you old enough to remember when Dan Devine coached the Packers? The '82 Series, the Milwaukee Brewers and Robin Yount? You don't have to answer in that order."

She stood there looking at me with her head tilted the way a little dog's does when listening to Jimi Hendrix' "Star Spangled Banner" at full blast on the stereo.

"Do you want a back rub or not?" she asked, a little irritated. "I'da thought you'd be more interested in your Grampa right now than me. He did just die, ya know."

"There's not much to be interested in, Grampa being dead and probably as uninteresting as he'll ever be," I said. "But I take your point. Yes, I'd like a back rub very much. The couch OK?"

"Couch, floor, bed, wherever you're comfy," she said.

I took off my T-shirt and laid face down on the couch, eyes closed. She started with my neck, and immediately I saw the Milky Way and all the galaxies right before me projected on my eyelids. Her hands were cool and smooth and gentle, like those of an angel with a degree in orthopedic nursing. She called it a deep massage, and I thought that was appropriate since it felt as though she was massaging my very soul. She could have answered every question I had just asked and I would not have been able to comprehend them. She closed this act by taking her fingers and digging invisible trenches up the back of my neck through the hairline.

I was no longer interested in her answers. I could have joined Grampa right there and then and been happier for the experience. Suddenly, she slapped me hard on the butt and said: "Feel better?"

"I think with that single act you just made up for a miserable childhood in the space of 15 minutes," I said. "Do that again and I might start thinking life is worth living without TV. I'm sorry. I shouldn't even joke about that. But it was quite enjoyable."

"Quite enjoyable," she said nasally, mocking me. "Quite enjoyable. You talk like some snobby Englishman who just got a blow job from his snobby English wife. You feel great, admit it. You're starting to feel like a human being, not some appliance. How long have you been like this?"

By now I was sitting up, shirtless with my back to the couch. She was sitting in the middle, just enough space between us to let me know I had another 20 yards to go before I hit pay dirt. I tried humor to loosen her up.

"I have simply chosen to ignore the temporal while I consider the deeper meanings of popular culture phenomena such as the notion of bestowing unspeakable wealth upon a family of poor, uneducated hill folk who cannot possibly have the imagination to enjoy themselves with money," I said.

"OK, so I'm gonna get bullshit talk," she said, clearly getting angry. "You know, I know you wanna sleep with me real bad. But I don't know anything about you. Nothing, except you eat bad and yer fat and you watch a lot of TV. Before I sleep with a man I wanna know something about him. I just gave you a real nice back rub, but I still don't know enough about you to muss your hair, let alone have sex with you. I don't even know your name."

"Oh, that's easy. My name is Ho Chi Minh," I said, desperately trying to evade the line of questioning. "Look, it had been my intention to find out more about you. You're in my house, after all. I didn't want to say much about myself. There isn't much to tell. Really. Just a lot of boredom and reruns. Hey, I maybe could give you Jed Clampett's story. It's much more interesting. You know, he was a poor mountaineer who barely kept his family fed, then one day he was shooting at some food and up from the ground ..."

"Fine, spend the rest of your life whacking off to that girl's poster on your wall," she said.

"I would do no such thing," I said. "I have too much respect for Farrah as an artist."

"Then whack off to 'Cock Sucking Bikers' magazine," she said, taking me back just a bit. How did she know about that one? "Yes, I did notice your pornography stuffed under the bed. I am the curious sort, ya know. What if yer Grampa in heaven could see you jacking off to that kind of stuff? Man, you are one sad case."

Well, thanks a lot for that image of Grampa watching me gratify myself, Pinky Lee. That won't make the experience any stranger, now will it?

Still, I was powerless to argue with her.

Once again, she had turned everything around. I was going to be forced to reveal something about myself. But I had a vivid imagination, and I figured I could come up with enough sad stories to make her leap into the sack in sympathy. Yes, I would use pity to get laid if that's what it took. By now, the thought of Grampa's death, awful though it was, had been replaced by the thought of having sex. I was a sad case. Was I ever. And I had only begun to explain my situation to her in a last ditch attempt to bed her.

I allowed my face to fall a bit, put a faraway look in my eyes as though I was traveling way, way back to some painful events in my life, and I think I even heard myself sob just a little.

With that bit of stagecraft out of the way, I was ready for the delivery.

"I don't know what happened to me," I said sadly. "I never had a chance at love. I think it was when I was a kid. My parents weren't terribly emotional but even when they were they were extremely undemonstrative. They didn't hug me. They didn't hug each other. They didn't kiss me on the forehead.

"Maybe it was some kind of religious thing, I don't know. They were just very reserved. But now that I think of it, I don't remember ever being hugged by my mother, except once when there was a huge blizzard and I had to walk home from my job at Leonid's pizza place, which was then known as 'Luigi's Pizzatorium.' It took an hour. When I walked in the front door of the house covered with snow and ice, she ran up to me, gave me a big hug, and even patted my back as she did so. But then she stepped back as though she had violated some unwritten protocol. She looked embarrassed, walked away and said supper would be ready in half an hour.

"Meanwhile, my father was to passion what mannequins are to humanity. The great part was he never yelled at me when I was a kid, no matter what I did. Or what anybody did for that matter. You know, I'll never figure out how Grampa could have a blank slate of a kid like my father. Maybe my father was that way because Grampa was nuts. Don't get me wrong, my father was a good man. He loved building model ships. Volunteer firefighter, president of the church council, but he made Mr. Spock from the old—and I might add the best—"Star Trek", look like a hysterical maniac. The only time I ever saw him angry was when I drank all of his Holy Water and baptized the dog in the bath tub. He clobbered me with a pliers because he believed I was mocking the religion he loved. He opened up a cut that bled but really didn't demand any attention. An hour later, he just came up to me, said, 'Sorry. I overreacted,' and stuck out his right hand to shake. That was it. If he ever hugged me, I don't remember that, either.

"Of course, by the time I got to high school I had already developed an appetite which made me big, but not athletic. This made me very unpopular date material, so romance was never really part of the picture for me.

"In the end, I guess I, I guess I ..." I trailed off. This was the hard part: selling the hurt. "I just never felt loved, and as a result I never learned how to love, and I just decided to quit life. Because what is life without love? Isn't that why we're here? To be loved?"

I bowed my head and looked at the floor. I pursed my lips as though to keep from breaking down. Jeffrey Hunter had nothing on me for this performance. I breathed deeply, sniffed, and waited for her to come and comfort me. If she did that, I had her in my trap.

By this moment, of course, Grampa's death might as well have been in 1957.

"Well, well, well," she said, smiling faintly and tilting her head back to look at me through the slits of her eyes. "Well, well, well. So you're the little lost boy who no one ever loved. Mama didn't hug you. Daddy didn't hug you. The girls wouldn't hug you. Boy, I'll bet if this little shithole town had a strip joint, you'd be their best customer, and all the waitresses would feel your eyes crawling up their legs as they poured drinks. That was the saddest attempt to get sympathy I've ever heard. Man, your problem is you've lived so little you haven't even been hurt enough to have the blues. You don't deserve to be depressed, but you are. You're a fake. You just never bothered to try."

As she spoke, in my mind I heard the whistling of bombs dropping as they exploded my feeble hopes of having sex. She was hard to pin down. She had a dumb act. And she had a smart act. She had a Midwestern accent. And she had a Southern accent. She was seducing me. She wasn't seducing me.

"You know, I asked you before why you never asked why I was hitch-hiking," she said. "It's very dangerous, you know. So since you're looking for sympathy, let me bend your ear with a true story that happened to me, and I don't have the blues. I'm not depressed. I'm sure this story's been told by millions a girls all over the country. But it happened to me, not them. See, when I was real little, everybody knew I was gonna be pretty. I think one'a the reasons my parents gave me this goofy-ass name is they thought it would help me win the Miss America pageant someday. Those damn Miss Americas always got some weird three-word name, just like Lee Harvey Oswald.

"So with looks like mine and a name like Pinky Lee Grushecky, I mighta just started wearin' a diamond tiara when I was 14. Thing was, older men always acted real creepy around me. One time on Christmas Eve, I's about 16, I was wearin' a real pretty red dress that I had picked out when my

113

momma took me to the Boston Store in Milwaukee. I was so proud of that dress, 'cause I knew it made me look pretty but it was also real Christmassy. That dress made me happy.

"Yer probably already figurin' out where this story is goin', but I'll finish it for you anyway. So my relatives come over fer Christmas Eve just like they did every year, and everybody's huggin' and drinkin' and sayin' merry Christmas and I'm feelin' like this is the first Christmas where I'm almost as good as an adult, even though I missed Santa. My daddy even let me have some brandy and Cokes so I could join in with the rest of the partiers. I was gettin' kinda woozy, but I's havin' a good time. So my Grampy, he comes over to me and asks if he could have a word with me. Why not? He's my Grampy! Maybe he's got a special present fer me, I'm thinkin'. So he takes me into a corner and he says: 'Pinky Lee. Don't tell yer daddy I said this. But yer gettin' real sexy.' And he starts touchin' my dress along the neckline until he grabs my breast. Then he puts both arms around me, puts his hand on my ass and sends his horrible old tongue down my throat. I'd a liked ta thrown up right there and then. I pulled away, ran upstairs and took that dress off. Threw it right in the garbage.

"Later, I told my daddy what happened and he slapped me. He says in this real mean, spooky voice, 'Don't you ever talk that way about your grandfather again.'

"It shouldn't have surprised me when one night I was asleep and Daddy came in after me himself. He started pullin' down my covers and pullin' up my nightie, but before he could do anything else I reached over onto my night stand and stabbed him in the cheek with a pen that I used to write down my dreams. My own daddy.

"While he was rollin' around screamin', I just grabbed whatever I could and hit the road. Stole his wallet, too, so I could have some money. Been hitchin' for years ever since. Never trusted anyone or anything enough to stay in one spot very long. Now, like I said, I got a right to be depressed. People I loved and trusted hurt me bad.

"That changed the way I looked at things. The world got kind of ugly for me, and men, well, men have never seemed the same. You can't trust yer daddy, you can't trust any man. I can't get even with my Daddy and my Grampy even though I'd like to. But instead, I'm gettin' even with every man I can, one at a time. Since I got you sent to jail for shopliftin', I figure we're even. But if I don't fall fer yet shit, don't be surprised. I've seen it all."

"My, my, my," I said. "I thought my line of crap was well conceived, but you've really got me boxed in. If I questioned a story like that, I look as bad as your old man. It is interesting, though, how I get to go to jail because your father's a scumbag. I'm sure there's some wonderful logic to that which my inferior mind simply cannot comprehend."

"Fuck you, you asshole," she said. She just stared vacantly across the room and I saw a small tear crawl down her cheek. I think I hurt her.

I guess I was supposed to say I was sorry, but I just wasn't terribly experienced in the practice of apologies. Besides, my day seemed full already. It wasn't yet 11 a.m., and already I needed a beer. I was confronted with the issues of the death and incest before I had even gotten dressed for the day.

You never, ever ask yourself how things could possibly get worse in these situations because all you need to do is think about the question to find out.

In this case, I did not have to wait long. Pinky Lee and I sat on couch staring at each other like two sumo wrestlers waiting for the other one to make a move. But the trance was broken by a knock at the screen door. I got up to answer the knock, knowing that getting up once again killed my chances for sex. It would take a long time to build the mood again, if I had indeed built a mood to begin with. If it had been Ed McMahon at the door offering me $12 million from Publisher's Clearinghouse, it would have been worth the effort of getting up. But this is my life we're talking about, so a good thing could not be waiting for me at the door. And it wasn't.

It was, who else? Foilhead Eddie. He had with him a box, a sort of heavy wooden crate a little bigger than a case of beer, and it looked as though it had been buried in the back yard for several years.

"He should take this with him," Eddie said, standing solemn and still like the robot Gort in the movie, *The Day the Earth Stood Still*. He was also carrying a wooden crate.

"Take what with whom?" I asked, trying desperately to be pleasant through my anger with a man who I figured could very well be carrying a gun. "I'm afraid the day has gotten off to such a rough start that I am unable to decipher the thoughts of even the most harmless psychotics, Eddie. So bear with me. Please tell me what the hell you're talking about. Speak slowly. I'm not a very quick study when it comes to comprehending other people's delusions."

"Your grandfather, he was a veteran, you know that," Eddie said. "He defended our country from Hitler. He would have defended it if the Democrats had taken over with their one-world conspiracy, too. Am I right?"

"For the sake of argument, if not the appeasement of a potentially violent madman, I'll say yes, he might have fought the Democrats if they had marched into Hammertown with United Nations troops," I said, backing away from the door slightly. "Am I to take your meaning to indicate that there are firearms in that box you are carrying?"

"They are the weapons of a military man," Eddie said. "He should be buried with them."

In all the years I knew Grampa, I never once saw him carry or use a gun. He said only that by the time the war was over, he was grateful he lived in a country where you didn't have to carry a rifle from town to town to defend yourself. He didn't go hunting like 99 percent of the men in Hammertown. He didn't target shoot. Guns were simply not a part of his life.

In Eddie's eyes, no one should be without firearms, even if they were dead. So when he came into the house, set down the crate and opened it, it was no surprise that there was enough firepower to defend a small town. I didn't know much about guns, but it appeared that they were all in decent shape. Still, even the idea of a gun with a dead man made me nervous.

I was a child of the '60s, and I remembered how JFK and Martin and Bobby got killed by guns. As a result, I was not enthusiastic about having this weaponry in my house.

"Pick one out," Eddie said. "You can bury it with your Grampa. An old soldier needs a gun."

"Eddie, don't get me wrong, but I think there's something inappropriate about sending a man to heaven or wherever with a gun," I said, staring horrified at the number of firearms that were in the possession of a man who wore aluminum foil on his head. Ain't the Second Amendment grand?

"Isn't there some kind of metal detector at the gates, anyway? He'd never be able to get into heaven with one of these."

"Pick one," Eddie said, his voice rising ominously and insistent. "Pick one. He was my friend. He needs a gun."

"OK, Eddie," I said. "Look, do you have any recommendations? I mean, these look all the same to me. They're handguns, right? Or it that one an Uzi? I think I recognize it from TV. Hey, these aren't loaded, are they?"

"Course they're loaded, man," Eddie said. "Gun ain't much good without rounds in it, is it? Gotta have it loaded. Safeties are on, though."

"Eddie, look, my Grampa is dead. He doesn't need a gun. He needs a casket, a minister, some mourners and several cubic feet of dirt. A gun seems a little incongruous," I explained. I might as well have been talking to the terriers next door.

Just then, Pinky Lee, who thus far had watched the exchange silently, broke in.

"Look, just take the damn gun," she said. "It can't hurt anything. Let Grampa be buried with a gun. He might even have gotten a kick out of the idea. I think he'd have liked it."

"Thank you so much for weighing in," I said. "But in fact I think I knew my grandfather just a little better than you did, and he didn't seem to like guns, that's all. I don't want any guns in the house. There could be some kind of accident."

"Well, now that your Grampa's gone I think the chances are there won't be an accident," she said. "Besides, we're putting it in his casket, anyway."

"He needs it," Eddie said.

"Fine," I said. "If you think he needs it. Give that one to me."

Eddie handed me the gun. An Uzi? A Glock? I didn't know. And he picked up the crate.

"It would be an honor if I could speak at the funeral," he said. "He was my friend. He was my compadre. He accepted what I said about my ability to transmit my thoughts to other people. He listened to me. I want to pay him an honor. It's what friends do for fallen comrades."

The thought of a man in a red plaid flannel shirt and denim overalls with a wool cap lined with aluminum foil speaking over my grandfather's coffin which contained a loaded gun sounded like one of the more absurd ideas I had heard even during the surreal last 24 hours.

"Sure thing, Eddie," I said, having lost control of the entire situation. "You can speak at Grampa's funeral. But please, try to look presentable. And when you write your speech, please remember you're speaking to Grampa's loved ones, or loved one, I should say, who is still adjusting to the loss. I just don't need an NRA rally."

"I shall respect your wishes," Eddie replied solemnly.

Chapter 12
Grampa's Funeral

If Grampa had wanted a church funeral, he was out of luck. He had done much to alienate the local clergy over the years, his Christmastime raccoon costume being the least of his means of doing so. In fact, his running commentaries on the padre's sermons during the few services he attended made him highly unpopular with the entire parish, not to mention the priest, so it was unlikely that we could appeal the priest's decision to the parish council. It didn't help our case that Grampa asked that he be buried without pants.

It also didn't help that Jerry had procured a kangaroo for the event in honor of Grampa's eccentric ways. Somehow, a kangaroo seemed to make sense to him in this instance. The marsupial was in the custody of Charlie, who now wanted to be known as "Charles," his station in life having improved since his employ by Jerry. Jerry led the creature on a leash everywhere, and Charles would be charged with maintaining the kangaroo's good behavior at the service, which would be held at the Homer Funeral Home and Tanning Salon in downtown Hammertown.

Since Hammertown is rather small, even death doesn't create enough business to allow a profit. So one day Mr. Homer, as he was always respectfully called as a representative of death, saw a tanning bed when he was staying at the YMCA in Milwaukee during a visit to his cousin, and he could not help but notice the parallels between tanning beds and coffins.

The only difference between the tanning beds and the coffins he sold was you didn't nail the tanning beds shut, he joked. Needless to say, with such a keen eye for a business opportunity, Mr. Homer was very liberal about the types of services that were held in his chapel. Mr. Homer's manner was that of a grim, gaunt undertaker. He always seemed serious, even when telling one of his flinty jokes. Physically, however, Mr. Homer looked more like a New Jersey stevedore. His thick arms, muscular, he explained, were from digging graves himself until he had the money to buy equipment.

His physique would have better fit an interior lineman for the Wisconsin Badgers. The tattoo on his left forearm, the head of a grinning Holstein cow, always managed to humor the newly bereaved when Mr. Homer wore his short-sleeved white business shirts during funeral planning sessions.

Despite his size and musculature, Mr. Homer was considered by many in town to be a gentleman, which was to say they thought he was a sissy. The fact that he was not known to use foul language or follow the Green Bay Packers brought about a general belief that he might even be gay. The fact that he would repeatedly say, "oh my, oh my," when confronted with a crisis situation further fueled theories about his manhood and sexuality.

But Mr. Homer was well-respected in Hammertown, not only because of his physical stature—he occasionally worked as a bouncer at the County Fair—but because his position conveyed a certain portfolio of intelligence and wisdom. The understanding was that anyone who had death as a business partner must be very smart. But Mr. Homer was also a shrewd businessman, and he was not in the habit of turning away business because of the presence of non-native species like, say, kangaroos.

Obviously, having explained the tanning bed/funeral parlor relationship, the kangaroo requires equal time for explanation. Jerry, it seems, was very impressed with Grampa's Dada sensibilities in the short time they had been in contact. A guy with Jerry's connections always knows somebody who knows somebody, and he arranged to have the kangaroo shipped from some dumpy roadside circus in Utah to Hammertown to be present at Grampa's funeral. The kangaroo's name was Billie, and it was believed to be a female.

She—it—wore a little red vest with yellow embroidered swirls. She also wore a red bellboy's hat and smelled like a wet dog.

"Why, Jerry? Why?" I asked when I saw Billie, knowing the explanation would be unfathomable. "Why, after I entrusted you with the planning of my grandfather's funeral, did you see fit to include a kangaroo in this most serious of human rituals?"

"Well, first of all, I didn't think a Thompson's Gazelle would have the same effect," Jerry explained. "And there was no way we could ship a rhino in time."

I stared at him as though my gaze could cause invisibility.

"OK, look. How well did you really know the old guy?" Jerry asked.

"I knew him all my life, and I knew he was just this side of criminally insane," I said. "There wasn't much more to know. He liked Metamucil and masturbating, the latter of which encourages me because that probably means my special appendage will not be useless when I am in my dotage. Why, pray, did you think you knew him better?"

"I didn't know him at all," Jerry said. "But you didn't have to know him to know he was telling the world to screw off with his oddball behavior. He wasn't crazy. He knew exactly what he was doing. Sure, he was a little gratuitous. But he lived by stream of consciousness, and sometimes that defied social convention. He did whatever came into his mind, as long as it didn't hurt anyone. He wore grass skirts in public, for God's sake. A man like that simply cannot have a regular, standard-issue funeral. So I called a buddy of mine and asked if he knew somebody who could send me a kangaroo. I think a kangaroo symbolizes this man's life. Kangaroos are happy creatures that make people laugh. Even their name is funny.

"Say it: Kangaroo. Kang-ga-rooo. Concentrate on the ooo sound. Like baboon. Baboon is funny too, right?"

I was not responding, although I somehow saw some logic in what he said. And that was very frightening. It was as though Grampa's presence inside my head was growing stronger. I regained my composure.

"This is insane," I protested. "Kangeroos don't attend funerals. They aren't guests at dinner parties and they aren't the best man at weddings. In short, they are not a part of human society. They are animals, Jerry. You may note that unlike us, they have fairly pronounced tails and they have no language that we can discern. Go back to high school biology. Use that Rutgers education of yours. Kangaroos are of a different phylum and genus. They cannot reason and they don't even have the intelligence to understand your moronic television show. They have fur and they shed and shit and piss and rut indiscriminately, although that may be the one characteristic they share with my grandfather."

"I'm just trying to help," Jerry said so earnestly that it could not have been faked. "I just want your Grampa to go out in style. C'mon. It's the new Jerry. I care about people. Indulge my need to be good."

"With a kangaroo at a funeral?"

"Yes, with a kangaroo," he said. "Be glad I didn't buy the race car casket. Look, Billie's a nice girl—uh, animal. We'll keep her on a leash and Charles will hang onto her the whole time. What could go wrong?"

"Don't ever ask me that question again," I warned, speaking through clenched teeth. "Fine. Billie comes to the funeral. But she doesn't get to speak, and she stays on the leash no matter what. She is not a pallbearer. She is a piece of living furniture. She has no role in this ceremony, do you understand?"

"Now you're getting the hang of it," Jerry said. "I think Grampa would be proud of you. I think he'd laugh like crazy if he knew what we were doing for him."

"Shut up," I said. But I resigned to agree with him.

And so three days after his demise, we held Grampa's funeral before a crowd of about a dozen people, including myself, Pinky Lee, Jerry, Charles and his wife, Dottie, Billie the kangaroo, Leonid, Grampa 's one-time boss in the pizza industry, an old woman named Alice Murphy who took it upon herself to mourn the passing of every resident of Hammertown, and, of course, Foilhead Eddie, who would deliver a eulogy of some kind. Mr. Homer agreed to officiate.

I had decided that Grampa would be cremated, meaning that Eddie would get back the gun he wanted Grampa to have right after the funeral service. Even Eddie agreed that putting the gun in the furnace with Grampa might be a little dangerous.

The Homer Funeral Home and Tanning Salon was little more than a glorified garage. It was a spacious building, large enough for a small, windowless chapel that could hold about two dozen mourners, a "work room" where bodies were prepared, a tiny dark business office. Another room on the other side of the building held eight tanning beds.

In the event there was a need for a larger room for a funeral service than the chapel could handle, the rotunda of City Hall could be used assuming it was not a church-sanctioned affair. For Grampa, there was no need to worry about needing the space of City Hall.

Homer's building had a small, dark, wood-paneled foyer with well-kept black Naugahyde couches lining the outside walls, with tasteful oak end tables on either side of each couch. Table lamps with ruffled shades provided the dim light. Art of the kind found at "starving artist" sales at a Holiday

Inn allowed mourners and tanners to view sailing ships, sunsets, waving fields of wheat, a snowy mountain range and, of course, the de rigueur rural Wisconsin wildlife portrait of a 13-point buck deer.

A small bumper sticker reading "I'm a Packer Backer" was stuck to the cash register. Homer took cash and credit, which further added the feel of a roadside diner to the tanning salon and funeral parlor.

When you entered the building from Wilson Street, Hammertown's main thoroughfare, you first saw a glass counter at the opposite wall, and a cash register. This, of course, was for the benefit of the tanning business, since Mr. Homer did not expect to be paid immediately in cash for funerals, but he did for tanning sessions. Inside the glass case were items needed for tanning: goggles, oils and white towels. Mr. Homer once said that he thought about selling sympathy cards at the front counter, too, but he decided that doing so would be "too obvious."

Once you were in the foyer, you had a choice between a door on the left and a door on the right. If you wanted to tan, you went through the door on the left. If you wanted to go to the chapel, you went to the door on the right. Sometimes, mourners were embarrassed to walk into the tanning salon. But those who came for the tanning never seemed to be put off when they walked into the chapel in the middle of a funeral, even if they were clad only in a skimpy swimming suit.

"Ooops," they'd giggle. "I don't wanna go in like, one of those boxes. I wouldn't get much of a tan if I was, like, underground."

Hardy har har.

Mr. Homer also liked to joke that he hoped he never accidentally went in the wrong room and buried a tanner in a tanning bed. This is what passed for humor in Hammertown, and the joke was told and retold hundreds of times.

No bikini-clad tanners walked into Grampa's funeral. But even if they had the affair could not have been anymore bizarre. To start, there was a kangaroo in there. But in spite of Jerry's promises, it got worse. Unspeakably worse. In fact, it had all the characteristics of an air show disaster.

The service was scheduled for 1 p.m. It was to be a simple affair. Mr. Homer would say a few generic prayers from a Protestant prayer book, Foilhead Eddie would deliver his eulogy, and I, as the last surviving relative, would say a few words. We'd have another prayer, we'd walk up to the open casket to say goodbye to Grampa one last time, and then we'd leave him for

Mr. Homer to cremate. Our job finished, we would file out of the building, maybe stop off and get a tan.

On paper, it looked fine. But it went quite a bit differently.

Grampa, lying in state in his Lincoln garb—well, half of it anyway, was at the front of the chapel in front of the altar in a brown casket with silver handles. Mr. Homer had worked his magic to straighten out Grampa from his, um, sitting position so that he could lie supine in his coffin.

The Lincoln suit—minus his pants—seemed like the most logical clothing for his funeral, and it was certainly more appropriate for departure from this world than his goat suit. Since the affair was an open casket, and as Grampa had no pants on, Mr. Homer had to find some way to conceal an erection that stubbornly remained pointing skyward even in death. He simply took Grampa's flattened stove-pipe hat and placed it over the other-worldly boner.

Other than the fact that the guest of honor was pantless and a kangaroo was fidgeting in the front row at the end of a leash held by a moron in a suit two sizes too small, it seemed like a normal funeral. Even Foilhead Eddie's eulogy was, at first, coherent, if occasionally disjointed.

Eddie had taken off his foil because he said he did not care who heard his thoughts, he was in mourning and his sadness would do them no good. He had showered, shaved and put on a pressed, clean charcoal gray suit.

It was very warm that day, and the room was unbearably stuffy. Since no one except Jerry was used to wearing decent clothing, it seemed even warmer than it was. As everyone was seated, Mr. Homer opened the door of the chapel and then the front door of the building in order to get the air circulating. A nice breeze rolled through the room, and even Grampa seemed more comfortable.

Upon opening the doors, the service began. Since his organist was vacationing Up North, as the natives called the area, Mr. Homer turned on a tinny-sounding boom box in the back of the room that played appropriate hymns like *A Mighty Fortress is Our God* and *Nearer My God to Thee.*

The music was a detail that Grampa had missed in his funeral plan. I guessed that if he had thought about it, he would have asked that *Pop Goes the Weasel* be played repeatedly throughout the service.

When the music started, Homer nodded at Eddie, who had been straining to get into the pulpit like a horse at the starting gate of the Kentucky

Derby. Eddie sprinted up, the pages of his eulogy drifting behind him like dead sparrows dropping from the sky. He stopped, turned around and picked them up, but now the pages were out of order. Eddie, who was not a professional speaker, would soon find out why one should always number the pages of his speech.

He stepped up to the podium, fumbled some more with the papers, tapped them hard on the end to straighten them up, and cleared his throat. As he was about to speak, he suddenly reached into his breast pocket. Of course, I assumed it was a gun and that we would all soon be as dead as Grampa. But it wasn't a gun. It was a portable police radio. Eddie turned it on, set it on the lectern and then began a disjointed tribute to Grampa that was punctuated by the sounds of crimes and misdemeanors from the Hammertown metropolitan area.

"What is life?" Eddie began. "Why are we here? Is life necessary? If so, why? Do we have a choice but to be here, or can we ask ahead of time not to be born, choosing instead to float aimlessly through the cosmos like chunks of food in the dishwater? Do we ever really know what our purpose was for walking this planet?"

Suddenly, in the midst of this deep meditation, the radio squawked. "Fifty seven, ah, fifty seven, what's your twenty?"

Eddie paused, waiting for a response. "Just passing the Mobil on Highway 10, heading west," said the disembodied voice, which sounded like our cop friend from the day before. "What's up?"

"This man, this war hero, Donald Q. Peck, did not ask not to be born, which should be obvious, because he lived to an old and dignified age," Eddie continued. "And because he was born ..."

"Ah, we got a report of some kids throwing bananas at passing cars from the parking lot at Booby's Booze Ranch," the dispatcher interrupted.

"Because he was born ..."

"I gotcha base. You say bananas? When I was a kid we used to throw apples. That was more American, I think."

"... many people lived because he died. I mean because he was born ..."

"Guy who throws apples at cars becomes a cop, huh?" the dispatcher said. "Jeez, throwin' bananas they might become head of the Highway Patrol."

I tried to stop Eddie's delivery, suggesting that he turn off the police monitor. But he was clearly confused and, as always, potentially dangerous, so the interruption was probably unwise. It was impossible to guess why Eddie brought a police radio to a funeral. My guess was that he believed this was a way to remain vigilant against whatever invisible government forces might try to come and take his beloved guns away.

"Gotta know where the cops are," Eddie said hurriedly, trying to explain the radio's presence. Then he resumed. "Now this man, who we all called Grampa, even though he wasn't our Grampa, was my friend. Yet I do not believe he was born simply to be my friend. But I am glad he spent some time here for that purpose. Because we all need companionship. We all need friends and family ..."

Pinky Lee nudged me.

"Eddie wears foil on his head, remember?" I whispered. "He's talking like a crazy man. No one needs anyone. They need TV and beer and cheese sticks."

Eddie went on: "But this man was also a hero, and we all need heroes, too. He was more than a hero, because even though he did heroic things, he never sought recognition..."

"Can you go to Kmart and check out a shoplifting incident?" It was the dispatcher again. "They're holding a man now."

"Don't look at me," I whispered to Jerry. Pinky Lee was snickering.

"Sure base. What was the guy stealing? Bananas?"

Pinky Lee burst out laughing and tried to mask it as a wail. No dice. Her outburst was creating an infectious round of nervous laughter among me and Jerry. Charles just glared at us and gave the kangaroo's leash a yank, as though Billie was giggling, too. Alice Murphy sat two rows behind us and shushed us.

I turned around and looked at her. "This is my grandfather's funeral," I said. "I can snicker or wail or whisper or play rock, paper, scissors if I so desire, you old busybody."

Now the kangaroo was making grunting noises and fidgeting. Charles held onto the leash with both hands as Billie began snuffling and straining on the leash.

"Subject was apprehended trying to walk out with a box of adult diapers," said dispatch.

"But he also had an odd way about him, a way which many could not understand," Eddie continued.

"Diaper Boy got a name?" Thirty-seven asked.

"Shimilanski, Robert C., common spelling," said dispatch. In a place like Hammertown, spelling names like Shimilanski was considered common.

Please, please, please let me get through this without hysterical laughter, I thought, my focus shifting away from the dead man in the room and to the notion of someone stealing adult diapers. That was sure a lot worse than Tic Tacs. I made eye contact with no one. In a pew a row over, Leonid sat dabbing his eyes with Kleenex, muttering: "I am sorry I yelled, Hula Lincoln. You were good man. You do not deserve to be dead. I hope Leonid did not kill you by making your heart sick."

Mrs. Murphy shushed Leonid, too. Mr. Homer stood solemnly in the back of the chapel, hands folded behind his back.

"Listen, dispatch, if this guy's got pooper problems I don't want to pick him up in a clean car. Get the other car to grab him."

"No can do," dispatch said. "He's after the banana kids."

"OK, but I'm not cleaning anything up," Thirty-seven said. "That guy shits in here, it's maintenance's problem."

And with that, the police radio fell silent. Hammertown's squad cars were engaged in the fight against crime, and now Eddie could finish his eulogy in peace. He looked down, turned a page, and began reading, focusing on the page in case the radio went off again. He didn't want to lose his place.

"Dear Union Carbide," he said, and then he stopped, frozen. A protest letter he had written regarding the production of insecticide had worked its way into the stack of papers that made up Eddie's speech. Pinky Lee was pinching me to keep me from laughing. Jerry had his head in his hands, and Charles was petting the increasingly agitated Billie. Leonid was still muttering and crying, and Mrs. Murphy called from the back row that we should all stop laughing and have more respect for the dead.

"Sorry, Mrs. Murphy," I said giddily. "We were just thinking about clowns."

That was it. We all lost it. The three of us burst into gales of open laughter as a confused Leonid and stunned Eddie looked on. It appeared Eddie was about to make one last try at finishing his eulogy. He collected himself, took a deep breath, and tried to speak. But it was not to be. Grampa would join Shakespeare and Churchill and FDR and Miles Davis in the next world without the benefit of full eulogy.

Hammertown being a small town, people knew each other quite well. And they knew each other's pets. People joked that you could always tell when a stranger was in town because that was the only time the dogs barked. Nearly everyone in Hammertown had a dog, and nearly everyone let them walk around unleashed. The unwritten rule was that dogs could defecate wherever they chose because everybody would be picking up the same amount of dog shit off their lawn, more or less.

Dogs sometimes walked right into stores and businesses to visit with people, and only the restaurants kept them out for obvious health reasons. So it was on that warm, lazy afternoon in Hammertown that two horse-like mutts from the neighborhood, Lester and Peewee, happened by the tanning salon and funeral home. They wandered in, as they sometimes did during funerals, and sniffed around looking for crumbs or interesting insects that also had made their way into the building. Their entrance was not viewed with any alarm by Mr. Homer, who had seen this before, knew the dogs and saw nothing inappropriate in their attendance.

But then, Mr. Homer had never had a kangaroo in his chapel before.

The mongrels both had detected Billie's scent the minute they walked into the building, but they could not identify the creature without visual contact. That didn't take long. Lester spotted Billie first, and, using his best dog reasoning, he began barking as though he had tracked down Satan himself. Peewee, alerted to the situation by Lester's barking, headed straight for poor Billie, who was just about to drag Charles out of his pew. The dogs barked like Robert Johnson's hellhounds, until they pounced right on the kangaroo.

Billie fought back violently, assuming in kangaroo-think, of course, that these wild dingoes were going eat her alive. Her fight-or-flight instincts kicked in and she broke free of Charles' grip on the leash, not before tearing the sleeve right off of his polyester suit jacket.

Billie hopped around the room instinctively looking for some brush to hide in, but as this was a chapel and tanning salon there was none. The dogs were reluctant at first to attack her because of her size and because to Lester and Peewee she was a biggest cat they had ever seen.

Mr. Homer, seeing what was taking place, scooped up his boom box and headed out the door to phone the police. The rest of us were yelling all at once, a cacophony of "Billie, no!" and "Peewee, Lester, get away from there!" and "Noooo!" Everyone was shouting except Charles, who was staring at the severed sleeve he held in his hand as though his arm had been torn off. Eddie, permanently thrown off by yet another interruption, began shouting something in German while remaining cemented to the floor behind the podium.

Grampa just lay there as though he were sunning himself, as always. I thought for a moment we should have laid him in state in a tanning booth.

It didn't take long for the dogs to corner Billie, and by now everyone was so afraid of what was likely to be a violent encounter among members of the animal kingdom that we, as human non-participants of this Darwinian battle, did nothing at all but shout commands, which none of the animals could have understood or obeyed under the best of circumstances. Kangaroos are, of course, known for their vicious kicks, and the cornered Billie took a swipe at Lester, sending him sailing about five feet. With Lester out of the way, she headed out of the corner in the direction that Lester had flown. Peewee, meanwhile, was taking bites out of Billie's tail, which was thrashing wildly.

The dogs pressed their attack, moving toward the middle of the chapel. Billie leaped to avoid Lester's jaws and fell onto Grampa's bier, toppling him out of his capsized casket to the floor. He landed on his back, and without the benefit of the concealing stovepipe hat, we all got one last look at Grampa's erection, not that anyone wanted to see it in the first place.

Lester jumped and knocked Billie backwards just enough to allow Peewee to grab her by the throat. It looked bad for Billie until Eddie took action.

Eddie, cursing auf Deutsch, or auf something anyway, saw Grampa's gun tumble out of the casket with his body. He ran to the gun and fired a single shot, which gave the animals pause, but only momentarily. He fired again, this time hitting Peewee smack in the ass. Peewee yelped and retreated to the pews, licking his wound. He would not survive the gunshot.

The smell of blood in the air, Lester was not about to give up. That is until Eddie fired a shot into his skull that sprayed Billie's vest with dog blood and brains. And that was that.

Except for a few bite wounds, Billie was relatively unharmed. Her bell-boy cap had been tipped to a jaunty angle in the conflict, and she continued hopping about the chapel long after the dogs had joined the Choir Invisible.

Pinky Lee, who had her arms around me, shouted to Jerry to go help Charles with Billie.

"That poor animal's been panicked," she said. "I hate to see animals in that state. You've got to do something, Jerry. That kangaroo is your responsibility."

Charles was struggling to calm poor Billie down, but the dog attack had quite an effect on her nerves and she had slipped the leash. She was hopping about the room wildly, with Charles half scolding and half pleading, "Oh, Billie, hop stopping, I mean stop hopping, girl."

Mr. Homer was running around the chapel, shouting, "Oh my, oh my," but his shouts had little effect in bringing reason and order to a scene which Salvador Dali would have thought strange and unreal.

As Charles and Jerry corralled Billie, Mr. Homer finally decided the best thing to do would be to pick Grampa up and put him back in his casket. It seemed like a waste, since he would shortly be transferred to an incinerator without the casket, but I ran over to help him scoop up the dead old man.

Eddie looked at the carnage and tossed the gun on the floor like Schwarzenegger at the end of an action movie. He walked over to me and stuck his chin out, and I was glad he had already thrown down the gun.

"I told you he had to have a gun with him," Eddie said, shaking his head as he walked out. "You never know when you need a gun. You just never know. Soldiers hang onto their guns, and police hang onto their pieces no matter what."

Chapter 13
Facing Life Without Grampa

We retreated to my house after the funeral, but not before stopping off at the Booze Ranch for replenishment of vital supplies. The Hammertown Humane Society came to pick up the dogs' carcasses, but they didn't know what to do with a live kangaroo, so the Hammertown police dropped their pursuit of petty thieves and banana throwers long enough to capture the exhausted animal and eventually put her in the same jail cell where I had been held the day before. They agreed to hold Billie until someone from the Milwaukee County Zoo could arrive to place her in the Australia exhibit until her nomadic owners could be tracked down.

Meanwhile, Booby's parking lot was covered with bananas and banana peels, the product of the hooliganism that was reported to police earlier. According to Booby, the young thugs had broken into a delivery truck that was headed for some grocery store in Little Rose. The kids stole several boxes of bananas before the truck driver, a Memphis native who had stopped in for a pint of peppermint schnapps but wound up talking about the Packers with Booby, had any idea what was going on. In fact, neither he nor Booby noticed what was going on until the cops showed up.

Sometimes it's interesting to think about what is going on in the rest of the world at the very moment you are suffering a loss or celebrating a victory. But in the case of Grampa's funeral, we had known exactly what was going on in at least one part of the world, Booby's Booze Ranch, because Eddie's police radio told us what was going on before Booby himself knew.

There you have it. We were mourning an old man while the youth of Hammertown threw bananas at passing cars. Life indeed goes on.

In Hammertown, it was always customary for people to visit the home of the deceased after the funeral. For some, this ritual represented a chance to secretly pilfer gewgaws and small valuables while pretending to offer support to the bereaved. For others, it was something of a social event, a chance to eat cake and drink coffee and have a few beers. As for the beer, it has been said that the people of Hammertown are always looking for a party, that they would throw up toasts to a successful gall bladder surgery. So it was fitting that we had stopped at Booby's to get the beer and wine that would be needed to entertain the guests who hadn't bothered to show up at the funeral but who would expect food and drink after the fact.

Naturally, given the burlesque scene, someone had to slip on one of the banana peels in the parking lot on the way into the store. That person, of course, had to be the most obese, most unable-to-recover one in the group, which meant that I myself hit the asphalt with a sickening thud just a few steps shy of Booby's door.

Once I hit I was hoping I had some injury that might get me sympathy from Pinky Lee without causing any real or permanent damage. I didn't hit my head, but Jerry and Pinky Lee couldn't tell from their angle. I decided to milk it.

I lay there, staring at the sky, and I began singing incoherently.

"Take me out to the ball game, take me out to the Cracker Jack," I sang, then shifted to free association. "When does Steve come to pick me up in the van? I want to go to the beach. Did you ever pet a horse? They're soft and they don't bite. Say, you're pretty. Will you marry me?"

As I had hoped, Pinky Lee came to my aid and cradled my head. Jerry went to get help from Booby.

"Oh baby, are you OK?" she said. "Did you hit your head? Oh God, please don't turn retarded on me."

I looked straight into her eyes. "Mommy?" I said. "Can I have sea monkeys for a pet? Does this bus go to the cannery?"

"Oh, God," she said, starting to cry. "We gotta get him to a doctor."

Jerry and Booby came out of the store, and Booby was visibly upset to see me lying prone in his parking lot.

"Aw, Jeez, he's gonna sue my ass off," Booby said. "Goddamn kids and those bananas. I ain't got time to clean this mess. It smells like a goddamn fruit salad out here. And look at the flies. Hey, I wonder if I paid my liability insurance."

"I'm sure your concern is heartfelt," Jerry said. "But perhaps you could summon medical help for this man."

No. No doctors. I did not like encounters with the medical profession, except for pretty nurses with cool hands, and my performance today could not be validated by any reputable physician. I had probably bruised my butt, but that was it. I decided to start coming around lest I be caught in my charade of mental defect by banana.

"Oh, man, what happened?" I said, moving up to lean on my elbows. "Don't tell me I slipped on a banana peel. How slapstick. How humiliating. Hey, Booby, what's with the bananas all over the place? Were you attacked by chimpanzees?"

"It was kids," he said. "Same as chimps."

"You OK, darlin'?" Pinky Lee said. "I'm worried about you."

I looked her straight in the eye, and I kissed her. "Yeah, I'm fine," I said. "But I seem to have pulled a muscle right here ..." I guided her hand to my personal banana.

"You pig, you didn't hurt that," she said in a manner that showed both anger and some humor. Maybe I had a chance with her tonight after all. My poor Grampa had died and I hurt myself in a liquor store parking lot. Those incidents had to be good for something. A pity lay. A mercy hump. Whatever it took.

"You know, you are just like a horny 14-year-old. You're pathetic," she said. "Pathetic."

"Yes," I said, giving her my best doe-eyed look. "I'm pathetic and pitiful and so scared to be alone. I just need to be loved."

"There's a difference between being loved and being laid," she said, helping me up.

"What an odd notion. Please, tell me more," I said. "I've seen no research to indicate love and being laid are at all related. I'm fascinated. I want to learn more about love. Will you teach me? Let's start with the screwing part."

"It's a subject you don't need to worry about, honey," she said. "You'll never learn it. It ain't gonna happen for you anytime soon."

"But a man without love is not a man at all," I said, mocking her. "I shall die without love. Why go on? Please, stab me in my lonely heart."

"Yer problem would be solved if I stabbed you in the nuts," she said. "Man, yer a pig."

"Well, if I can't have love, then I must have beer immediately," I said. "Perhaps I can just numb my senses and forget my terrible pain with a case of Point Bock beer. Let us proceed to the alcohol emporium posthaste that I may find the potion to drown my deepest sorrows and then fall into a beer-soaked slumber and have delirious fantasies about caressing your tight little blue-jeaned ass."

"I'll smack you if you so much as dream about me," she said.

"I wonder where you're sleeping tonight," I responded pleasantly. "With that attitude it won't be at my house."

When we entered Booby's, Jerry was lost in the wine aisle looking for something decent to drink. A man of his wealth was used to something better than "zinfandel" or "liebfraumilch," but this being Hammertown, he was having a hard time finding something potable. Booby, upon seeing me walk in, immediately came out from behind the counter and shook my hand, an unusual move for a man who believed human contact was a form of weakness. He had a motive, of course.

"Hey, buddy, how ya doin'?" he said. "Guess that spill out in the lot wasn't so bad after all, huh? You prob'ly wouldn't wanna sue me over something like that, what with no permanent damage or nuthin'."

"I don't know, Booby," I said. "I can't seem to feel my feet, and my legs seem so heavy, so heavy," I said, staggering slightly. "I'll have to have a doctor take a look. Maybe see one of those TV lawyers."

"Naw, naw, c'mon, you ain't gonna wind up in a wheelchair, boy," he said. "Yer too tough fer that. Little fall can't hurt a big guy like you. You coulda played for The Pack, my friend. Say, I'll tell ya what, I'll let you and yer friends have a little shopping spree here on me. Just, ah, here, just write a little note on this piece a paper and say everything's fine and you won't sue ol' Booby, then go home and get yerself nice and shitfaced on me." His voice dropped to a whisper. "Maybe you can even get some drunk booty tonight."

"Don't count on it, Fat Boy," Pinky Lee said, having overheard our conversation from several feet away as she examined a bottle of Jägermeister.

I took the paper Booby was offering and leaned over on his counter to write my waiver.

The paper was Booby's stationery, a tasteful little design with Booby's logo and a martini glass tilted to one side. Under the logo was a slogan: "Booby's Booze Ranch: All the Booze You Can Choose."

I wrote the waiver, signed it with an X and handed it to Booby. Then I walked over to a bottle of single-malt scotch and, just to horrify Jerry and

Booby, said: "How does this taste with Coke? What the heck do I care? It's free. I'll take it anyway. Say, Booby, can I come and fall in your parking lot next week? Say, do you sell Sterno here? I haven't had Sterno in weeks."

Pinky Lee picked out a six-pack of beer with jalapeno peppers in it along with the Jagermeister she had been eyeing. I saw her carrying the two items and asked whether she was planning to puke on my couch or on my carpet since the two items seemed to make a combination that would have the effect of Epicac. She replied that she would puke on my fat head, and we enjoyed a chuckle over the exchange. Ha ha.

I, meanwhile, chose the single-malt scotch, five cases of Miller Lite for guests, a case of Point Bock for me, and two bottles of Boodles gin with Martini and Rossi vermouth for martini time. I loved martini time. I was most creative at martini time. If I had any friends, they would be impressed with me during martini time. The great part about martinis is when you're drinking them you don't care if you have friends or not. After enough of them, you didn't care of you have arms or legs, either, since you weren't going to get far using either of them after the gin had taken your nervous system hostage.

"Hey, do you have nice clothes here, or just booze? I mean as long as I'm raiding the place," I asked cheerfully.

"Just booze, pal," Booby said. "Don't milk it. I gotcher waiver now."

Jerry grabbed a dusty case of Chilean Merlot, pronounced it passable, and we headed for the door thanking Booby.

"Hey, just look out fer them bananas out there," he said.

Armed with enough alcohol to keep a Russian platoon loaded for a weekend, we headed back to my place to hold the "mourning party." Leonid, who really was mourning, had promised to send over a dozen pizzas. Mrs. Murphy brought cupcakes and cherry Jell-O molds with—what else?— bananas suspended inside. Our neighbors, the hippies with the yappy dogs, brought over a big tray of brownies. Foilhead Eddie, whom we did not expect to see at the house, brought a large garbage bag full of potato chips that no one wanted to eat because of their container and their brand anonymity and because they came from a man who was obviously unbalanced.

It looked like Grampa would have a well-attended mourning party, and it looked like everyone who showed up would wind up suitably hammered. Now that's how you mourned in Hammertown. I put a picture of Grampa, fully clothed in his army uniform, on top of the TV so it would seem like he was with us. I should have put out his hula skirt, but I forgot in the rush of the moment.

What was most interesting about the event was Eddie's reaction to my other next-door neighbors. They arrived before Eddie with their tray of brownies and a sympathy card that had a lily on the front.

They introduced themselves as the Georges, Tom and Ellie. As I met them I realized I had never bothered to learn their names. They said they worked at The Chips. Name and occupation. That's all I needed to know. Tom was wearing blue jeans, a Grateful Dead tie-dyed T-shirt and cowboy boots. Ellie was wearing a tan gauze dress that allowed you to see her shapely, but hairy, legs when the light was just right, and she was barefoot. There's just something about barefoot women in gauze dresses, no? With his fu manchu mustache and John Lennon glasses, and with her long, straight center-parted hair and bare feet they looked like walking clichés of '60s counterculture, the couple on top of the cake at a hippie wedding.

I was surprised to see them, given their feelings about me and my Grampa and my feelings about their stupid dogs and their gas guzzling SUVs. I was even more surprised by their cordiality. Oh God, I thought, I hope they don't want to be friends. Friends come over to talk. Friends borrow things they don't return. For the moment, though, I accepted their gesture of kindness.

"We're really sorry about your grandfather," Tom said, looking genuinely sad. "I know we complained about him a lot, but we actually thought he was pretty cool. I mean, he did whatever he wanted to do. That's righteous, man. That old dude wanted to shock the world, rock the world and sock the world, and man did he ever. Jeez, he had a big schlong, too. It was pretty weird looking out the window and seeing that thing almost glowing in the sun. You're awful lucky to have his genes, if you know what I mean. Or maybe it's your girlfriend over there who's lucky."

"Well, thank you very much," I said awkwardly. "I didn't expect to see you here, but it's very kind of you to come. Uh, she isn't my girlfriend, by the way."

"Oh, that's, like, too bad, 'cuz you'd make such a nice couple," Ellie said. "We'd love to get to know another couple. This town's such a bummer.

Everybody's so stuck up. We don't have many friends here, but I think we could really swing with you and your chick over there."

"Swing?"

Tom looked over at her with a glance that said "shut the hell up, man" and she just smiled and walked into the kitchen with the tray of brownies. I saw her introducing herself to Pinky Lee and they hit it off right away. Swing? I didn't want to start thinking about that. Things were already complicated enough.

I walked into the kitchen and gobbled down a couple of brownies, having more or less forgotten to eat that day. I rifled a Point Bock down my throat.

Pinky Lee and Ellie were setting out all the food for the guests with Mrs. Murphy, and it suddenly occurred to me that my house was filled with strangers who were trying to help me. This was contrary to my notion of human selfishness, but I convinced myself that they all felt there was something in this for them. Like free hootch, or maybe the chance to cadge a memento.

I got another beer, tossed down another brownie and headed toward the living room. I saw the picture of Grampa I'd placed on the coffee table and realized that he'd be taking his second dump of the day right about then. Good ol' Grampa.

Charles was sitting on the couch with Jerry, and Jerry was asking him if he ever wondered why he was put here on earth. Charles said it was to serve Jerry. I did not want to hear any part of that conversation.

Meanwhile, when Foilhead Eddie arrived and saw Tom and Ellie, his eyes narrowed and he almost let out a Christopher Lee as Dracula hiss. Or was it Peter Cushing? I could never get those two straight. In any event, the presence of the Georges was clearly upsetting to Eddie, and I wanted to keep an eye on him just in case.

"Eddie, ya wanna beer?" I said, trying to sound like the friendly guy next door. "Nice job at the funeral. You did the best you could."

"There is evil here," Eddie said. "Evil. Danger."

"Look, Eddie, if you're going to start fighting bats or ocelots or invisible Vietcong, please go and entertain them at your own home," I said. "I don't think I can handle anymore strangeness today, and it is my grandfather's funeral. Tell the demons to get lost, OK? Keep nice and cool, OK, Edward? You're not packing heat, are you? Eddie?"

Oh, shit. He was. In the hip pocket of his suit. It bulged from the suit and looked like he himself had an erection.

"Just stay away from your neighbors," he said, and he took a beer.

"Does that mean you, too? "

"Beware. "

All right, I thought. Let's get the tough part out of the way. I had to make a few brief remarks and make people think I was grateful to have their support in my time of need. In fact, all I could think was that I was missing "Hogan's Heroes" to keep company with a man with a gun, a guilt-ridden gameshow host, a moron, some hippies and a girl who either did or did not want to sleep with me.

This was certainly more work than I had planned for the day.

When it seemed that everyone who was going to come had arrived, Eddie offered a toast:

"To a man who was a man. Man was he a man-to-man man." Then he began to riff, using the "Mr. Ed" theme song as a basis. It was the second time in two days that song had been part of my life and I wondered if that was some kind of cosmic hint that my favorite talking horse would be returning to the airwaves on one of the cable networks. Eddie continued as my mind wandered:

"A man is a man who can who can, and no one can stop a man who can ..."

"Thank you, Eddie, we're all very touched," I said. "Now, if I could just say a few words that I might have said at the funeral if the dogs hadn't attacked the kangaroo."

Everyone gathered in the living room and stood or sat rapt, hanging on my every word. I actually kind of enjoyed the attention, but the feeling was fleeting.

"There's been a lot of talk around here the last few days about our purpose on Earth," I said. "I don't think anyone ever really knows. I, for example, don't believe that God put me here so that I could sit here and watch TV all day. On the other hand, we can't all be performers. There has to be an audience. And I guess I'm the audience. My purpose is to laugh at other people's bad jokes, enjoy their sitcom scripts and drink the beer they make. That's all. I accept my role. Many people get into trouble when they have been designated as part of the audience and they decide they must be on the stage themselves. But they don't belong there.

"They don't have any real talent, none worth sharing, anyway, and so in a way, to be assigned to be a member of the audience for life's theater and then to try to become an actor yourself is not only foolish, it is in defiance of your mission. Your mission is assigned, and you do it. There's no fighting it. That's why some people work on the floor of the factory and some become president. They were pre-ordained before they came here. Pre-destination. Performers and audience. Just like John Calvin said. At least that's who I think it was.

"Of course, I have never seen much sense in the Protestant theology. But I am willing to concede they may have had a point with predestination. Who among us can change our fate?"

What the hell was I talking about? I'd had a few beers, but certainly nothing that would make me feel this light-headed. I could hold my alcohol. I was a Harnmertownian. But I pressed on. I had them. I was a performer, at least for the moment. Unfortunately, the performance was a bit on the metaphysical side. Jerry was looking at me with his face twisted and his head tilted.

Charles looked at me as though I was speaking Esperanto. The George's were nodding their heads in agreement, as though they were listening to some motivational speaker, and Pinky Lee just sat in Grampa's chair and grinned. Eddie stood stiffly by the door like he was waiting for something, a bus, a pizza, or maybe a tyrannosaurus in a green tutu.

I suppressed a mysterious giggle, took a swig of Point Bock, and then I resumed after belching.

"My grandfather decided he didn't want to be a part of the cosmic schematic. Somewhere along the line he decided he would defy human and heavenly convention and do whatever he pleased. He decided not to accomplish his mission. In fact, he didn't even care what his mission was. He simply followed his own sensibilities, and he didn't give a flying fuck what anyone else thought, including his Maker. Such actions can be quite dangerous in the afterlife, I believe, but I think God will cut Grampa some slack. He lived the way he wanted to, and he got away with it. He didn't hurt anyone, he paid his taxes, and sometimes he wore a tutu."

I took another swig and continued.

"My grandfather asked the important questions about life. For example, he wanted to know how, in the short-lived TV show 'Manimal,' did the guy know which animal to turn himself into in a pinch? He wondered how the guy knew how to turn into a cobra instead of a diamondback rattler, or why not a constrictor instead of a deadly poisonous snake? What gave him the ability to make a snap judgment on turning himself into a marmoset or a mongoose or a civet? The choices were endless, and Grampa figured this guy didn't have a zoology degree. With Grampa in the house, such important matters could be debated."

Once again, the need to suppress laughter was becoming urgent. I was feeling so good, I wasn't going to let a little nervous laughter get in the way of a great speech. But I was beginning to lose control. I was going to laugh soon. Tom offered a little support. He held his palms down flat to the floor as if to say, you're all right.

"Keep goin', dude, we're with ya," he said.

"But maybe that was Grampa's mission after all," I continued. "He asked questions no one else thought of, and he showed us that we can become performers, that we can defy what's expected of us and take whatever role we please, that we don't just have to be the audience. Just like 'Manimal,' we can be a two-toed or three-toed sloth or even a civet. The choice is ours. So maybe, without even knowing it, Grampa was assigned a task that he actually completed. After all, you can fight City Hall, but you can't fight heaven. God's will will be done. So maybe that's his life lesson."

I paused again. Swallowed hard. "Alas, poor Grampa, I knew him well, Horatio. To be or not to be. That is the question. For $1,000 and a Jeep Grand Cherokee, right Jerry? What dreams may come when we have shuffled off this mortal coil? That is the $64,000 question ..."

I burst. Through pursed lips a snicker turned into a sputter which transformed into a doubled-over belly laugh. I started asking myself what I had drunk so far, and then it occurred to me: the brownies. I had just eaten half a tray of pot brownies that the Georges had brought over. Tom and Ellie looked at me as though they recognized my situation. Tom gave me the thumbs up.

"Way to go, dude," Tom said. "That Shakespeare shit is heavy, man."

"To be to be do," I said, cackling and breaking into song. "To be do da da, da da da da da. Shakespeare in the night, exchanging glances ..."

Pinky Lee, who hadn't eaten any brownies, came over and brought me to a chair.

"OK, baby, it looks like we're in for a silly night," she said. "Lemme know if you get the body rushes and you think yer gonna throw up. Happens sometimes with pot, ya know."

"Purina cat chow, chow chow chow," I said, my stomach beginning to hurt from the maniacal laughter. "Man, whatever that stuff is, it's good enough to make soccer interesting, and that is no mean feat. May I sing for you? *Old MacDonald had a farm, with a chick chick here. Chim cheree. Did I tell you I love you yet? I love your little kitty ears.* Shh. Do I hear the whine of a test pattern on TV? I love TV."

The crowd moved into the kitchen rather than watch me in what probably looked like delirium tremens and endless babbling. Eddie stood by the door, not moving, but looking increasingly edgy. Off in the distance, I thought I heard sirens, but I assumed those sirens were in my head—or maybe in Eddie's head. Pinky Lee just sat with me and laughed with or at me.

Sometimes she even gave me a little tickle to make things worse.

"We gotta get all those giggles outta you," she said, poking me to make me squirm.

The sirens kept coming, but I kept giggling. I felt like I was on some carnival midway ride that wouldn't stop. But Eddie managed to break the spell in his own way. He reached into his pocket and pulled out the gun.

Oh, shit. We're all going to die. No more Hillbillies. No more Farrah. No more chance at sex with Pinky Lee. I thought about death. I thought I should cross myself just in case, but if I died stoned, would they let me into heaven or send me straight to the Lake of Fire? It's horrible to be so cooked when someone pulls out a gun.

"Freeze! FBI!" he said. "Don't move or I'll blow your head off, dope boy."

I hit the deck and laid face down on the floor. This was so unfair. I get stoned once in a million years and the goddamned FBI comes down to bust me. Wait a minute. This was Foilhead Eddie. He's just delusional. He can't be the FBI.

Jeez, I sure was thinking like a dopehead.

The sirens in the distance had closed in. In fact, the wailing was coming from two black unmarked cars that were now parked on my front lawn. Red and blue lights flashing and all.

At least I wouldn't have to explain all this to the neighbors.

Pinky Lee was lying on top of me. Unfortunately, not for the purposes I had hoped. I couldn't see the others in the kitchen, and I assumed they were on the floor, too. I saw Eddie charge in there and bring Tom George out by the collar with a weeping Ellie right behind.

"Fuckin' pig, man, chill out," he said." 'Tcher hands off me."

I was transported to 1969 for a moment. I saw spiraling shapes and heard The Jefferson Airplane singing *We Can Be Together*. "I Dream of Jeannie" on TV. Groovy. Up the system, Tom. See you in Chicago. Intensify the struggle on every front.

"I'm sorry, everybody," Eddie said in a clear voice I had not previously heard. "This doesn't involve you. This is federal business. Please go about your business of mourning and drinking legal alcoholic beverages. I'm afraid I'll have to take the brownies with me."

Just then, two local cops walked in right behind some guys I assumed to be Eddie's federal agent colleagues. I looked up from the floor, which had become quite comfortable, and saw the same cop who had driven me and Jerry to jail the day before. He didn't seem to recognize me or Jerry or Charles. He was too breathless over the big FBI bust. The Feds took Tom to one car, and Ellie went with the G-Man in the second car.

Eddie told the cops he would meet him at the station house. Eddie looked at me and said: "I'm very sorry I had to do this at your Grampa's party. He was a good man, and he deserves a commendation. He's been watching these dirtbag drug peddlers for me for a long time. Did you know they had a huge dope farm out in the woods and they've been distributing across the Midwest? No wonder kids are always so messed up around here, throwing bananas and whatnot."

"But Eddie, you're insane," I pleaded.

"No, I'm undercover," he said, flashing his shield. "I'm acting insane. And I will be grateful to stop wearing foil on my head. You ever put aluminum foil on your head? Ever wear it all summer long? Ever stay up all night flashing mirrors at the sky to make the town think you're nuts? I should have gone to acting school, not law school. I would have made more money and I would only have had to wear foil on my head for certain scenes. And maybe I could have slept with some starlets. But I decided to serve instead."

"So you used an old stereotype of the mentally ill to cover up the fact that you were a cop?" I said. "Ingenious, if a bit cruel to the mentally ill. I mean, foil?"

"The mentally ill are all around us," he said as though he was speaking to an audience of junior high school kids. "But you never know when one of them is actually an undercover cop."

"Armed with this knowledge, I feel so much safer, Eddie," I said. "See ya around, I guess."

He turned and left without further insight into the mentally ill or the possible fates of Tom and Ellie. My head, meanwhile, was now officially in a spin. Grampa was a narc. Eddie was FBI.

The Georges were dealers. And all the while, I'd just been watching TV.

"Take care of our dogs," Ellie shouted to me as she was escorted out.

The dogs? The terriers? I was now the custodian of these irascible hairballs with the high-pitched barks? No dice. Oh, God, I needed another brownie.

Next door, about a half-dozen dark-suited Feds had arrived and they searched the George's house, pulling everything apart looking for who-knows-what. Personally, I never believed dope should be anything but legal. I didn't use it much myself, because it would have meant going out and looking for it, but I didn't see the problem with marijuana. Every dope head I'd ever met was pretty mellow. But maybe the George's were selling crack or heroin or cocaine. For all I knew about what was going on, they could have been selling nuclear secrets to the Australians.

As I worked to comprehend the day's events, Pinky Lee helped me up to the couch. As she leaned over I got a clear shot of her breasts. Yummy. Only then did it occur to me she was wearing the same halter top and short shorts she'd been wearing when we met. She was a hitcher. Where was she going to get a change of clothes? I made a mental note to take her to look for some clothes the next day, assuming she would still in the vicinity.

Leonid and Mrs. Murphy came into the living room and told me they had to leave.

"We're sorry about everything," said Mrs. Murphy, who wasn't. The news of this incident would be all over town by day's end.

"I must go to pizza place and help them close up," Leonid said. "I am sorry about storm troopers. I thought this happened only in Russia, like

KGB. Police everywhere in Russia. I am not happy that your grandfather was working with police because I came here to escape such collaboration with authorities. But maybe he did it for money, so that's OK. Doing bad things for money is good capitalism. I go now. I take Mrs. Murphy home and go to my restaurant."

They left, and only Jerry, Charles, Pinky Lee and I remained. Still under the heavy influence of tetrahydrocannabinol, I couldn't help but notice the texture of the wallpaper. It's funny how you never look at the things that surround you until you're on some drug. Jerry stood in front of the TV, hands in his pockets and lips pursed. He was nervous about the awkward silence that had fallen on the room, and he felt the need to make everything better, seeing as he was such a nice guy these days.

"Hey, I was downstairs kind of snooping around, but I've got an idea," he said. "Anyone up for a game of Hungry, Hungry Hippos? Monopoly? There's all kinds of stuff down there."

"I've got a better idea," I said. "Let's watch some TV."

And we did. "Rockford Files." James Garner was a genius.

Chapter 14
What Next?

Resigned to the idea that I would not be making any physical transactions with my halter-topped tormentor, I sat with the others that night and drank to the point of passing out. This was a good move, I thought, since the resulting hangover would make me ornery enough for some pretty nasty poison pen letters the next day.

Prior to my passing out, there had been a "Twilight Zone" marathon on one of the cable networks, and I was in the perfect mood for a little "Zone." My favorite episode was the one where Robert Redford played Death and he tricked Gladys Cooper into coming out of her apartment to die. The rest of the shows in the marathon had faded into an alcoholic blur, but before I lost consciousness, I bet myself that if Robert Redford came to take Grampa, Grampa would have pissed on his shoes.

The next morning, I had to piece together the rest of the previous evening. Pinky Lee apparently led me up to bed and undressed me, but I have no recollection of the event. When I woke up I had a headache, the shakes, I was incredibly horny and there was little I could do to improve that situation. Alcohol always did that to me that day after—made me horny, that is, which is ironic, since few people would want anything to do with someone as hungover as I was, even if I was Robert Redford.

I needed greasy food immediately. Eggs, bacon and toast with real butter. Black coffee.

Aspirins and apple juice. Give me all of 'em and I would be as right as rain. I just couldn't stand upright long enough to try to cook anything.

The hangover is a peculiar phenomenon. When people are drinking heavily, somewhere in their head a light goes on that says if they drink anymore they'll feel awful the next day. But they continue to drink, almost in defiance of what is to come the next morning, and they make it worse for themselves but they manage to convince themselves it was all worth it. In Hammertown people even joked about their alcoholic blackouts.

144

Hangovers made me groggy and as I got older it always took two days to get over them. The worst part about this one was that I had the same song running in my head over and over. It was the theme from "Love, American Style."

In polite society, people get drunk by accident. In Hammertown, you were always drinking for the same purpose: To get hammered. There wasn't anything else to do in a small town like ours. People always said Hammertown was a nice place to raise kids, which is good because there sure wasn't anything else to do. Those of us without kids were left supremely bored. I never understood the charms of small towns. If they're so great, how come more people don't live in them?

I stayed in Hammertown partly because of Grampa, partly because I owned the house, but mostly because my lifestyle would have been the same if I had lived in my hovel in Hammertown or in a Manhattan penthouse. TV, beer, and cheese sticks. Even Hammertown had these things. For the first time, though, I was starting to think I might have to leave my hometown just to see what was out there.

Without Grampa, nothing was holding me back.

These were the ideas that were floating through my head that morning as I tried to negotiate what promised to be a difficult morning after. Leaving was a decision for another time, though. Right now, I had to write a letter for Charles as I promised I would. It bears repeating simply because it's one of my favorite efforts.

So I sat down and wrote the letter to Charles' nemesis, Steve. This hangover was particularly savage, and I thought my IQ had dropped about 50 points as a result.

That was an appropriate way to feel if I was going to write a letter in Charles' voice. It beat hitting myself in the head with a two-by-four to get into character.

And so I wrote, in the best credibly semi-literate Charles prose:

"Dear Steve:

"Your are so damm stuck up and stupid just becauze you got to be superviser your to good for your old freinds who knew you when you were just a dope smoking kid in the clearing in the woods like the rest of your freinds. What you don't want to know is I am making fun of you behind your back and so are everyone else, yes,

all your freinds are laughing because you don't know how stupid you look in that white coat with supervisor on it like a Super Man costume or something when it just covers your tiny dick and your stuck up ways you did not have when you were in the woods drinking and smoking dope, yes I mean marijuana and you should tell those bosses you suck ass on all the time what you really are, just another Hammertown woods doper. You told me last Wensday I should not challenge your so-call authority but who can respect someone who is no better than the rest of us except he has a superviser badge and a white coat insted of a blue coat like all the rest of us you used to hang around with and drink and listen to Zepplin in the woods with us, and that is why you don't have the so-called authority over us even if you are our so-called boss because we will never respect what you have become. You probably don't even think the Moody Blues is cool anymore either because you're listening to Kenny Gee or some dickish light jazz group like all your bigshot frends drinking there white wine talking like their big when their not.

"You always wanted to be a astronat when we hung in the woods, but you did not become a astronat, you became a geek in a white coat who forgotten all the people he grew up with and should feel shame. You will never be better than the rest of us, you fag jerk asshole.

"Yours truly Charles, your former freind. (Not Charlie to you. Charles.)

"P.S. I screwed your slut wife Tina years ago when you were away at superviser school and she said she would come back to my huge dong someday probably when she is tired of your tiny worm prick and she can get her hands on your superviser money. Think about that the next time you are screwing her that she is thinking of me and my big shlong. That is why she is moaning not because of you. I'm married now but I could screw Tina any time I want."

Frankly, I found writing beneath my station more difficult than I thought. Try it sometime. Just go against everything you know and try to write like an idiot or a TV sitcom writer. But as difficult as it was to write, I was sure this letter would do the job for Charles, and I was looking forward to handing it over and watching the damage be done to his enemy. I didn't like people like this Steve guy. Of course, I didn't like homophobic rednecks like Charlie, either. Or people in general, for that matter.

But people like Steve, bullies who took on airs in a place like Hammertown, needed to be destroyed, and I was more than happy to give an assist.

Since I was on a roll, I thought I would take care of a matter of personal business. It seems that some cable network executive decided to remove "The Outer Limits" from its late night lineup and replace it with back-to-back episodes of "One Day at a Time." Mind you, I like looking at Valerie Bertinelli as much as the next guy, but spend ten minutes watching Bonnie Franklin engaging in what passed for comic dialog with Pat Harrington made one yearn for the peace only death could bring. And back-to-back episodes are more punishment than any viewer should have to bear, so I took it upon myself to begin a campaign that would, if not save "The Outer Limits," at least put "One Day at a Time" in a much-deserved television tomb.

I knew that network executives, even those at the rinky-dink cable networks, didn't pay much attention to letter writers. They view people who protest their lineup changes in the same way that the rest of society viewed those losers who fought so hard to save that awful "Beauty and The Beast" show. It required a certain knack to get their attention and make them know you were serious.

First, being a guy with some time on my hands, I found out who was responsible for making programming decisions at the network in question. Then, being the resourceful type, and again, with a lot of time on my hands, I found the home address of the nitwit. Getting the letter at home is always unnerving, because it makes them feel like they're being watched. You don't want them to focus too much on how you found them, though, or they'll just disregard you as a garden-variety stalker. That's why a letter like this needed a certain flair.

To wit:

"Mr. Michael T. Parker
Executive Vice President for Programming
American Cable Company
High Falls, WI
"Dear Mr. Parker:
"Judging by a recent decision you made to remove 'The Outer Limits' from your airwaves, or cablewaves, if you will, I must assume that you have been ingesting a lower quality of opium than usual. Perhaps your drug of choice was laced with some brain damaging compound such as rat poison, which, although symbolically

appropriate to your breed, has affected your ability to comprehend the weight your decisions have on the discriminating viewing public.

"Clearly, any decision to remove such quality programming as 'The Outer Limits' and replace it with 'One Day at a Time' can only be the product of a decision made by an opium eater. Frankly, your drug problem is of no concern to me, that is, until it gets in the way of my viewing pleasure. Then I must act.

"Please don't confuse me with stalkers or other mental defectives who haunt your vermin-infested industry. Simply think of me as a consultant who wants to help you, someone you can lean on when your drug-induced hallucinations make it too difficult to perform your duties. Think of me as a consultant who is always watching, watching your network, that is, and who is available to you at a moment's notice any time of the day or night. You see, I care about you, your career and your well-being, and I know that making a decision to resurrect 'One Day at a Time' for any reason must be a cry for help, a cry for the drug rehabilitation you so desperately need. Please take my word for it: If you continue on this path, we will shortly be watching 'Cagney and Lacey' on your network, and there will be riots in the streets. Your career will be ruined, and I will be very, very upset. But we can avoid all of this.

"If the opium, or perhaps the crack cocaine, has not already driven you to sell your clothing, then it is not too late. Put 'The Outer Limits' back on your network, and forever remove 'One Day at a Time' from the airwaves. It will be a wise move professionally and personally. Trust me. I know."

Much of this letter could be read as a veiled threat, but there is nothing that I couldn't defend to the authorities if I had to. Still, a subtle postscript always lets the reader know the seriousness of the situation. And so I added:

"P.S.: The traffic on Route 7 must be murder when you leave work at about 7:15 p.m. each night. I can recommend some alternate routes to your home that would get you there faster."

Finally, in the case of network executives, I always find that the dramatic gesture goes over big. That's why I sign these types of letters in blood. If I have time, I might even tape bits of food like corn or peas to the letter. Maybe even a lock of hair if I'm a bit shaggy. I assure you that I am as sane as the next person. But I know ways to get attention through the written word and sometimes a few props.

Having finished my writing for the day, I looked over at the sleeping Pinky Lee and wondered if I hadn't got so drunk the night before if I would

148

have had a shot at her when she got drunk herself. It was a moot point, but one that had to be considered, seeing as I had an attractive semi-nude woman in my bed and I had not had sexual relations with another person, living or dead, since my days with the IHOP waitress.

"Hey, Sleeping Beauty, if you don't want a handsome prince to come over and slobber all over you and start humping your leg to wake you up, you might want to consider moving under your own power," I said. "And might I add that you look radiant this morning. Say, if I came over to you right now and just breathed on you, would you throw up for me?"

"If yer tryin' to get in my pants, it ain't workin' for me, fat man," she said. "You don't show a lot of gratitude for someone who had to be carried up to bed whinin' about yer Grampa bein' dead. Man, you are a sloppy drunk. How the hell did you even get up this morning?"

"You should see what I'm like hung over, dearest," I said. "As for my early rising, I find that if I get up before the hangover sets in, before I am fully sober, it can come to me gradually rather than attack all at once. But now that you mention it, I think I'm about to expel gas due to last night's gustatory activities. I hope you don't mind. Perhaps you should brace yourself."

She rolled over and put her pillow over her face. "Let 'er rip, jerk," she said, her voice muffled by the pillow's foam stuffing.

I didn't, of course. I'm too well-bred for such behavior.

"What have you been doing while I was sleeping?" she asked. "Hey, wait a minute, if you were coppin' feels on a sleepin' woman, you're lower than I thought. God, you are a creep."

"Oh, I'm even lower than you think, but I can assure you I did not touch you during your alcohol-induced coma," I said. "It just wouldn't be sporting. However, if you'd like me to come over there right now …"

"Don't bother," she said. "Where's Jerry? I smell toast and coffee."

"Well, that might be toast and coffee, or it may be something I belched up just now, but in any case, if someone is making breakfast I am more than willing to eat it in spite of my condition," I said, holding out my arm. "Care to join me, madama?"

"I'm gonna shower and find some clothes," she said. "I'll come down later."

"Good luck finding clean clothing," I said. "Right about now I'm kind of sorry I'm not a cross-dresser because I'm sure I might have had something tasteful for you. But feel free to rummage about for whatever apparel I might have that would be tight to your lovely form."

As I went downstairs, I could tell that Charles had already come over to begin his day serving Jerry. In fact, Charles was making breakfast from items Jerry had given him the money to purchase the night before while I was dozing.

"Well, the sun also rises and so do you, finally," Jerry said in his talk show host voice.

"Say, can we interest you in some food? Or do you think you might have a problem holding it down?"

I looked at Charles, who was at the stove, wearing an unfamiliar apron that said "Colleje Gradiate" on it. "Eggs, Charles, over-medium and if you've got any bacon make sure it can still squeal. I hate burnt bacon. And toast. I see somebody made coffee. Bless them and their kin."

"You want yer boast tuttered, I mean toast buttered, or with oleo?" Charles asked.

"Who could ever want oleo?" I said. "Those Illinois flatlanders? The 'eat smart' people at the hospital? This is the Dairy State. Give me butter, and lots of it. I want to hear my arteries whistling after breakfast. I want to feel the chair groan under my weight as I eat. I want my cardiovascular system to scream for mercy, mercy which is not coming, only more cream and more butter. Say, I hope you bought some krullers for after the main course."

"Yes, we thought of everything," Jerry said. He was quiet for a moment, and he was looking straight at me as though he was examining the scab from a wound on a remote part of his body.

"So this is it for you, huh?" he said.

"This is what? Breakfast? If that's what you're asking, frankly I could use a little more, maybe some muffins or a jelly doughnut. Have you ever had prime rib with eggs? A rich man like you should be eating prime rib every day. It's not just for dinner anymore, you know."

"I sense that you know what I'm talking about, but you are uncomfortable with the topic," Jerry said, once again the serious-looking anchor man. "Your lifestyle is miserable, your life is meaningless, and you are completely happy with yourself as long as you are abjectly unhappy. How do you do it? How do you look at yourself in the mirror? With that huge gut and those skinny legs, you look like a beach ball on a golf tee. You hate everything and everybody, and yet you seem content. How do you do it? Don't you want to change?"

"Yes, I want to follow the path of a world-famous game show host, a man who has insulted and lost three wives on his show, a man who used his best friend's testicular cancer as a continuing joke about having blue balls," I said. "Oh, yes, I want to be like you, Jerry Most, I want to be famous for being a big prick and then have an epiphany on the road to Hammertown and become someone whose ego, not his undeveloped sense of morals, is driving him to be good and kind so that he will now be loved instead of hated. Yes, Jerry, oh yes, I want to be just like you. I want to change. But first, hand me that salt shaker. These eggs need a little pick-me-up."

"You know, you don't have to be nasty about it," he said. "I just thought you'd like to get out of here. Don't you want to leave? Even for a while?"

"And do what?"

"I don't know. See the country. Meet new people. Maybe even have a life," he said. "I'll pay for it. My treat."

"What a guy. Jerry Most is sharing the wealth so that he can touch the life of just one person. I guess that makes it all worth it, eh, Jer Bear? What are you, running for Miss America? I'm afraid you don't have the legs for it."

It turned out that Pinky Lee had been listening to this conversation from the stairs. She was standing behind me as I sat at the kitchen table when she decided to enter the fray. She put her hands on my shoulders and dug in her nails. It gave me kind of a kinky thrill, but that was clearly not her intent. She let go and then walked behind Jerry, who was sitting across the table from me, and leaned up against the counter with a look that said I was in for a lecture from a woman who was wearing the same shorts she had been wearing since I met her, and the same underwear for all I knew, along with a stained old XXX Large T-shirt of mine from Booby's Booze Ranch. Charles was still cooking, though it was not clear for whom. I thought maybe he'd keep going until his Master Jerry told him to stop. I had a picture in my mind of 144 scrambled eggs filling every plate and bowl in my house before Jerry remembered to tell him to knock off.

But here was Pinky Lee, a woman who was not screwing me, a woman with whom I had no real relationship, a woman who had gotten me thrown in jail, preparing to tell me how I needed to change my life. Oh, goody. I couldn't wait for this.

"You know what yer problem is?" she said. "You hate people."

"Bull's-eye, Ms.Grushecky," I said. "You are far more perceptive than your limited education should allow. Yes, I hate people. And now that Grampa is dead, I can say without hesitation that I hate everyone in the whole goddamned human race. Including both of you. I would include Charles, but I think his devotion to Mr. Most renders him subhuman and not part of the discussion. Now, will someone pass me the krullers? I've got to stoke the hate machine."

"Yer just sad and pathetic, you know that?" she said. "No wonder you ain't been laid since Arnold Ford was president. It's not that yer fat and ugly. A lot of women can overlook that if the guy is a sweetheart. But yer fat and ugly and mean. Jee-sus, you'd think girls'd be lining up for a chance to be abused by you."

"Your reference to my sex life, or lack of same, seems a bit of a low blow for someone that, I'm guessing, has been laid about 9,314 times in the last few years, and that's just by boozed-up drifters. There's no telling how many married men, bar pickups and pizza delivery men would be added to that number."

She lunged across the table in a futile attempt to shove the kruller I was biting into my nose. Jerry grabbed her as she began shouting: "You fat bastard. You are such a fat bastard. I don't know why I ever told you anything about myself. You fucking fat rat. I hope you never get fucked for the rest of yer miserable life. I hope yer balls fall off. I hope some hooker rips 'em off and her pimp shoves them down your throat ..."

"Oh, Miss Pinky Lee, our first disagreement," I squealed. "How romantic. Can we have sex now that everything is out in the open?"

"OK, OK, you two," Jerry broke in. "I don't think we're getting anywhere."

"Jerry Most, in a very special role, a role that just may break your heart, the mediator of good feelings," I said. I was becoming truly abusive. My poison pen was becoming my poison tongue. Fuck them. What were they going to do for me?

"Look," Jerry said. "You don't have to be an asshole about this. I just figured that with your Grampa's death and with all your neighbors gone that you might want a change of scenery. A vacation. I don't think even you know what you want. I just can't figure out what your problem is, but I'm here to help, pal. The new Jerry, you know."

I don't know whether it was Jerry's saccharine new persona, or whether I was still pissed off from being sent to jail for breath mints, or whether sadness over Grampa's death had manifested itself in rage, but I let loose all at once, and I think I scared my house guests. It was a great performance, and very therapeutic.

"Want to know what my problem is with my colleagues in the human race? I'll tell you. It's that we have evolved to such an advanced state, yet we still behave like apes. The big push the little around, the rich screw the poor. It's always, 'Me first.' The list of what I hate about this culture is so long we'd need to talk straight through to lunch for me to get to all of it. But I'll give you an idea. What's really getting to me is the assholes in gas guzzling SUVs who drive on your ass at 80 miles an hour on the highway because they know if there's a crash they live and you die. And the same goes for the so-called 'knights of the road,' the semi drivers, who treat all vehicles in front of them as though they were flies on their windshields. It's 'Get out of the way or die,' for these Neanderthals.

"These people are bullies, low-life scum who only feel good about themselves because they drive big vehicles and make enough money to move to neighborhoods where they are so far from the city they're guaranteed not to see a black or a brown person or a car more that's more than two years old. I hate people because for years they were only willing to sell their dignity on a game show for a nice patio set, and now they're willing to risk their very lives on shows like yours, yet they all profess some religious pomposity that makes me want to puke blood. I'm sick of people who leave their cell phones on in theaters and operas, people who give you a dirty look when you tell them to shut the fuck up when they're talking during a movie.

"I'm tired of people who insist that they have 'smoker's rights' in all public places, and I'm tired of the ninnies who insist on fighting with the smokers about where they smoke. I'm sick of the smokers who dispose of their butts as though the whole world is an ashtray.

"I'm tired of silly suburbanites who are so quick to leap onto the next status-ridden fad that they are willing to embrace the most ridiculous game in the world, soccer, for themselves and their kids. Soccer, for God's sake, and I'm sick to death of people who worship that sissy pseudo-Eurosport so blindly that they 're willing to call sports editors at newspapers they don't even subscribe to, let alone read, and demand more coverage of European soccer or worse yet, their stupid kids' peewee league soccer scores. I'm sick to the point of retching of people who say baseball is boring because they're too stupid to understand it. I hate living in a world where 'artists' like Madonna are considered anything other than homely exhibitionists instead of a pop icons. I hate people who insist on referring to those lowing cattle Celine Dion and Mariah Carey as 'divas' when they've never heard a real diva sing.

"I'm sick of the pretensions of the so-called middle class and their spoiled children who have cell phones of their own so they can tell each other what kind of socks they're wearing to school. And what about advertising? Ad people rule the English language. Who else could come up with, 'The soup that eats like a meal?' How the hell does soup eat? Or waiters who ask, 'How's your food tasting?'

"You're staring at me, but oh, there's more, there's more. I'm on a roll. I haven't been able to vent like this in years. Let me tell you, there is a special place in hell for the people who ding your car doors in parking lots or who steal your parking space just as you're about to pull in. And speaking of school—I did just mention school, didn't I?—well, I predict that schools will do a lot better and cost a lot less the minute we fire every ratty-cardigan wearing 'educator' from the principal to the superintendent. Did I mention politicians yet? Just nod if you're following me.

"Anyway, politicians, especially local politicians, are some of the most unemployable people on the face of the earth. Yet at least they presume to do something for the good of their community, and some of them, especially the ones who understand pure power politics, manage to get things done. So even though in some cases politicians are some of the lower life forms on the planet, the people I really loathe are their idiot constituents who say they don't vote because in their enlightened opinion, 'All politicians are crooks.' Do you know how easy it is to get elected in this country? For God's sake, that psychopath Ted Bundy could have said from prison that he was going to cut the capital gains tax and the personal income tax and he could have been elected governor of Florida the next day.

"You don't have to be smart to be elected in this society, just cynical enough to tell the SUV-driving, cell-phone-calling, mall-walking, selfish buffoons who make up the majority of this lumpen proletariat society that you'll get government off their backs and cut taxes. Of course, when they bitch that the garbage isn't being picked up or the roads have potholes or their schools are using closets for classrooms, well, then, it must be those corrupt politicians who are screwing it up. It couldn't possibly have anything to do with their own selfish impulses to cut spending, cut taxes and still get decent government service.

"We're pro-life and pro-capital punishment. We're a God-fearing country, but churches are hiring marketing consultants to try to lure people back into the pews. And while I'm at it, I'm tired of ignoramuses who don't read a newspaper opining about constitutional law and tax policy on talk radio, and people who get their political information from only slightly better-informed TV talking heads.

"I hate people who pull out in front of you when you're driving even though there's no one behind you, and then turn left and hold you up. I believe there is a special place in hell for people who pass in the parking lane on a city street. I hate people who think *Respect* is Aretha Franklin's only song and the fact that *Stairway to Heaven* is still played on radio stations with as much frequency as it was in 1976 while not even country stations will play the great music of Lyle Lovett or John Hiatt. I despise people who mow their lawns at 7:30 on a Saturday morning or use their snow blower on any day at 6:30 a.m. so they can clear their driveway to go to the gas station. I resent people who pull up at someone's house and honk the horn rather than get out of the car and actually greet their passenger. I hate people who cut in line, who cut you off when driving and who make comedians like Roseanne popular. But they're all out there waiting for you every day, and I, for one, cannot and will not tolerate their nonsense any longer. They are ruining this country, this society, this culture.

"The fact is, ladies and gentleman, we are not a dumb country, yet we choose to remain ignorant and even glorify ignorance in the mass media. We're not stupid, we're just intellectually and culturally lazy. And rude. Oh, God, are we rude. And vulgar. How can we make fun of the French when we can't tell each other what time it is without using the word 'fuck'? And have you ever see some of the T-shirts at a county fair? For God's sake, don't let the kids see 'em unless you want to explain to your six-year-old why she can't go on the mustache ride advertised on some would-be comic's chest.

And what about those 'I'm with Stupid' T-shirts? They're still selling them. After all these years there are people who think those are clever.

"My point is that we're not interested in advancing as a culture and as a society, we just want a quicker way to toast a bagel and we want an espresso machine and we want plenty of mindless comic-book action movies. We want more money, although we lack to imagination to know what to do with it once we buy the SUV, the home theater and some jewelry. We are a culture of monsters, worse than any of the invading tribes at the fall of Rome and more profane than them as well. And we're going down, down, down by our own hand by our own worship of the lowest common denominator. I'm not saying I'm better than other people. I'm saying I want to avoid contact with them at all costs. They will exist whether I am here or not. But as long as I avoid them, I can pretend they're not there. It's just me and my TV and my beer. There. I've probably missed a few points, but I think I've summarized my view of the human condition succinctly. Any questions?"

"Yeah," Charles said. "You want some more eggs?"

"Thank you, Charles, I've had my fill," I said. "In fact, I think it's fair to say I've had a bellyful." I picked up the *Hammertown Telegraph-Herald* that was lying unopened on the table and flipped the pages to the obituaries. This time, I actually knew someone on the page. And it appeared they had not fooled with my tribute to Grampa, which made me think I should have embellished even more. Hey Grampa, you're somebody today. On the opposite page, they included a brief news story about the funeral and Billie and the dogs. I threw the paper up in front of my face with a snap and crack of newsprint and I pointedly began ignoring my company. My company decided it was not to be ignored.

"So that's it, eh, Fat Boy?" Pinky Lee said. "Yer just quittin'. Yer not gonna live yer life. Yer just too good for the rest of us so you can just rot in your stupid smelly house."

"Why do I have to live my life with the rest of the hoi polloi?" I asked. "The Holy Fathers of Orthodoxy lived in the desert without companionship, and they did just fine. Their motives were spiritual enlightenment and a desire to get closer to God. My purpose is far less noble, and I am much less deserving of their heavenly wisdom, but I, too, can survive quite nicely without knowing whether or not bell-bottoms have come back into style, and that is probably about the only valuable information to be gleaned from today's pop culture. I just want to be left alone. Why can't anyone understand why I want to be left alone?"

Jerry, who had that dog-like expression on his face again, looked as though he was formulating a response. Either that or he had gas. He kept inhaling, saying "I" as though he was about to speak, and then letting all the air out. Pinky Lee had walked into the living room in apparent disgust, which was fine with me, since pleasing her wasn't getting me anywhere anyway.

She had turned the TV on loud, and from the sound of it she was watching CNN, which was probably as much of a surprise to her as it was to me. Charles, good old Charles, was throwing out the extra eggs he had made, muttering, "What a waste, what a waste." I suggested he put them in his pocket and feed them to the waifs at home, but he ignored me.

"Jerry, you look like you want to say something," I said, encouraging him. "Did I strike a chord? Are you going to join me in my quest for hermitdom? Of course, if you joined me, we wouldn't be hermits. I don't think hermits can have roommates. Please, explain it all to me. You are a game show host, icon of this culture, which means you have wisdom and knowledge. Speak to me. Charles, why don't you say something? Somebody say something. I'm going mad from the oppressive silence. How about it Charles? What is your purpose in life? You've been listening to all of us. Why are you here?"

"To serve Jerry Most," he said, scraping food into the garbage can. "I'd just be a drunk jailbird without Jerry Most. I can even talk better since I met Jerry Most. I don't screw up my letters anymore. He cured me. He gave me confidence."

"Listen to that, Jerry, it's your first disciple," I said. "Say, did you give him pieces of silver? Let's hear all about your curative powers. I'm in the presence of a mystic."

"You're a real asshole," Jerry said. That was it.

"And?"

"And nothing. You're just an asshole," he said. "It's not complicated. There are a million people like you. I know. I was an asshole, too, a bigger asshole than you'll ever be. But even I don't have such a dark view of society. At least not anymore."

"Ah, so we're competing. OK, want to go to the playground and push down some little girls?"

"C'mon, knock it off for a minute," he said. "You've seen me on TV. Everyone has. I'm a big hit, a national star, and ..."

"Actually, I avoided your show like ebola," I said. "I saw your show as a sign of these awful, awful times, when people would risk their lives for merchandise. The documentation of the fall of western civilization will note that the harbingers of the decline were rap music, the cancellation of the first 'Star Trek' and the premiere of your show."

"OK, fine. You didn't watch the show. But you know what a jerk I was. I hurt people. People I loved. My wives, women who gave me sex, just to get ratings. People loved to hear me talk about how they snored or they had long toenails or how one of them used to throw up after every meal and come back to bed without brushing her teeth."

"You never said that on TV, pal. Which one was it? Who's the puker? I'm calling *The Star* or *The Enquirer*. Or would that be *Playboy*? Or all of them? Wait right here. I'll need a quote."

"Anyway, anee-way, the point is, I think I've changed. I've really changed since I came here to Hammertown," Jerry said with a nauseating earnestness and seriousness.

"Yes, of course you've changed. You've become stupider. Hammertown does that to people. Why, right now, you've got an urge to go ta da mall 25 miles away ta look fer a new gas grill so you kin cook da brats out in da backyard fer da Packers game, dehr, 'aina?" I said, affecting my best Wisconsin yokel accent. "Or maybe ya wanna go down ta da bar and do some tequila shots. Say, d'ya wanna go downtown and get one a'dem Packer flags fer yer car? When's deer huntin' season? Oh, screw da season, let's just go out and kill tings."

Jerry was getting frustrated with me, but I was unsympathetic to what he was trying to prove. I had lived here most of my life, and I was not about to attribute mystical qualities to the dump. The only change one went through in places like Hammertown was a mental numbness that grew until there was no need to think about anything other than getting the groceries. The staleness of the place overwhelmed any sense of introspection or intellectual growth.

I admit that I was beginning to get gratuitously mean, but it was a catharsis. I had never been able to tell anyone my feelings for this dump, and now it was coming out all at once. For the moment, I was the performer and Jerry, and possible Pinky Lee, was the audience.

Charles—well, Charles seemed happily oblivious to my diatribe. He was doing the dishes.

"You and your elitist, thumb-sucking mumbo jumbo can fuck off," Jerry said finally. "If you want to take me on in a little battle of shit, let me know. I've chewed up and spit out better than the likes of you. But I'm not going to, because that's over. I'm a new Jerry Most. The trip across country did what I wanted it to do. It cleared my head and made me see what a complete asshole I've been. I'm actually ashamed, and I don't know how to make amends, but I'm going to. I've certainly got the money to do it, more than I could or should be able to spend in a lifetime. So now I'm going to try to do some good to undo all the bad I've done, and I'm going to start with you."

"Oh, goody. Can I have a pony? Or a monkey? What about a monkey? Can I, huh? Can I have a monkey, Mr. Rich Talk Show guy?"

"Y'know, I should just let you stay here and die in your own misery, but I'm not going to do that," Jerry said. "I'm going to change your life, too. You'll see I was right. There's no reason to sit around here and be a loser and a mope. Sure, people are jerks. I'm surprised it took you so long to figure that out. But do you want to let them win? Do you want to let them take over the world, or do you want to fight back and take a piece of the action?"

"I want to watch TV."

"No, no you can't watch TV. You're going to come with me. We're going to rent or buy an RV, we're going to travel the backroads, and we're going to come back here and we'll see if you don't look at this place differently. And if you don't, if you still hate your hometown and all the people in it, I'm going to play the role of genie. I'm going to grant a wish. I'm going to get you on my show, 'Die Trying,' and let those baboons tear through your flesh and give you the spectacular death you seem to long for. Whattaya say, pal? You've got nothing to lose. It's all on me."

Just then, Pinky Lee re-emerged from the living room.

"Did I hear someone say road trip?" she said. "That's my life. The road. Let's go."

"Oh, this won't be just any road trip, dearie," I said. "Jerry's going to change my life by showing me America. And if it doesn't work, I get to be eaten by baboons. I'm sure you, of all people, would find entertainment value in that."

"No!" she cried with emotion that I was sure was mocking me. "I don't wanna see my bay-bay eaten by monkeys."

"They're not monkeys, they're baboons," I instructed. "There's a difference. Nor are they chimpanzees or orangutans. They are baboons. Very advanced primate societies, and highly efficient killers. I'll be dead before I hit the ground when one or two of them rip my jugular out. I'm almost looking forward to this. And all for the benefit of ratings. A noble end if there ever was one."

"Well I'm not gonna let no damn monkeys or baboons or whatever you call them eat my bay-bay, so you ain't goin' on that show," Pinky Lee said. "I wanna be an old woman with you."

"No doubt to continue torturing me well into my dotage, I'd guess. If we stay together until we're old, do you think we can finally have sex when we're 90?"

"We can have sex anytime you want if you don't go on this stupid show."

"Your affection for me is touching. And speaking of touching ..."

She walked up to me, looked me in the eyes and suddenly, with the swiftness of a cobra, she grabbed my crotch. "Yes?"

"Jerry, I think she makes a good point," I said. "There's no reason to take any silly risks. Why, I've got my whole life ahead of me. There's a lot of TV to watch, and, well, there's just a lot of sex to be had. Am I right, my darling?"

"You're right," she said. "But not right now."

"Of course not. We have company. But later ..."

"Yes, later. When it's bedtime." She let go of my member.

"You mean after 'M*A*S*H?' I said blankly, still hypnotized by the feeling of someone else's hand on my penis.

"Yes, and I'll be that nurse, what's her name? Hot Lips? I'll be her fixin' you up just right. Butchoo have to promise not to go on Jerry's awful show. I don't want you to die."

"Right now I'd promise to give up 'Petticoat Junction' for you," I said, making a pledge I could never hope to keep. Of course, that's what guys do to get laid, isn't it? I also didn't intend to keep my promise not to go on Jerry's show. I knew damned well that she'd blow me off as soon as the novelty of my warm and giving persona wore off, and she'd be hitchhiking again. Maybe she'd even get picked up by Rolf, the truck driver who took away my IHOP waitress.

"When you talk about skippin' TV shows, I know you're serious," she said.

Yes, serious. Very serious. Serious I am. That's what I was thinking. What I said was: "I knew from the moment I saw your halter top and decided to pick you up that you were special. Maybe you're even my soul mate."

Believe me, if you haven't already figured it out, I don't usually talk this way. But even though she had been taunting me all day, I still felt like I could pull this off. And the more I thought about it, the more I needed to pull it off. Hell, I'd recite Shakespeare for a chance at the old in-out, for laying pipe, for doing the nasty.

But my fantasies soon gave way to a knock at the door. It was the cop. Again. I never did catch his name, but I made a point to this time. It was Schmidt. Sergeant Schmidt. Hey, almost like Sergeant Schultz on "Hogan's Heroes." I left Jerry and Pinky Lee in the kitchen and went to the door. Sergeant Schmidt was standing in the screen porch.

"Now what?" I said pleasantly through the screen door, making a point of not opening it.

"I have some very sad news," Sergeant Schmidt said. He took off his cap.

"Oh my God. My grandfather! He's dead, isn't he? You're going to tell me my beloved Grampa is dead? It was those kids with the bananas, wasn't it? What did they do to him, the bastards? I'll kill them. I'll find them all and kill them. Oh God, oh God, no, this can't be happening. Please tell me I'm dreaming. He hated bananas. "

"Well, of course your grandfather 's dead, I just ..."

"Oh God, it's true, it's true? He is dead," I said, falling to the floor and biting at the carpet. "Why couldn't it have been me? Why him? He was so full of life! He could have touched so many other lives. Why, why, why?"

"Hey, pal, your Grampa was buried yesterday," Sergeant Schmidt said, obviously confused. "I don't know what's going on here."

"Wait a minute, officer, I think you're right. Yes ... yes I was at a funeral yesterday and yes, it was for my Grampa. It was very nice. Flowers, an undercover cop as a eulogist and, of course, a kangaroo." I straightened up and smiled. "OK, what other sad news to you have to tell me?"

"It's the kangaroo," he said grimly. "He's dead."

"She."

"She's dead. We found her in the cell where we were holding her this morning, and she was dead."

"Oh God, she committed suicide from the shame of being locked up. Why didn't you check on her? Did she hang herself? Did she take poison? I need answers."

"I don't know," he said, getting annoyed. "It was a kangaroo. And it's dead. Sorry pal. There wasn't anything we could do. Those guys from the zoo said they couldn't get here till the weekend, and she just couldn't stand being in the cell. Who could blame her?"

Just then Jerry, having heard the word kangaroo, came into the room.

"What's wrong with Billie?" he said excitedly. "I'm gonna owe somebody a lot of dough if anything happened to that giant rat."

"Oh Jerry, it's terrible, she's, she's dead," I said. "They think it was suicide. Oh, there is too much tragedy in my life."

"No, we don't think it's suicide," Sergeant Schmidt said. "I don't know. Maybe she had some damned kangaroo disease. Maybe the dogs bit into some organ or something and that killed her. But she's dead."

"Shit," said Jerry, going for the animal rights award for sympathy. "Where is she?"

"We buried her out in the woods," Sergeant Schmidt said. "We really didn't think to call you ahead of time. If it's any consolation, we left her in her little vest and hat. We said a little prayer and we dumped her in a hole near the clearing. We didn't think you would want to do it, and we didn't have any other place to put her."

"Shit," said Jerry again. "Shit, shit, shit, shit."

"What's the matter, Jer? I thought you had the money to pay for this," I said.

"Sure I do, but this guy who owns Billie said it was like his own kid, or at least like a pet, and he's going to want a lot more money for that hairy purse than I'm willing to pay," he said. "He's gonna shake me down but good."

"Jer?"

"What? Shit. What do you want?"

"You could just not tell him. I mean, you don't even know where he is. Do you want the cops to put out an all-points bulletin for some cheesy circus just to let the owner know his kangaroo is dead? Maybe he can carry on without that information, always thinking that Billie is happy somewhere, boxing little people or something."

"It seems awfully cold."

"If it was a child, it would be cold. It's a kangaroo. A fucking kangaroo. A mangy, ill-kept marsupial that is in a better place. Forget about it."

"Well, I would hate to be the one to break it to the guy. OK, let's forget about it."

"Good, Jerry, good. Maybe later on we can go put some kangaroo food on the grave, if that will make you feel better. Of course, Sergeant Schmidt would have to show us where it is."

"Aw, ya can't miss it," Schmidt said. "It's where the dirt's piled up real good. You'll see it."

"Terrific. Then Jerry, later you and I will go to Billie's grave and say a few words on the passing of the kangaroo," I said. "Fair enough?"

"Fair enough."

"Thank you, officer," I said. "Now, if you run into any other circus animals, say a zebra or a bear in a pointy hat riding a unicycle, well, just run it over for me, will you?"

"I tell ya, I've seen just 'bout everything on dis job," he said. "Ya know, dere was one time when Hank Johnson shot a bear down by the garbage dump 'cuz it wouldn't let nobody in there ta dump da garbage and ..."

I closed the door so I did not have to hear the rest of that quaint local legend.

"I'm going to watch a little TV, and then we can go see Billie's grave," I said. "I think we should get there before the raccoons dig her up. That could be kind of nasty."

"Poor Billie," Pinky Lee said. "I can just imagine her sitting in that jail cell. I feel so bad for her. I should have gone to her and brought her a coconut or whatever kangaroos eat."

"That's funny, you didn't bring me any coconuts when I was in jail, Miss Pinky," I said. "I guess I'd get more attention from you if I had pointy ears and a little pouch on my belly."

"I think I can take care of all of this if I write a big check," Jerry said. "I'll just assume that Billie was more of a pet than part of the circus act. But still, people get very close to pets. I'm going to write a huge check to Billie's owner and they can buy a whole flock of kangaroos."

"You mean a herd?" I said.

"Herd, flock, school, I don't care, as long as Billie's owner gets new kangaroos," Jerry said. "I feel guilty, and when I feel guilty, I write big checks."

"You're a saint, Jerry, a saint, I say," I told him. "Quick, Pinky Lee, get me the Vatican. We've got to kill Jerry so he can be canonized right away. We'll make his checkbook a relic and all will come to worship it. He can be the patron saint of bankruptcy."

"Shut up," she said. "I'm trying to watch TV."

"Hey, just so you know, sweetie, they don't have any cartoons on that station," I called to her. "Scooby Doo doesn't do the news."

"Fuck you."

"Please?"

"It must take a lot of energy, negative energy, to keep up this nasty facade," Jerry said, breaking up another of our little lovers' spats. "I think you can be a better person. Look, no one was worse than me, and now look. I've seen what I was, and I want to be something different. I don't even know how I'm going to do it, but I'm going to try."

"OK, you try. Me, I'm going to watch TV."

"Look, I'm not going to give up on you," Jerry said. "Are the woods walking distance? Can we walk to Billie's grave from here?"

"If it is where I think it is, yeah."

"Then let's go for a walk and talk."

"That's a little more exercise than I'm used to, but fine. But only if you buy me a salted nut log candy bar at the gas station on the way."

"I'll buy you two."

"I love hanging with millionaire game show hosts. Say, as long as you're buying, I wonder if they have stereos at the gas station, too, or just gas and candy bars."

"Let's just go."

I slipped on my Milwaukee Brewers windbreaker, gave Pinky Lee a huge wet kiss on the cheek, and said, "Bye, honey. Don't wait up." She elbowed me in the gut and Jerry and I left her with Charles, who was now polishing the sink fixtures.

As we walked down my street, I introduced Jerry to Hammertown by pointing out the stories in every house.

"There's Jack Bemick's house. He got caught molesting the little girls in the neighborhood. No one knew until one of them, Debbie Schwister, went home and told her mother that he gave her the nick name 'Little Lumps' and she thought it was funny. Her mother did not. No one pressed charges against Jack because it was thought that maybe some of the other daddies were doing the same things. Awful man. Should be dead. Oh, and there's Bob David's house. He used to get drunk and chase his kids down the street with a butcher knife and threaten to kill them before they could become miserable bastards like him.

"Of course, there's Bobby Hauser's house. He was an older kid than me. He told me and my friend Steve he had some really cool comics he would show us at his house. But when we got to his room he pulled out a knife and made us show him our penises. He said if we told anyone he would beat the hell out of us. I guess I would have to look out for him, having told you and all, but Eddie is in prison right now, and I'm guessing many of his colleagues are showing him their penises. These two bungalows here, not much happened, except that between the two adjacent households, three people died young of liver cancer. Wonder how they got so lucky.

"Over here, that's Bob Leonard's old house. He used to be a cop here until he rousted some kids who were necking in a car out by the woods. Turns out he scared the young man in the car, who was armed and didn't know Bob was a cop. Kid shot Bob in the face, and Bob died on the way to the hospital. Later, the kid hung himself before his trial."

We walked on in silence. It was a small town. There was only so much scandal.

"Not much more to show you before we get to the woods, except that house there, the one with the yellow aluminum siding. That's where my high school sweetie, Carol Ann, lived. I almost lost my virginity in that house, so I always get a little randy every time I pass by because I can remember all that groping and feeling and coming and going. My old high school sweetie moved to Fargo and is, I understand, quite happy. Good for her."

Jerry had been walking with his hand on his chin, as though he was actually interested in my little hometown travelogue. Occasionally he'd nod and say: "Mmmm, hmmmm." I was kind of glad he didn't make fun of all this, since it was all part of my life, for whatever that was worth.

As we got to the edge of the woods, Jerry turned around and surveyed the little bit of Americana I had described.

"You're not the only one with a strange neighborhood," he said. "America is one strange neighborhood."

"Thank you Dr. Most. I thought I would need pills to get over this feeling."

"I've got some thinking to do."

"You're going to cure dysfunctional neighborhoods with a game show? You may be onto something. Give away prizes if you get help for your molesting problem and can answer questions about American presidents. A Blazer if you get yourself into rehab, and a Rolex if rehab sticks for more than six months."

Jerry became silent, ignoring my lame witticisms. And this was my A-list material. We walked to the clearing and found Billie's grave. The dirt was loose over it, and it looked so hastily dug that I suspected the cops would get calls from the first person who found it, thinking that a human body was buried there by a mass killer or a jealous husband. I didn't know whether or not to cross myself.

Billie was an animal, but this was a grave.

The cops didn't mark the poor animal's grave for fear that the local kids would use it as a gathering spot—"Meet us by the kangaroo grave! Bring beer!"—and they did their best to camouflage it. They failed.

Jerry just stared at the mound of loose dirt as though he was having some sort of moment of clarity. I was looking at the grave and wondering how long it would take before I could go back home and watch TV.

Suddenly, Jerry looked at me, serious as Walter Cronkite during Vietnam.

"You're going on the show," he said. "I'm going to see to it that you get your chance to live or die on my program. And either way, everyone, even you, will learn from the experience. You're miserable, and you don't even know it. So if you die, you get your secret wish granted. If you live, you get a lot of money and get to change your life. But first, we're going to take a little cross-country trip so you can see humanity isn't as bad as you thought. Then maybe, just maybe, you'll end this death-by-boredom lifestyle and start living. Either that or it's death by baboon on national TV. What's it gonna be, pal?"

As I stood over the makeshift grave of a dead kangaroo, I knew I had to do it.

Chapter 15
A Road Trip Before I Die

The road trip is a curiously American phenomenon, going back much farther than Ike's Interstate Highway System. The pioneers moved west when things got tough back east and there was a chance to grab some land and make it big. Or maybe they were escaping from the law. They might even have been pursuing religious freedom.

Me? I was going west for the chance to be eaten by baboons on a game show. I bet no one had ever gone west for that reason in the entire history of humankind. Sure, lots of people had been eaten by mountain lions and fatally bitten by rattlesnakes on the way out there, but it certainly wasn't their idea to die that way when they set out. I'll bet that not one soul ever went west to be intentionally eaten by predatory animals, especially predators not native to the area. After careful consideration of my situation, I thought I just might make my mark on the world after all.

Mind you, I never thought I'd actually be eaten by baboons or kangaroos or cannibalistic serial killers when I got to California. But after a while, I began to think Jerry was right. Sometimes, you have to blow up your life, change everything, start over, get a clean sweep and all of those other life-changing cliches. I was beginning to feel a little uptight and tied down in Hammertown anyway.

In fact, I felt like a loaded handgun on the coffee table at a frat party. Eventually, I was going to go off, and then who knew what would happen? So I thought that maybe leaving town would take the pressure off of me. I could relax. I deserved it. My Grampa was dead, after all.

Even if I didn't intend to die by baboon, a free chance to travel the country combined with the opportunity to go on national TV and challenge nature was a little hard to resist, even for someone who had long since lost interest in any stimulus more challenging than trying to discern the subtle subplots of "Get Smart."

In the final analysis, a free trip across country was just a chance for me to get my fair share. No one had ever given me anything, so why not a free trip and a shot at big cash and prizes.

So here I was, ready to take the road trip of my life. Or even the road trip to end my life. The stakes certainly made the whole thing a little more exciting than a trip to the Travelodge in Mitchell, South Dakota.

All of this meant I would miss all television reruns except those I could watch on the motel TV. But like those pioneers of the days of yore, I was prepared to make sacrifices, even the ultimate sacrifice of forgoing the "Hillbillies." Jethro could wait.

I packed light—a few books, the one suit I owned, a bunch of T-shirts and two pairs of jeans. Oh, and one pair of shorts, for when it got hot. Like most fat people, I did not like wearing shorts because of the looks I got. My bulbous, varicose legs looked like a road map written on a marshmallow and could likely kill the appetite of even the most voracious and compulsive eater, so I tried to be considerate. But sometimes it's just too hot for big-boy pants.

Jerry had rented a camper-trailer that was the size of a Milwaukee bungalow so that we could stay as far away from the real outdoors as possible. At night, even with the camper, he promised we'd stay at quaint motels to get a closer look at the local population. Pinky Lee, after some deliberation with Jerry that went into the wee hours for several nights in a row, decided to join us.

Although I had given up on the notion of ever bedding her, something deep inside suggested that the road might lead to some romantic situations that would bring us just a little closer. No dice, as it eventually turned out.

We decided on a seating chart. Charles would drive, with Jerry riding shotgun. Pinky Lee and I would be in the back, where there were seats, a small rest room, and two bunks. Perhaps that would give me my chance!

I closed up the house, but didn't bother to lock it. No one in Hammertown would enter it, save for high school kids who would eventually use it for a love nest when they discovered it was available. Locking it would be futile, anyway. The kids were like raccoons breaking into a garbage can—they would do what they had to do, and they had all day and night to do it. More power to 'em, I thought. Let them make a love nest. No one else was ever going to get laid there.

We climbed aboard the camper enthusiastically.

"Let's set a course for adventure," I said sardonically.

"Oh, you're gonna get an adventure," Pinky Lee said, licking her lips.

"Bite my ass, tease," I said. I was already becoming crude and resentful.

"Now, boys and girls, we've got a long way to drive, let's not fight," Jerry said. "Charles, let us cast off the anchor, or cast it on, or whatever you do with the anchor when you want to sail away."

"We towin' a boat?" Charles said.

"Sorry, my limited friend, I was using naval terminology and I forgot that our little town here is landlocked," Jerry said. "Let's just get out of here. Set sail."

"Are we there yet?" I asked. "Can we have ice cream?"

"I'll give you something to lick," Pinky Lee said.

"Fuck you."

"Knock it off, wise guy," Jerry said to me. "Don't make me come back there."

"Fine, I'll just sit back here with my coloring book and not talk to anyone," I said. "Just tell her not to tease me."

"Don't tease him."

"Oh, I won't tease him," she said, looking at me with a grin and licking her teeth. The word "him" sounded like "eeum."

"She's doing it! She's looking at me sexy. Make her stop looking at me."

"This is getting old fast," Jerry warned. "You know, I don't have to bring two people back to California with me. You could always get out now and we could forget everything."

"What? No baboon death? Not on your life, Jerry. You can't talk me out of it now. I can just feel their glorious fangs ripping into my neck. And on national TV, yet. I owe you for this one, Jerry, I really do. Although I may have to pay you back from beyond the grave."

"It's my pleasure, my friend," Jerry said. "I hope everything works out the way you want it to. I really do."

"Well, as soon as I figure out what it is I want, I'll let you know."

As we cruised out of town, we passed The Chips and Charles thought he saw his old nemesis, Steve.

"Izzat Steve? Izzat Steve?" he said with an enthusiasm sounding like a dog who had just seen his owner's car pulling into the driveway. "Hey Steve! Steve! Steve, com'ere, buddy. Look who I'm with! It's Jerry Most!"

Charles had stopped the van so that Steve, once he recognized Charles, could walk up to the vehicle. Charles leaned out an open window and seemed very happy to see Steve, now that he was hanging with a big shot. Unfortunately, what Charles didn't know was that I had mailed the poison pen letter to Steve and signed Charles' name, using a crayon for credibility's sake.

I pretended to sleep. I did not want to see what would happen. Jerry was muttering under his breath: "Must we stop? Can't we just get out of here? Do we have to have a reunion before we go?"

"Be nice, Jerry," I whispered. "You're a nice guy now."

"Hey, Steve! Good ta see ya, old buddy!" Charles said as Steve approached. "How're they hangin'?" Remarkably, Charles was not speaking in spoonerisms in spite of his excitement, but as Steve approached the camper it looked like two lovers approaching each other in a meadow in slow motion. Except that suddenly one of the lovers, Steve, stuck out his fist and took a running punch at poor Charles, who was more confused than hurt.

"You stupid, rat-ass motherfucker," Steve said. I guess hello was out of the question under the circumstances. "You take back that you fucked my wife. You take it back. How could you write something like that? She never fucked no one but me. Never, you fuck. And even if she did, it wouldn't have been you, you sick fuck retard."

"Who, who, who said I w-w-wucked your fife?" said a clearly agitated Charlie. "I never fucked nobody but my wife, and that was just try to have kids."

"Oh yeah, then how did you know she thinks I have a worm dick, you lying sack of shit? We're having some problems, but there's no reason to go and fuck my wife and make things worse. Every man has problems down there sometimes. I'm working on it, you bastard."

Oh-oh. Good guess on my part about the penis problems. How could I have known a letter pulled out of my ass would be so accurate? It's a gift, I guess. While I decided not to take a role in this morality play, Jerry decided to play the role of town marshal.

"Now boys, you've been friends for a long time," Jerry said, not knowing what he was talking about. "I'm sure you went out in those woods and had some fun drinking Old Milwaukee and listening to Journey. I want you both to go back to those days and remember your friendship. Steve—is that your name, Steve?—I want you to apologize for hitting Charles. If Charles said he didn't have sex with your wife, as his employer I am satisfied that he did not."

"Charlie's workin' for you? The game show guy where people are s'posed to get killed?"

"Yes, Charles in now in my employ. And he is a good man."

Charles sat in the driver's seat wiping blood from his nose, but seemed otherwise unhurt.

He said: "Yeah, Steve, did you ever think this would happen? That I would wind up hanging with a famous star? If I'm hanging with a famous star, I wouldn't need to woo your scrife. I could get some famous Hollywood starlet. That is if I wasn't married. But I don't even think yer wife is all that pretty. I wouldn't screw her with yer wormy dick."

"Hey, watch it," said Steve.

"He meant nothing by it, Steve," Jerry said. "Here. Take $500 and go out and buy your wife a pretty dress. I had originally intended to punish you for your poor treatment of Charles, but I have changed my ways. And it would appear you have enough problems now, anyway. Use the money, do something fun, and try to explode your life, OK?"

"I don't know about exploding anything, but I'll take the cash," Steve said, reaching across Charles to take it from Jerry's hand. Steve leaned back from the camper and looked at Charles. "I'm sorry, buddy," he said. "I've been a real prick for a lot of years since I became a boss. I just lost my head. But now that you're hanging with a famous game show host, we're peers, so I won't be shitty to you anymore."

"Thanks, pal," Charles said. "Let's go get a twelver and hit the woods for old times when I get back. I'm going to California. With Jerry. But I'd like to see you when I get back."

"You got it," Steve said.

Charles said goodbye and started to pull away slowly. But suddenly, Steve was running alongside the camper and tapping on the window. Charles stopped again and rolled down the window and addressed Steve.

"What's wrong, buddy?" Charles said.

"Well, it's just that, if you didn't write the letter, who did?" ·

Jerry looked back at me but said nothing. Fortunately, Charles' simple thought process prevented him from using deductive reasoning and fingering me for the crime.

"I don't know, man," Charles said. "Do you suppose there's another Charles in town sleeping with your wife?"

Steve's mind reeled at the very notion. "Well if there is, I'm gonna find 'im," Steve said ominously. "I'll kill the man who violated our sacred vows between me and my bride."

Finally, I had to break in. The poor galoot was suffering. Although that would normally not be of my concern, since I was the source of his pain, I offered a plausible explanation.

"The Chips is a big company," I said. "There are a lot of people who are probably jealous of your success, someone who wants desperately to wear a white jacket like yours. Someone who's so jealous they can't stand it probably just wrote you that letter to make you feel bad. Just don't let anyone know that it worked, then the jerk won't have the satisfaction of knowing he got to you."

"Yer probably right," Steve said, obviously relieved. "But how did they know about ..."

"Good guess, that's all," I said. "Maybe the person who wrote it has the same problems, ah, down there, as you said."

"Yeah, right. Hey, thanks. Hey, ain't you the guy who lives with his naked Grampa?"

"Lived. Grampa's dead."

"Aw, sorry, man. He was weird, but he meant no harm."

"Thanks for the condolences."

Finally, Charles started to pull away again, but I made him stop. I had some unfinished business to accomplish.

"Hey, Steve. Steve."

"Yeah?" he said, running back to the driver window.

"You know, if the letter wasn't just a prank, if there really is a guy schtupping your wife, well, I'm sure she still loves you the best, and I'm sure she sees past your, uh, deficiencies. So don't worry. Now let's hit the road, Charles. Cal-if-orn-ia here we come, right back where we started from ..."

Steve looked as though he was going to cry as we pulled away.

"You are such a fucking asshole," Pinky Lee said.

"I know. It's probably one of the things that attracts you."

"I'd be more attracted to a garter snake."

"I'll bet you would. I'll bet you would."

She smacked me on the shoulder and I was rubbing away the pain as I saw the wooden sign in the shape of a hammer that said: "Thanks for Visiting Hammertown. Please Come Again!"

Now why would anyone want to do that twice?

The camper was silent for 90 seconds before Jerry abruptly announced the need for a theme song for the trip. He said before we left town we should see if there were CDs we could buy for the trip. I, of course, was not enthusiastic about returning to the scene of my crime, but I did not want my musical selections to go unrepresented. A trip in a camper with a CD player and three people you weren't sure you liked could be a living hell if you don't have the right music.

So we passed the woods, which seemed quiet at the moment—no banana throwing adolescents hiding in the trees—and headed off to Kmart. Charles pulled into the parking lot and, still unfamiliar with the size of his vehicle, ran into three abandoned shopping carts, crushing one with a satisfying crunch. He parked at the end of the lot rather than try to angle park the beast, and we all disembarked like some trailer park family heading off the decorate the living room.

"Pick whatever you want," Jerry said. "I'm paying."

"Good, then can I get appliances, too?" I said.

"I mean CDs," he said flatly.

"If anyone buys a disc by that talentless exhibitionist Madonna I reserve the right to buy the entire Tom Waits catalog," I said. "I warn you, I will get the better end of the deal. *Earth Died Screaming* is a lovely ballad."

"OK, OK, no Madonna, no Tom Waits," Jerry said. "Try to select discs that you love and would like to share with everyone else—something we might be able to tolerate if not enjoy. OK? Can we do that?"

"Great," I said. "Hey, wait until you hear the Buzzcocks' *Orgasm Addict*. It's really pretty—you know, a late night romance song. 'He's always at it. He's an orgasm addict.' You'll love it."

"I'm lookin' for some Willie Nelson," Pinky Lee announced. "Anybody see some Willie? I want some Willie."

"I'll give you some Willie," I said with a leer.

"Shut up," she said. "Pencil dick."

"You'll never know."

"You can't stop me from buying some Willie Nelson."

"No, I can't. But if I hear 'On the Road Again' just once I will murder you all in your sleep and leave you all in a ditch near a reservoir."

"Fuck you," Pinky Lee said.

"Pinky Lee's ultimate argument closer. 'Fuck you.' Have you ever tried using 'piss off?' It's got kind of a British feel to it. You know. Kind of classy."

Since I was concentrating on my repartee with Pinky Lee, I didn't notice that Rip, the security guard I had met a few days prior, had joined us as we entered the shopping mecca that is Kmart. He was wearing a security guard hat with a badge on it, and when he saw me he stopped, cocked the hat back, and folded his arms. He looked like Barney Fife about to write a parking ticket to an old woman.

"Hey, Fat Boy," he said. "I thought we told you not to come 'round here no more."

"Is that the royal 'we' you are referring to? Has the Queen of Kmart banned me from her realm? Or are you the Queen. You don't look like a queen. Or maybe, hey, wait a minute, you are ..."

"Shut the hell up, Fat Boy. I just want you to know I'm gonna be watching you every minute yer here. You steal one Tic Tac, and it's off to jail. You steal a radial tire, out. You go after a salad spinner, and yer a dead man, you ..."

"Why the hell would I steal one radial tire? Or how? Do I stuff it in my pants?"

"Just know yer bein' watched, aina?"

"Yah, and so."

Jerry leapt to defend my honor. "I will vouch for this man, mister ... Mr. Rip," he said. "I am purchasing everything for this group, so shoplifting cannot be a factor in this visit. I will pay for everything."

"Hey, will you buy me that goony guard hat, Jerry?" I said.

Rip made a move toward me, but Jerry stopped him. He pulled out a wad of cash and handed Rip a $100 bill. "Here's a little something for the Christmas party next year," Jerry said. "But you can spend it on something else if you can't wait until then."

"Hey, ain't you that guy on the TV show? What's yer name? I know, Monty Hall, yer on that death show," Rip said. "Wow, a celebrity in my Kmart. A celebrity handing out $100 bills. You s'pose you could get me on yer show? I'd like to drive a race car into a wall, maybe buy me a Jacuzzi for my backyard with my survival money."

"We'll see," Jerry said, not bothering to identify himself. "Why don't you write down your name on this business card and we'll get back to you."

Rip wrote his name on the back of the business card from a used car salesmen Jerry had met during his earlier travels and handed it back to Jerry, hyperventilating in his excitement to the point of a wheeze. After he recognized Jerry, Rip softened considerably toward me and he shook Jerry's hand.

"I'm gonna assume this dirtbag won't act up as long as you're here," he said. "I'll just leave you folks be. No famous game show host would let someone steal from a Kmart."

He disappeared into the store gripping the C-note with both hands.

"Now, can we find some music and get on the road?" Jerry asked.

I knew my audience, and I knew what they'd hate. So the first disc I picked was Bob Dylan's *Blonde on Blonde*. That was for the cretinous Pinky Lee, who would say: "This guy sings terrible. You can't dance to this. Turn it off." Then there was The Ramones' *Rocket to Russia*; Sex Pistols' *Never Mind the Bullocks*; Miles' *Sketches of Spain*, for those quiet, introspective moments; The Beach Boys' *Pet Sounds*, because I intended to sing every song on the album while drunk; *London Calling*, by the Clash; *Beware of the Dog*, one of the screechiest blues records ever made, recorded by a gentleman named Hound Dog Taylor; and the two greatest albums ever recorded, *Born to Run* and *Darkness of the Edge of Town*, of course, by Bruce Springsteen. I thought those selections represented a good cross-section of my moods. The Kmart had a remarkable selection, actually.

Jerry brought some Jimmy Buffet, which I thought was a good idea, and he also picked up a box set of old soul tunes. Ominously, he chose a few gospel selections as well.

Pinky Lee, as could be expected, chose trash. Soundtracks, mostly. *Cats. Phantom of the Opera. A Chorus Line.*

"Hey, if you like Broadway shows you should get the soundtrack to 'Glengarry Glen Ross,'" I said.

"I didn't see that one, but if you like it I'm sure it sucks," she said.

Jerry urged Charles to pick a few selections for himself. I dreaded what he would choose. I had visions of myself listening to *The Best of Sesame Street* or something by Ted Nugent. In fact, his choices were great: *Step Inside This House* by Lyle Lovett and *Guitar Town* by Steve Earle.

Maybe this road trip wouldn't be so bad after all.

We all went up to the cash register with our selections, and we waited in line behind people buying George Foreman grills and fishing equipment and light bulbs and toilet paper and cheap throw rugs. Jerry was going to pay in cash, so the transaction wouldn't take that long. But it took just long enough, especially when it came time for the cashier to make change. It took her longer to do that than it took us to pick the music.

While we were waiting in line, I saw Tic Tacs hanging on a rack for the traditional impulse buy. Or in this case, impulse steal. I grabbed a box of spearmint and a box of peppermint and slid them into my pocket. This wasn't to impress Pinky Lee. This was for me. I was balancing the scales of justice.

When we got back to the camper and we all took our places, I sat there grinning and nodding my head.

"What's with you, weirdo?" said Pinky Lee.

"Tic Tac, my dear?" I said. "They're minty."

"You're pathetic," she said.

Chapter 16
On The Road Again

Road trips are always better in the abstract than they are in reality. The road trip in your mind does not have construction projects which mean it will take you three hours to get through Chicago. The road trip in your mind does not account for the agonizing need to urinate after drinking eight beers between Point A and Point B. The road trip in your mind does not account for the fact that your ass really begins to hurt after sitting for 200 miles or so.

The road trip of your mind has you looking for Springsteen's *Thunder Road*. But the real thing has you yearning for a Burger King at the next exit so you can pee, get something to eat and maybe buy a newspaper that has more than 12 pages.

These were the elements of our road trip. But the undercurrent of the personal dynamics certainly made it a bit more interesting. For example, would this high level of togetherness serve to bring me and Pinky Lee close enough so that I could have sex with her? Would Jerry figure out what he really wanted to do with his life as he stared at the yellow lines of the road and navigated for Charles? Would Charles turn out to be a psychotic killer and gut us all like deer while we slept?

All of these matters crossed my mind as we drove, but the problem was we hadn't even made High Falls yet. High Falls, the town's namesake, hadn't been high since the glacial age. In fact, the falls were more of a series of cascades outside of town. High Falls was a typical backwater burg but was the biggest town in the area, and we decided we would stop there to begin our search for the "real people" Jerry claimed he knew, the real people who would help me understand that life was worth living, that there was no reason to wish that I could be ripped apart by baboons or any other savage primate.

We had gotten a late start out of Hammertown, but we decided to head out and get a few hours' travel in anyway. High Falls was the first "major" population center on our map, so we went there with the intention of going downtown and getting to know the people there right away. It was almost as though we were politicians trying to get in touch with our constituents during an election year. Not much time, a few handshakes, a brief conversation and it's off to the next podunk town.

High Falls is a place with one main street to speak of, University Avenue, and the biggest crime problem facing local authorities is to prevent young denizens from "cruising" it at night.

High Falls was the kind of place where there was believed to be a gang problem because young men hung out on street corners all night. In fact, standing on a street corner is all there is for a young person to do there. Unless there was a tire fire at the dump on the edge of town, there was little to watch or do in this slice of Small Town America.

Since High Falls' University Avenue is right off the main highway, we headed straight into town. Pinky Lee was sleeping, a string of saliva flowing uninterrupted between the corner of her mouth and her left shoulder. I focused in on the sight so that the mental picture would entertain me at low moments, or when I was failing to nail her again.

"We're going to find a good bar, a local bar," Jerry said. "You'll see there are very many good souls in the world. Even at a bar."

"Blackie has said this many times," I said. "I just never believed him."

"Who's Blackie?" Jerry said.

"You really were wasted when we met, weren't you?" I said. "Blackie is the man who got you so drunk at the bar in Hammertown where we were first introduced. Say, while I'm thinking of it, what did you do with that nice car you drove into town? You didn't leave it there, did you? The locals will be putting their fingerprints all over it."

"Had it shipped back by my staff," Jerry said. "That's what staff is for."

"That must be a very rewarding job, being part of a 'staff,' playing fetchit for a famous game show host," I said. "And from which home for the self-esteemless did you extract these proud specimens who live only to get Jerry Most another mineral water or take out his dry cleaning? I'm sorry, Charles, I'm not referring to you, of course."

"I'm not offended," he said. "For me it's an honor to serve Jerry Most. It is my purpose in life. That and being a member of the American Legion Post."

"Well, I guess that's better than being an ant," I said. "Slightly, anyway. Ants can't watch TV, I suppose. Although I wonder what Ant TV would be like. Do you suppose there would just be a lot of propaganda glorifying the queen? That wouldn't be very interesting."

Jerry, obviously getting irritated again, interfused my stream of conscious rambling just before I started talking about any politics.

"So what's your contribution to society, smart ass? How have you made the world a better place? Go ahead, tell me what makes you so superior to Charles and the rest of us?" Jerry said.

"Me? Well, first of all, I'm a well-known TV personality and I have a staff of people who rely on me for their paychecks," I said. "They take out my dry cleaning and pick up my Jaguars when I'm too drunk to drive myself. And they don't mind it because they love me and I'm famous and I'm as close to fame as they'll ever get. It validates them. In a sense, I give them identity. No, I give them life itself."

"Godammit, sometimes I'd like to break your teeth," Jerry said, waving at me over the front seat as though he was taking a swipe at me. "Can you stop being sarcastic for one second? Can you have one conversation that doesn't turn into an insult contest?"

"Um, no."

"There you go again," he said. "This whole trip is about life, why we're here. What we do and why we do it. I'm trying to be serious."

"And failing miserably."

"Charles, would you stop the camper and drop this guy off on the side of the road?"

"I would be honored," Charles said.

"Charles would be honored," I said. "It's his purpose in life. Of course, think of all the ratings points you'll lose if I don't go on your show. Ah, but that's not what this is about, is it? It's not about ratings. It's about Jerry Most having the power over life and death, about being a nice guy for a change and granting baboon death to someone who professes not to want to live anymore. Jerry, leaving me on the side of the road would not be nice for either of us. There are no baboons in Wisconsin to eat me, and even if there were, there would be no cameras to capture the action. I would simply have to hitchhike home and instead be skinned alive by the denizens of these parts. It's a lose-lose situation, Charles."

As we argued we were moving closer to High Falls, and the lights of the used car lots and convenience stores roused Pinky Lee slightly, but only enough to have her cut the string of spittle and rub it on the upholstery. It was momentarily quiet. I was looking out the window for the skyline of High Falls until I realized towns like High Falls don't have skylines. Jerry sat in front sighing repeatedly. Obviously, he was trying to regroup.

"What is a man?" he started, then paused.

Oh crap, not this again.

"What is a man if his chief good and market of his time be but to sleep and feed? A beast, no more," Jerry said in his best Shakespeare in the park accent. "Shakespeare, from Hamlet."

"Well, some guys just give up livin' and go dying little by little piece by piece," I said, in my best Springsteen baritone. "Some guys come home from work and wash up and go racin' in the streets. Springsteen. From the *Darkness* album."

"You got an answer for everything."

"Yeah, it's just usually the wrong one."

Pinky Lee, waking now at the thought that alcohol must be nearby, blinked and looked out the window to get her bearings.

"You know, there's a bed back there you could have been drooling on instead of sleeping sitting up," I said. "Though it was sweet watching you drool like that."

"I was not drooling," she said.

"'Fraid so, dear," Jerry said.

"Fuck you both. Let's get a drink," she said.

"A capital idea," I said. "But can we make sure the bar has a TV so I have even the remotest chance of picking up a rerun or two? Or maybe even a ballgame?"

"It's your road trip," Jerry said. "Whatever you want."

We drove past several bars, none of which seemed to match our personal expectations of what a decent gin mill looked like from the outside. I wanted a bar that had a neon Hamm's beer sign on it. Pinky Lee wanted a sports bar. And Jerry was looking for something called a "cocktail lounge" so that it might be just classy enough to have a decent single-malt scotch, but homey enough to feature regular hometown folk. I won.

The establishment I chose was called "Lorraine's C-U There," and it had an old Schlitz sign in front. An old Schlitz sign was an indication that the bar was authentic, given that Schiltz left Milwaukee decades ago and no one but no one ever drank the stuff they were calling Schlitz these days. Any bar with a sign that old was not a pretentious bar. It was a place where the locals fled their spouses and ate fish fries and watched TV to avoid the crushing loneliness of doing it at home.

We lumbered into the lot and, seeing no motorcycles or broken glass on the pavement, determined that it was safe for a major star like Jerry Most to enter the premises and leave unharmed.

When we walked into the place, I knew it was the right one. Although anti-smoking laws had been passed a long time ago, vestigal smoke still hung in the air from smokers whose cancer had killed them decades before. There were two pool tables in the back and the cushions were bare in spots but Pinky Lee and Jerry thought they'd hit a few balls after a while. All the cues were, upon inspection, as warped as an old man's finger.

The entire place was done in red—deep, absorbent red that made the whole joint look like the devil's waiting room when the neon lights hit the walls just right. The juke box, a CD juke box, contained mostly modern country music, the worst of that breed of dreck. There were three people in the bar, all men in their 50s and 60s, each of them prematurely creased with deep wrinkles that made them look like catcher's mitts that had been left outside all summer. They were seated equidistant from one another, one at each end of the bar and one in the middle.

They were engaged in a conversation that would have been more appropriate to a cozy, intimate booth in the back of the bar. But it was clear that they owned this place, or they may as well have owned it. This was their hangout, their home-away-from-home, their lair, the one place where they could escape the outside world. It was also clear after a while that they sat so far away from each other because they were sitting on the stools that had been designated by the management as "their" stools. No one else could sit in these stools, even when it was crowded. These three boozehounds kept the place going during the week, and they were rewarded with permanent perches. The problem was, they were all seated so far apart that the only way they could sit in their personal stools and still converse was to shout to each other. Moving the stools closer was out of the question. If they had thought about why, they might have cited the feng shui. Bad luck could come from moving the stools. A drunk driving rap on the way home. Maybe getting picked up by a woman intent on robbing old drunks. There was no need to risk any of this. So they sat there every night and shouted at each other about sports, wives, popular culture and the price of booze until closing time.

This arrangement would not have been much of a problem except that we sat ourselves at the bar and immediately got caught in the conversational crossfire. These gentleman did not change their habits when guests were in the room. The one in the middle seemed to initiate all conversations, and the others would jump in the minute they agreed or disagreed.

Lorraine, a jolly, round, profane, black-haired woman with a beehive 'do, was tending bar, something she had done at least 12 hours a day for probably the past 20 years. Lorraine could have run for mayor and won without ever leaving the place. Everyone knew her, and she was always good for a free drink when she though you looked a little down and out. She was like a mom offering chicken soup to her ill children.

"Ya look like a buncha weary travelers," she said. Looking at Pinky Lee, she added: "Ah, honey, you got drool crust on the left comer of your mouth. At least I hope that's drool crust, haw, haw, haw." She winked at me, and I could feel myself blush.

Meanwhile, the man in the middle of the bar, who called himself "The Hitman," was spouting off about the pathetic nature of team nicknames, and we ordered our drinks from Lorraine over the sounds of his ranting.

"The Milwaukee Bucks," he said, spitting the name. "Look, it's a team with great tradition. But Bucks? You shoot bucks, you don't fear them. Other teams come into town, they look at a stupid deer on the home uniforms, and that's it. Oooh, it's a buck. Everybody look out. Hide the salt lick. They shoulda given the thing fangs, or maybe had him carrying a machete or something. That would show everybody that the Bucks mean business."

"You said it, Hitman," said the man on the left.

"Fuckin'-A right, Hitman," said the man on the right. "Ya fuckin' shoot da Bucks."

"And the fuckin' 76ers," Hitman said, obviously on his first roll of the evening. "What the hell is that? It's numbers? Not threatening at all. How can numbers scare you? Unless they're on your bar bill, right Lorraine? Hey, c'mere and gimme a smooch. I haven't had it in awhile."

"76ers. Shit," said Rightie.

"No smooches for you till you're too drunk to recall 'em," Lorraine said. "If you're drunk I know you won't try to take things any farther than a smooch."

"Hey, Lorraine, I could use a smooch right here," said Lefty, cackling and pointing to his crotch.

"Say, Otto," said Lorraine. Lefty's name was Otto? "Wanna know the scariest words you'll ever hear? You're cut off. No more drinks. No more sex. Like those words? Wanna hear 'em for real? Then talk about me smooching yer nuts again and see what happens. I know life without sex is a reality for you. But can you really face life without beer?"

"Dear God, I am so sorry," said Otto/Lefty. "Hey, whattya say I clean yer grease trap for you this weekend to make it up to you?"

"Ferget about it," Lorraine said. "Besides, I don't want you eatin' outta there, weirdo. You'd get sick and sue me."

By this point, Jerry and Pinky Lee decided they had had enough of the conversation, and they retreated to the back of the bar to play pool. Charles, whose silence was becoming annoying, went in back with them, and he sat quietly in a corner reading a Bible. It's always comforting when your designated driver brings a Bible into a bar.

As they dismissed themselves to play pool, I told them I was going to stay at the bar and listen to this conversation among the locals. I had a sense that the guy who called himself Hitman was a kindred spirit, a long-lost brother in bitterness and bile, and I wanted to hear more. I hadn't even noticed that the TV was showing an "I Dream of Jeannie" rerun, the Hitman had drawn my attention so quickly. Anybody who thought about the lameness of sports mascot names had to be a very clear thinker. I moved in closer to be able to hear him better over the ambient noise of the bar.

"Hey, Fat Boy, don't get too close," he warned. "I ain't queer, ya know."

"Of course not," I said. "I was just fascinated by your discussion of the buck as a mascot."

"You patronizing me, boy?" he said, turning dark. "You think 'cause you rolled into town from Madison or Milwaukee or Minneapolis you can just sit there and be amused at the comments of a failed sportswriter, maybe even get him to buy you a drunk? Fuck you. Go back to Chicago."

"Actually, I'm from Hammertown," I said meekly.

"Oooh, city slicker, Hitman," said the guy on the right.

"Hammertown, eh?" said Hitman. "I have a brother-in-law lives in Hammertown. Haven't seen him in years. He's a real asshole."

"What's his name? Maybe I know him," I said, trying to draw nearer to the subject of my study.

"I just told you he's an asshole," he snapped. "What the fuck do I care if you know him or not? His name's Dick Head. There. Know him?"

"Dick Head," Otto sputtered. "There ain't no Dick Head, Hitman."

"No shit? Omigod I've been conned. I better call my sister right away. She ain't Mrs. Head after all," Hitman said. "Fucking moron, I was being clever. No wonder you didn't understand it."

"Hey, Otto, I got a brother named Shit Head, too," said the guy on the right. "Head's are a big family in Hammertown."

"Bite my ass," said Otto.

"That fat ass? Man, if I bit that it would take you three days to find out about it," said the guy on the right.

The guy who called himself the Hitman regained control of the conversation by asking me what I was doing in town. I told him I was on a cross-country trip with a famous game show host that was supposed to culminate in a baboon attack on my person during a national TV show.

"That guy you're with, he's a game show host?" Hitman said. "Jeez, I gotta watch more prime time TV other than ESPN."

"Yes, he's pretty well known," I said, hoping I would impress this curmudgeon for reasons I still don't understand. Maybe I just viewed Hitman as a father figure.

"So which one-ayou is boinkin' the blond," he asked, displaying his level of interest in the famous game show host. "I bet she's a real hellcat in the sack."

"Actually, none of us are," I said.

"Yer not homos are ya? Lotta homos in the TV business."

"Why is that always the assumption that you're gay if you're not constantly rutting with every woman who walks into a bar?" I said. "Isn't there more to being a man? "

The three of them looked at me as though I had just spoken blasphemy in the halls of the Vatican.

"What the hell else is there to bein' a guy?" Hitman said. "Drinkin', sports and screwin'. Screwin' women, that is. Every once in a while you read a book to break up the pattern. But it should be a sports book."

It sounded to me as though Hitman was living the same sort of fulfilling life that I had been back in Hammertown. He had sports. I had TV reruns. I ordered another beer and Lorraine brought me two, having spotted someone who was obviously in this conversation for the long haul. It was with that simple act that I understood what made her so popular. In the back of the bar I could hear Jerry and Pinky Lee laughing and joking as they played pool. Pinky Lee had filled the juke box with five dollars and made a series of picks that betrayed a distinct lack of imagination.

Your Cheatin' Heart? How clichéd.

It suddenly occurred to me that Jerry and Pinky Lee had grown closer in recent days. They cast a lot of knowing glances at each other, and their giggling at the pool table sounded as though they had been doing more than just a little friendly bonding over the past week or so. At the moment, however, I was not concerned about my prospects with Pinky Lee. I had become fascinated by Hitman and his attitude, his morose take on life. It sounded as though the Hitman and his pinheaded friends were very similar to me. I wanted to prove to Jerry that I was not the only unhappy soul who had trapped himself in a tiny world of his own to avoid interaction with the real one, and Hitman would prove my point for me. But I had to engage the two in conversation without involving Heckle and Jeckle. Hitman was about to resume his sermon, though, so I just sat back and absorbed the wisdom of someone who had been beaten back by the world even worse than I had.

"Kid," he said, looking at me. Kid was better than Fat Boy, but I couldn't tell what he was about to uncork on me. "Kid, you ever have a dream? You ever want something so bad it was all you could think about but for whatever reason the Fates never saw their way clear to give it to you?"

He was trying to open me up. I decided to play along. Sort of.

"Yes," I said quietly. "But I don't like to talk about it."

"Fuck you, kid, you gotta talk about it," he said. "I'm talkin' about my dreams, you could do me the courtesy of doin' the same."

"Yeah, do the same, kid," said the man on the right, Otto or whatever his name was.

"Well, it's kind of embarrassing," I said.

"Nothing's embarrassing in a bar," Hitman said. "Especially this one, right Lorraine?"

"Cripes, no," she said as she wiped out beer glasses. "We're all pals in here."

"OK, kid, so go on, tell us your dream," Hitman said.

"Well, ever since I was a kid, I dreamed of having X-ray vision," I said. "It was kind of a super-hero thing. But I never got X-ray vision. I knew I could never fly, either, but I thought there was an off chance I could become like that stretchy guy in the Fantastic Four. No dice. Invisibility was out of the question, too. So once I got out of that phase, in my twenties, I wanted to produce TV shows for a while, but I never figured I'd make it in Hollywood, being from a small town like Hammertown and all. So now, while I watch TV for hours on end, I dream of being a cabaret singer. I just love show tunes."

"Jee-sus H. Christopher," Hitman said. "What the fuck is wrong with you? You some kinda goddamn weirdo?"

"Is it so wrong to idolize Joel Grey?" I said. "Must we always worship the athlete?"

"Shut the fuck up before I puke," Hitman said. "Jeez. A cabaret singer. What the fuck. X-ray vision. Whattya you, nuts, gay or what? Whatsyer name, anyway?"

"Raskolnikov, and I'm on the lam," I said. "But I swear to God I didn't touch the old bitch."

"What the hell is he talkin' about Hitman?" Otto said.

There was a brief pause as Hitman took a long pull from his beer and ordered another one. He pulled a quarter out of his pocket and began spinning it on the bar. Tammy Wynette was singing *Stand By Your Man*, Charlie was reading his Bible and Pinky Lee and Jerry were goofing around trying trick shots at the pool table, oblivious to the world. Lorraine was at the right side of the bar, smoking cigarettes and watching "Eight is Enough," which had just come on the TV suspended above the bar.

Hitman stared blankly at the bar as he spoke.

"He's just a clever lad putting on the old drunks with literary allusions and bizarre tales of his youth," Hitman said. "Think yer foolin' anyone, Fat Boy? Think yer funny? Think yer hangin' with a bunch of old drunks too addled to figure out when they're being mocked? I got news for you, pally.

I coulda been working for the *Chicago Tribune* right now if I hadn't let my ex-wife talk me into staying in this shithole until the kids graduated from high school. I had an offer. Take my column, 'Designated Hitman,' to the sports pages of the Trib. Syndication was even a possibility. But I gave it all up to stay here and give the kids a sense of home. Keep 'em away from the traffic and the crime. 'Course, the kids moved away the minute they graduated. Why wouldn't they? They live in Milwaukee, Chicago, D.C. My wife, who is now my ex, dumped me after the last one left the house, and here I am, stuck writing my column for beer money for a newspaper in a podunk town. Yeah, I made some stupid decisions, pal, but I ain't stupid. Bitter, I'll give you bitter. But I'm entitled. I can't say I used to be somebody, but I can say I coulda been somebody. Say, you wanna see one o' my columns? "

"Do I have a choice?" I said, still making friends.

"No, you do not," he said.

"Then it would be my pleasure, Mr. Hitman. Or is it Mr. Designated?"

"Fuck you and read, turd."

I was surprised. I did not expect to find decent writing in a local rag in High Falls, Wisconsin. But the Hitman was pretty good, if a little unpolished. And I thought it was a shame he didn't get to make it big, because our writing styles were so similar. Here, dear reader. Take a look at this column and see what you think. It is difficult to imagine how one could gin up the psychotic passion necessary to write about sports this way. Clearly the product of a tortured soul, no?

The headline was "Soccer and Other Sissy Sports," and it contained some of the best insight into popular culture and sports that I have ever seen. To wit:

"Is Hitman the only person on Earth who wishes death to rain upon the Euro-trash goon who created the game of soccer? Of course not. Hitman's readers are intelligent, discerning members of the sports cognoscenti who would have nothing to do with a sissy sport like soccer. They hate it as much as the Hitman and would indeed exhibit their maniacal rage at the person who foisted the sport of the bored on the rest of the world.

"After the preceding statement I can already see the soccer wimps going to their computers to write Hitman nasty letters replete with death threats and questions about Hitman's manhood. But they should use the time to learn how to turn a double play or drive the lane in traffic.

"The soccer weenies always use the same arguments, and the Hitman will refute them one by one so that we may launch our campaign to rid the United States of the silliest game—and I do mean game, since I can't bear to call it a sport—ever invented. For example, I can predict that every soccer doofus in town will say that 'soccer is the most popular game in the world.' Well, prostitution is the world's oldest profession, but you don't see screwing as an Olympic sport, do you? (Although Hitman would get many gold medals if it was.)

"OK, maybe soccer is hot stuff in loser countries like Finland or Bosnia or Argentina. But where would you rather live, in a country where you can watch Major League Baseball, NCAA basketball and the National Football League? Or in a country where dysentery reigns and the banks close for the World Cup? I'll take the good old US of A and a ballgame on a warm summer night any time.

" 'Oh, but Hitman,' the soccer sissies will squeal, 'soccer is a game that allows every child to develop his or her coordination and learn teamwork. It's not like baseball or football where only the best kids get to play.' Oh yeah? Ever see one of those soccer dweeb coaches screaming at a six-year old on a Saturday morning? That's real healthy. For God's sake, if you're going to have your kid get browbeaten by a stranger three days a week, at least make sure he or she is learning to hit or throw a curve ball. At least there's the possibility of a pot of gold at the end of that rainbow.

"As far as developing athletic skills through soccer, all Hitman can say is that he lettered in the sport in high school. That should tell you something. Hitman was an overweight underachiever who threw like a girl. But Hitman got his letter in soccer because everybody who couldn't run fast or throw or catch went out for soccer—and made the team. It was an easy letter. The fact is, you have all the skills you need to play soccer by the time you're four years old. You can run and you can kick? You're a soccer player."

As I was reading, I realized the bar had gone silent, as though everyone was waiting for me to praise the Hitman's column. The backroom, where Jerry and Pinky Lee had been playing pool, was quiet, except for a little giggling. Hitman and the two men at the bar were just staring at me, waiting for me to say something. "I like it so far," I said. "But I haven't finished it."

I resumed reading.

"Now, soccer is king of the weenie sports, no doubt about it, but there are others in the court of weeniedom. Take women's basketball. Please. Why do they shoot like they're desperately trying to beat their brother at Horse—and failing? Why is this dreck cluttering the airwaves? I'd rather watch Australian Rules Football. But just don't make me watch women stomping up and down the court and mugging for the camera like Jordan every time they hit an uncontested layup.

"But as bad as soccer and women's basketball are, they pale in comparison with that sequined drama known as figure skating. Who the hell decided that this was sport? Now, don't get me wrong. Hitman loves seeing leggy women perform in weird positions at high speed. But normally he has to pay for that sort of thing and it's not called sports. Sure, I can hear all the women figure skating fans squealing at once: 'Oooooh, that's not fair. You have to be an athlete to be a good figure skater. These people practice for years and years.'

"Listen to me folks. Ballet requires athleticism, too, and I actually like it. But I don't have to read about it on the goddamned sports page, do I? And it's not cluttering up prime time that would be better used to broadcast a college football game or maybe an old western.

"You wanna make figure skating a sport? Put some guys on the ice whose mission is to keep these waifs from performing the Bulgarian Triple Flip or whatever they call those moves. See what happens when you put one of the guys from the Philadelphia Flyers front line on the ice with some glittering twit named Elvis. You'll see blood and broken bones. You'll see some body checking. And if you like to watch ice skaters perform whilst airborne, you ain't seen nothing until you see the goon squad launch a figure skater like a rag doll.

"I know you agree with me, fellow readers. But we are losing the battle. Every time I turn on TV there's some kind of 'rock and roll shootout on ice' figure skating show playing during prime time. Yes, we are losing the battle. Soon, figure skating and soccer will be the national sports, and women's basketball will replace men's college basketball on TV during the long winter months. Then we will be bored. We will be cold. And we will pray for our own deaths.

"So go to hell, all of you. I'm done. Hitman needs to drink about 15 beers to kill the pain of life in this miserable town."

I didn't quite know what to think. This was either brilliant prose or the rantings of an old man whose time had come and gone. I hadn't really thought much about soccer or women's basketball or figure skating. But I didn't view them as harbingers of the end of Western Civilization. Still, the bitterness and bile of his writing made the whole thing sensible to me.

"Whattya think, kid?" Hitman said. "It's the truth, ain't it? I got something there, don't I? That could go in the *Tribune* or the *Times* or even that stinking paper in Milwaukee that never responds to my job applications. Bastards. Fuck 'em all. I stayed here so the kids could have a steady life without moving around, and the first thing they did was move outta this podunk town as soon as they got old enough. Now I'm stuck writing great stuff for a crappy paper in a crappier town."

Just then, Jerry walked in, with Pinky Lee on his arm and Charlie following a respectful three paces behind. He had overheard our conversation.

"Hitman, I think I can fix this," he said.

"Fix what? "

"Your situation. Your desire to play to a bigger audience."

"How you gonna do that, pool boy?"

"The editor of the *Los Angeles Times* is one of my best friends," Jerry said. "I could make a call and get you an interview there. How'd you like to live in LA?"

"Man, I'd take a job in Hell if it meant getting out of this rathole," Hitman said. "Are you serious, or are you just yankin' my chain? Because if you're yankin' my chain, fuck you in advance."

"I am dead serious," Jerry said. "Get some of your material together and drop it off at the High Falls Plaza hotel in the morning. I'll take it to him myself."

"Sheeit, Hitman, yer gon' to LA," said Otto, who was very drunk and speaking in quick bursts to get the words out before he forgot what he was talking about. "I'm coming with."

"You got a wife and kids, dickhead," Hitman said. "You're stuck here. Just like me. This town is our prison. Lorraine gimme some poison, will you? I'm planning a jail break."

"You been drinking poison all night," she said.

"Then it's true. The Hitman is invincible. So I can live forever in this dump. How nice."

The man on the right, whose name was Philly, as it turned out, was also very drunk, and he had been bobbing his head up and down like one of those glass birds that drinks from a cup of water on top of your refrigerator.

"Hey, you OK?" Lorraine asked him. "I don't wanna be cleaning any upchuck tonight. I do not want this afternoon's lunch on this evening's floor. Am I understood?"

Too late.

A cascade of beer, dinner, lunch and breakfast erupted from his mouth onto the floor and the edge of the bar. The room gave out a collective groan.

"Jesus H, can't you hold your liquor anymore?" Otto said.

Philly looked down at his handiwork and threw up again.

"Aw, Jee-sus," Lorraine said. "Don't go looking at it, Philly. That'll just make you puke again. Otto, get him out of here."

A young couple walked in just then and quickly turned around and left. Otto didn't move to assist his drunken friend.

"Ya drunken bum, yer costing me business," Lorraine said.

"On the contrary," Hitman said. "He and I and Otto are keeping you in business. We are also keeping you company. Those two were good for two beers before they were loose enough to go to an apartment and engage in clumsy drunk sex followed by betrayal and heartbreak and perhaps even an attempted suicide by one of the parties."

No one had fed the juke box in some time, and the room had taken on the feel of a party that had been over a few hours before. Lorraine was fetching a mop and some rags, Philly had his head on the bar, Hitman was re-lighting a cigar in spite of local smoking ordinances, and Otto sat on his stool looking as though he was waiting instructions for further action. He reached over the bar and poured himself another beer from the tap, placed both forearms on the bar and sighed.

Philly had moved himself a few stools away from the stool where he had vomited and he called to Lorraine that he would help her clean up. He got off the stool and fell, taking two stools to the floor with him. Finally, Otto ran over to assist him.

"One, two, three, four, five, six, seven, eight, nine, TEN," Hitman said. "It's a knockout. Haw, haw, haw."

"That's sympathetic of you," I said archly.

"Hey, pal, there's nothing in the world funnier than watching a man's orbit decay," Hitman said. "Unless it's watching a guy fall off a bar stool. Hee hee hee ooh. That was a good one tonight, Philly."

Philly tried and failed to gurgle a response.

At this point, Jerry decided that he and Charles and Pinky Lee would retire to the hotel. Pinky Lee had both arms around Jerry's elbow like an anaconda that had gone about trying to squeeze an elephant and only got a grip on the leg. She was licking Jerry's ear. I had hoped she was going to have indiscriminate sex with me, not a rich guy who could get anyone he wanted. No dice.

"Hey, Hitman, send me some stuff," Jerry said. "I'll get you to the *Times*, just wait and see."

"Yeah, yeah, yeah, make me a big star, game show boy," Hitman said. "I'll send you my portfolio."

During this period I was looking at Pinky Lee, trying to make eye contact with her. She was just looking up at Jerry's ears with her hands cupping his shoulder until he pivoted and headed toward the door that Charles was holding open. I told them I was going to stay behind and talk to Hitman, we all said good night and off they headed toward the hotel.

It's not that I wanted to stay and talk to Hitman. I wasn't sure he was going to do anything to change my mood. I just didn't want to go to bed. I kind of liked being in bars, and this one seemed so perfectly unpretentious that I almost felt as much at home as I would on my own couch. For a moment I thought about my couch. I wondered if it missed me. I wondered if teenagers were screwing on it. That made me think I should get it cleaned when I got home. I ordered myself and Hitman another beer and we stared at the TV.

Lorraine had changed the channel until she found something tolerable. Of course it was a M*A*S*H rerun. I had nothing against M*A*S*H, but it seemed that no matter where I went, M*A*S*H was playing in reruns. I had heard that one station in Milwaukee had even played it consistently after the 10 o'clock news for 12 years. The world of classic sitcoms was so rich with material that it seemed a waste to run M*A*S*H all the time.

Otto and Philly left, Philly barely on his own steam, and Lorraine had decided to clean the whole bar, not just the area where Philly had puked, in preparation for closing. She was humming *Raindrops Keep Falling On*

My Head, which was one of the few non-country selections on the juke box. Hitman was silently puffing on his cheap cigar looking like a parody of the rough and tumble old-time sportswriter. He opened his mouth to speak, and I expected him to begin spouting off on sports again. But he didn't.

"Did you ever wonder why they didn't give Toucan Sam from that Fruit Loops cereal his own cartoon show?" he asked. "The guy was a natural talent. Kind of a James Mason sophistication about him. Maybe that was the problem. He was too classy."

"Well, I think it had something to do with congressional pressure not to let cartoon characters sell cereal to kids," I said. "Otherwise Quisp, Quake and Tony the Tiger would have had their own shows. Imagine a Cap'n Crunch show. That would have been boring."

"What the hell do you know," Hitman snapped. "You probably don't even know Cap'n Crunch from Roger Maris, ya fat moron."

"No, I don't know much about Hibbing, Minnesota-born Roger Eugene Maris other than the fact that he had a .260 lifetime average in a 12-year career with Cleveland, Kansas City, New York, and of course the tragic trade to St. Louis," I said. "Oh yes, 275 home runs, 851 RBI and 1,325 career hits. I understand he led the league in RBIs in 1960 and 1961, and I've heard he also broke Babe Ruth's single season home run record. I also have a poster of him in my bedroom. But what do I know? I'm just a fat moron, an intellectual inferior to a drunken down-and-out sportswriter in a small, dingy town."

"You got a poster of him on your wall?" he asked, as if I had just told him I had an ant farm in the living room. "What, do ya still live with yer ma? In any case, it appears you do possess human intelligence. I'm impressed. Lorraine, get this man a beer on me."

"I'll take a scotch," I said. Hey, he was buying.

"Your interest in Maris is both admirable and rare, but I was especially interested in your offhand references to breakfast cereal characters," Hitman said. "Who'd you like better, Quisp or Quake?"

"Quisp."

"A fellow Quisp man, eh? Well let me shake your hand."

"Say, since you're so interested in cereal, has it ever occurred to you how these products ever came to be in the first place?" I asked. "I've always wondered how a guy went to work in the morning and said, 'Honey, I'm going to create a cereal based on a cartoon character and children all over the world will love me.' Did they debate whether Quisp or Quake would be better names? And who came up with Count Chocula? Was that the result of a bout with marijuana and Dracula movies? Who would think a derivative vampire would be a good character to vouch for something for children to eat?"

"Ya know, kid, I feel like we have met before," Hitman said. "Let's talk about TV shows. Ya like TV?"

"I saw one once in a museum in Chicago. Does it really exist? Can a box really get pictures from the air? Tell me this miracle is so!"

"Yeah, yer a real hoot. But I'm serious. I mean, how did a guy walk into his boss's office and say, 'Boss, I got it. It's a show about a talking horse. But he's not just any talking horse. He can try out for the Dodgers and drive a laundry truck without getting into a fatal accident.' How can that guy pitch something like that and keep his job? Or his freedom for that matter?"

"Well," I said, "I'd like to meet the guy who told his boss that a family of beings that looked like Frankenstein and Dracula and a little boy who looked like the werewolf would capture the hearts of all America? And of course, there are the magic shows: 'I Dream of Jeannie' and 'Bewitched.' Then some executive at CBS came downstairs and shouted: 'They've got a genie and a witch on ABC and NBC! What have we got? What're you clown's working on?' And a quick-thinking writer shouted, 'Ah, uh, a Martian!' and the other writers breathed a sigh of relief as their jobs were saved and America was once again entertained."

"Did you ever figure out 'My Mother the Car?' "

"No."

"What about 'Chicken Man?' Wasn't that the one with Charles Nelson Reilly where he played some inept super hero? Remember? Alice Ghostly was his mother?"

"I don't recall that one real well."

"Maybe it was a fever dream," I said.

The conversation was dying out without even talking baseball. Hitman looked like he was getting sleepy, and Lorraine was nowhere to be seen, so it didn't appear we'd be drinking anything else. Hitman didn't want to go home, which was obvious by the way he nursed his beer. Maybe he was bored with his conversations with Philly and Otto and Lorraine, but he was probably afraid to break up the team and go somewhere else to talk.

"So, whattya do, kid? What brings you to this shithole?" he said.

"Well, what I do and what brings me here are two different things," I explained. "What I do is write. Poison pen letters, that is. And why I'm here is to go on a long road trip so I can go on Jerry Most's game show, 'Die Trying'—maybe you've seen it—and have a chance at ending my miserable life on national TV by being eaten by baboons. I'm having some misgivings about that last part these days, but other days I think it would be just as well to let any predatory creature gnaw my flesh. You're pretty miserable. Your life didn't turn out the way you wanted. Haven't you ever thought you'd end it all if someone would do it for you? Suicide by baboon?"

"Yeah, I hate my awful, lonely life in this dump, I really do," he said. "But holy shit man, you've got to keep up the struggle. That's what life is all about, the struggle. If we were meant to be happy all the time we'd still be in Eden. But we aren't. So we fight to be happy, and sometimes we win. And we try to fight but still be good people. And we wait for that moment where it all pays off. In my case, I've had to wait longer than I thought, but there's a reason I'm still here in High Falls instead of being in Chicago or Los Angeles. Some of it is just bad decisions on my part, or failure to recognize opportunity. But maybe it was neither. Maybe I was supposed to stay here because my life was not about becoming famous or writing for a big newspaper. Maybe some kid will be inspired to sportswriting because of the Hitman, and that's what my life is about. Maybe I'll be dead before he gets to thank me when he wins the Pulitzer. But just wondering about all this makes me keep going. You gotta keep going, too.

"Look, you religious?" He didn't wait for an answer. "Don't try to read the Big Guy's mind, kid. We don't know why we're here. We may never find out. But even if you hate it, you've got to stick around. It's all about redemption, kid. Don't you want redemption in your life?"

"Some people live for money, some people live for sex, and yes, some people live for redemption," I said. "I, on the other hand, live to watch TV. Not a noble existence, I admit, but so what if I want to end it?"

"Cause Maris fought to the end, kid, even when he got the cancer," Hitman said. "He didn't want to go."

Hitman got up and pulled a five dollar tip out of his hip pocket. "Hey, kid," he said. "If you do wind up fighting baboons or bats or whatever, I'll be rooting for you. Maybe that's your destiny, but just don't give up the fight."

"Thanks MacArthur," I said. "Or Rockne, I mean. I'll keep you in mind as I pursue that destiny. Or at least as it pursues me. But I have one question before you fade off into the inky High Falls night. What if it really was my destiny to be eaten by baboons on TV? What if there was some cosmic lesson in all that? What if I and the baboons had been born to boost the ratings of a TV show to save the job of a network executive who gave lots of money to a charity that wound up curing cancer? What if I was supposed to give myself up to cure cancer?"

"Go ta hell, ya fat mope," he said. He wadded up the five dollar bill and threw it on the bar.

Lorraine had returned from the mop closet. "Give this guy a stiff one," Hitman said. "He'll need it." Then he walked out.

"So what'll it be, money man?" she said. "Hitman's buying."

"Got battery acid?" I said.

"Just cheap gin and bad jokes," she said.

"Just give me the gin with some vermouth and present it to me in a martini glass. I thought it was a really classy move to drink a martini after having held down a scotch. "Oh, and turn up the TV," I said. "The Partridge Family" was on, and I always thought that Danny Bonaduce was a real hoot.

Lorraine made my martini in a highball glass and kept the change. She set the glass in front of me and said it was last call. Then she disappeared again into the back room while I watched TV. Lorraine had turned off all the neon signs in the window, shut down the juke box and turned off the light over the pool table. The place was as dark as my living room. During a commercial break I looked outside. No one was awake in High Falls. At least if they were they weren't walking around downtown. Of course, it didn't have to be 2 a.m. for that to be the case; it was usually deserted at midday since the mall opened up on the edge of town.

I stared out the window at a little shop called "Susan's Sew Good," a tailor. Next door was a Christian Science Reading Room. Next to that was another bar, closed too, called "Tommy's Tip Top Tap." I wondered if the people who showed up for work at places like that were happy, or they were miserable and wondering why the hell they were born. Did Susan wonder about the greater meaning of things as she hemmed up a pair of pants? Who knew? In spite of my religious conviction that God loves us all, I felt alone and depressed, a sure sign that it was closing time and the alcohol had had its effect. Time to go home. Or at least to the hotel.

I threw the martini down the hatch, set the glass on the on the bar, shouted a weak goodbye to Lorraine and walked out into the coolness of the night, the late part of the evening that Tom Waits called *The Heart of Saturday Night*. The whole city looked like the set of a "Twilight Zone" episode: empty, eerie and desolate. It was probably a nice town during the day, but right now it looked like Beirut without the charm. I entertained my deep case of melancholy as I walked slowly to the hotel, which was a few blocks away.

I had quite a little buzz going, and I had that warm glow of security that a night of responsibly drinking martinis, beer and scotch can provide. I walked down the street absently humming the theme from "Mannix" and was looking for a nice all-night greasy spoon to get a cheeseburger. I saw a building about two blocks ahead that appeared to be light enough to be a restaurant, so I headed off in that direction, switching to the theme from "Petticoat Junction" and fantasizing that Meredith MacRae was on my arm.

It certainly didn't seem like the kind of night that would end with me in a coma. But most nights that end that way come on without warning. It's always when you're feeling best that you get the news of the brain tumor, or in this case, the savage beating. The details of the event I'm about to describe are a little sketchy, of course, because I spent much of my time bleeding and getting kicked.

But as near as the police could tell, it went like this.

I was heading eastbound on University Avenue, looking for the restaurant, when three scruffy white males dressed in denim jackets and baggy pants and black T-shirts with pictures of white rap artists on them, probably between the ages of 15 and 18, appeared out of a doorway.

"Awright homo, give us alla yer money," said the largest of the herd, brandishing what appeared to be a Gary Gaetti model Little League baseball bat. They were wearing blue scarves over their heads, which gave them the appearance of a gang, or at least a club. The smallest of the group had to keep pushing his scarf up to keep it out if his eyes. The other two had terrible complexions; the one with the baseball bat had a whitehead on his nose that gave him the appearance of a young rhinoceros. It was tough to take them seriously, especially since they were carrying a Gaetti bat.

"Actually, I'm not gay, although I wouldn't be ashamed to tell you if I was," I explained. "In fact, I'd be proud. But I'm just a broke and broken and slightly drunk heterosexual. I even have a Farrah Fawcett poster on my wall at home to prove it. Not prove that I'm drunk, that is. Prove that I'm heterosexual. I view Farrah as the pinnacle of womanhood, someone your generation might equate with, say, Kathy Lee Gifford."

"Shuttup, pussy," said the middle one, trying to assert himself and impress the others with his own tough guy stylings. He kicked me in the shin. "Just give us your fucking wallet now or we'll beat the piss outta ya, aina?"

"Who's Anna?" I asked, stalling for time in the vain hope that someone would happen upon this situation and cause the young toughs to flee before things got complicated. No dice.

"Think yer funny, Fat Boy?" he responded. "Let's kick his ass."

"Let's get his wallet first," said the little one, pushing his scarf up. "I need some smokes."

"Hand it over, you tub of shit," said the kid with the bat. "I'll bust yer cranium just for the hell of it."

"Is this some gang initiation?" I asked. "I didn't know High Falls had become cosmopolitan enough for gangs. Jeez, you've got all the disadvantages of a big city and none of the advantages. Have you ever considered a move to a bigger city—say, I don't know, the Quad Cities, where the arts scene is a little better?"

The kid with the bat, whom I mentally dubbed Bat Boy, took a nice swing and hit me in the gut, knocking the wind out of me. At that point, I decided to reach into my hip pocket and pulled out my wallet. There was no use in fighting these little goons. Besides, as a matter of habit I always stick my money in a money clip in my right front pocket, not in my wallet, when I'm out for a drink.

So the only contents of my wallet were my driver's license, a few gas station credit cards, a picture of Grampa in a beekeeper's suit, and a condom that I had carried since 1976 as a symbol of my inability to get laid.

That, as it turned out, was my undoing.

The kid with the bat took the wallet and handed it to the little kid, who reported the lack of cash but said there was a rubber in the wallet. After this, my memory starts to get hazy.

"You cocksucker, you didn't carry any money?" Bat Boy said. "You are so fucking dead."

"I knew that before I met you guys," I said.

Bat Boy swung the bat and hit me in the gut again, then pulled the Three Stooges act. As I bent over, he swung up and hit me in the face, immediately bringing a shower of blood. As I swung my head back up from the impact of the blow, I fell over backward and hit the back of my head on the concrete. Then all three began kicking me and they began hooting like baboons. Oh, shit. I hadn't planned things this way, to die on a street in a dumpy little town like this. I couldn't fight back, but I refused to give in. In fact, my poison tongue instinctively joined battle.

"You little shits, there are better ways to compensate for your inability to cope with your own ridiculous and dangerously homophobic fears and the fact that your fathers have been touching you indecently since you were four years old," I groaned. "You are yokels who will never leave this miserable burg unless it's to get sex therapy in a state prison. If I were you, I'd kill myself now before life gets too hard to handle, before the alcoholism and the drug addiction and the death by drunk driving."

They were kicking me and kicking me and hooting when headlights suddenly appeared and they took off running.

"You stupid shit hicks," I screamed. "This is bullshit. You mug people in New York or Washington or Chicago. It's not part of the deal here, in Small Town America. And by the way, here's the money, you brainless little bastards."

I struggled to my knees, took out my wad of cash from my pocket and threw it in their direction.

"You're so fucking stupid you can't get a robbery straight. How does it feel to be such fuck ups? Come on. Come back and get your money. I'll just give it to you just to make you feel like total dumb shits."

Apparently I felt as though I had gotten sufficient licks in, because that is when everything went black. It turned out that while my brain was healing, things had really gotten strange.

Chapter 17
"Is This Hell?"

I slept the sleep of the damned, which is to say I was in a coma for a few days and suffering from bizarre dreams that occasionally replayed the beating and at other times led me to believe I was watching reruns of "Here Come the Brides" forever. I kept hearing the theme: "The bluest skies you've ever seen are in Seattle." I knew the melody, but those were the only words I had, and they kept ringing through my mind as the memories of the High Falls toughs kicked me again and again.

The world outside of my head was of no consequence to me, which was different from my usual life only in that I was asleep, or comatose.

During this sleep, or whatever they call it, I was also tormented by unspeakable demons who told me it was my fault the networks cancelled "Pete and Gladys" with Harry Morgan in the 1960s, and that my failure to act promptly caused Bob Crane to be mysteriously bludgeoned to death in a Phoenix hotel room. Doctors said I lay in bed moaning, "I know nothing, I see nothing" in a faux German accent—meaning, obviously, that the ghost of John Banner, best known as the beloved Sgt. Schultz in "Hogan's Heroes," was visiting my hospital room. Did he have something to do with the murder after all those years of taking crap from Hogan and the gang? It was too preposterous and frightening to consider.

But Grampa was there, too, in my dream. In fact, he was one of the first images I saw after the last few blows hit my head. We were standing in what appeared to be an urban used car lot, but the salesmen were standing on their desks in their underwear yelling, "EXTRA, EXTRA" like old-time newspaper boys and making no apparent attempt to sell any of the junkers in the lot. Gramps was wearing a tuxedo and a space helmet with a reflective shield, and even though I couldn't see his face I knew it was him. He was riding a giraffe—he finally got his giraffe. It was an image so utterly believable for my grandfather that even the memory of it makes it hard to believe

201

the vision was merely a product of my deepest unconscious thoughts. Who else could it have been?

"Grampa, it's good to see you," I said. I'm embarrassed to say that's all I could muster considering I was talking to a dead man. "So, ah, do you know where we are?"

"I can't believe I ate the whole thing," he said, his voice echoing behind the helmet.

"What thing?"

"Ring around the collar," he screeched as the giraffe reared back and whinnied like a horse.

"Grampa?"

"Those dirty rings. You try soaking them out and scrubbing them out, but you still get ring around the collar."

"Am I to take it you will only be responding in commercial scripts?"

"Parkay."

I took that to be a yes. It was entertaining, even if it wasn't all that informative, and I continued trying to talk to him to get some idea of what was going on. I didn't know if I was alive or dead or dreaming or awake.

"Grampa, can you tell me anything about where we are? Are we in heaven? Are we in hell?"

"Certs with retsyn is two, two, two mints in one."

"I'm addicted to retsyn, you know. It's why my breath was always so fresh. I didn't tell you because I didn't want to worry you. But now that you're dead I guess it doesn't matter."

"Plop, plop fizz, fizz, oh what a relief it is."

He made a motion with his arm, as if I should follow him somewhere. But whether it was a dream or real life, I was not going to follow a man in a space helmet riding a giraffe even if he was my grandfather. It was just one of those things I didn't have to be taught in school. It was instinct.

"Grampa, I don't think so," I said. "You haven't been gone long enough for me to miss you, but I know I will. But I'm not coming with you. I've felt dead for a long time, but I'm not sure I'm ready for the real thing. I get the feeling that if I go where you go, I'll be dead. And then what?"

"*Me vidi malgrandon birdon*," he said.

Instinctively I thought understood his dialect of Esperanto. I think he was saying, "I saw a little bird."

202

Grampa then stuck out his tongue, which stretched like a thick rubber band, and licked the inside of his helmet, leaving a gooey smear on the face shield that obscured his crazy grin. It was a nauseating sight, but at some level it made me happy because I knew Grampa was in that special place where he could continue his work as a behavioral freak of nature for all eternity. Seeing him with a giraffe and a space helmet made me wistful, but I realized he had access to the biggest toy box in the universe and he intended to make the best of it. I wish I had asked him if they had TV; it might have made my decision to follow him a little easier.

Anyway, I was comforted by this notion, even as the giraffe grew wings and flew away and I knew I would never see him again. Grampa shrieked: "Madge! I'm soaking in Palmolive?!" and the giraffe rose into the green sky and lighted on a nearby Fotomat hut, then flew back over me with Grampa howling, "At Ford, we've got a better idea!" As the flying giraffe passed overhead, Grampa dropped something that floated down like a leaf dropping from a tree. He and his mount were out of sight when I picked it up off of the hood of a green '75 Pinto with plaid interior.

It was a photograph of a baboon. Just the face of the baboon, not the whole body, but the animal was baring its teeth, four-inch fangs, really, in a dominance display. What was unnerving was not the size of the ape's incisors, but the fact that he was wearing a little gold crown, a crown bejeweled with what appeared to be bits of fecal matter. I figured that Grampa had decorated the crown, and I remembered his warning to the people he greeted at Kmart when he wore the turban: "Don't look at the jewel! It will hypnotize you." It must have been his old friend, the King of Baboons, and he was not engaging in a display of dominance, he was laughing a big baboon laugh, apparently at me.

I don't believe in dream interpretation, especially when the dreams are generated by some severe blows to the head. But I thought that even in the surreal sleep I was in, Grampa was able to speak to me from beyond the grave, and he gave me an important message. The problem was, I couldn't for the life of me decipher the message, except that I shouldn't stare at the balls of shit on the crown of a laughing baboon if I didn't want to be hypnotized. I'm afraid I was far too literal to understand whether this was a warning or just a sound piece of advice from beyond the grave. So if the dream or hallucination or vision or whatever it was was meant to be a message to me, I didn't receive it. I guess Grampa had wasted the trip down here to appear in my dream.

I don't remember much else about the comatose times, except that at one point I dreamed that my right hand had turned into a TV remote and all I had to do to change the channel or turn up the volume was give it a little twist. The bad news was, in my dreams the only thing on every channel was shows about the diets of North American shore birds.

Otherwise, the whole thing was like a long, dark nap. Every once in a while I'd hear echoing voices like the ones you hear on soap operas. They would call my name, and they would tell me to wake up, but no dice. Once, I swear I even felt someone sticking my hand in warm water, and another time someone with cold, hairy hands was in my personal "red zone" as they say in football. But I was too knocked out to enjoy it or not enjoy it, depending on whom the hands belonged to.

Later, when I had recovered somewhat, the doctors told me I had been out for about a week. They said that while they knew I would eventually come out of the coma, they weren't sure what kind of brain damage I had suffered. Knowing that gave me a lot of entertainment until I was finally released from the hospital. As long as they didn't know whether or not I was brain damaged, I had a nice little control device at my disposal. When things got boring, I'd just start shrieking and clawing at the air, screaming, "Get them out of here, aaahhh, they're on me, they're on me, get 'em off, get 'em off," and then they would give me some interesting form of sedation that made staring at "Golden Girls" a lot more fun.

But I haven't mentioned the surreal sight I witnessed when I came out of the coma.

Everything I described up until now seemed as normal as a Saturday afternoon cutting the lawn by comparison.

As I heard my name being called and I actually managed to open my eyes, I saw two people dressed in blinding white suits. Angels in leisure suits! No dice. It was two people I had gotten to know pretty well in the last few weeks: It was Jerry and Pinky Lee. I saw them leaning over my face, visions of white, and I said: "Oh shit! I've died and gone to hell! Oh, man, this is not fair. I went to confession. I stayed on the couch all day. I didn't hurt anyone. Oh, Lord, give me another chance."

Jerry wiped my brow with a silk handkerchief and Pinky Lee patted me in my special place knowing that a semi-comatose guy wouldn't be much trouble. Even though I was near death she insisted on taunting me.

"Whoa, pal, you're not in hell, you're still here on Earth," Jerry said.

"Same thing," I said.

"Well, I see you've got your sense of humor back already," he said, grinning. "You had us worried for a while. We couldn't let you get attacked on my show if you were already dead or even just comatose. I'm told baboons don't like carrion. They like the hunt. Of course I'm no baboon expert."

"Thanks for your concern," I said, suddenly remembering my mission. "How long have I been here, and how long have you been here, and why aren't you making your game show? Where is the TV remote and can I get a beer in here?"

Pinky Lee went over to a chair in a corner of my room and opened up a black gym bag that was sitting there. She pulled out a sixer of Milwaukee's Best, and I wanted to marry her immediately.

"It's kinda warm, but I was saving it for when you woke up," she said. "You like this stuff, right?"

"Sweetie, I'm so desperate for a beer right now I'd drink a Coors," I said. "Well, OK, nobody's that desperate. But yes, this is one of my brands. Thanks."

"Yer welcome," she said. "Welcome back to the real world."

"I never thought I would hear those words uttered from a woman wearing a white leisure suit with a matching halter top," I said. "But then again, I don't get out much. Now, would someone explain to me our current circumstances? Give it to me slow, I've been out of town for a while."

Just then a nurse entered the room. She was tall, dark-haired with big brown eyes and long, long skinny legs. She was also very angry.

"Who gave this man beer?" she demanded. "He has just gotten out of a coma and the last thing he needs is alcohol. Why didn't anyone even bother to tell me he had awakened? I've got to explain all of this on my shift report. Oh, where's the doctor? I'd better tell him what's happened."

She reached over to take the beer from my hand.

"You'll take my beer when you pry it from my cold, dead fingers," I said.

"That can be arranged," she said.

Jerry, ever the would-be diplomat, walked over and put his hand on her shoulder.

"Ma'am, I'm Jerry Most, the famous but soon-to-be-former host of 'Die Trying,'" he said. "I can assure you we have been taking good care of him in your absence. As for the beer, I apologize. We simply missed our friend and we were eager to celebrate his return to the realm of the living."

She stood there staring at him, giving him the "ohmigod it's a TV star" look, but she said nothing. Jerry reached into his pocket and pulled out a wad of cash.

"Here you go, Clara Barton, a little something for the ward Christmas party," he said, tucking in her hand. "Everything's fine, because Jerry Most is here. Now, run along so we can tell our friend some exciting news."

She drifted out of the room, never taking her eyes off Jerry. It was hard to believe that Jerry had been hanging around the hospital without her ever knowing or noticing until now. Maybe she had seen him but simply couldn't bring herself to believe that a celebrity had virtually taken up residence in her ward. In any event, it didn't appear she would be any further trouble.

Meanwhile, something Jerry said was still hanging in the air. The "famous soon-to-be-former host of 'Die Trying.'" What the hell was that supposed to mean?

The two of them just stood there looking at me and smiling this eerie, unnerving gaze, like some cult members who became amused when you decide to debate them on their beliefs.

"What?" I said.

"We're so happy," said Pinky Lee.

"Oh, for God's sake, you're getting married," I said. Visions of smoke stacks crumbling and rockets crashing to the ground crowded my head.

"No, we're not getting married, partner," Jerry said. "We are married. Sorry we couldn't invite you to the ceremony, but you were nursing a pretty nasty head wound. We brought some champagne to celebrate. Dom Perignon. Want some?"

"What the hell? I've only been in a coma for seven days," I said. "But then again, I'm not sure this isn't some kind of brain-injury related dream. You two got married?"

"But that's not the good news," Pinky Lee said, flashing a diamond the size of a beer bottle cap. "The good news is our new life after the show ends."

"You've decided to become lion tamers?" I said.

"It's a new show," Jerry said, beaming. "We've found religion since we've found each other. I never cared about another person before—that is until I met this beautiful creature. She brought me closer to God, and that's where I came up with the idea for the new show."

"Don't tell me, it's a cooking show, right?"

"No, goofball," Jerry said. "Honey, tell him."

"It's gonna be called 'Try Living,'" she said. "Get it? Jerry's going from 'Die Trying' to 'Try Living.' Ain't that a great idea?"

"You know, I can't tell you the number of times I've turned on TV and said to myself, 'Sports and entertainment is fine, but what we really need is a religious show with no theology or doctrine hosted by people who have never opened a Bible in their lives,'" I said. "Congratulations! You're filling a real need on TV."

"Thanks, pal," Jerry said. "I knew you'd approve."

I swear, my biting sarcasm is wasted on most people in this world.

"So what about your old show?" I said to Jerry. "Am I still going to be on it? Or will I be your first guest on the new show. Now that I think about it, that's not a bad idea, having a guy get torn apart on a religious show. Maybe instead of having baboons eat me, you could have a mob stone me for heresy."

"No way, friend," Jerry said. "'Try Living' is going to have songs and stories and Bible readings and prayers. It's going to lift everyone's spirit and make them try living a new life with God. It's not going to be one of those shows where we condemn people for sinning. That demo is already watching other shows. We're going to have a whole new untapped audience of happy religious people who don't want to worry about hell and the consequences of sin. It's going to be a feel-good show. No one's going to be stoned on our show. That is, unless we need to spike the ratings. Haw, haw, haw."

"But don't you have a contract for the highly rated old show?" I asked. "Doesn't the network still want to see people try to cheat death and fail?"

"Sure I do," he said. "That's where you come in. Up until now, no one's been seriously hurt on the show. But if you go on and get attacked, God forbid, even killed, well, you can bet that's a one-way ticket to cancellation.

Legal will insist on it if the network insurance companies don't. That way, I get out of the contract, and, after an appropriate time of public soul searching and mourning, I'll do some TV talk shows, and then I'll announce the new show. By the way, the first show will be dedicated to your memory or your recovery, depending on how good a job the monkeys do. Man, Pinky Lee and I will be on the front cover of *People* magazine so fast those network PR people won't even have time to burn out a press release."

"So in other words, I get killed by baboons—not monkeys, by the way— to help you get out of a contract and start a religious show."

"The plot has some interesting symbolism, doesn't it?"

I closed my eyes. I began wishing I hadn't come out of the coma. Having been unconscious and apparently near death for as long as I had gave me a new sense of life. Not in the sense that Jerry's stupid happy chat religious show would, but just in the sense that, hey, you get one life, so don't short-change yourself needlessly by taking stupid chances. Like, say, tangling with a baboon troop.

On the other hand, I had made so little use of the life I had that at this point I thought I might just as well take my chances on Jerry's show. If I could survive a battle with baboons, I might gain the kind of celebrity that leads to big screen TVs and getting laid.

"So I take it we're going to Africa," I said, just trying to keep the conversation going.

"Naw, we can't do that," Jerry said. "It's not in the budget. The network wouldn't go for sending an entire crew to Africa."

"So where else so we find a bunch of baboons with taste for human flesh to attack me for the sake of your ratings?" I said. "I don't think they allow that sort of thing at the downtown Y anymore."

"You'll never believe where we've scouted out a place," he said. "Remember the clearing in the woods near Hammertown?"

"I've been there many times, but ..."

"That's the place, my friend. You're going home to meet your fate," he said. "Isn't it great? Isn't it ironic? We're bringing baboons to the wilds of Wisconsin, and you're going home to meet them. It's all been cleared with local and state officials. Remember, I have staff to take care if that sort of thing. The battle will take place in the woods. Your woods. You'll be on your home turf. Whattya say, partner?"

If I didn't exactly feel like my life was worth living, I just wasn't sure I felt like dying. So I said: "Yeah, sure, why not? At least I'll have home field advantage against those glorified chimps. Baboons, I mean."

"I am so proud of you, baby," said Pinky Lee.

"I'll bet you are," I said. "But next time I pick up a hitchhiker, I'm kind of hoping she's a little more normal than you. A crack addict, maybe."

"Hey, watch it, fella, "Jerry said with mock seriousness, "you're talking about my bride."

It took all the strength I could muster, but that statement hit me like a finger down the throat the morning after a bender.

I felt it coming on suddenly, but I sneezed blood all over Jerry's white suit. I guess I wasn't quite healed yet.

Chapter 18
Escape From the Planet of the Baboons

After my release from the hospital, the road trip had pretty much ended. Instead of going to LA via America, I went back to Hammertown to meet Jerry, Pinky Lee, Charles, the "Die Trying" crew, and my fate. I arrived by helicopter and landed on the front lawn of City Hall before a group of gawking Hammertownians I had never met before and whose acquaintance I did not care to make now.

I was whisked into a limousine, where the mayor told me I would be the guest of honor in a parade.

"It ain't the Fourth of July yet, but it ain't every day one of ours gets to go on TV and battle gorillas," he said.

"Baboons," I said.

"What'd you call me?"

"Just joking, your worship."

So there I was, back in my own hometown, a place I had never really hoped to see again, it having been a bad enough place to have been born in the first place, and this would be the place where I was to die, or at least die trying, or even try dying. Whatever.

It was at least a glorious return; I was in a limousine convertible at the back of a parade with "Miss Hammertown," a 17-year-old named Heather Emily Hornsby with aspirations to someday become "Alice in Dairyland," an honor bestowed to the few women who could adequately represent the state's proud dairy industry. The mayor sat in the front seat, and Charles was handling the driving duties. It was good to see old Charles again, and for him this was something of a triumphant return.

This remarkable parade in my honor included both high school marching bands from Hammertown and Little Rose. Since there were no songs appropriate to the baboon, the bands played animal theme songs like *Crazy Elephant Walk, Pop Goes the Weasel, Hold That Tiger* and, for some reason, Black Sabbath's *Ironman*.

Most of the baboons were being kept in the woods in an undisclosed location that every high school kid in town knew about. But for purposes of the parade and for promoting the big event, someone put two of the creatures in a little cage pulled by a sad-faced clown on a bicycle. They sat inside their tiny enclosure staring in bored and abject helplessness.

As for the show and the use to which the baboons would eventually be put for my benefit, the "Die Trying" producers had gotten their hands on two dozen baboons and sent them off to a special area of the woods to hang out until showtime. Armed guards formed a perimeter around the baboon territory to prevent the sharp-toothed primates from wandering into town and, say, harassing mourners at the Homer Funeral Home and Tanning Salon.

While they seemed content to have the guards throw their food into the middle of the clearing, they did get bored, and that occasionally sent them into a frenzy. You could hear them howling and hooting everywhere. Baboons communicate through their howling, and different howls indicate different messages. In this case, I guessed that the howls meant: "Please don't let them make us wear pointy spangled hats and ride unicycles in a roadside circus." After a while the constant woofing and hooting and howling was worse than the constant November to February whine of snowmobiles. Or the equally oppressive March to October roar of riding lawnmower engines.

But the hooting usually stopped after the report of a rifle shot. No one in Hammertown had ever heard anything like the howls of hungry, irritable baboons. Hammertown was, after all, part of the far North American climate, an area unlikely to house a habitat for wild apes of any kind, let alone those with four-inch fangs. So gun owners were naturally attracted to the baboon compound.

Once in a while, a local hunter would sneak through the perimeter, either through their knowledge of the woods or by bribing a guard, and take a few pot shots at one or two of the hairy killers. In the Hammertown metropolitan area, it is tradition that any sign of fur or horns seen in the wild means you point and shoot. Normally, this also means some furry creature would receive a bullet through the skull. And the idea of something in the woods with four-inch fangs, something so close to The Missing Link as to be close kin to some gun owners, drove the hunters nuts. A dead baboon would mean an exotic trophy of the kind that would be irresistible to even the most inhibited and responsible of the gun-wielding half-wits who infest North Woods towns.

So the sound of gunfire and the subsequent baboon casualties reached a half-dozen until the "Die Trying" security staff took further precautions to save what was left of the troop. First, they herded them into a tight circle in the clearing. In fact, it was the very clearing where Billie the Kangaroo was buried. Then they surrounded the area with extra guards and trip wires designed to alert the baboon security team to any intruders entering the area or any baboons leaving. They also brought guard dogs, which added to the general clamber as dogs and baboons traded threats.

Meanwhile, the parade, which was led by the very cop who arrested me in the very car that Jerry threw up in—now presumably cleaned—consisted of the high schools' bands, the clown-drawn baboon trailer, our limousine, one containing Jerry and Pinky Lee, a camera crew, a few press cars, and three show horses with panels advertising "Dealin' Dick's Pre-Owned Cars." It drew as big a crowd as any event could in Hammertown. Many of the crowd was non-native species, people who had rolled into town in anticipation of my bloody demise. The locals were at work, for the most part, and management at The Chips wasn't giving off days for parades. As a small town, it was difficult to draw hordes, or even dozens, of onlookers. The fact that the event was hastily organized didn't help.

But a parade it was, and it was for me, so I waved to everyone as though I was the president. I wished I had a top hat and a cigarette holder. Better yet, I wished I had a beer. I made pig noses at children, and I whinnied like a horse at the old women. I drew an eyeball on my palm for use when waving. It was my little tribute to Grampa, who would have loved all of this.

As we passed a group of high school kids playing what we used to call hooky, one of them threw a banana at the car, hitting Miss Hammertown and tilting her crown to an awkward angle. She remained poised and continued smiling while she adjusted the crown and the mayor screamed curses at the perpetrator.

It was a nice parade.

It ended in the parking lot of Booby's Booze Ranch, which was now completely free of banana peels and remains of other tropical and domestic fruits. There, Booby greeted me with a 40-ounce bottle of Miller High Life and a big smile.

"Hey kid, yer puttin' this town on da map," he said. "I got people comin' in from all over wantin' to buy some alcohol for when you go on TV and get et. Man, yer good for business. Anytime you want to get eaten by chimps, you let me know."

"Baboons."

"Hey, I don't care if it's squirrels. I say we have somebody eaten every week out der in da woods."

"Look, I have always been willing to give my life for business and higher profits, so I'm so pleased to hear my situation might benefit you," I said. "I just hope I get free products until I meet my dreadful fate."

"Nuthin's free, pally," Booby said. "But I'll give you a substantial discount. How's zat sound?"

"Your sentimentality makes me weep," I said. "I'll be needing more than this bottle to get me through tonight. I've got a lot to do before I go on national television with the 'F Troop.'"

"Ah, hell, go on and take a case a beer," he said. "Just don't go tellin' anyone Booby's giving away free booze."

Just then a few high school girls walked up to me tentatively with little pads of paper. They had been watching me and Booby, but they refused to say anything. Finally, I looked at them and said: "Boo."

They giggled nervously.

"Are you the monkey man?" the taller of the two asked.

"Some say we are all descended of the apes, dear girl, but I am probably more man than ape, although I have a great deal of hair on my back," I replied. "Still, how far are any of us from our vestigial savage selves? Right now, for example, I'd like to bite you in your pretty little neck. But society forbids such action. So what can I do for you, besides bite you, that is?"

"Can we, can we ..." she said.

"Can you buy me a drink? That depends on your age, which I'm guessing falls short of the minimum, although no judge would convict me if I went ahead anyway and claimed ignorance," I said. "May I complete another sentence for you?"

"Look Fat Boy, we just want your autograph," said the shorter and obviously more pugnacious one. "We just never met a celebrity before. We don't care much about your battle with the monkeys."

"Baboons."

They held out their little pads and I signed the tall one's "Roger Maris" and the shorter one's "John Wayne Gacy." How would they know? It's not as though they were going to look up the names in the phone book. Or a history book.

I stood milling about the parking lot not knowing quite what to do. Going home seemed to make a lot of sense, since I lived there. But the network insisted that I stay in a Holiday Inn Holidome in Little Rose. They wanted what might be my last night to be as luxurious as possible, and I expected that TV camera would be following me around watching my every move right up until the time the show started.

One of the camera men got a little too close to me as I finished talking with the girls, and nearly smacked me in the head with the camera lens. I protested that he was getting too close, but he just said: "Contract says you gotta let us do what we gotta do, and this is what we gotta do, so shut up and take the money, Fat Boy."

Fat Boy. There it was again. If I survived the baboon attack I was determined to go on a diet. A cheese sticks and beer diet. Then I'd grow a beard, but I wouldn't trim it, and I'd let my fingernails get to be about six inches long and tell everyone I was Howard Hughes. Well, this is what Grampa would have done, anyway. That's what made him remarkable. Me, I'm unremarkable. I'll just run into some apes, put up some kind of a fight, survive, and go back to my couch and be home in time to watch the "Hillbillies."

Still, this cameraman's attitude irritated me. So as he was shooting me as I walked toward Jerry, I suddenly turned around and whipped out my male member. Then I chased him as I tried to piss on his shoes.

"Hey, whoa, pal, you can't do that sort of thing anymore," Jerry said. "You're a celebrity. People are going to expect a different kind of behavior out of you. The want to look up to you."

"If people want to look up to me, then the world is in a lot of trouble," I said. Once again, I thought of Grampa. What would he have done to tell the world to piss off? Sure, I'll go on their show and fight the apes, I thought, but

I didn't think I had to give in to the idea of celebrity along the way. I wanted to remain the same anonymous figure I had always been.

Grampa, I thought, just give me a little of your sense of "screw you," and I can live through this whole thing. I closed my eyes for a moment, and I saw Grampa talking to me as a 15-year-old. We were in his garage, and he was pounding nails into a six-foot-high series of two-by-fours that were connected to form something like Stonehenge.

"Always remember, boy, as long as they think you're nuts, no one will touch you. How many lunatics get mugged every day? None. Because lunacy is scary to the so-called sane people. Behave poorly and they will assume you are nuts. Once they assume you are nuts, they will leave you alone. If you're ever attacked, shit yourself and say you're from Neptune. Your attackers will hurry off."

I guess I should have thought of that back in High Falls when the young toughs clobbered me.

Having told me about the advantages of acting unbalanced, Grampa had moved his sculpture out to the front yard. In front of it he placed a hand-painted sign identifying his creation as the "Hardonatron." The sign said that the device was guaranteed to maintain the male erection for three weeks simply by rubbing against it.

"They think I think this is a Hardonatron, even though scientists have worked for years to create such a device and failed," he had said, pointing to some bemused neighbors. "But I am going to put it here in the front lawn and be guaranteed that no one will ever bother to break into my house. The criminal element knows that people who put weird Hardonatron devices on their front lawn do not have anything worth stealing."

The same goes for people who place electric water fountains in their driveway, or who place hotel key cabinets on their front lawn, items that all found their way into or onto Grampa's yard, which was also my yard, at one point or another in his continuing quest to be left alone by attracting attention to himself.

When any of my friends asked about Grampa, I simply said, well, you know, he was a decorated veteran, I think the war took a lot out of him, at least that's what my mom always said.

But after all these years of thinking Grampa as a nude sunbathing nuisance, it turned out he had the right idea. He didn't like people anymore than I did, and in the end he was probably irritated that he spent any time trying to save them or their country. He would have done well in a cave or in the desert. And now I decided to take a few notes from his book. I should have done it long ago.

Thinking of all these things, I let my pants drop all the way to my ankles, then I stepped out of them.

"Hey, what the hell are you doing?" Jerry said. "There are people all over the place. The cameras are rolling. You want them to think you're nuts?"

"My ass needs air," I said.

"Your ass, my ass," he said. "Don't pull this on me. I've got a lot tied up in you."

"Where's Pinky Lee?" I asked. "I wanted her to see my ass before it gets eaten by monkeys."

"All she's going to see right now is your ass with my foot in it," he said.

It was a side of Jerry I hadn't seen before, and I knew my behavior was beginning to work. "Jerry, Grampa knew the King of Baboons, do you?" I asked. "I want to have an audience with him."

"Shut up and get in the limo. We're taking you to the Holidome in Little Rose," Jerry said.

Oh, that'll help. Get me to the Holidome.

While I was exposing my posterior to the greater world, one set of eyes took me right back to high school and the beginning of this nightmare that was my life. I saw a vaguely familiar woman. But it wasn't Pinky Lee.

It was Carol Anne Doerfler. Herself!

It had been so long without any contact between the two of us that I thought she might be dead. She looked as beautiful as the fantasies I had created during our long separation.

I was shocked. I was embarrassed. I was still in love. Damn.

"What are you doing?" she said, ignoring the obvious.

Well, in love though I might still be, I was also quite bitter. She had ruined my concept of love and togetherness and made me the man I was. She had an out-sized role in my life, and seeing her brought forth a torrent of conflicting emotions. I had always thought that maybe one day we'd be together, but I new it was adolescent fantasy.

Still.

Here I was, a famous guy who could have gotten any girl I wanted due to my newfound celebrity. And there was the object of my desire. Carol Anne Doerfler in the flesh! It might have been a good time to pull up my pants, walk over to her, embrace her and ask how she was.

But I didn't answer her.

I simply waved my ass in her general direction, bowed and walked away. I got in the car.

Fuck her.

But afterward I was torn. All these years of wanting to see her, to be with her, to hold her, blew up in my face. I needed to distract myself from what just happened, so I began a conversation with Jerry.

"Say, Jerry, did you ever notice that no matter how you say it, the word 'prong' sounds dirty?" I said, looking straight into the camera. "For example, Jerry, why don't you hand me the prong? Does your hardware store have any prongs? Prong. There are other words that sound dirty, too. Just tell some junior high kid that you'd like him to get a ream of paper from the supply closet. Ream. I could go on and on."

All of this was being recorded for posterity by the same cameraman whose shoes I had attempted to piss on earlier. I called him close to me, claiming to want a close-up. When he was about six inches from my face, I blew the contents of my nose onto his lens.

"You crazy asshole!" he said, but before he could come after me Jerry yelled to Charles to drive me to the Holidome. Charles sped away, and as he did, he gave me a strange look.

"I know whatcher doing," he said. "Yer tryin' to get out of yer date with the baboons cuz you don't wanna die."

"Charles, you may or may not be right about that," I said. "But I'd really like to stop off at my house before I go to the Holidome. I want to get some stuff out of there."

"I s'pose," he said. "I'll just consider it yer last request."

"Charles," I said, pulling up my pants, "you are a beautiful man, and I love you very much. I mean that. Could I kiss you?"

"Only if you would like to wind up in a ditch," he said.

"OK, never mind. Screw the Holidome. Just take me home, big guy."

And so he did.

Chapter 19
Home Sweet Love Nest

As Charles pulled into the driveway, I could see that I was not wrong in my prediction that the kids would discover the place empty and use it for humping, bong hits, shotgunning beer and whatever else they pleased. In fact, as I entered my home it appeared from some of the materials on the kitchen table, it seemed that at least one of the more enterprising youths had been operating a crude palm reading and Tarot card operation using their own home-made cards. I picked one card up off the floor that had a skull and crossbones on it and the inscription: "You're screwed."

We would soon see.

Charles was still waiting in the car, and I poked my head out the front door and asked him to contact Jerry to see if I could take care of a few matters at home before I reported to the Holidome. He nodded and got on his phone, had a brief conversation, and came back to the front door.

"I'll be back in about an hour and a half," he said. "I'm going to run a few errands myself. Jeez, it smells like something died in there."

"It's just my rotten soul. Don't worry," I said.

I thanked him and he left. Then I took a quick inventory of the place, and while it appeared that nothing was stolen, it did appear that some interesting activities had been taking place in my absence. Banana peels were everywhere, and it looked like some of the smokers had been putting out their cigarette butts on my walls. On one wall of the dining room, someone had burned the words "Luv Docter" and made a haphazard attempt at engraving a heart.

From the stack of condoms on the floor beneath it appeared that some of the young lovers in the crowd had tried to stick their used condoms inside the heart using the natural adhesive.

Wrappers from fast food places littered the living room carpet as well as boxes from Leonid's Excellent Good Pizza. The requisite beer can pyramid had fallen, leaving a three-feet deep pile of Miller Lites and Old Milwaukees in front of my fireplace, which itself was stuffed with underwear that they had attempted to burn to make the place more romantic. Someone had also adopted the quaint habit of partiers from generations ago when he or she apparently wore a lampshade as a hat, then stepped on it when it fell to the floor. Someone had plugged the drain and urinated in my bathroom sink.

Based on all that I had seen, I did not want to go upstairs and check on my bedroom, and I assumed the bed hadn't been thrown out the window because I hadn't spotted it out on the lawn. But I had to pick up to my computer and write one more poison pen letter. I walked upstairs, past the bras and panties and a large raccoon suit that was lying on the landing. It looked like one of Grampa's, but someone had ripped the ass end out. I did not want to know why.

My room smelled awful, a nauseating combination of bleach and sweat and beer and dirty sheets. But both Roger and Farrah appeared intact, with the exception that some philistine had written "nice nips" on my Farrah poster and highlighted her protruding breasts with a felt-tipped pen.

My computer, thankfully, was largely untouched, probably because it was so old I used it only as a word processor, not a gamebox.

I could have—should have—been angry about this violation of my home. But anger requires work, and often leads to revenge, which means more work, and in the end, I just didn't see how getting upset was going to fix anything. And what had I expected when I left the door unlocked?

But I had begun to consider my situation, and I determined that whether or not I survived a baboon attack, I needed to get a few last words in. A last poison pen letter, one last chance to tell friends and enemies and acquaintances and people I would never meet just how I felt about a world I had more or less resigned from years ago. I knew I only had an hour or so before Charles returned, so I didn't spend much time tidying the room. I sat down, and I began writing what could only have appeared to be a suicide note to anyone who wasn't aware of the circumstances under which I was writing.

To read it now will give you a very good idea of my frame of mind before and immediately after I picked up a hitchhiker on the way to the beer depot.

Since the letter was aimed at the entire world, or at least American culture, I didn't know to whom I should address it. The United Nations

General Secretary? The President of the United States? The Speaker of the House? God? No, you don't write poison pen letters to God. I settled on the presidents of all three networks, with a copy going to the presidents of the "major cable" networks.

I wrote my "last" poison pen letter with the provision that it had to be read by Jerry Most on "Die Trying" after my contest with the baboons, whether or not I survived.

"Dear Sirs, Madams and Undecideds:

"As I write this, a group of bloodthirsty mammals are grooming each other, picking fleas and nits from each other's coats, so that they can look their baboony best when they try to rip my throat out on national television so that an entire generation will have one of those cultural touchstones every generation must have in order to identify itself and distinguish itself from generations past.

"When I was young, one of the culturally defining moments was the Beatles' appearance on The Ed Sullivan Show. *For me, another moment was seeing a post-Star Trek William Shatner shilling for Promise Margarine. It was then that I knew nothing was sacred in this world. Captain Kirk battles Klingons, he doesn't offer them a butter substitute to the masses. But what do you care? You make money by creating memories and then smashing them. The margarine shilling transformed into something worse: T.J. Hooker. How could he live with himself? How can anyone live with themselves in this consumer-driven 'I got mine, fuck you' kind of society?*

"How can I even ask the question? You live with yourselves the same way the rest of this rotten world lives with itself. You're just a reflection of a society so sick it thinks it's normal. Society doesn't want Chris Elliott's brilliant 'Get a Life' TV show because its humor is a little too absurd, so you cancel it, but then 'Married With Children' celebrates its 200th show. And it's all because it's about giving 'em what they want, car chases as drama and lame insults as humor.

"But you don't stop there. You steal our past by using the music of our youth to sell sport utility vehicles and adult diapers. OK, maybe they haven't used pop songs to sell adult diapers, but it's only a matter of time before Carly Simon's Anticipation falls to ad reps selling Pampers for Men, or maybe Ex-Lax. It had already been used to pitch ketchup years ago, but the statute of limitations has worn out on that one. Time to drag it out again.

"And the public, the mass lumpen proletariat, lets these vulpine copywriters force them to associate drain cleaners with songs they grew up with because they,

too, would sell their memories and their souls for the chance to make money so they can buy a new microwave oven and lawn furniture for the vacation cabin in the wilderness, which itself is just down the road from the waterslide theme park.

"We are a nation of vulgarians, and no one cares. In fact, we revel in it. No one cares about their neighbors, their community or the government. They just want their fair share and something to watch on TV to keep them from thinking about how miserable and meaningless their existences have really become. They want TV programs like 'Wheel of Fortune' that don't challenge you too much, and they want radio stations that play Eagles and Supertramp six-packs."

"And so I will entertain you tomorrow night on prime time national television. I will do battle with baboons for your entertainment, and if you're lucky, they'll kill me and you'll be able to talk about it for a few days.

"But just know this. Even as I'm being eaten, I am mocking you. I stopped living years ago. I stopped caring about anything other than reruns on TV when I realized that no matter how hard you worked, no matter how hard you tried, in the end it was dog eat dog, me versus you, each of us against the rest of the world. And we're all losing. The difference is I know it. You don't, because you've chosen to allow entertainment and material gain to be your Everest; you want merchandise because it is there.

"So as I fight off primates, just know that I'm laughing. Because my point about this culture has been proven. I'm proof of how low we're willing to go. And a smiling nitwit named Jerry Most will give you the play-by-play, complete with snide comments about my weight and complexion. Here's a hint about his opening line: he'll openly speculate that my fat meat will give the baboons heart attacks.

"Enjoy the show, and enjoy your life ... or die trying."

I was missing something. I needed to add something. A post script. So I did.

"P.S. Just so you know, I knew all along baboons were unlikely to attack a human. They prefer grubs and small mammals. Their four-inch fangs could indeed tear apart an unsuspecting leopard, but that would only be in defense. Since I know this was going to be read by Jerry after my baboon battle, I hope you all feel good about yourselves and your viewing habits."

Oh, and this: "P.P.S. Hey Jerry, I'll bet this kills the evangelism show, huh? You might want to look into a career in computer programming or electronics repair."

I couldn't wait to hear Jerry read that last line on camera in his flashy white suit.

My work here was done. I printed out the letter, sealed an envelope using water from the filthy toilet, I don't know, for extra effect. I walked out of my room, but walked back in to salute Roger and wink at Farrah. One way or the other, I wasn't sure I would ever be back.

As I walked down the stairs, I tripped on the raccoon costume and smacked my head against the wall. I instinctively added two and two, came up with four and realized there was no brain damage this time. There was, however, a nice raspberry on the back of my head that would look great on a big-screen TV.

I went to the front door, saw that Charles had not yet arrived, then checked the clock and realized I had a half-hour to kill. Perfect. There had to be a decent rerun on cable. And there was. I opened a warm can of beer that had been left on an end table, and settled back to watch "Adam 12."

But just as the dispatcher was saying, "One Adam 12, One Adam 12, see the man about a robbery," I heard someone walking up to the screen door. Now what? Can't a man spend his last moments at home in peace?

Not when he picks up hitchhikers named Pinky Lee. And here she was. She was tapping lightly on the frame of the screen door.

"You home? Can I come in?" she said.

"Well, it seems everyone else has, I suppose there's no reason to keep you out," I said. "Want a can of beer? They're warm, and some have been opened and have cigarette butts in them, but I don't suppose you're the type that's picky. Just pick one up off the floor."

"Don't be a dickhead," she said.

"Boy, this is going to be like dialog from Casablanca," I said. "Don't worry, we'll always have Hammertown."

"Look, I wanted to explain."

"Explain what? Quantum mechanics? Why Samantha the witch can't remove another witch's curse? The popularity of pro wrestling? I want to learn."

"I shouldn't have come here."

"OK, Ilse Lund, you shouldn't have come. So whattya want?" I guzzled the beer, belched and smashed the can against my head. That hurt a bit, but I didn't let on. I was trying to make a point.

"Who's Elsie Lund?"

"Never mind. Now whattya want? I'm busy. I gotta lift weights. Work out. I got a baboon match coming up."

"Are you pissed about me and Jerry getting married? You seem so bitter."

"Are you sure you haven't seen 'Casablanca'? Look, I've been bitter ever since they cancelled 'The Rat Patrol.' I learned you couldn't trust anyone then. I've never been the same. But I've never been bitter about human relationships. I don't care much for them to begin with. But you don't want to know that, do you? You just want me to say everything is great so you won't feel bad anymore, especially after the baboons rip my face off and make me look like the Phantom of the Opera. You don't want to feel guilty after I'm dead. In fact, I think you feel real shitty because you taunted me into believing I had a chance at some kind of twisted romance with you and then you dumped me for a rich guy, a game show host, no less. Look, that's human nature. All things being equal, I'd have taken the rich guy, too. But in this case, all things aren't equal. Jerry's good looking, and I'm a fat, balding putz with adult-onset acne, a subsistence income and a bad case of misanthropy, thanks to you and so many others. Not much competition, I'd say. Don't worry about it. I'm no good at being noble, but it doesn't take a lot to know that the problems of two little people don't add up to a hill of beans in this crazy world."

"Why are you talking weird? Are you losin' it?"

"C'mon kid, you mean you've never heard me do Bogie?"

"Who?"

I sighed and rummaged for another beer. Warm or not, I needed a beer.

"Look, I just wanted to let you know I really did like you, and I'm glad you picked me up. You really changed my life. I just want to thank you."

"Oh, well, you're welcome. I've always wanted to turn someone's life around. Now I can die happy."

"You're making this harder than it has to be, but I'm going to do it."

Incredibly, she lifted off her shirt, slipped out of her blue jeans and stood there in her underwear. Her body was more spectacular than I had pictured. I was, of course, incredibly aroused, but equally confused.

"Ah, if I'm not mistaken, that ring means you and Jerry Most are married," I said, a little out of breath. "What does your religion say about this sort of thing? I know mine tends to frown on it."

"I wanted to do this before we got married, but you were in a coma," she said. "I feel like I have to do this."

Yes, it was odd. It was uncomfortable. It was against my belief in the sacred vows of marriage. But what the hell, I wasn't married, she was. She took me by the hand and led me to my room and took off the rest of her clothing. I practically fell on top of her on the bed.

I'm not going to go into the gory details because it would be ungentlemanly and because, unfortunately, I was a bit flatulent because I was nervous and that was embarrassing, even for me. Let's just say that being with her was worth the wait. And I generated enough memories of the incident to last me for a lifetime, assuming the baboons didn't kill me or rip off my manhood. She even let me call her Ilse.

But something odd did happen as we lay in bed. Apparently, whoever drew on the Farrah poster also knocked her loose from her masking tape mounts. Because out of the blue, she fell off her perch on my bedroom wall, a position she had held for decades.

I thought that was eerie and symbolic. In any case, I thought about going for seconds when a car horn started honking from the driveway and Charles's voice started calling. He was anxious to get us to the hotel because, it turned out, Jerry had promised to let Charles's wife and kids come so they could swim in the Holidome pool. Until then I had been unaware that Charles had progeny. The thought frightened me.

"Get's low—shit—let's go," Charles said. "Shit's owetime. Dammit. Sorry, honey. It's almost showtime."

She kissed me on the nose and we got up to get dressed.

"Don't tell Jerry, kay?" she said.

"It'll be our little secret," I said. "Now let's go. Charles says it's showtime."

Chapter 20
Godzilla Versus the Baboons

I fell asleep in the limo on the way to the Holidome. I was groggy but when we arrived I maneuvered my way through the lobby to the room and into bed. When I awoke in The President's Suite the next day I had a massive hangover. The television was blaring, and it was broadcasting a Godzilla movie. Perfect. Today the American public would see me as Godzilla.

I would finally, if briefly, have an identity. I would forever be known as "that monkey guy," which was better than being known as who I really was, a loser who didn't care anymore. Godzilla was throwing boulders at some kind of turtle creature when the phone rang. It was Jerry.

"That was quite a show you put on last night, sport," he said. "Should I have my staff bring you some aspirins and orange juice? Always worked for me, you know, back when I was still drinking. Of course, I'm not doing that anymore since I've found religion. It feels good, pal, it really does. Hey, are you there?"

I wasn't. I had placed the phone on the night stand and let him babble without an audience. Godzilla dove under water to attack the turtle creature. I wiped my hands across my face and brow and got up to go to the bathroom. I could hear Jerry's voice buzzing from the phone, so I stuffed the phone in the drawer next to the Gideon Bible.

I got to the bathroom and noticed a headache and the shakes, but no nausea. That's what I call fighting trim.

All of this deserves some explanation, I suppose. After I rode with Charles and his family to the Holidome the day before—the kids sang, "Hey Hey, we're the Monkees" all the way there—I was mobbed by several local and even more national reporters, all asking the same stupid questions, like:

"How does it feel?" Given a choice between them and the baboons, I would have taken the baboons, even if they were rabid.

"How the hell would I know?" I said. "I haven't felt anything in years."

"Is the baboon a monkey or a gorilla or what?

"I think it's a member of the fish family."

"Do you want to die?

"My spirit died years ago. My body's an empty shell, like a pod."

"What do you think of Jerry Most's religious conversion?"

"I think this is a real breakthrough for game show hosts. I predict they'll be playing 'Concentration' in heaven as soon as he dies."

"How will you spend your last night?"

"Ah, that's a tough one. I'll say, watching pornography, whacking off and eating cheese sticks." I don't think that one made it to the air.

"Do you think you're a role model?"

"Yes. Anyone who wants to be ripped apart by primates should look up to me."

"What's your astrological sign?"

"I believe I'm a marmoset. Larry the marmoset. I'm on the cusp."

"Have you met the baboons yet?"

"I met them at the weigh in, and later, and we did bong hits together. They're pretty cool."

"What weight in?"

"The one at the Ali -Frazier fight. The Thrilla in Manila."

"Are you nuts?"

"No, I am Ironman. Haven't I said that before?"

"What do baboons eat besides humans?"

Trick question. I was saving that one for after they realized they'd been duped.

"I believe they eat whale meat. But it's hard for them to get their paws on whale meat in Africa, so normally it's marshmallow circus peanuts, which they get by begging from rich tourists on safari. They especially like banana flavor, naturally."

"If you survive, what other death-defying tricks will you try?"

"I'm going over Frostbite Falls in a Hovercraft."

"Anything with animals?"

"I may wrestle with a Thompson's Gazelle or a Greater Kudu. Depends on who's ranked higher and how high the purse is ..."

"What do you do for a living?"

"I'm in the umbrella repair business, and I have a TV degree in creative writing from the Sally Struthers Institute."

"Is it true you write nasty stalker letters to celebrities?"

"That is not true. I only send them harmful rays using mind power. Can you feel them?"

"Did you really send a threatening letter to the president?"

"I once called him a phony dipshit, but he was on TV in my living room and couldn't hear me. Unless he is illegally reading my thoughts, we have had no communication."

"Do you consider yourself a role model?"

"Did you get here late? Yes. I am a role model for all those who want to face down the worldwide baboon threat but have not had the courage. Follow me, and we will be victorious."

This went on for about ten minutes until some "Die Trying" staff people pulled me away and led me to a makeshift green room. I was a little disappointed by my answer to the last question. I could have told them about how I really am a role model for the new America, the prosperous America that avoids human contact, especially with dangerous agents such as neighbors. I'm a role model for all those people who think that minivans and big houses don't make up for the meaninglessness of it all. I'm a role model for the disconnected, those people who have no connection to this society. I could have said all that, but I decided I'd save that for the "News Hour with Jim Lehrer."

Finally, the mob broke up and I was delivered to the green room, a trailer, actually, near the scene of the battle. It was a very nice. A large screen TV. A wet bar that later turned out to be the reason for debilitating hangover. A couch for lounging, and a few occasional chairs for occasional guests. The place smelled like new carpet and I spent a lot of time sneezing as a result. The sneezing made me very uncomfortable, and when I'm uncomfortable, I drink. Of course I drink when I'm comfortable, too. But being uncomfortable brings more urgency to the drinking, so I was drinking quickly.

A phone rang again shortly after I rifled my first single-malt scotch. It was Jerry checking in on me.

"Ready to die trying, sport?" he said, cheerily. I could hear his wife talking in the background, and I felt smug.

"Well, ah, actually Jerry, I've decided to back out," I said. "I had a vision of Grampa bathing in a vat of wet Metamucil. Well, it looked like Grampa, anyway, but he had those spooky eyes like a fly, and he told me I should shave my head, put my hair in a paper bag, and, well, it gets a little foggy after that, but I remember he said not to do this."

There was a long pause. I could hear the TV over the phone. Jerry was watching the Golf Channel.

"You OK?" he said.

"Of course I'm OK," I said. "If I wasn't OK I would go out and battle baboons."

"Look, asshole, I told you I've got a lot riding on you," he said. "Don't fuck with me. We're all set, and you're going out into the woods where you spent your childhood and see what the baboons do to you."

"Are you quoting Jesus, Jerry?" I said.

"Fuck you," he said darkly.

"I can guarantee Jesus never ever said that," I said. "Are you sure you're ready for this evangelism thing? You're awfully angry and profane. Maybe you should become a chef instead of a preacher. Or what about small engine repair?"

I heard him slam down the phone, and within a few seconds I heard harsh footsteps pounding down the Holidome corridor. I poured another scotch, a tumbler-full actually—no need to waste time going back to the bar again and again—and suddenly, Grampa was looking over my shoulder saying: "Have some fun, boy. They're going to dick you anyway." There was an insistent pounding at the door. It was Jerry.

"Open up, Fat Boy, we've got to have a talk," he yelled through the door.

"Oh, Mr. Allnut, our first quarrel," I said, doing my best Hepburn.

"Open the fucking door or I'll have my staff open it," he said.

"I'm ironing my cape. I'm not decent," I said, pouring more scotch into the tumbler. This was getting fun. Everything Grampa had ever told me, on the few times when he was lucid, anyway, was beginning to make sense. If you want to control events, behave in a strange manner. People will pretty much do anything you want once you start acting strangely. So I stripped naked, took a kitchen knife from the galley, and, just like Richard Hell, gently carved the words "YOU MAKE ME" into my chest, only the

"E" in the word "make" didn't turn out too well and it looked more like "YOU MAK ME," which confused Jerry all the more. That act was kind of dumb, I guess, because it really stung and I would probably get tetanus if the baboons didn't get me first. Or maybe the baboons would get tetanus. But I had a point to make, even if I myself didn't know what it was. Small rivulets of blood rolled down my chest and I wiped them off with a couch cover which I placed over my head like an Egyptian pharaoh. Then I went to the door and let Jerry in. A few staff members entered with him.

"Oh, for God's sake, he's out of his fucking mind the night before the biggest show of my life," Jerry wailed.

"Do you have some Metamucil, Buddha?" I asked. "I need to force a big dump. I've been farting all day. Want some scotch? Which one of you staff guys is Robin? I'm assuming Jerry is Batman. Or maybe he's Green Lantern. Jerry, what was Green Lantern's special power? Did he have a sidekick? Lemme see your ring."

"All right, all right, all right, calm down," Jerry said. "Come on. You're just fine. I think someone has the jitters. A little stage fright. It's OK, I get the butterflies, too, and I'm a professional."

"It's not that," I said. "It's just that I think I'm allergic to primates. I don't want to get hives the first time I get attacked on TV. I hate the hives."

"OK, have your fun," he said. "Act goofy. Be your Grampa. Enjoy yourself at my expense. Drink everything. Find a hooker and get laid. I'll even have my staff send one up here. But if you don't care about yourself, then care about me and Pinky Lee. We've got to start that new show. I've got to get rid of this abomination. I want to be a positive force in American culture. I want redemption."

"I almost forgot, this isn't about me being eaten, it's about you," I said. "Fine. But if I pull this off with the baboons, I want one of those foot massagers as a prize. And an electric garage door opener. And a garage."

"I'll give you the Hope fucking diamond, just promise me you'll show up and battle the chimps."

"Baboons. Hamadryas baboons. Natives of Africa's rocky steppes."

"Whatever."

"Can I have an ice cream cone?"

"You can have ice cream, you can have gin, I don't care. I'll have staff get some."

"Can I have a pony?"

Jerry looked around the room, which had slowly filled with staff. All were wearing blue nylon windbreakers with "Die Trying Staff" on them. Some of the staff were making themselves at home, opening the refrigerator, taking out beers and using the phone. Two of them turned on one of the big screens and sat down to watch an old Robin Williams comedy special on HBO. You could tell it was old, anyway, because he was really funny. Finally, Jerry spotted Charles standing at the door like a guard at Buckingham Palace.

"Charles, Charles, I want you to keep an eye on him," Jerry shouted from across the room. Charles approached Jerry looking like a drunk trying to pretend he was sober, which is exactly what he was at that moment. Charles, it turned out, had stopped off at Booby's on the way home to pick up the kids, and he had procured two pints of peppermint schnapps, apparently to make his wife think his breath was minty fresh, not loaded with alcohol molecules. I had my drinking buddy for the night.

"Worry about me," he said, focusing his eyes slowly. "I mean, don't worry about me. What did I just say?"

"Oh, for God's sake, are you drunk?" Jerry said.

"I just have a bittle luzz … a little buzz going," he said.

"Look, I need you to keep an eye on our friend here," Jerry said. "Can you handle that? Can you keep him out of trouble? Can you keep him from hurting himself?"

"Yersecret's shafe," he burped, "with me."

"I'll take that as a yes, because I have no choice," Jerry said.

"I'll be fine," I said. "Boys! Hey, everyone in the room. We're all going to the Holidome bar, which I believe is called the Waikiki Room with a Hawaiian decor, for a big drinking festival on Jerry's nickel. Mai Tai's all around!"

A collective cheer went up among the dozen young staff people in the room.

"Asshole," Jerry said under his breath. "But I'll tell you what. I'll pay for everything you want to do if you promise not to leave the Holidome."

"Sounds like Leonid's going to do great business tonight," I said. "We're ordering pizzas from his place 30 miles away so we can give him a huge tip on you."

"Fine, have fun," he said, turning around and heading toward the door as if he had just been told his Porsche was on fire. "I've got a lady waiting.

I'll see you later on the set. Remember, we're at the clearing where they buried that kangaroo."

"Bye, Jerry, bye. Hey everyone, Jerry's taking off, say bye," I shouted. "Charles, I want you to order 15 pepperoni pizzas from Leonid's and have staff pick them up. You and I are going to get drunk."

"I think I already did," Charles said.

"Then let's get drunker," I said.

"Gotcha," he said.

The rest of the night disappeared into a series of martini chugs, beer bongs, Mai Tai funnels, one pantless hula dance by Charles on top of a cocktail table, and many baboon-like woofs in salute to me. The party naturally attracted some of the local talent, and I wound up having my second sexual experience of the day—I hope I showered; I don't remember—in the men's room with a part-timer named Mina who may or may not have had three eyes and an angel tattoo on her breast that said, "Moo Bossy" and had the head of a Guernsey cow. I also remembered that she offered to make a "YOU MAK ME" carving a permanent tattoo if I came to her house. I believe I declined.

Charles' wife came looking for him at one point. She was a woman whom they refer to as "handsome" in these parts when they're afraid to say she's ugly. She appeared angry and worried, and she was surrounded by her children, all of whom were dripping wet and ready to go home. But a large bouncer-type staffer came to her and said Charles was in Jerry's suite at a production meeting and would be there all night. He said Charles said to go home, and she shook her head slowly and left.

The rest is a blur. I remember laughing a lot more than I have in years, maybe in my life, and I remember thinking that this was the kind of life I could get used to, and that maybe I should have a series where I fought baboons. It was a great last night on Earth.

The next thing I knew I was waking up to a blaring Godzilla movie, and the smell of eggs, burnt toast and coffee was in the air. The large staffer who dealt with Mrs. Charles came over to me with a spatula in his hand.

"Breakfast, cowboy?" he asked. His name was Spaniel.

"I'll need to throw up first," I said.

"Go to it," he said. "I'll have a plate on the table for you."

"Where's Charles?" I asked.

"He felt guilty and had someone drive him home. From the looks of his wife, I'd say he's dead now," Spaniel said.

I got up and went to the bathroom and put my finger in my throat in a successful attempt to vomit. I cleaned up and went to the breakfast table.

So began what was to be my first last day on Earth. Or not.

Chapter 21
"Just a Few Questions Before You Die"

The format for "Die Trying" was fairly loose, since the only real purpose of the show was to get people to do stupid and dangerous things for the purpose of monetary and material gain. But the producers, and the legal department, I guess, decided there should be a few minimal standards for contestants before anyone got to taste death. The point was to make it look like a competition while at the same time making sure some person who should not hold a driver's license didn't wind up scuba diving in a reef full of sharks.

So after a brief interview to allow the audience to bond with the contestant and learn what made him or her decide to play, a few trivia questions are asked, and if they were correctly answered, the contestant got a chance to fight death. The questions were usually along the lines of "Which president was shot at Ford's Theater?" or "What is the boiling point of water?" Contestants got as much time as they needed, which often lead to dead spots as they searched their brain for whatever reasoning tools they had left after having gone through decades of the American education system and general TV numbness.

The network had been pumping up this event for weeks, and it was going to be broadcast live.

Normally, they taped these things weeks ahead of time so they could show teasers to promote the show. They figured in this case that a semi-suicidal, or at least terminally indifferent, fat guy fighting monkeys, um, baboons, would mean that blood would be spilt. Good for the ratings, of course.

I spent most of my time watching TV on those big screens while eating Jell-O and potato chips and trying not to think about the nausea.

Rumor had it that protesters would attempt to stop the show, and they were trying to figure out what room I was staying in so they could spirit me off to wherever protestors spirit their victims. Protester World Headquarters, maybe?

Spaniel, who had kept an eye on me after everyone left the night before, watched TV with me, and every once in a while he'd walk around the suite as though he was expecting someone to burst in. He would look out the window, check the peephole on the door, and then come back and sit down. I felt like I was some kind of international spy. Or maybe Alexander Mundy in "It Takes a Thief."

Anyway, about two hours before showtime, there was a knock at the door.

"I'll get that," I said.

"Very funny," Spaniel said.

It was a huge makeup artist named Tippy who had a pronounced limp and a voice that sounded like Gary Cooper.

"What the hell do I need a makeup artist for?" I said. "I didn't know I'd have to look my best when doing battle."

"Jerry says he doesn't want your face to wash out," Spaniel said. "Tippy knows what he's doing. You'll look great."

Tippy took me to a chair where he could more easily apply his art. He kept calling me "partner," and I half expected someone in a black suit and cowboy hat to leap out from behind a chair and start shooting.

"You're going to be dazzling," he said. "Just sit still, partner. Let Tippy work his magic. You'll leave a great looking corpse if the monkeys don't get your face."

"Baboons."

"It's important to look good when you're on TV, even when you're wrestling with animals," Tippy said. "You don't want some old history teachers of yours to think you turned into a slovenly loser, do you? You could even get job offers."

"Well, I guess there's a lot of call for baboon fighters," I said.

"How long you been fighting baboons?" he asked.

"Since my return from the dog dimension," I said. "Previously, I existed only as a sound wave from a Pete Townshend chord at a Who concert, invisible, yet ever present and very powerful. But then I took human form to teach you all about the dangers of television and primates."

"TV's not dangerous, partner," he said. "TV's your friend. You shouldn't talk about it that way. I don't know about monkeys."

"Baboons. I'm sorry, I've been quarreling with TV ever since they cancelled 'The Addams Family,'" I said. "What people don't know is that an evil breed of apes actually runs the major networks, and they've infiltrated cable, too. Only public TV had the smarts to put up ape repellant and keep themselves from being taken over."

"You have an interesting imagination, partner," he said.

"It's not imagination, it's delusions," I said.

Our conversation was interrupted by Spaniel, who said it was time to go to the set. First I had to get dressed, which meant putting on a royal blue Spandex suit with the "Die Trying" logo on it. It looked like Superman gone long to seed. I put it on without putting on underwear. I didn't want the visible underwear lines to ruin the look.

"Good to meetcha, partner," Tippy said. "You look dyno, just dyno. Go get 'em." He paused.

"Say, you think you'll need one of these?" he said, pulling a stun gun from his make-up vest.

"Naw, no weapons allowed," I said.

"You're a brave one, partner," he said. "Good luck."

Spaniel whisked me down the hall out a back entrance to the waiting limousine. There had been no signs of mobs at the hotel, but Spaniel wasn't taking any chances. I started singing *Doo Wah Diddy* in a loud falsetto just to irritate him just in case someone got curious. It attracted no attention, largely because there was no one around the Holidome at the moment, and because most people got sick of *Doo Wah Diddy* years ago.

Charles was behind the wheel of the limo when we got there, looking a bit chagrined and a bit sore.

"Anything the matter, Charlie Boy?" I asked cheerily as I climbed in.

"Skillet head," he said quietly.

"Got a bad headache, huh? Drank a few too many Mai Tais?"

"I don't know what I drank, but when I got home my wife hit me in the head with a skillet, a cast-iron skillet," he said. "She don't like me drinking no more. Hurts like hell."

We headed straight over to the woods, a ride of about 25 minutes from the Holidome through Little Rose to the freeway and then back to Hammertown. It was a bright, sunny day, a bit warm but not uncomfortably so.

The road was littered with the usual billboards for waterslides and "shoppes" where tourists could pick up souvenirs of the local culture. Pewter miniature hammers, Hammerhead baseball caps and little snow globes with "The Chips" factory still looking like the old hammer factory. The only interesting billboard was one aimed at me, one sponsored by the Hammertown Chamber of Commerce which normally promoted Hammertown's economic development. It had a picture of a chimpanzee on it that said "Hammertown is proud of you, Monkey Man!"

So I guessed I would be known as Monkey Man as long as I lived in Hammertown.

As we pulled into Hammertown, it was apparent that something different was taking place because of the heavy traffic. Every parking space in town had been taken up, and cars were lined all the way up the woods, even though only "Die Trying" staff would be allowed anywhere near the event.

As we got closer, the protestors figured out I was the one in the limo, and they attacked.

"You should be ashamed! You're exploiting these poor baboons," one shouted.

"But I'm yummy," I said. "They'll enjoy my meat very much."

"You're sick," shouted another.

"Ya think?"

"What if baboons don't want to be on TV?" shrieked one earth mother.

"You'll have to talk to their agent."

Someone was wearing a gorilla suit and was carrying a sign that said: "I am the president." I did not know whether that person was on my side or not.

Charles drove us slowly past the crowd and got us to the clearing. Light standards were everywhere, and staff was scurrying as if planning for an ambush. Jerry, wearing a tasteful black beret, was supervising and Pinky Lee stood by his side in a pair of pink short shorts, a "Die Trying" T-shirt and a "Try Living" baseball cap with a halo over the logo—they weren't wasting any time—with a pony tail pulled through the back. She was hanging on

Jerry's neck. She was also barefoot and looked luscious. My Spandex suit strained as I gazed at the sight.

Spaniel led me straight to Jerry, who greeted me with a two-handed hand shake. His wife said hello without looking at me, but I sensed there was still some real electricity between us.

"In one hour, you're on national TV," Jerry said.

"Oh, goody, will I meet Zsa Zsa Gabor?" I asked.

"No, smart guy, but if you don't play ball you might meet Wally Cox," he said. "Wally Cox, as you may know, is dead at the present time."

"I'll take Charlie Weaver to block," I said. "Don't worry, you'll get what you want from me. Just make sure the baboons are ready to rumble."

"They've been woofing out here all day, filthy bastards," he said. "Never thought I could hate baboons like this. Always picking at each other."

The baboons had been wandering about the clearing for the past couple of days or so acclimating themselves to the area. They were penned in by the secured area, although they didn't show any desire to go anywhere. They were gathering around a shady area where the cops had buried Billie the kangaroo and where the kids usually came to smoke dope, drink and copulate. The baboons hadn't been fed—that way they would be meaner and hungrier. They didn't look mean or hungry. From a distance, they didn't look any different than a family that had just moved into town.

The rest of the wait was as dull as you'd expect. I had my own director's chair with my own name on it, which I got to keep if I survived, and I just sat there watching my baboon enemies and reading old copies of "People" magazine. I wondered if they would be doing a story about me. One thing for sure, I wouldn't let them take my picture with a baboon. A marmoset, maybe, but after today, no baboons.

I wondered if Grampa was watching all this from beyond the grave, and I farted in a sort of greeting to him just in case.

They had sealed off the entire clearing as a battleground for me and my hairy friends, using the plastic crowd control fencing that keeps people in line at rock concerts. I would be the only one allowed to enter. I surveyed the ground as I waited for my cue, and generally I just paced after I was done with magazines.

While Jerry was in makeup, Pinky Lee sidled up to me as I leaned against the barrier. She ran her finger down my spine and it gave me a chill.

"What're you gonna do next time you see a hitcher, baby?" she asked.

"Fake a seizure and run her over," I said.

"C'mon, this is more than you're done in your entire life," she said.

"So?"

"Whattya mean, 'so'?" she said. "Your life was nothing before you met me."

"I liked it that way," I said. "And by the way, you call this something?"

"Look, someday you'll thank me for all this," she said, licking her lips in that annoyingly seductive fashion. "And I know you'll remember me."

"You're assuming that I'm not going to be killed," I said.

"Nobody's getting killed today," she said. "There's a reason you're here. Some cosmic reason."

"Does it have to do with beer?"

"I don't know. I just got a hunch is all."

Right about then Charles and Spaniel found me and said it was time to prepare to go on the air. Spaniel led me to a stage area where the staff had set up a makeshift game show set. A stagehand mic'ed me and set me down in another director's chair, which was separate from another director's chair, presumably Jerry's, by a round Formica coffee table.

"Could you say a few words to check the mic?" another stagehand said.

"Come and listen to ma story 'bout a man name Jed, a poor mountaineer barely ..."

"Thank you."

"I was singing my song."

"Thank you."

Jerry mounted the stage right about that time, and he was all TV grins. He reached out and shook my hand again as though he had never seen me before, and he stood over me and pointed his finger down at my head.

"This guy shouldn't be fighting baboons, he should be screwing 'em! Of course, maybe that's how he was born in the first place—when his dad screwed a monkey!" he said, and the stage crew and staff laughed heartily. "In fact, maybe we should give this guy some rubbers. You never know."

"Baboon," I corrected one last time. "You meant to say my dad may have screwed a baboon to cause my conception. Not a monkey."

It was the old TV Jerry. Apparently he intended to ease the transition once he moved to "Try Living." I wasn't going to play along.

"I can't screw primates or anything else," I said. "I had your wife earlier today. You know, she really ought to get that mole in that special place looked at by a dermatologist."

Jerry just stared at me. "I don't think the baboons are going to have a chance to get you before I do," he said through his teeth.

But it was too late for him to kill me. The show's goofy theme was starting, and we were now on national TV. Oooh, goody.

It was the usual blah, blah, blah let's welcome our guest, what do you do for a living, are you ready-type chatter that I had always ignored on "The Match Game" and which seemed no more interesting even though I was the subject of said banter. I was completely tuned out, not because I was nervous, but because it seemed just as banal in person as it did on TV. I suddenly burst into some inappropriate laughter because, as I explained, I was thinking about clowns.

Finally, Jerry said the magic words: "Are you ready?"

"Not really," I said. "Can I go potty?"

"Well, as you know, we have to ask you a few questions before we know if you're worthy to die trying," he said. "Answer the questions and you can face death. Let's go. Number one. What crime show starring two female detectives replaced 'Lou Grant'?"

Through my teeth I said: "One of the worst shows ever on TV, 'Cagney and Lacey.'"

"Terrific," he said. "Now name Jimmy Carter's vice president."

"That would be Walter 'Fritz' Mondale," I said smiling smugly.

"Great. Now you're almost there. Let's go to sports," he said.

Oh, good. My trivia wheelhouse. I could already taste death or merchandise, whichever came first.

"Name the first player to break Babe Ruth's single season home run record," he said, winking.

I was supposed to get this right or the whole show would be screwed up because you can't fight death without answering the questions correctly.

"Ahhh, that's a tough one," I said. "Ummm. Michael Jordan?"

Jerry's eyes flamed a bit. I thought I had him. I thought I escaped his little TV hell. But he suddenly smiled.

"Ooh, that's too bad," he said. "The answer is Roger Maris. I heard you were a big baseball fan. You should have known that one."

"Well, um ..."

"But don't worry," he said. "I didn't say you had to answer the questions correctly, I said you had to answer them."

"So I still get a chance at cash and merchandise?"

"Sure thing. JUST AS SOON AS YOU FIGHT THE BABOONS OR DIE TRYING! LET'S GO, GO, GO!" he yelled, a little more enthusiastically than usual. I think that comment about his sweetie smarted a bit.

A staff member, not Spaniel, led me to an opening in the barrier around the clearing. He then took a piece of meat and rubbed it all over my Spandex outfit.

"Hey, I was planning to wear this to a wedding this weekend," I protested.

"Gotta give the animals some scent," he said.

"I think I'll be ripe enough once I get out there," I said.

"He's ready," the staff member said.

"LET'S GET IT ON!" Jerry shouted.

The idea was for me to run into the middle of the baboon troop until they either perceived me as a predator or they just got pissed off from the harassment of a fat guy who smelled like meat.

So there I was in a Spandex suit running toward a troop of baboons. Somehow, this wasn't the type of ending I had envisioned when I said I wanted to die by being attacked by a troop of baboons.

I ran through the troop a few times and got little more than a few curious glances. But finally, the alpha male got angry and he picked something up from the ground—it looked like a stick or something—and started to run after me. I ran. He chased. And America cheered. A few others followed, grabbing more sticks, but they started hitting each other over the head with them. I was still running around and when I turned and I saw the alpha male, King Baboon himself, moving around in circles, staggering then falling backwards and woofing. The others were staggering, too. It was hilarious.

This was TV, and the people expected a show, so I ran toward the baboons woofing myself.

They got up and started twirling in circles again. A few threw more sticks at me, which, it turned out, were Billie the kangaroo's bones. They were found, apparently, when the baboons were digging around for grubs and other baboon food. The incompetent cops had left Billie in an extremely shallow grave, and in the final insult she was exhumed by grub-searching simians.

King Baboon, meanwhile, would make attempts to come after me but could never make it more than a few steps. I couldn't help myself. Here I was, facing death by baboon, and I was laughing. Laughing in the face of death, I guess, but actually laughing in the face of stoned baboons.

Apparently, the staff had failed to thoroughly check the site where the grand fight was to take place.

Had they looked, they would have found dozens of half-empty beer cans and lime vodka bottles left by generations of high school students. One baboon was even studying a condom—used, of course, and, oh, God, Mr. Baboon don't put your nose in there! It was great TV.

Meanwhile, the baboons had also been nibbling at the roaches and little marijuana plants and that had grown from years of the beer and lime vodka and screwing parties held by all those high school students of Hammertown who were now owners of car washes and convenience stores and were members of the Chamber of Commerce and Rotary Club if they weren't in jail.

The killer baboons were cooked. Stoned. Seriously fucked up. They wanted some cheese sticks and Moody Blues tunes, not human flesh.

Wanting to make the entire situation worse, I got close enough to one of the zoned-out animals and he allowed me to give him a piggyback ride. Wheee.

A few "Die Trying" staff eventually brought me back to the stage area, where Jerry was laughing.

"This ought to do it, Fat Boy," he said in my ear. "This show is dead. And you didn't even have to die. In fact, there's some great merchandise waiting for you!"

"That's kind of nice, I suppose," I said. "I was hoping for more action."

"Oh, you'll get it now," he said. "You're somebody now. Every chick in America is going to want to nail you. You were on TV. It doesn't matter that you're fat and ugly, fighting baboons in a TV game show or fighting crime on a drama, you're big stuff as long as you're on TV. That's how you become somebody, my friend. On TV. You don't really exist until you're on TV."

I wasn't so sure about that.

Chapter 22
What Have We Learned?

A few months passed after my appearance on network TV and my decision to chronicle the events of that time. My life remained largely the same, in spite of Jerry's promise of gaining self-esteem and identity through TV appearances. I used the money I made on the show to have my house professionally cleaned, and I did some minor remodeling by putting a wet bar with a beer tapper in the living room. And I bought a big screen TV, of course, and a huge new couch with Scotchguard fabric protectant in case of accidents.

It turns out I decided not to leave Hammertown after all. I had everything I wanted, so why put everything in boxes and get an apartment in Chicago?

Things changed, though. People said hello to me when I went to the liquor store, and I guess I became something of a celebrity in Hammertown. This sometimes meant I got the best table at Leonid's Best Good Pizza.

But my life was the way I wanted it. The same as always. Pizza. Cheese sticks. Beer. TV. It turned out TV didn't get me laid, but that was partly my fault. You don't meet many women sitting in your own living room day after day.

Of course, without Grampa and Foilhead Eddie and my dope-growing neighbors, things got kind of dull around town. But then again, I had all the adventure I ever needed whenever I turned on my TV. Murder. Sex. Crime. You name it. TV has it all. And I had a big TV in my own living room.

But I still didn't feel like I had much of an identity even after my national TV appearance.

Jerry and Pinkie Lee became famous televangelists, and their show "Try Living" became a big hit on cable TV, although nowhere as big as "Die Trying."

Hitman never went to Los Angeles because, as he put it, "I'm too rooted in this shithole town." So he never left High Falls.

So in the end, everybody got what they wanted, more or less.

One morning as I sipped my coffee I opened the *Telegraph-Herald* and I saw something next to the obituaries I had never seen before.

My name.

Under "Police File," a list of arrests used by town gossips, it read: "Leo Burt Peck, Hammertown, fined $68 for shoplifting Tic Tacs at Kmart."

There it was. My name was in the local newspaper.

I was somebody after all.

THE END

About the Author

Bill Zaferos is a first-time author and writer who managed to channel his mental illness into creativity by writing *Poison Pen* during a manic high. He wrote the novel in a few months and then left it on a closet shelf for 15 years before allowing friends and family to read it. With their encouragement, Zaferos finally sought publication of the novel and, well, here it is.

He has been a newspaper political reporter, a political consultant and public relations and advertising executive. He grew up an asthmatic kid who watched a lot of '60s and '70s television shows, and he especially loved the original "Star Trek," "The Outer Limits," "The Twilight Zone" and the Watergate hearings.

Zaferos is a diehard baseball fan with split loyalties to the Milwaukee Brewers and Boston Red Sox. He is also a music devotee, especially to the music of The Who and Bruce Springsteen with a little of The Clash, Sex Pistols, Miles Davis and many others alongside. He has seen Springsteen in concert dozens of times, having lost track of the count after about 45 or 50.

Zaferos is a journalism and political science graduate of the University of Wisconsin-Madison, and he received his M.A. at Marquette University. He lives in downtown Milwaukee – not the suburbs – with his wife, Tracey Carson.

To contact the author, please visit www.poisonpenbook.com.

CPSIA information can be obtained
at www.ICGtesting.com
Printed in the USA
FFHW010209010519
52160618-57528FF

9 781595 986597